NEW YORK REVIEW BOOKS
CLASSICS

RANDALL JARRELL'S BOOK OF STORIES

RANDALL JARRELL (1914–1965) was born in Tennessee and graduated from Vanderbilt. A poet, novelist, translator, and critic as well as writer for children, Jarrell was a prolific author whose best-known works include the poems collected in *The Woman at the Washington Zoo* and *The Lost World*, the academic comedy *Pictures from an Institution*, the children's story *The Bat Poet*, and *Poetry and the Age*, a group of essays. An influential critic who, as poetry reviewer for *The Nation*, helped to launch the careers of Robert Lowell and other contemporaries, Jarrell taught for many years at the University of North Carolina, where he was much revered. He died in a car accident in 1965.

D1165836

RANDALL JARRELL'S BOOK OF STORIES

AN ANTHOLOGY

Selected and with an Introduction by
RANDALL JARRELL

NEW YORK REVIEW BOOKS

New York

This is a New York Review Book
Published by The New York Review of Books
435 Hudson Street, New York, NY 10014

Library of Congress Cataloging-in-Publication Data
  Randall Jarrell's book of stories / selected and with an introduction by Randall
Jarrell.
    p. cm. — (New York Review Books classics)
  ISBN 1-59017-005-9 (pbk. : alk. paper)
  1. Short stories—Translations into English. 2. Short stories, English. I. Title:
Book of stories. II. Jarrell, Randall, 1914–1965. III. Series.

  PN6120.2 .B59 2002
  808.83'1—dc21

                            2002000741
ISBN 978-1-59017-005-2

Book design by Lizzie Scott
Printed in the United States of America on acid-free paper.

10 9 8 7 6 5 4

CONTENTS

INTRODUCTION

1.

S TORY, the dictionary tells one, is a short form of the word *history*, and stands for *a narrative, recital, or description of what has occurred*; just as it stands for *a fictitious narrative, imaginative tale; [Colloq.] a lie, a falsehood.*

A story, then, tells the truth or a lie—is a wish, or a truth, or a wish modified by a truth. Children ask first of all: "Is it a *true* story?" They ask this of the storyteller, but they ask of the story what they ask of a dream: that it satisfy their wishes. The Muses are the daughters of hope and the step-daughters of memory. The wish is the first truth about us, since it represents not that learned principle of reality which half-governs our workaday hours, but the primary principle of pleasure which governs infancy, sleep, daydreams—and, certainly, many stories. Reading stories, we cannot help remembering Groddeck's "We have to reckon with what exists, and dreams, daydreams too, are also facts; if anyone really wants to investigate realities, he cannot do better than to start with such as these. If he neglects them, he will learn little or nothing of the world of life." If wishes were stories, beggars would read; if stories were true, our saviors would speak to us in parables. Much of our knowledge of, our compensation for, "the world of life" comes from stories; and the stories themselves are part of "the world of life." Shakespeare wrote:

> This is an art
> Which does mend nature, change it rather, but
> The art itself is nature . . .

and Goethe, agreeing, said: "A work of art is just as much a work of nature as a mountain."

In showing that dreams both satisfy our wishes and punish us for them, Freud compares the dreamer to the husband and wife in the fairy tale of "The Three Wishes": the wife wishes for a pudding, the husband wishes it on the end of her nose, and the wife wishes it away again. A contradictory family! But it is this family—wife, husband, and pudding—which the story must satisfy: the writer is, and is writing for, a doubly- or triply-natured creature, whose needs, understandings, and ideals—whether they are called id, ego, and superego, or body, mind, and soul—contradict one another. Most of the stories that we are willing to call works of art are compounds almost as complicated as their creators; but occasionally we can see isolated, in naked innocence, one of the elements of which our stories are composed. Thomas Leaf's story (in Hardy's *Under the Greenwood Tree*) is an example:

> "Once," said the delighted Leaf, in an uncertain voice, "there was a man who lived in a house! Well, this man went thinking and thinking night and day. At last, he said to himself, as I might, 'If I had only ten pound, I'd make a fortune.' At last by hook or by crook, behold he got the ten pounds!"
>
> "Only think of that!" said Nat Callcome satirically.
>
> "Silence!" said the tranter.
>
> "Well, now comes the interesting part of the story! In a little time he made that ten pounds twenty. Then a little after that he doubled it, and made it forty. Well, he went on, and a good while after that he made it eighty, and on to a hundred. Well, by-and-by he made it two hundred! Well, you'd never believe it, but—he went on and made it four hundred! He went on, and what did he do? Why, he made it eight hundred! Yes, he did,"

continued Leaf, in the highest pitch of excitement, bringing down his fist upon his knee, with such force that he quivered with the pain; "yes, and he went on and made it A THOUSAND!"

"Hear, hear!" said the tranter. "Better than the history of England, my sonnies!"

"Thank you for your story, Thomas Leaf," said grandfather William; and then Leaf gradually sank into nothingness again.

Every day, in books, magazines, and newspapers, over radio and television, in motion-picture theaters, we listen to Leaf's story one more time, and then sink into nothingness again. His story is, in one sense, better than the history of England—or would be if the history of England were not composed, among other things, of Leaf's story and a million like it. His story, stood on its head, is the old woman's story in *Wozzeck*. "Grandmother, tell us a story," beg the children. "All right, you little crabs," she answers.

Once upon a time there was a poor little girl who had no father or mother because everyone was dead and there was no one left in the whole world. Everyone was dead, and she kept looking for someone night and day. And since there was no one on earth, she thought she'd go to heaven. The moon looked at her so friendly, but when she finally got to it, it was just a piece of rotted wood. So she went on to the sun, and when she got there, it was just a dried-up sunflower. And when she got to the stars, they were just little gold flies stuck up there as if they'd been caught in a spider web. And when she thought she'd go back to earth, it was just an upside-down pot. And she was all alone. And so she sat down and cried. And she's still sitting there, all alone.

The grandmother's story is told less often—but often enough: when we wake into the reality our dream has contradicted, we are bitter at returning against our wishes to so bad a world, and take a fierce pleasure in what remains to us, the demonstration that it is the worst of all possible worlds. And we take pleasure also—as our stories show—in repeating over and over, until we can bear it, all that we found unbearable: the child whose mother left her so often that she invented a game of throwing her doll out of her crib, exclaiming as it vanished: "Gone! gone!" was a true poet. "Does I 'member much about slavery times?" the old man says, in *Lay My Burden Down*; "well, there is no way for me to disremember unless I die." But the worst memories are joyful ones: "Every time Old Mistress thought we little black children was hungry 'tween meals she would call us up to the house to eat. Sometimes she would give us johnny-cake and plenty of buttermilk to drink with it. There was a long trough for us they would scrub so clean. They would fill this trough with buttermilk and all us children would sit round the trough and drink with our mouths and hold our johnnycake with our hands. I can just see myself drinking now. It was so good. . . ." It is so good, our stories believe, simply to remember: their elementary delight in recognition, familiarity, mimesis, is another aspect of their obsession with all the likenesses of the universe, those metaphors that Proust called essential to style. Stories want to *know*: everything from the first blaze and breathlessness and fragrance to the last law and structure; but, too, stories don't want to know, don't want to care, just want to *do as they please*. (Some great books are a consequence of the writer's losing himself in his subject, others are a consequence of his losing himself in himself: Rabelais's "do what you please" is the motto of how many masterpieces, from Cervantes and Sterne on up to the present.) For stories vary from a more-than-Kantian disinterestedness, in which the self is a representative, indistinguishable integer among billions —the mere *one* or *you* or *man* that is the subject of all the verbs—to an insensate, protoplasmic egotism to which the self is the final fact, a galaxy that it is impracticable to get out of to other galaxies. Polarities like these are almost the first thing one notices about fiction. It is as much haunted by the chaos which precedes and succeeds order as by order; by the incongruities of the universe (wit, humor, the arbitrary, accidental, and absurd—all irruptions from, releases of, the Unconscious) as by its likenesses. A story may present fantasy as fact, as the sin or *hubris* that the fact of things punishes, or as a reality superior to fact. And, often, it presents it as a mixture of the three: all opposites meet in fiction.

The truths that he systematized, Freud said, had already been discovered by the poets; the tears of things, the truth of things, are there in their fictions. And yet, as he knew, the root of all stories is in Grimm, not in La Rochefoucauld; in dreams, not in cameras and tape recorders. Turgenev was right when he said, "Truth alone, however powerful, is not art——" oxygen alone, however concentrated, is not water; and Freud was right, profoundly right, when he showed "that the dream is a compromise between the expression of and the defense against the unconscious emotions; that in it the unconscious wish is represented as being fulfilled; that there are very definite mechanisms that control this expression; that the primary process controls the dream world just as it controls the entire unconscious life of the soul, and that myth and poetical productions come into being in the same way and have the same meaning. There is only one important difference: in the myths and in the works of poets the secondary elaboration is much further developed, so that a logical and coherent entity is created."

2.

A baby asleep but about to be waked by hunger sometimes makes little sucking motions: he is dreaming that he is being fed, and manages by virtue of the dream to stay asleep. He may even smile a little in satisfaction. But the smile cannot last for long—the dream fails, and he wakes. This is, in a sense, the first story; the child in his "impotent omnipotence" is like us readers, us writers, in ours.

A story is a chain of events. Since the stories that we know are told by men, the events of the story happen to human or anthropomorphic beings—gods, beasts, and devils; and are related in such a way that the story seems to begin at one place and to end at a very different place, without any essential interruption in its progress. The poet or storyteller, so to speak, writes numbers on a blackboard, draws a line under them, and adds them into their true but unsuspected sum. Stories, because of their nature or—it is to say the same thing—of ours, are always capable of generalization: a story about a dog Kashtanka is true for all values of dogs and men.

Stories can be as short as a sentence. Bion's saying, *The boys throw stones at the frogs in sport, but the frogs die not in sport but in earnest,* is a story; and when one finds it in Aesop, blown up into a fable five or six sentences long, it has become a poorer story. Blake's *Prudence is a rich, ugly old maid courted by Incapacity* has a story inside it, waiting to flower in a glass of water. And there is a story four sentences long that not even Rilke was able to improve: *Now King David was old and stricken in years; and they covered him with clothes, but he got no heat. Wherefore his servants said unto him, Let there be sought for my lord the king a young virgin: and let her stand before the king, and let her cherish him, and let her lie in thy bosom, that my lord the king may get heat. So they sought for a fair damsel throughout all the coasts of Israel, and found Abishag a Shunamite, and brought her to the king. And the damsel was very fair, and cherished the king, and ministered to him: but the king knew her not....* The enlisted men at Fort Benning buried their dog Calculus under a marker that read, *He made better dogs of us all;* and I read in the paper, a few days ago: *A Sunday-school teacher, mother of four children, shot to death her eight-year-old daughter as she slept today, state police reported. Hilda Kristle, 43, of Stony Run, told police that her youngest daughter, Suzanne, "had a heavy heart and often went about the house sighing."*

When we try to make, out of these stories life gives us, works of art of comparable concision, we almost always put them into verse. Blake writes about a chimney sweep:

> A little black thing among the snow
> Crying " 'weep! 'weep!" in notes of woe!
> "Where are thy father & mother, say?"—
> "They are both gone up to the church to pray
>
> "Because I was happy upon the heath,
> And smil'd among the winter's snow,
> They clothèd me in the clothes of death,
> And taught me to sing the notes of woe.
>
> "And because I am happy & dance & sing,
> They think they have done me no injury,
> And are gone to praise God & his Priest & King,
> Who make up a Heaven of our misery—"

and he has written enough. Stephen Crane says in fifty words:

> In the desert
> I saw a creature naked, bestial,
> Who, squatting upon the ground,
> Held his heart in his hands
> And ate of it.

> I said, "Is it good, friend?"
> "It is bitter—bitter," he answered;
> "But I like it
> Because it is bitter,
> And because it is my heart."

These are the bones of stories, and we shiver at them. The poems in this book have more of the flesh of ordinary fiction. A truly representative book of stories would include many more poems: during much of the past people put into verse the stories that they intended to be literature.

But it is hard to put together any representative collection of stories. It is like starting a zoo in a closet: the giraffe alone takes up more space than one has for the collection. *Remembrance of Things Past* is a story, just as Saint-Simon's memoirs are a great many stories. One can represent the memoirs with the death of Monseigneur, but not even the death of Bergotte, the death of the narrator's grandmother, can do that for *Remembrance of Things Past*. Almost everything in the world, one realizes after a while, is too long to go into a short book of stories—a book of short stories. So, even, are all those indeterminate masterpieces that the nineteenth century called short stories and that we call short novels or novelettes: Tolstoy's *The Death of Ivan Ilyich*, *Hadji Murad*, *Master and Man*; Flaubert's *A Simple Heart*; Mann's *Death in Venice*; Leskov's [*The*] *Lady Macbeth of the Mzinsk District*; Keller's *The Three Righteous Comb-Makers*; James's *The Aspern Papers*; Colette's *Julie de Carneilhan*; Kleist's *Michael Kohlhaas*; Joyce's *The Dead*; Turgenev's *A Lear of the Steppes*; Hofmannsthal's *Andreas*; Kafka's *Metamorphosis*; Faulkner's *Spotted Horses*; Porter's *Old Mortality*; Dostoyevsky's *The Eternal Husband*; Melville's *Bartleby the Scrivener*, *Benito Cereno*; Chekhov's *Ward No. 6*, *Peasants*, *In the Ravine*.

And there are many more sorts of stories than there are sizes. Epics; ballads; historical or biographical or autobiographical narratives, letters, diaries; myths, fairy tales, fables; dreams, daydreams; humorous or indecent or religious anecdotes; all those stories that might be called specialized or special case—science fiction, ghost stories, detective stories, Westerns, True Confessions, children's stories, and the rest; and, finally, "serious fiction"—Proust and Chekhov and Kafka, *Moby-Dick*, *Great Expectations*, *A Sportsman's Notebook*. Most of this book is "serious fiction," some of it (Frost, Brecht, Blake, Wordsworth) serious fiction in verse; but there is a letter of Tolstoy's, a piece of history and autobiography from Saint-Simon; and there are gypsy and German fairy tales, Hebrew and Chinese parables, and two episodes from the journal of an imaginary Danish poet, the other self of the poet Rainer Maria Rilke. For there are all kinds of beings, and all kinds of things happen to them; and when you add to these what are as essential to the writer, the things that don't actually happen, the beings that don't actually exist, it is no wonder that stories are as varied as they are.

There are two extremes: stories in which nothing happens, and stories in which everything is a happening. The Muse of fiction believes that people "don't go to the North Pole" but go to work, go home, get married, die; but she believes at the same time that absolutely anything can occur—concludes, with Gogol: "Say what you like, but such things do happen—not often, but they do happen." Our lives, even our stories, approach at one extreme the lives of Prior's Jack and Joan:

> If human things went Ill or Well;
> If changing Empires rose or fell;
> The Morning past, the Evening came,
> And found this couple still the same.
> They Walked and Eat, good folks: What then?
> Why then they Walk'd and Eat again:
> They soundly slept the Night away:
> They did just Nothing all the day...

Nor Good, nor Bad, nor Fools, nor Wise;
They wou'd not learn, nor cou'd advise:
Without Love, Hatred, Joy, or Fear,
They led—a kind of—as it were;
Nor Wish'd, nor Car'd, nor Laugh'd, nor Cry'd:
And so They liv'd; and so They dy'd.

Billions have lived, and left not even a name behind, and while they were alive nobody knew their names either. These live out their lives "among the rocks and winding scars/ Where deep and low the hamlets lie/Each with its little patch of sky/And little lot of stars"; soundly sleep the Night away in the old houses of Oblomov's native village, where everybody did just Nothing all the day; rise—in Gogol's Akaky Akakyevich Bashmachkin, in the Old-World Landowners—to a quite biblical pathos and grandeur; are relatives of that Darling, that *dushechka*, who for so many solitary years "had no opinions of any sort. She saw the objects about her and understood what she saw, but could not form any opinion about them"; sit and, "musing with close lips and lifted eyes/ Have smiled with self-contempt to live so wise/And run so smoothly such a length of lies"; walk slowly, staring about them—or else just walk—through the pages of Turgenev, Sterne, Keller, Rabelais, Twain, Cervantes, and how many others; and in Chuang T'zu disappear into the mists of time, looming before us in primordial grandeur: "In the days of Ho Hsu the people did nothing in particular when at rest, and went nowhere in particular when they moved. Having food, they rejoiced; having full bellies, they strolled about. Such were the capacities of the people."

How different from the later times, the other pages, in which people "wear the hairs off their legs" "counting the grains of rice for a rice-pudding"! How different from the other extreme: the world of Svidrigaylov, Raskolnikov, Stavrogin, where everything that occurs is either a dream told as if it were reality, or reality told as if it were a dream, and where the story is charged up to the point at which the lightning blazes out in some nightmare, revelation, atrocity, and the drained narrative can begin to charge itself again! In this world, and in the world of *The Devil*, *The Kreutzer Sonata*, *The Death of Ivan Ilyich*, everything is the preparation for, or consummation of, an Event; everyone is an echo of "the prehistoric, unforgettable Other One, who is never equaled by anyone later." This is the world of Hofmannsthal's *A Tale of the Cavalry*, where even the cow being dragged to the shambles, "shrinking from the smell of blood and the fresh hide of a calf nailed to the doorpost, planted its hooves firm on the ground, drew the reddish haze of the sunset in through dilated nostrils, and, before the lad could drag her across the road with stick and rope, tore away with piteous eyes a mouthful of the hay which the sergeant had tied on the front of his saddle." It is the world of Nijinsky's diary: "One evening I went for a walk up the hill, and stopped on the mountain . . . 'the mountain of Sinai.' I was cold. I had walked far. Feeling that I should kneel, I quickly knelt and then felt that I should put my hand on the snow. After doing this, I suddenly felt a pain and cried with it, pulling my hand away. I looked at a star, which did not say good evening to me. It did not twinkle at me. I got frightened and wanted to run, but could not because my knees were rooted to the snow. I started to cry, but no one heard my weeping. No one came to my rescue. After several minutes I turned and saw a house. It was closed and the windows shuttered . . . I felt frightened and shouted at the top of my voice: 'Death!' I do not know why, but felt that one must shout 'Death!' After that I felt warmer . . . I walked on the snow which crunched beneath my feet. I liked the snow and listened to its crunching. I loved listening to my footsteps; they were full of life. Looking at the sky, I saw the stars which were twinkling at me and felt merriment in them. I was happy and no longer felt cold . . . I started to go down a dark road, walking quickly, but was stopped by a tree which saved me. I was on the edge of a precipice. I thanked the tree. It felt me because I caught hold of it; it received my warmth and I received the warmth of the tree. I do not know who most needed the warmth. I walked on and suddenly stopped, seeing a precipice without a tree. I understood that God had stopped me because He loves me, and therefore said: 'If it is Thy will, I will fall down the precipice. If it is Thy will, I will be saved.' "

This is what I would call pure narrative; one must go to writers like Tolstoy and Rilke and Kafka to equal it. In the unfinished stories of Kafka's notebook, some fragment a page long can carry us over a whole abyss of events: "I was sitting in the box, and beside me was my wife. The play being performed was an exciting one, it was about jealousy; at that moment in the midst of a brilliantly lit hall surrounded by pillars, a man was just raising his dagger against his wife, who was slowly retreating to the exit. Tense, we leaned forward over the balustrade; I felt my wife's curls against my temple. Then we started back, for something moved on the balustrade; what we had taken for the plush upholstery of the balustrade was the back of a tall thin man, not an inch broader than the balustrade, who had been lying flat on his face there and was now slowly turning over as though trying to find a more comfortable position. Trembling, my wife clung to me. His face was quite close to me, narrower than my hand, meticulously clean as that of a waxwork figure, and with a pointed black beard. 'Why do you come and frighten us?' I exclaimed. 'What are you up to here?' 'Excuse me!' the man said, 'I am an admirer of your wife's. To feel her elbows on my body makes me happy.' 'Emil, I implore you, protect me!' my wife exclaimed. 'I too am called Emil,' the man said, supporting his head on one hand and lying there as though on a sofa. 'Come to me, dear sweet little woman.' 'You cad,' I said, 'another word and you'll find yourself lying down there in the pit,' and as though certain that this word was bound to come, I tried to push him over, but it was not so easy, he seemed to be a solid part of the balustrade, it was as though he were built into it, I tried to roll him off, but I couldn't do it, he only laughed and said: 'Stop that, you silly little man, don't wear out your strength prematurely, the struggle is only beginning and it will end, as may well be said, with your wife's granting my desire.' 'Never!' my wife exclaimed, and then, turning to me: 'Oh, please, do push him down now.' 'I can't,' I exclaimed, 'you can see for yourself how I'm straining, but there's some trickery in it, it can't be done.' 'Oh dear, oh dear,' my wife lamented, 'what is to become of me?' 'Keep calm,' I said, 'I beg of you. By getting so worked up you're only making it worse, I have another plan now, I shall cut the plush open here with my knife and then drop the whole thing down and the fellow with it.' But now I could not find my knife. 'Don't you know where I have my knife?' I asked. 'Can I have left it in my overcoat?' I was almost going to dash along to the cloakroom when my wife brought me to my senses. 'Surely you're not going to leave me alone now, Emil,' she cried. 'But if I have no knife,' I shouted back. 'Take mine,' she said and began fumbling in her little bag, with trembling fingers, but then of course all she produced was a tiny little mother-of-pearl knife."

One of the things that make Kafka so marvelous a writer is his discovery of—or, rather, discovery by—a kind of narrative in which logical analysis and humor, the greatest enemies of narrative movement, have themselves become part of the movement. In narrative at its purest or most eventful we do not understand but are the narrative. When we understand completely (or laugh completely, or feel completely a lyric empathy with the beings of the world), the carrying force of the narrative is dissipated: in fiction, to understand everything is to get nowhere. Yet, walking through Combray with Proust, lying under the leaves with Turgenev and the dwarf Kasyan, who has ever wanted to get anywhere but where he already is, in the best of all possible places?

In stories-in-which-everything-is-a-happening each event is charged and about to be further charged, so that the narrative may at any moment reach a point of unbearable significance, and disintegrate into energy. In stories-in-which-nothing-happens even the climax or denouement is liable to lose what charge it has, and to become simply one more portion of the lyric, humorous, or contemplative continuum of the story: in Gogol's *The Nose* the policeman seizes the barber, the barber turns pale, "but here the incident is completely shrouded in a fog and absolutely nothing is known of what happened next"; and in *Nevsky Avenue*, after Schiller, Hoffman, and Kuntz the carpenter have stripped Lieutenant Pirogov and "treated him with such an utter lack of ceremony that I cannot find words to describe this highly regrettable incident," Pirogov goes raging away, and "nothing could compare with Pirogov's anger and indignation. Siberia and the lash seemed to him the least punishment Schiller deserved. . . . But the whole thing somehow petered out most strangely: on the way to the general, he went into a pastry-cook's, ate two pastries, read something out of the *Northern Bee*, and left with his anger somewhat abated"; took a stroll along Nevsky Avenue; and ended at a party given by one of the directors of the Auditing Board, where he "so distinguished himself in the mazurka that not only the ladies but also the gentlemen were in raptures over it. What a wonderful world we live in!"

One of these extremes of narrative will remind us of the state of minimum excitation which the organism tries to reestablish—of the baby asleep, a lyric smile on his lips; the other extreme resembles the processes of continually increased excitation found in sex and play.

3.

There are so many good short narratives of every kind that a book of this size leaves most of their writers unrepresented. By saying that I was saving these writers for a second book I tried to make myself feel better at having left them out of the first. For I have left out all sagas, all ballads, all myths; a dozen great narrators in verse, from Homer to Rilke; Herodotus, Plutarch, Pushkin, Hawthorne, Flaubert, Dostoevsky, Melville, James, Leskov, Keller, Kipling, Mann, Faulkner—I cannot bear to go on. Several of these have written long narratives so much better than any of their short ones that it seemed unfair to use the short, and it was impossible to use the long. Hemingway I could not get permission to reprint. Any anthology is, as the dictionary says, a bouquet—a bouquet that leaves out most of the world's flowers.

I disliked leaving out writers, but I disliked almost as much having to leave out some additional stories by some of the writers I included. I have used so many of the writers who "came out of Gogol's *Overcoat*" that *The Overcoat* is in a sense already here, but I wish that it and *Old-World Landowners* were here in every sense; that I could have included Chekhov's *The Bishop*, *The Lady with the Dog*, *Gooseberries*, *The Darling*, *The Man in a Shell*, *The Kiss*, *On Official Business*, and how many more; that I could have included Kafka's *The Penal Colony* and *The Hunter Gracchus*; and that I could have included at least a story more from Lawrence, Tolstoy, Verga, Grimm, and Andersen. With Turgenev's masterpiece all selection fails: *A Sportsman's Notebook* is a whole greater and more endearing than even the best of its parts.

Here, then, are thirty stories. Some of them are realistic, some fantastic; from the heights of some of the stories the abysses of others may seem infinitely removed. It is the reader who joins them. What Proust wrote is true: "In reality, each reader reads only what is within himself. The book is no more than a sort of optical instrument which the writer offers the reader to enable the latter to discover in himself what he would not have found but for the aid of the book."

—RANDALL JARRELL

RANDALL JARRELL'S
BOOK OF STORIES

FRANZ KAFKA

A COUNTRY DOCTOR

I WAS IN great perplexity; I had to start on an urgent journey; a seriously ill patient was waiting for me in a village ten
miles off; a thick blizzard of snow filled all the wide spaces
between him and me; I had a gig, a light gig with big wheels,
exactly right for our country roads; muffled in furs, my bag of
instruments in my hand, I was in the courtyard all ready for
the journey; but there was no horse to be had, no horse. My
own horse had died in the night, worn out by the fatigues of
this icy winter; my servant girl was now running round the
village trying to borrow a horse; but it was hopeless, I knew
it, and I stood there forlornly, with the snow gathering more
and more thickly upon me, more and more unable to move.
In the gateway the girl appeared, alone, and waved the lantern; of course, who would lend a horse at this time for such a
journey? I strode through the courtyard once more; I could
see no way out; in my confused distress I kicked at the dilapi-
dated door of the year-long uninhabited pigsty. It flew open
and flapped to and fro on its hinges. A steam and smell as of
horses came out from it. A dim stable lantern was swinging
inside from a rope. A man, crouching on his hams in that
low space, showed an open blue-eyed face. "Shall I yoke up?"
he asked, crawling out on all fours. I did not know what to
say and merely stooped down to see what else was in the sty.
The servant girl was standing beside me. "You never know
what you're going to find in your own house," she said, and
we both laughed. "Hey there, Brother, hey there, Sister!" called

the groom, and two horses, enormous creatures with power-ful flanks, one after the other, their legs tucked close to their bodies, each well-shaped head lowered like a camel's, by sheer strength of buttocking squeezed out through the door hole which they filled entirely. But at once they were standing up, their legs long and their bodies steaming thickly. "Give him a hand," I said, and the willing girl hurried to help the groom with the harnessing. Yet hardly was she beside him when the groom clipped hold of her and pushed his face against hers. She screamed and fled back to me; on her cheek stood out in red the marks of two rows of teeth. "You brute," I yelled in fury, "do you want a whipping?" but in the same moment reflected that the man was a stranger; that I did not know where he came from, and that of his own free will he was help-ing me out when everyone else had failed me. As if he knew my thoughts he took no offense at my threat but, still busied with the horses, only turned round once towards me. "Get in," he said then, and indeed everything was ready. A magnif-icent pair of horses, I observed, such as I had never sat be-hind, and I climbed in happily. "But I'll drive, you don't know the way," I said. "Of course," said he, "I'm not coming with you anyway, I'm staying with Rose." "No," shrieked Rose, fleeing into the house with a justified presentiment that her fate was inescapable; I heard the door chain rattle as she put it up; I heard the key turn in the lock; I could see, moreover, how she put out the lights in the entrance hall and in further flight all through the rooms to keep herself from being dis-covered. "You're coming with me," I said to the groom, "or I won't go, urgent as my journey is. I'm not thinking of paying for it by handing the girl over to you." "Gee up!" he said; clapped his hands; the gig whirled off like a log in a freshet; I could just hear the door of my house splitting and bursting as the groom charged at it and then I was deafened and blinded by a storming rush that steadily buffeted all my senses. But this only for a moment, since, as if my patient's farmyard had opened out just before my courtyard gate, I was already there; the horses had come quietly to a standstill; the blizzard had stopped; moonlight all around; my patient's parents hurried out of the house, his sister behind them; I was almost lifted out of the gig; from their confused ejaculations I gathered not a word; in the sickroom the air was almost unbreathable; the neglected stove was smoking; I wanted to push open a window; but first I had to look at my patient. Gaunt, without any fever, not cold, not warm, with vacant eyes, without a shirt, the youngster heaved himself up from under the feather bedding, threw his arms round my neck, and whispered in my ear: "Doctor, let me die." I glanced round the room; no one had heard it; the parents were leaning forward in silence waiting for my verdict; the sister had set a chair for my handbag; I opened the bag and hunted among my instruments; the boy kept clutching at me from his bed to remind me of his entreaty; I picked up a pair of tweezers, examined them in the candlelight and laid them down again. "Yes," I thought blasphemously, "in cases like this the gods are helpful, send the missing horse, add to it a second because of the urgency, and to crown everything bestow even a groom—" And only now did I remember Rose again; what was I to do, how could I rescue her, how could I pull her away from under that groom at ten miles' distance, with a team of horses I couldn't control. These horses, now, they had somehow slipped the reins loose, pushed the windows open from outside, I did not know how; each of them had stuck a head in at a window and, quite unmoved by the startled cries of the family, stood eyeing the patient. "Better go back at once," I thought, as if the horses were summoning me to the return journey, yet I permitted the patient's sister, who fancied that I was dazed by the heat, to take my fur coat from me. A glass of rum was poured out for me, the old man clapped me on the shoulder, a familiarity justified by this offer of his treasure. I shook my head; in the narrow confines of the old man's thoughts I felt ill; that was

5

my only reason for refusing the drink. The mother stood by the bedside and cajoled me towards it; I yielded, and, while one of the horses whinnied loudly to the ceiling, laid my head to the boy's breast, which shivered under my wet beard. I confirmed what I already knew; the boy was quite sound, something a little wrong with his circulation, saturated with coffee by his solicitous mother, but sound and best turned out of bed with one shove. I am no world reformer and so I let him lie. I was the district doctor and did my duty to the uttermost, to the point where it became almost too much. I was badly paid and yet generous and helpful to the poor. I had still to see that Rose was all right, and then the boy might have his way and I wanted to die too. What was I doing there in that endless winter! My horse was dead, and not a single person in the village would lend me another. I had to get my team out of the pigsty; if they hadn't chanced to be horses I should have had to travel with swine. That was how it was. And I nodded to the family. They knew nothing about it, and, had they known, would not have believed it. To write prescriptions is easy, but to come to an understanding with people is hard. Well, this should be the end of my visit, I had once more been called out needlessly, I was used to that, the whole district made my life a torment with my night bell, but that I should have to sacrifice Rose this time as well, the pretty girl who had lived in my house for years almost without my noticing her—that sacrifice was too much to ask, and I had somehow to get it reasoned out in my head with the help of what craft I could muster, in order not to let fly at this family, which with the best will in the world could not restore Rose to me. But as I shut my bag and put an arm out for my fur coat, the family meanwhile standing together, the father sniffing at the glass of rum in his hand, the mother, apparently disappointed in me—why, what do people expect?—biting her lips with tears in her eyes, the sister fluttering a blood-soaked towel, I was somehow ready to admit conditionally that the boy might be ill after all. I went towards him, he welcomed me smiling as if I were bringing him the most nourishing invalid broth—ah, now both horses were whinnying together; the noise, I suppose, was ordained by heaven to assist my examination of the patient—and this time I discovered that the boy was indeed ill. In his right side, near the hip, was an open wound as big as the palm of my hand. Rose-red, in many variations of shade, dark in the hollows, lighter at the edges, softly granulated, with irregular clots of blood, open as a surface mine to the daylight. That was how it looked from a distance. But on a closer inspection there was another complication. I could not help a low whistle of surprise. Worms, as thick and as long as my little finger, themselves rose-red and blood-spotted as well, were wriggling from their fastness in the interior of the wound towards the light, with small white heads and many little legs. Poor boy, you were past helping. I had discovered your great wound; this blossom in your side was destroying you. The family was pleased; they saw me busying myself; the sister told the mother, the mother the father, the father told several guests who were coming in, through the moonlight at the open door, walking on tiptoe, keeping their balance with outstretched arms. "Will you save me?" whispered the boy with a sob, quite blinded by the life within his wound. That is what people are like in my district. Always expecting the impossible from the doctor. They have lost their ancient beliefs; the parson sits at home and unravels his vestments, one after another; but the doctor is supposed to be omnipotent with his merciful surgeon's hand. Well, as it pleases them; I have not thrust my services on them; if they misuse me for sacred ends, I let that happen to me too; what better do I want, old country doctor that I am, bereft of my servant girl! And so they came, the family and the village elders, and stripped my clothes off me; a school choir with the teacher at the head of it stood before the house and sang these words to an utterly simple tune:

> Strip his clothes off, then he'll heal us,
> If he doesn't, kill him dead!
> Only a doctor, only a doctor.

Then my clothes were off and I looked at the people quietly, my fingers in my beard and my head cocked to one side. I was altogether composed and equal to the situation and remained so, although it was no help to me, since they now took me by the head and feet and carried me to the bed. They laid me down in it next to the wall, on the side of the wound. Then they all left the room; the door was shut; the singing stopped; clouds covered the moon; the bedding was warm around me; the horses' heads in the open windows wavered like shadows. "Do you know," said a voice in my ear, "I have very little confidence in you. Why, you were only blown in here, you didn't come on your own feet. Instead of helping me, you're cramping me on my deathbed. What I'd like best is to scratch your eyes out." "Right," I said, "it is a shame. And yet I am a doctor. What am I to do? Believe me, it is not too easy for me either." "Am I supposed to be content with this apology? Oh, I must be, I can't help it. I always have to put up with things. A fine wound is all I brought into the world; that was my sole endowment." "My young friend," said I, "your mistake is: you have not a wide enough view. I have been in all the sick-rooms, far and wide, and I tell you: your wound is not so bad. Done in a tight corner with two strokes of the ax. Many a one proffers his side and can hardly hear the ax in the forest, far less that it is coming nearer to him." "Is that really so, or are you deluding me in my fever?" "It is really so, take the word of honor of an official doctor." And he took it and lay still. But now it was time for me to think of escaping. The horses were still standing faithfully in their places. My clothes, my fur coat, my bag were quickly collected; I didn't want to waste time dressing; if the horses raced home as they had come, I should only be springing, as it were, out of this bed into my own. Obediently a horse backed away from the window; I threw my bundle into the gig; the fur coat missed its mark and was caught on a hook only by the sleeve. Good enough. I swung myself onto the horse. With the reins loosely trailing, one horse barely fastened to the other, the gig swaying behind, my fur coat last of all in the snow. "Gee up!" I said, but there was no galloping; slowly, like old men, we crawled through the snowy wastes; a long time echoed behind us the new but faulty song of the children:

> O be joyful, all you patients,
> The doctor's laid in bed beside you!

Never shall I reach home at this rate; my flourishing practice is done for; my successor is robbing me, but in vain, for he cannot take my place; in my house the disgusting groom is raging; Rose is his victim; I do not want to think about it any more. Naked, exposed to the frost of this most unhappy of ages, with an earthly vehicle, unearthly horses, old man that I am, I wander astray. My fur coat is hanging from the back of the gig, but I cannot reach it, and none of my limber pack of patients lifts a finger. Betrayed! Betrayed! A false alarm on the night bell once answered—it cannot be made good, not ever.

Translated by Willa and Edwin Muir

ANTON CHEKHOV

GUSEV

1.

IT WAS GETTING dark; it would soon be night.

Gusev, a discharged soldier, sat up in his hammock and said in an undertone:

"I say, Pavel Ivanych. A soldier at Suchan told me: while they were sailing a big fish came into collision with their ship and stove a hole in it."

The nondescript individual whom he was addressing, and whom everyone in the ship's hospital called Pavel Ivanych, was silent, as though he had not heard.

And again a stillness followed. . . . The wind frolicked with the rigging, the screw throbbed, the waves lashed, the hammocks creaked, but the ear had long ago become accustomed to these sounds, and it seemed that everything around was asleep and silent. It was dreary. The three invalids—two soldiers and a sailor—who had been playing cards all the day were asleep and talking in their dreams.

It seemed as though the ship were beginning to rock. The hammock slowly rose and fell under Gusev, as though it were heaving a sigh, and this was repeated once, twice, three times. . . . Something crashed onto the floor with a clang: it must have been a jug falling down.

"The wind has broken loose from its chain . . ." said Gusev, listening.

This time Pavel Ivanych cleared his throat and answered irritably:

Anton Chekhov

"One minute a vessel's running into a fish, the next, the wind's breaking loose from its chain.... Is the wind a beast that it can break loose from its chain?"

"That's how christened folk talk."

"They are as ignorant as you are then.... They say all sorts of things. One must keep a head on one's shoulders and use one's reason. You are a senseless creature."

Pavel Ivanych was subject to seasickness. When the sea was rough he was usually ill-humored, and the merest trifle would make him irritable. And in Gusev's opinion there was absolutely nothing to be vexed about. What was there strange or wonderful, for instance, in the fish or in the wind's breaking loose from its chain? Suppose the fish were as big as a mountain and its back were as hard as a sturgeon: and in the same way, supposing that away yonder at the end of the world there stood great stone walls and the fierce winds were chained up to the walls ... if they had not broken loose, why did they tear about all over the sea like maniacs, and struggle to escape like dogs? If they were not chained up, what did become of them when it was calm?

Gusev pondered for a long time about fishes as big as a mountain and stout, rusty chains, then he began to feel dull and thought of his native place to which he was returning after five years' service in the East. He pictured an immense pond covered with snow.... On one side of the pond the red-brick building of the potteries with a tall chimney and clouds of black smoke; on the other side—a village.... His brother Alexey comes out in a sledge from the fifth yard from the end; behind him sits his little son Vanka in big felt overboots, and his little girl Akulka, also in big felt boots. Alexey has been drinking, Vanka is laughing, Akulka's face he could not see, she had muffled herself up.

"You never know, he'll get the children frozen ..." thought Gusev. "Lord send them sense and judgment that they may honor their father and mother and not be wiser than their parents."

"They want resoling," a delirious sailor says in a bass voice. "Yes, yes!"

Gusev's thoughts break off, and instead of a pond there suddenly appears apropos of nothing a huge bull's head without eyes, and the horse and sledge are not driving along, but are whirling round and round in a cloud of smoke. But still he was glad he had seen his own folks. He held his breath from delight, shudders ran all over him, and his fingers twitched.

"The Lord let us meet again," he muttered feverishly, but he at once opened his eyes and sought in the darkness for water.

He drank and lay back, and again the sledge was moving, then again the bull's head without eyes, smoke, clouds.... And so on till daybreak.

2.

The first outline visible in the darkness was a blue circle—the little round window; then little by little Gusev could distinguish his neighbor in the next hammock, Pavel Ivanych. The man slept sitting up, as he could not breathe lying down. His face was gray, his nose was long and sharp, his eyes looked huge from the terrible thinness of his face, his temples were sunken, his beard was skimpy, his hair was long.... Looking at him you could not make out from what class he came, whether he were a gentleman, a merchant, or a peasant. Judging from his expression and his long hair he might have been a hermit or a lay brother in a monastery—but if one listened to what he said it seemed that he could not be a monk. He was worn out by his cough and his illness and by the stifling heat, and breathed with difficulty, moving his parched lips. Noticing that Gusev was looking at him he turned his face towards him and said:

"I begin to guess.... Yes.... I understand it all perfectly now."

"What do you understand, Pavel Ivanych?"

"I'll tell you.... It has always seemed to me strange that terribly ill as you are you should be here in a steamer where it is so hot and stifling and we are always being tossed up and down, where, in fact, everything threatens you with death; now it is all clear to me.... Yes.... Your doctors put you on the steamer to get rid of you. They get sick of looking after poor brutes like you.... You don't pay them anything, they have a bother with you, and you damage their records with your deaths—so, of course, you are brutes! It's not difficult to get rid of you.... All that is necessary is, in the first place, to have no conscience or humanity, and, secondly, to deceive the steamer authorities. The first condition need hardly be considered, in that respect we are artists; and one can always succeed in the second with a little practice. In a crowd of four hundred healthy soldiers and sailors half a dozen sick ones are not conspicuous; well, they drove you all onto the steamer, mixed you with the healthy ones, hurriedly counted you over, and in the confusion nothing amiss was noticed, and when the steamer had started they saw that there were paralytics and consumptives in the last stage lying about on the deck...."

Gusev did not understand Pavel Ivanych; but supposing he was being blamed, he said in self-defense:

"I lay on the deck because I had not the strength to stand; when we were unloaded from the barge onto the ship I caught a fearful chill."

"It's revolting," Pavel Ivanych went on. "The worst of it is they know perfectly well that you can't last out the long journey, and yet they put you here. Supposing you get as far as the Indian Ocean, what then? It's horrible to think of it.... And that's their gratitude for your faithful, irreproachable service!"

Pavel Ivanych's eyes looked angry; he frowned contemptuously and said, gasping:

"Those are the people who ought to be plucked in the newspapers till the feathers fly in all directions."

The two sick soldiers and the sailor were awake and already playing cards. The sailor was half reclining in his hammock, the soldiers were sitting near him on the floor in the most uncomfortable attitudes. One of the soldiers had his right arm in a sling, and the hand was swathed up in a regular bundle so that he held his cards under his right arm or in the crook of his elbow while he played with the left. The ship was rolling heavily. They could not stand up, nor drink tea, nor take their medicines.

"Were you an officer's servant?" Pavel Ivanych asked Gusev.

"Yes, an officer's servant."

"My God, my God!" said Pavel Ivanych, and he shook his head mournfully. "To tear a man out of his home, drag him twelve thousand miles away, then to drive him into consumption and ... and what it is all for, one wonders? To turn him into a servant for some Captain Kopeykin or midshipman Dyrka! How logical!"

"It's not hard work, Pavel Ivanych. You get up in the morning and clean the boots, get the samovar, sweep the rooms, and then you have nothing more to do. The lieutenant is all the day drawing plans, and if you like you can say your prayers, if you like you can read a book or go out into the street. God grant everyone such a life."

"Yes, very nice, the lieutenant draws plans all the day and you sit in the kitchen and pine for home.... Plans indeed! ... It is not plans that matter, but a human life. Life is not given twice, it must be treated mercifully."

"Of course, Pavel Ivanych, a bad man gets no mercy anywhere, neither at home nor in the army, but if you live as you ought and obey orders, who has any need to insult you? The officers are educated gentlemen, they understand.... In five years I was never once in prison, and I was never struck a blow, so help me God, but once."

"What for?"

"For fighting. I have a heavy hand, Pavel Ivanych. Four Chinamen came into our yard; they were bringing firewood or something, I don't remember. Well, I was bored and I knocked them about a bit, one's nose began bleeding, damn the fellow.... The lieutenant saw it through the little window, he was angry and gave me a box on the ear."

"Foolish, pitiful man ..." whispered Pavel Ivanych. "You don't understand anything."

He was utterly exhausted by the tossing of the ship and closed his eyes; his head alternately fell back and dropped forward on his breast. Several times he tried to lie down but nothing came of it; his difficulty in breathing prevented it.

"And what did you hit the four Chinamen for?" he asked a little while afterwards.

"Oh, nothing. They came into the yard and I hit them."

And a stillness followed.... The card-players had been playing for two hours with enthusiasm and loud abuse of one another, but the motion of the ship overcame them, too; they threw aside the cards and lay down. Again Gusev saw the big pond, the brick building, the village.... Again the sledge was coming along, again Vanka was laughing and Akulka, silly little thing, threw open her fur coat and stuck her feet out, as much as to say: "Look, good people, my snowboots are not like Vanka's, they are new ones."

"Five years old, and she has no sense yet," Gusev muttered in delirium. "Instead of kicking your legs you had better come and get your soldier uncle a drink. I will give you something nice."

Then Andron with a flintlock gun on his shoulder was carrying a hare he had killed, and he was followed by the decrepit old Jew Isaiychik, who offers to barter the hare for a piece of soap; then the black calf in the shed, then Domna sewing at a shirt and crying about something, and then again the bull's head without eyes, black smoke....

Overhead someone gave a loud shout, several sailors ran by, they seemed to be dragging something bulky over the deck, something fell with a crash. Again they ran by.... Had something gone wrong? Gusev raised his head, listened, and saw that the two soldiers and the sailor were playing cards again; Pavel Ivanych was sitting up moving his lips. It was stifling, one hadn't strength to breathe, one was thirsty, the water was warm, disgusting. The ship heaved as much as ever.

Suddenly something strange happened to one of the soldiers playing cards.... He called hearts diamonds, got muddled in his score, and dropped his cards, then with a frightened, foolish smile looked round at all of them.

"I shan't be a minute, mates, I'll ..." he said, and lay down on the floor.

Everybody was amazed. They called to him, he did not answer.

"Stepan, maybe you are feeling bad, eh?" the soldier with his arm in a sling asked him. "Perhaps we had better bring the priest, eh?"

"Have a drink of water, Stepan ..." said the sailor. "Here, lad, drink."

"Why are you knocking the jug against his teeth?" said Gusev angrily. "Don't you see, turnip head?"

"What?"

"What?" Gusev repeated, mimicking him. "There is no breath in him, he is dead! That's what! What nonsensical people, Lord have mercy on us ...!"

3.

The ship was not rocking and Pavel Ivanych was more cheerful. He was no longer ill-humored. His face had a boastful,

defiant, mocking expression. He looked as though he wanted
to say: "Yes, in a minute I will tell you something that will
make you split your sides with laughing." The little round
window was open and a soft breeze was blowing on Pavel
Ivanych. There was a sound of voices, of the plash of oars in
the water.... Just under the little window someone began
droning in a high, unpleasant voice: no doubt it was a
Chinaman singing.

"Here we are in the harbor," said Pavel Ivanych, smiling
ironically. "Only another month and we shall be in Russia.
Well, worthy gentlemen and warriors! I shall arrive at Odessa
and from there go straight to Harkov. In Harkov I have a friend,
a literary man. I shall go to him and say, 'Come, old man, put
aside your horrid subjects, ladies' amours and the beauties of
nature, and show up human depravity.' "

For a minute he pondered, then said:

"Gusev, do you know how I took them in?"

"Took in whom, Pavel Ivanych?"

"Why, these fellows.... You know that on this steamer
there is only a first class and a third class, and they only allow peasants—that is the riffraff—to go in the third. If you
have got on a reefer jacket and have the faintest resemblance
to a gentleman or a bourgeois you must go first class, if you
please. You must fork out five hundred rubles if you die for
it. Why, I ask, have you made such a rule? Do you want to
raise the prestige of educated Russians thereby? Not a bit of
it. We don't let you go third class simply because a decent
person can't go third class; it is very horrible and disgusting.
Yes, indeed. I am very grateful for such solicitude for decent
people's welfare. But in any case, whether it is nasty there or
nice, five hundred rubles I haven't got. I haven't pilfered government money. I haven't exploited the natives, I haven't
trafficked in contraband, I have flogged no one to death, so
judge whether I have the right to travel first class and even
less to reckon myself of the educated class? But you won't

catch them with logic.... One has to resort to deception. I put on a workman's coat and high boots, I assumed a drunken, servile mug and went to the agents: 'Give us a little ticket, your Honor,' said I...."

"Why, what class do you belong to?" asked a sailor.

"Clerical. My father was an honest priest, he always told the great ones of the world the truth to their faces; and he had a great deal to put up with in consequence."

Pavel Ivanych was exhausted with talking and gasped for breath, but still went on:

"Yes, I always tell people the truth to their faces. I am not afraid of anyone or anything. There is a vast difference between me and all of you in that respect. You are in darkness, you are blind, crushed; you see nothing and what you do see you don't understand.... You are told the wind breaks loose from its chain, that you are beasts, Pechenegs, and you believe it; they punch you in the neck, you kiss their hands; some animal in a sable-lined coat robs you and then tips you fifteen kopecks and you: 'Let me kiss your hand, sir.' You are pariahs, pitiful people.... I am a different sort. My eyes are open, I see it all as clearly as a hawk or an eagle when it floats over the earth, and I understand it all. I am a living protest. I see irresponsible tyranny—I protest. I see cant and hypocrisy —I protest. I see swine triumphant—I protest. And I cannot be suppressed, no Spanish Inquisition can make me hold my tongue. No.... Cut out my tongue and I would protest in dumb show; shut me up in a cellar—I will shout from it to be heard half a mile away, or I will starve myself to death that they may have another weight on their black consciences. Kill me and I will haunt them with my ghost. All my acquaintances say to me: 'You are a most insufferable person, Pavel Ivanych.' I am proud of such a reputation. I have served three years in the Far East, and I shall be remembered there for a hundred years: I had rows with everyone. My friends write to me from Russia, 'Don't come back,' but here I am going back to spite them ... yes. ... That is life as I understand it. That is what one can call life."

Gusev was looking at the little window and was not listening. A boat was swaying on the transparent, soft, turquoise water all bathed in hot, dazzling sunshine. In it there were naked Chinamen holding up cages with canaries and calling out:

"It sings, it sings!"

Another boat knocked against the first; the steam cutter darted by. And then there came another boat with a fat Chinaman sitting in it, eating rice with little sticks.

Languidly the water heaved, languidly the white seagulls floated over it.

"I should like to give that fat fellow one in the neck," thought Gusev, gazing at the stout Chinaman, with a yawn.

He dozed off, and it seemed to him that all nature was dozing, too. Time flew swiftly by; imperceptibly the day passed, imperceptibly the darkness came on. ... The steamer was no longer standing still, but moving on further.

4.

Two days passed, Pavel Ivanych lay down instead of sitting up; his eyes were closed, his nose seemed to have grown sharper.

"Pavel Ivanych," Gusev called to him. "Hey, Pavel Ivanych."

Pavel Ivanych opened his eyes and moved his lips.

"Are you feeling bad?"

"No ... it's nothing ..." answered Pavel Ivanych, gasping. "Nothing; on the contrary ... I am rather better. ... You see I can lie down. ... I am a little easier. ..."

"Well, thank God for that, Pavel Ivanych."

"When I compare myself with you I am sorry for you ... poor fellow. My lungs are all right, it is only a stomach cough. ... I can stand hell, let alone the Red Sea. Besides I take a critical attitude to my illness and to the medicines they give me for it. While you . . . you are in darkness. . . . It's hard for you, very, very hard!"

The ship was not rolling, it was calm, but as hot and stifling as a bathhouse; it was not only hard to speak but even hard to listen. Gusev hugged his knees, laid his head on them and thought of his home. Good heavens, what a relief it was to think of snow and cold in that stifling heat! You drive in a sledge, all at once the horses take fright at something and bolt. . . . Regardless of the road, the ditches, the ravines, they dash like mad things, right through the village, over the pond by the pottery works, out across the open fields. "Hold on," the pottery hands and the peasants shout, meeting them. "Hold on." But why? Let the keen, cold wind beat in one's face and bite one's hands; let the lumps of snow, kicked up by the horses' hoofs, fall on one's cap, on one's back, down one's collar, on one's chest; let the runners ring on the snow, and the traces and the sledge be smashed, deuce take them one and all! And how delightful when the sledge upsets and you go flying full tilt into a drift, face downwards in the snow, and then you get up white all over with icicles on your mustaches; no cap, no gloves, your belt undone. . . . People laugh, the dogs bark. . . .

Pavel Ivanych half opened one eye, looked at Gusev with it, and asked softly:

"Gusev, did your commanding officer steal?"

"Who can tell, Pavel Ivanych! We can't say, it didn't reach us." And after that a long time passed in silence. Gusev brooded, muttered something in delirium, and kept drinking water; it was hard for him to talk and hard to listen, and he was afraid of being talked to. An hour passed, a second, a third; evening came on, then night, but he did not notice it. He still sat dreaming of the frost.

There was a sound as though someone came into the hospital, and voices were audible, but a few minutes passed and all was still again.

"The Kingdom of Heaven and eternal peace," said the soldier with his arm in a sling. "He was an uncomfortable man."

"What?" asked Gusev. "Who?"

"He is dead; they have just carried him up."

"Oh, well," muttered Gusev, yawning, "the Kingdom of Heaven be his."

"What do you think?" the soldier with his arm in a sling asked Gusev. "Will he be in the Kingdom of Heaven or not?"

"Who is it you are talking about?"

"Pavel Ivanych."

"He will be . . . he suffered so long. And there is another thing, he belonged to the clergy, and the priests always have a lot of relations. Their prayers will save him."

The soldier with the sling sat down on a hammock near Gusev and said in an undertone:

"And you, Gusev, are not long for this world. You will never get to Russia."

"Did the doctor or his assistant say so?" asked Gusev.

"It isn't that they said so, but one can see it. . . . One can see directly when a man's going to die. You don't eat, you don't drink; it's dreadful to see how thin you've got. It's consumption, in fact. I say it, not to upset you, but because maybe you would like to have the sacrament and extreme unction. And if you have any money you had better give it to the senior officer."

"I haven't written home . . ." Gusev sighed. "I shall die and they won't know."

"They'll hear of it," the sick sailor brought out in a bass voice. "When you die they will put it down in the *Gazette*, at Odessa they will send in a report to the commanding officer there and he will send it to the parish or somewhere. . . ."

Gusev began to be uneasy after such a conversation and to feel a vague yearning. He drank water—it was not that; he dragged himself to the window and breathed the hot, moist air—it was not that; he tried to think of home, of the frost—it was not that. . . . At last it seemed to him one minute longer in the ward and he would certainly expire.

"It's stifling, mates . . ." he said. "I'll go on deck. Help me up, for Christ's sake."

"All right," assented the soldier with the sling. "I'll carry you, you can't walk, hold on to my neck."

Gusev put his arm round the soldier's neck, the latter put his unhurt arm round him and carried him up. On the deck sailors and time-expired soldiers were lying asleep side by side; there were so many of them it was difficult to pass.

"Stand down," the soldier with the sling said softly. "Follow me quietly, hold on to my shirt. . . ."

It was dark. There was no light on deck, nor on the masts, nor anywhere on the sea around. At the furthest end of the ship the man on watch was standing perfectly still like a statue, and it looked as though he were asleep. It seemed as though the steamer were abandoned to itself and were going at its own will.

"Now they will throw Pavel Ivanych into the sea," said the sailor with the sling. "In a sack and then into the water."

"Yes, that's the rule."

"But it's better to lie at home in the earth. Anyway, your mother comes to the grave and weeps."

"Of course!"

There was a smell of hay and of dung. There were oxen standing with drooping heads by the ship's rail. One, two, three; eight of them! And there was a little horse. Gusev put out his hand to stroke it, but it shook its head, showed its teeth, and tried to bite his sleeve.

"Damned brute . . ." said Gusev angrily.

The two of them, he and the soldier, threaded their way to the head of the ship, then stood at the rail and looked up and down. Overhead deep sky, bright stars, peace and stillness, exactly as at home in the village, below darkness and disorder. The tall waves were resounding, no one could tell why.

Whichever wave you looked at each one was trying to rise higher than all the rest and to chase and crush the next one; after it a third as fierce and hideous flew noisily, with a glint of light on its white crest.

The sea has no sense and no pity. If the steamer had been smaller and not made of thick iron, the waves would have crushed it to pieces without the slightest compunction, and would have devoured all the people in it with no distinction of saints or sinners. The steamer had the same cruel and meaningless expression. This monster with its huge beak was dashing onwards, cutting millions of waves in its path; it had no fear of the darkness nor the wind, nor of space, nor of solitude, caring for nothing, and if the ocean had its people, this monster would have crushed them, too, without distinction of saints or sinners.

"Where are we now?" asked Gusev.

"I don't know. We must be in the ocean."

"There is no sight of land. . . ."

"No indeed! They say we shan't see it for seven days."

The two soldiers watched the white foam with the phosphorous light on it and were silent, thinking. Gusev was the first to break the silence.

"There is nothing to be afraid of," he said, "only one is full of dread as though one were sitting in a dark forest; but if, for instance, they let a boat down onto the water this minute and an officer ordered me to go a hundred miles over the sea to catch fish, I'd go. Or, let's say, if a Christian were to fall into the water this minute, I'd go in after him. A German or a Chinaman I wouldn't save, but I'd go in after a Christian."

"And are you afraid to die?"

"Yes. I am sorry for the folks at home. My brother at home, you know, isn't steady; he drinks, he beats his wife for nothing, he does not honor his parents. Everything will go to ruin without me, and father and my old mother will be begging their bread, I shouldn't wonder. But my legs won't bear me, brother, and it's hot here. Let's go to sleep."

5.

Gusev went back to the ward and got into his hammock. He was again tormented by a vague craving, and he could not make out what he wanted. There was an oppression on his chest, a throbbing in his head, his mouth was so dry that it was difficult for him to move his tongue. He dozed, and murmured in his sleep, and, worn out with nightmares, his cough, and the stifling heat, towards morning he fell into a sound sleep. He dreamed that they were just taking the bread out of the oven in the barracks and he climbed into the stove and had a steam bath in it, lashing himself with a bunch of birch twigs. He slept for two days, and at midday on the third two sailors came down and carried him out.

He was sewn up in sailcloth and to make him heavier they put with him two iron weights. Sewn up in the sailcloth he looked like a carrot or a radish: broad at the head and narrow at the feet. . . . Before sunset they brought him up to the deck and put him on a plank; one end of the plank lay on the side of the ship, the other on a box, placed on a stool. Round him stood the soldiers and the officers with their caps off.

"Blessed be the Name of the Lord," the priest began. ". . . As it was in the beginning, is now, and ever shall be."

"Amen," chanted three sailors.

The soldiers and the officers crossed themselves and looked away at the waves. It was strange that a man should be sewn up in sailcloth and should soon be flying into the sea. Was it possible that such a thing might happen to anyone?

The priest strewed earth upon Gusev and bowed down. They sang "Eternal Memory."

The man on watch duty tilted up the end of the plank, Gusev slid off and flew headforemost, turned a somersault in the air and splashed into the sea. He was covered with foam and for a moment looked as though he were wrapped in lace, but the minute passed and he disappeared in the waves.

He went rapidly towards the bottom. Did he reach it? It was

said to be three miles to the bottom. After sinking sixty or seventy feet, he began moving more and more slowly, swaying rhythmically, as though he were hesitating and, carried along by the current, moved more rapidly sideways than downwards.

Then he was met by a shoal of the fish called harbor pilots. Seeing the dark body the fish stopped as though petrified, and suddenly turned round and disappeared. In less than a minute they flew back swift as an arrow to Gusev, and began zigzagging round him in the water.

After that another dark body appeared. It was a shark. It swam under Gusev with dignity and no show of interest, as though it did not notice him, and sank down upon its back, then it turned belly upwards, basking in the warm, transparent water and languidly opened its jaws with two rows of teeth. The harbor pilots are delighted, they stop to see what will come next. After playing a little with the body the shark nonchalantly puts its jaws under it, cautiously touches it with his teeth, and the sailcloth is rent its full length from head to foot; one of the weights falls out and frightens the harbor pilots, and striking the shark on the ribs goes rapidly to the bottom.

Overhead at this time the clouds are massed together on the side where the sun is setting; one cloud like a triumphal arch, another like a lion, a third like a pair of scissors.... From behind the clouds a broad, green shaft of light pierces through and stretches to the middle of the sky; a little later another, violet-colored, lies beside it; next to that, one of gold, then one rose-colored.... The sky turns a soft lilac. Looking at this gorgeous, enchanted sky, at first the ocean scowls, but soon it, too, takes tender, joyous, passionate colors for which it is hard to find a name in human speech.

Translated by Constance Garnett

RAINER MARIA RILKE

THE WRECKED HOUSES;
THE BIG THING

IT IS GOOD to say it out aloud: "Nothing has happened."
Once more: "Nothing has happened." Does that help?

That my stove began to smoke again and I had to go out,
is really no misfortune. That I feel weary and chilled is of
no consequence. That I have been running about the streets
all day is my own fault. I might just as well have sat in the
Louvre. But no, I could not have done that. There are certain
people who go there to warm themselves. They sit on the
velvet benches, and their feet stand like big empty boots side
by side on the gratings of the hot-air registers. They are extremely modest men who are thankful when the attendants
in their dark-blue uniforms studded with medals suffer their
presence. But when I enter, they grimace. They grimace and
nod slightly. And then, when I go back and forth before the
pictures, they keep me in view, always in view, always within
that scrambled, blurry gaze. So it was well I did not go into
the Louvre. I kept on the move incessantly. Heaven knows
through how many towns, districts, cemeteries, bridges, and
passage-ways. Somewhere or other I saw a man pushing a
vegetable cart before him. He was shouting: "Chou-fleur,
chou-fleur," pronouncing the "fleur" with a strangely muffled "eu." Beside him walked an angular, ugly woman who
nudged him from time to time. And when she nudged him,
he shouted. Sometimes he shouted of his own accord too, but
that would prove useless, and he had to shout again immediately after, because they were in front of a house that would

buy. Have I already said that the man was blind? No? Well, he was blind. He was blind and he shouted. I misrepresent when I say that, suppressing the barrow he was shoving, pretending I did not notice he was shouting "cauliflower." But is that essential? And even if it were essential, isn't the main thing what the whole business was for me? I saw an old man who was blind and shouted. That I saw. Saw.

Will anyone believe that there are such houses? No, they will say I am misrepresenting. This time it is the truth, nothing omitted, and naturally nothing added. Where should I get it from? Everyone knows I am poor. Everyone knows it. Houses? But, to be precise, they were houses that were no longer there. Houses that had been pulled down from top to bottom. What *was* there was the other houses, those that had stood alongside of them, tall neighboring houses. Apparently these were in danger of falling down, since everything alongside had been taken away; for a whole scaffolding of long, tarred timbers had been rammed slantwise between the rubbish-strewn ground and the bared wall. I don't know whether I have already said that it is this wall I mean. But it was, so to speak, not the first wall of the existing houses (as one would have supposed), but the last of those that had been there. One saw its inner side. One saw at the different stories the walls of rooms to which the paper still clung, and here and there the join of floor or ceiling. Beside these room-walls there still remained, along the whole length of the wall, a dirty-white area, and through this crept in unspeakably ugly motions, worm-soft and as if digesting, the open, rust-spotted channel of the water-closet pipe. Gray, dusty traces of the paths the lighting-gas had taken remained at the ceiling edges, and here and there, quite unexpectedly, they bent sharp around and came running into the colored wall and into a hole that had been torn out black and ruthless. But most unforgettable of all were the walls themselves. The stubborn life of these rooms had not let itself be trampled out. It was still there; it clung to the nails that had been left, it stood on the remaining handsbreadth of flooring, it crouched under the corner joints where there was still a little bit of interior. One could see that it was in the paint, which, year by year, it had slowly altered: blue into moldy green, green into gray, and yellow into an old, stale rotting white. But it was also in the spots that had kept fresher, behind mirrors, pictures, and wardrobes; for it had drawn and redrawn their contours, and had been with spiders and dust even in these hidden places that now lay bared. It was in every flayed strip, it was in the damp blisters at the lower edges of the wallpapers; it wavered in the torn-off shreds, and sweated out of the foul patches that had come into being long ago. And from these walls once blue and green and yellow, which were framed by the fracture-tracks of the demolished partitions, the breath of these lives stood out—the clammy, sluggish, musty breath, which no wind had yet scattered. There stood the middays and sicknesses and the exhaled breath and the smoke of years, and the sweat that breaks out under armpits and makes clothes heavy, and the stale breath of mouths, and the fusel odor of sweltering feet. There stood the tang of urine and the burn of soot and gray reek of potatoes, and the heavy stench of aging grease. The sweet, lingering smell of neglected infants was there, and the fear-smell of children who go to school, and the sultriness out of the beds of nubile youths. To these was added much that had come from below, from the abyss of the street, which reeked, and more that had oozed down from above with the rain, which over cities is not clean. And much the feeble, tamed domestic winds, that always stay in the same street, had brought along; and much more was there, the source of which one did not know. I said, did I not, that all the walls had been demolished except the last—? It is of this wall I have been speaking all along. One would think I had stood a long time before it; but I'm willing to swear that I began to run as soon as I had recognized that wall. For that

29

is the terrible thing, that I did recognize it. I recognize everything here, and that is why it goes right into me: it is at home in me.

I was somewhat worn out after all this, one might even say exhausted, and that is why it was too much for me that he too had to be waiting for me. He was waiting in the little crémerie where I intended to eat two poached eggs; I was hungry, I had not managed to eat the whole day. But even then I could not take anything; before the eggs were ready something drove me out again into the streets, which ran toward me viscid with humanity. For it was carnival and evening, and the people all had time and roved about, rubbing against each other. And their faces were full of the light that came from the show-booths, and laughter bubbled from their mouths like matter from open sores. The more impatiently I tried to force my way forward, the more they laughed and the more closely they crowded together. Somehow a woman's shawl hooked itself to me; I dragged her after me, and people stopped me and laughed, and I felt I should laugh too, but I could not. Someone threw a handful of confetti into my eyes, and it burned like a whip. At the crossings people were wedged fast, shoved one into the other, and there was no forward movement in them, only a quiet, gentle swaying back and forth, as if they copulated standing. But although they stood, and I ran like a madman along the edge of the pavement where there were gaps in the crowd, yet in truth it was they who moved while I never stirred. For nothing changed; when I looked up I was still aware of the same houses on the one side and on the other the booths. Perhaps everything indeed stood fast, and it was simply a dizziness in me and in them which seemed to whirl everything around. I had no time to reflect on this; I was heavy with sweat, and a stupefying pain circled in me, as if something too large were driving along in my blood, distending the veins wherever it passed. And in addition I felt that the air had long been exhausted, and that I was now breathing only exhaled breath, which my lungs refused.

But it is over now; I have survived it. I am sitting in my room by the lamp; it is a little cold, for I do not venture to try the stove: what if it smoked, and I had to go out again? I am sitting and thinking: if I were not poor I would rent another room with furniture not so worn out, not so full of former occupants, as the furniture here. At first it really cost me an effort to lean my head on this arm-chair; for there is a certain greasy-gray hollow in its green covering, into which all heads seem to fit. For some time I took the precaution of putting a handkerchief under my hair, but now I am too tired to do that; I discovered that it is all right the way it is, and that the slight hollow is made exactly for the back of my head, as if to measure. But I would, if I were not poor, first of all buy a good stove, and burn the clean, strong wood that comes from the mountains, and not these miserable têtes de moineau, the fumes of which scare one's breathing so and make one's head so confused. And then someone would have to tidy up without coarse noises, and keep the fire the way I need it; for often when I have to kneel before the stove and poke for a quarter of an hour, the skin on my forehead tense with the close glow and with heat in my open eyes, I expend all the strength I have for the day, and then when I get among people they naturally get the better of me very easily. I would sometimes, when the crush is great, take a carriage and drive by; I would eat every day in a Duval . . . and no longer slink into crémeries . . . Would he too have been in a Duval? No. He would not have been allowed to wait for me there. They don't allow the dying in. The dying? I am now sitting in my room; so I can try to reflect quietly on what happened to me. It is well to leave nothing in uncertainty. I went in, then, and at first only noticed that the table at which I usually sat was occupied by someone else. I bowed in the direction of the little counter, ordered, and sat down at the next table. But then I felt him, although he did not stir. It was precisely this immobility of his that I felt, and I understood it all at once. The connection between us was established, and I knew that he was stiff with terror. I knew that terror paralyzed him, terror at something that was happening inside him. Perhaps one of his blood-vessels had burst; perhaps, just at this moment, some poison that he had long dreaded was penetrating the ventricle of his heart; perhaps a great abscess had risen in his brain like a sun that was changing the world for him. With an indescribable effort I compelled myself to look in his direction, for I still hoped it was all imagination. But then I sprang up and rushed out; for I had made no mistake. He sat there in a thick, black winter coat, his gray, strained face plunged deep into a woolen neckcloth. His mouth was closed as if it had fallen shut with great force, but it was not possible to say whether his eyes still saw: misty, smoke-gray spectacle lenses covered them, trembling slightly. His nostrils were distended, and the long hair over the wasted temples, out of which everything had been taken, wilted as if in too intense a heat. His ears were long, yellow, with large shadows behind them. Yes, he knew that he was now withdrawing from everything: not merely human beings. A moment more and everything will have lost its meaning, and that table and the cup, and the chair to which he clings, all the near and commonplace things around him, will have become unintelligible, strange and heavy. So he sat there and waited until it should have happened. And defended himself no longer.

And I still defend myself. I defend myself, although I know my heart is already hanging out and that I cannot live any longer, even if my tormentors were to leave me alone now. I say to myself: "Nothing has happened," and yet I was only able to understand that man because within me too something is happening, that is beginning to draw me away and separate me from everything. How it always horrified me to hear said of a dying person: he could no longer recognize anybody. Then I would imagine to myself a lonely face that raised itself from pillows and sought, sought for some familiar thing, sought for something once seen, but there was nothing there. If my fear were not so great, I should console myself with the fact that it is not impossible to see everything differently and yet to live. But I am afraid, I am namelessly afraid of this change. I have, indeed, hardly got used yet to this world, which seems good to me. What should I do in another? I would so gladly stay among the significations that have become dear to me; and if anything has to change at all, I would like at least to be allowed to live among dogs, who possess a world akin to our own and the same things.

For a while yet I can write all this down and express it. But there will come a day when my hand will be far from me, and when I bid it write, it will write words I do not mean. The time of that other interpretation will dawn, when not one word will remain upon another, and all meaning will dissolve like clouds and fall down like rain. Despite my fear I am yet like one standing before something great, and I remember that it was often like that in me before I began to write. But this time I shall be written. I am the impression that will change. Ah, but a little more, and I could understand all this and approve it. Only a step, and my deep misery would be beatitude. But I cannot take that step; I have fallen and cannot pick myself up again, because I am broken. I still believed some help might come. There it lies before me in my own handwriting, what I have prayed, evening after evening. I transcribed it from the books in which I found it, so that it might be very near me, sprung from my hand like something of my own. And now I want to write it once again, kneeling here before my table I want to write it; for in this way I have it longer than when I read it, and every word is sustained and has time to die away.

"Mécontent de tous et mécontent de moi, je voudrais bien racheter et m'enorgueillir un peu dans le silence et la solitude de la nuit. Ames de ceux que j'ai aimés, ames de ceux que j'ai chantés, fortifiez-moi, soutenez-moi, éloignez de moi le mensonge et les vapeurs corruptrices du monde; et vous, Seigneur mon Dieu! accordez-moi la grâce de produire quelques beaux vers qui me prouvent à moi-même que je ne suis pas le dernier des hommes, que je ne suis pas inferieur à ceux que je méprise."

"They were children of fools, yea, children of base men: they were viler than the earth.

And now I am their song, yea, I am their byword. . . . They raise up against me the ways of their destruction.

They mar my path, they set forward my calamity, they have no helper . . .

And now my soul is poured out upon me; the days of affliction have taken hold upon me.

My bones are pierced in me in the night seasons: and my sinews take no rest.

By the great force *of my disease* is my garment changed: it bindeth me about as the collar of my coat . . .

My harp is also turned to mourning, and my organ into the voice of them that weep."

The doctor did not understand me. Nothing. And certainly it was difficult to describe. They wanted to try electric treatment. Good. I received a slip of paper: I had to be at the Salpêtrière at one o'clock. I was there. I had to pass a long row of barracks and traverse a number of courtyards, where people in white bonnets stood here and there under the bare trees like convicts. Finally I entered a long, gloomy, corridor-like room, that had on one side four windows of dim, greenish glass, one separated from the other by a broad, black partition. In front of them a wooden bench ran along, past everything, and on this bench they who knew me sat and waited. Yes, they were all there. When I became accustomed to the twilight of the place, I noticed that among them, as they sat shoulder to shoulder in an endless row, there could also be other people, little people, artisans, char-women, truckmen. Down at the narrow end of this corridor, on special chairs, two stout women had spread themselves out and were conversing, concierges probably. I looked at the clock; it was five minutes to one. In five minutes, or say ten, my turn would come; so it was not so bad. The air was foul, heavy, impregnated with clothes and breaths. At a certain spot the strong, intensifying coolness of ether came through a crack in the door. I began to walk up and down. It crossed my mind that I had been directed here, among these people, to this overcrowded, general consultation. It was, so to speak, the first public confirmation of the fact that I belonged among the outcast; had the doctor known by my appearance? Yet I had paid my visit in a tolerably decent suit; I had sent in my card. Despite that he must have learned it somehow; perhaps I had betrayed myself. However, now that it was a fact I did not find it so bad after all; the people sat quietly and took no notice of me. Some were in pain and swung one leg a little, the better to endure it. Various men had laid their heads in the palms of their hands; others were sleeping deeply, with heavy, fatigue-crushed faces. A stout man with a red, swollen neck sat bending forward, staring at the floor, and from time to time spat with a smack at a spot he seemed to find suitable for the purpose. A child was sobbing in a corner; it had drawn its long thin legs close up on the bench, and now clasped and held them tightly to its body, as though it must bid them farewell. A small, pale woman on whose head a crape hat, adorned with round, black flowers, set awry, wore the grimace of a smile about her meager lips, but her sore eyes were constantly overflowing. Not far from her had been placed a girl with a round, smooth face and protruding eyes that were without expression; her mouth hung open, so that one saw her white, slimy gums with their old stunted teeth. And there were many bandages. Bandages that swathed a whole head layer upon layer, until only a single eye remained that no longer belonged to anyone. Bandages that hid, and bandages that revealed, what was beneath them. Bandages that had been undone, in which, as in a dirty bed, a hand now lay that was a hand no longer; and a bandaged leg that protruded from the row on the bench, as large as a whole man. I walked up and down, and endeavored to be calm. I occupied myself a good deal with the wall facing me. I noticed that it contained a number of single doors, and did not reach up to the ceiling, so that this corridor was not completely separated from the rooms that must adjoin it. I looked at the clock; I had been pacing up and down for an hour. A while later the doctors arrived. First a couple of young fellows who passed by with indifferent faces, and finally the one I had consulted, in light gloves, chapeau à huit reflets, impeccable overcoat. When he saw me he lifted his hat a little and smiled absent-mindedly. I now hoped to be called immediately, but another hour passed. I cannot remember how I spent it. It passed. An old man wearing a soiled apron, a sort of attendant, came and touched me on the shoulder. I entered one of the adjoining rooms. The doctor and the young fellows sat round a table and looked at me, someone gave me a chair. So far so good. And now I had to describe what was the matter with me. As briefly as possible, s'il vous plaît. For much time these gentlemen had not. I felt very odd. The young fellows sat and looked at me with that superior, professional curiosity they had learned. The doctor I knew stroked his pointed black beard and smiled absently. I thought I should burst into tears, but I heard myself saying in French: "I have already had the honor, monsieur, of giving you all the details I can give. If you consider it indispensable that these gentlemen be initiated, you are certainly able, after our conversation, to do this in a few words, while I find it very difficult." The doctor rose, smiling politely, and going toward the window with his assistants said a few words, which he accompanied with a horizontal, wavering movement of his hands. Three minutes later one of the young men, short-sighted and jerky, came back to the table, and said, trying to look at me severely, "You sleep well, sir?" "No, badly." Whereupon he sprang back again to the group at the window. There they discussed a while longer, then the doctor turned to me and informed me that I would be summoned again. I reminded him that my appointment had been for one o'clock. He smiled and made a few swift, abrupt movements with his small white hands, which were meant to signify that he was uncommonly busy. So I returned to my hallway, where the air had become much more oppressive, and again to pace up and down, although I felt mortally tired. Finally the moist, accumulated smell made me dizzy; I stopped at the entrance door and opened it a little. I saw that outside it was still afternoon, with some sun, and that did me ever so much good. But I had hardly stood a minute thus when I heard someone calling me. A female sitting at a table two or three steps away hissed something to me. Who had told me to open the door? I said I could not stand the atmosphere. Well, that was my own affair, but the door had to be kept shut. Was it not permissible, then, to open a window? No, that was forbidden. I decided to resume my walking up and down, for after all that was a kind of anodyne and it hurt nobody. But now this too displeased the woman sitting at the little table. Did I not have a seat? No, I hadn't. Walking about was not allowed; I would have to find a seat. There ought to be one. The woman was right. In fact, a place was promptly found next to the girl with the protruding eyes. There I now sat with the feeling that this state must certainly be the preparation for something dreadful. On my left, then, was this girl with the decaying gums; what was on my right I could not make out till after some time. It was a huge, immovable mass, having a face and a large, heavy, inert hand. The side of the face that I saw was empty, quite without features and without memories; and it was gruesome that the clothes were like that of a corpse dressed for a coffin. The

narrow, black cravat had been buckled in the same loose, im-
personal way around the collar, and the coat showed that it
had been put on the will-less body by other hands. The hand
had been placed on the trousers exactly where it lay, and even
the hair looked as if it had been combed by those women who
lay out the dead, and was stiffly arranged, like the hair of
stuffed animals. I observed all these things with attention,
and it occurred to me that this must be the place that had
been destined for me; for now I believed I had at last arrived
at that point of my life at which I would remain. Yes, fate
goes wonderful ways.

Suddenly there rose quite nearby in quick succession the
frightened, defensive cries of a child, followed by a low,
hushed weeping. While I was straining to discover where this
could have come from, a little, suppressed cry quavered away
again, and I heard voices, questioning, a voice giving orders in
a subdued tone, and then some sort of machine started up and
hummed indifferently along. Now I recalled that half wall,
and it was clear to me that all this came from the other side
of the doors and that work was going on in there. Actually,
the attendant with the soiled apron appeared from time to
time and made a sign. I had given up thinking that he might
mean me. Was it intended for me? No. Two men appeared
with a wheelchair; they lifted the mass beside me into it, and
I now saw that it was an old paralytic who had another,
smaller side to him, worn out by life, and an open, dim and
melancholy eye. They wheeled him inside, and now there
was lots of room beside me. And I sat and wondered what
they were likely to do to the imbecile girl and whether she
too would scream. The machines back there kept up such an
agreeable mechanical whirring, there was nothing disturbing
about it.

But suddenly everything was still, and in the stillness a
superior, self-complacent voice, which I thought I knew, said:
"Riez!" A pause. "Riez! Mais riez, riez!" I was already laugh-

ing. It was inexplicable that the man on the other side of the partition didn't want to laugh. A machine rattled, but was immediately silent again, words were exchanged, then the same energetic voice rose again and ordered: "Dites-nous le mot: avant." And spelling it: "A-v-a-n-t." Silence. "On n'entend rien. Encore une fois..."

And then, as I listened to the hot, flaccid stuttering on the other side of the partition, then for the first time in many, many years it was there again. That which had struck into me my first, profound terror, when as a child I lay ill with fever: the Big Thing. Yes, that was what I had always called it, when they all stood around my bed and felt my pulse and asked me what had frightened me: the Big Thing. And when they got the doctor and he came and spoke to me, I begged him only to make the Big Thing go away, nothing else mattered. But he was like the rest. He could not take it away, though I was so small then and might so easily have been helped. And now it was there again. Later it had simply stayed away; it had not come back even on nights when I had fever; but now it was there, although I had no fever. Now it was there. Now it grew out of me like a tumor, like a second head, and was part of me, though it could not belong to me at all, because it was so big. It was there like a huge, dead beast, that had once, when it was still alive, been my hand or my arm. And my blood flowed both through me and through it, as if through one and the same body. And my heart had to make a great effort to drive the blood into the Big Thing; there was hardly enough blood. And the blood entered into the Big Thing unwillingly and came back sick and tainted. But the Big Thing swelled and grew over my face like a warm bluish boil and grew over my mouth, and already the shadow of its edge lay upon my remaining eye.

I cannot recall how I got out through the numerous courtyards. It was evening, and I lost my way in this strange neighborhood and went up boulevards with interminable walls in one direction and, when there was no end to them, returned in the opposite direction until I reached some square or other. Thence I began to walk along a street, and other streets came that I had never seen before, and still other streets. Electric cars would come racing up and past, too brilliantly lit and with harsh, beating clang of bells. But on their signboards stood names I did not know. I did not know in what city I was or whether I had a lodging somewhere here or what I must do in order not to have to go on walking.

ROBERT FROST

THE WITCH OF COÖS

I STAYED the night for shelter at a farm
Behind the mountain, with a mother and son,
Two old-believers. They did all the talking.

MOTHER. Folks think a witch who has familiar spirits
She could call up to pass a winter evening,
But won't, should be burned at the stake or something.
Summoning spirits isn't "Button, button,
Who's got the button," I would have them know.

SON. Mother can make a common table rear
And kick with two legs like an army mule.

MOTHER. And when I've done it, what good have I done?
Rather than tip a table for you, let me
Tell you what Ralle the Sioux Control once told me.
He said the dead had souls, but when I asked him
How could that be—I thought the dead were souls,
He broke my trance. Don't that make you suspicious
That there's something the dead are keeping back?
Yes, there's something the dead are keeping back.

SON. You wouldn't want to tell him what we have
Up attic, mother?

MOTHER. Bones—a skeleton.

SON. But the headboard of mother's bed is pushed
Against the attic door: the door is nailed.
It's harmless. Mother hears it in the night
Halting perplexed behind the barrier
Of door and headboard. Where it wants to get
Is back into the cellar where it came from.

MOTHER. We'll never let them, will we, son! We'll never!

SON. It left the cellar forty years ago
And carried itself like a pile of dishes
Up one flight from the cellar to the kitchen,
Another from the kitchen to the bedroom,
Another from the bedroom to the attic,
Right past both father and mother, and neither stopped it.
Father had gone upstairs; mother was downstairs.
I was a baby: I don't know where I was.

MOTHER. The only fault my husband found with me—
I went to sleep before I went to bed,
Especially in winter when the bed
Might just as well be ice and the clothes snow.
The night the bones came up the cellar-stairs
Toffile had gone to bed alone and left me,
But left an open door to cool the room off
So as to sort of turn me out of it.
I was just coming to myself enough
To wonder where the cold was coming from,
When I heard Toffile upstairs in the bedroom
And thought I heard him downstairs in the cellar.
The board we had laid down to walk dry-shod on
When there was water in the cellar in spring
Struck the hard cellar bottom. And then someone
Began the stairs, two footsteps for each step,

The way a man with one leg and a crutch,
Or a little child, comes up. It wasn't Toffile:
It wasn't anyone who could be there.
The bulkhead double-doors were double-locked
And swollen tight and buried under snow.
The cellar windows were banked up with sawdust
And swollen tight and buried under snow.
It was the bones. I knew them—and good reason.
My first impulse was to get to the knob
And hold the door. But the bones didn't try
The door; they halted helpless on the landing,
Waiting for things to happen in their favor.
The faintest restless rustling ran all through them.
I never could have done the thing I did
If the wish hadn't been too strong in me
To see how they were mounted for this walk.
I had a vision of them put together
Not like a man, but like a chandelier.
So suddenly I flung the door wide on him.
A moment he stood balancing with emotion,
And all but lost himself. (A tongue of fire
Flashed out and licked along his upper teeth.
Smoke rolled inside the sockets of his eyes.)
Then he came at me with one hand outstretched,
The way he did in life once; but this time
I struck the hand off brittle on the floor,
And fell back from him on the floor myself.
The finger-pieces slid in all directions.
(Where did I see one of those pieces lately?
Hand me my button-box—it must be there.)
I sat up on the floor and shouted, "Toffile,
It's coming up to you." It had its choice
Of the door to the cellar or the hall.
It took the hall door for the novelty,

And set off briskly for so slow a thing,
Still going every which way in the joints, though,
So that it looked like lightning or a scribble,
From the slap I had just now given its hand.
I listened till it almost climbed the stairs
From the hall to the only finished bedroom,
Before I got up to do anything;
Then ran and shouted, "Shut the bedroom door,
Toffile, for my sake!" "Company?" he said,
"Don't make me get up; I'm too warm in bed."
So lying forward weakly on the handrail
I pushed myself upstairs, and in the light
(The kitchen had been dark) I had to own
I could see nothing. "Toffile, I don't see it.
It's with us in the room though. It's the bones."
"What bones?" "The cellar bones—out of the grave."
That made him throw his bare legs out of bed
And sit up by me and take hold of me.
I wanted to put out the light and see
If I could see it, or else mow the room,
With our arms at the level of our knees,
And bring the chalk-pile down. "I'll tell you what—
It's looking for another door to try.
The uncommonly deep snow has made him think
Of his old song, *The Wild Colonial Boy*,
He always used to sing along the tote-road.
He's after an open door to get out-doors.
Let's trap him with an open door up attic."
Toffile agreed to that, and sure enough,
Almost the moment he was given an opening,
The steps began to climb the attic stairs.
I heard them. Toffile didn't seem to hear them.
"Quick!" I slammed to the door and held the knob.
"Toffile, get nails." I made him nail the door shut,

And push the headboard of the bed against it.
Then we asked was there anything
Up attic that we'd ever want again.
The attic was less to us than the cellar.
If the bones liked the attic, let them have it.
Let them stay in the attic. When they sometimes
Come down the stairs at night and stand perplexed
Behind the door and headboard of the bed,
Brushing their chalky skull with chalky fingers,
With sounds like the dry rattling of a shutter,
That's what I sit up in the dark to say—
To no one any more since Toffile died.
Let them stay in the attic since they went there.
I promised Toffile to be cruel to them
For helping them be cruel once to him.

SON. We think they had a grave down in the cellar.

MOTHER. We know they had a grave down in the cellar.

SON. We never could find out whose bones they were.

MOTHER. Yes, we could too, son. Tell the truth for once.
They were a man's his father killed for me.
I mean a man he killed instead of me.
The least I could do was to help dig their grave.
We were about it one night in the cellar.
Son knows the story: but 'twas not for him
To tell the truth, suppose the time had come.
Son looks surprised to see me end a lie
We'd kept all these years between ourselves
So as to have it ready for outsiders.
But tonight I don't care enough to lie—
I don't remember why I ever cared.

Toffile, if he were here, I don't believe
Could tell you why he ever cared himself . . .

She hadn't found the finger-bone she wanted
Among the buttons poured out in her lap.
I verified the name next morning: Toffile.
The rural letter-box said Toffile Lajway.

GIOVANNI VERGA

LA LUPA *

SHE WAS tall, and thin; but she had the firm, vigorous
bosom of a brown woman, though she was no longer young.
Her face was pale, as though she had the malaria always on
her, and in her pallor two great dark eyes, and fresh, red lips,
that seemed to eat you.

In the village they called her *la Lupa*, because she had
never had enough—of anything. The women crossed themselves when they saw her go by, alone like a roving she-dog,
with that ranging, suspicious motion of a hungry wolf. She
bled their sons and their husbands dry in a twinkling, with
those red lips of hers, and she had merely to look at them
with her great evil eyes, to have them running after her
skirts, even if they'd been kneeling at the altar of Saint
Agrippina. Fortunately, *la Lupa* never entered the church,
neither at Easter nor at Christmas, nor to hear Mass, nor to
confess.—Fra Angiolino, of Santa Maria di Jesu, who had been
a true servant of God, had lost his soul because of her.

Maricchia, poor thing, was a good girl and a nice girl, and
she wept in secret because she was *la Lupa's* daughter, and
nobody would take her in marriage, although she had her
marriage-chest full of linen, and her piece of fertile land in
the sun, as good as any other girl in the village.

Then one day *la Lupa* fell in love with a handsome lad
who'd just come back from serving as a soldier, and was

---

* *La Lupa* means *the she-wolf*, and also *the prostitute, the enticer.*

cutting the hay alongside her in the closes belonging to the
lawyer: but really what you'd call falling in love, feeling your
body burn under your stuff bodice, and suffering, when you
stared into his eyes, the thirst that you suffer in the hot hours
of June, away in the burning plains. But he went on mowing
quietly, with his nose bent over his swath, and he said to her:
"Why, what's wrong with you, Mrs. Pina?"—In the immense
fields, where only the grasshoppers crackled into flight, when
the sun beat down like lead, *la Lupa* gathered armful after
armful together, tied sheaf after sheaf, without ever weary-
ing, without straightening her back for a moment, without
putting her lips to the flask, so that she could keep at Nanni's
heels, as he mowed and mowed, and asked her from time to
time: "Why, what do you want, Mrs. Pina?"

One evening she told him, while the men were dozing
in the stackyard, tired from the long day, and the dogs were
howling away in the vast, dark, open country: "You! I want
you! Thou'rt handsome as the day, and sweet as honey to me.
I want thee, lad!"

"Ah! I'd rather have your daughter, who's a filly," replied
Nanni, laughing.

La Lupa clutched her hands in her hair, and tore her temples, without saying a word, and went away, and was seen no
more in the yard. But in October she saw Nanni again, when
they were getting the oil out of the olives, because he worked
next to her house, and the screeching of the oil-press didn't
let her sleep at night.

"Take the sack of olives," she said to her daughter, "and
come with me."

Nanni was throwing the olives under the millstone with
the shovel, in the dark chamber like a cave, where the olives
were ground and pressed, and he kept shouting *Ohee!* to the
mule, so it shouldn't stop.

"Do you want my daughter Maricchia?" Mrs. Pina asked
him.

"What are you giving your daughter Maricchia?" replied Nanni.

"She has what her father left, and I'll give her my house into the bargain; it's enough for me if you'll leave me a corner in the kitchen, where I can spread myself a bit of a straw mattress to sleep on."

"All right! If it's like that, we can talk about it at Christmas," said Nanni.

Nanni was all greasy and grimy with the oil and the olives set to ferment, and Maricchia didn't want him at any price; but her mother seized her by the hair, at home in front of the fireplace, and said to her between her teeth:

"If thou doesn't take him, I'll lay thee out!"

La Lupa was almost ill, and the folks were saying that the devil turns hermit when he gets old. She no longer went roving round; she no longer sat in the doorway, with those eyes of one possessed. Her son-in-law, when she fixed on him those eyes of hers, would start laughing, and drag out from his breast the bit of Madonna's dress, to cross himself. Maricchia stayed at home nursing the children, and her mother went to the fields, to work with the men, just like a man, weeding, hoeing, tending the cattle, pruning the vines, whether in the north-east wind or the east winds of January, or in the hot, stifling African wind of August, when the mules let their heads hang in dead weight, and the men slept face downwards under the wall, on the north side. *Between vesper bell and the night-bell's sound, when no good woman goes roving round*, Mrs. Pina was the only soul to be seen wandering through the countryside, on the ever-burning stones of the little roads, through the parched stubble of the immense fields, which lost themselves in the sultry haze of the distance, far off, far off, towards misty Etna, where the sky weighed down upon the horizon, in the afternoon heat.

"Wake up!" said *la Lupa* to Nanni, who was asleep in the ditch, under the dusty hedge, with his arms round his head. "Wake up! I've brought thee some wine to cool thy throat."

Nanni opened his eyes wide like a disturbed child, half-awake, seeing her erect above him, pale, with her arrogant bosom, and her eyes black as coals, and he stretched out his hand gropingly, to keep her off.

"No! No good woman goes roving round between vespers and night," sobbed Nanni, pressing his face down again in the dry grass of the ditch-bottom, away from her, clutching his hair with his hands. "Go away! Go away! Don't you come into the stackyard again!"

She did indeed go away, *la Lupa*, but fastening up again the coils of her superb black hair, staring straight in front of her, as she stepped over the hot stubble, with eyes black as coals.

And she came back into the stackyard time and again, and Nanni no longer said anything; and when she was late coming, in the hour between evensong and night, he went to the top of the white, deserted little road to look for her, with sweat on his forehead;—and afterwards, he clutched his hair in his hand, and repeated the same thing every time: "Go away! Go away! Don't you come into the stackyard again!"

Maricchia wept night and day; and she glared at her mother with eyes that burned with tears and jealousy; like a young she-wolf herself now, when she saw her coming in from the fields, every time silent and pallid.

"Vile woman!" she said to her. "Vile, vile mother!"

"Be quiet!"

"Thief! Thief that you are!"

"Be quiet!"

"I'll go to the Sergeant, I will."

"Then go!"

And she did go, finally, with her child in her arms, went fearless and without shedding a tear, like a madwoman, because now she also was in love with that husband of hers, whom they'd forced her to accept, greasy and grimy from the olives set to ferment.

The Sergeant went for Nanni, and threatened him with jail and the gallows. Nanni began to sob and tear his hair; he denied nothing, he didn't try to excuse himself.—"It's the temptation," he said. "It's the temptation of hell!" and he threw himself at the feet of the Sergeant, begging to be sent to jail.

"For pity's sake, Sergeant, get me out of this hell! Have me hung, or send me to prison; but don't let me see her again, never, never!"

"No!" replied *la Lupa* to the Sergeant. "I kept myself a corner in the kitchen, to sleep in, when I gave her my house for her dowry. The house is mine, I won't be turned out."

A little while later, Nanni got a kick in the chest from a mule, and was likely to die; but the parish priest wouldn't bring the Host to him, unless *la Lupa* left the house. *La Lupa* departed, and then her son-in-law could prepare himself to depart also, like a good Christian; he confessed, and took the communion with such evident signs of repentance and contrition that all the neighbors and the busybodies wept round the bed of the dying man.

And better for him if he had died that time, before the devil came back to tempt him and to get a grip on his body and his soul, when he was well.

"Leave me alone!" he said to *la Lupa*. "For God's sake, leave me in peace! I've been face to face with death. Poor Maricchia is only driven wild. Now all the place knows about it. If I never see you again, it's better for you and for me."

And he would have liked to tear his eyes out so as not to see again those eyes of *la Lupa*, which, when they fixed themselves upon his, made him lose both body and soul. He didn't know what to do, to get free from the spell she put on him. He paid for Masses for the souls in Purgatory, and he went for help to the priest and to the Sergeant. At Easter he went to confession, and he publicly performed the penance of crawling on his belly and licking the stones of the sacred threshold before the church for a length of six feet.

After that, when *la Lupa* came back to tempt him:

"Hark here!" he said. "Don't you come again into the stackyard; because if you keep on coming after me, as sure as God's above I'll kill you."

"Kill me, then," replied *la Lupa*. "It doesn't matter to me; I'm not going to live without thee."

He, when he perceived her in the distance, amid the fields of green young wheat, he left off hoeing the vines, and went to take the axe from the elm-tree. *La Lupa* saw him advancing towards her, pale and wild-eyed, with the axe glittering in the sun, but she did not hesitate in her step, nor lower her eyes, but kept on her way to meet him, with her hands full of red poppies, and consuming him with her black eyes.

"Ah! Curse your soul!" stammered Nanni.

Translated by D. H. Lawrence

NICOLAI GOGOL

THE NOSE

1.

A MOST EXTRAORDINARY thing happened in Petersburg on the twenty-fifth of March. The barber, Ivan Yakovlevich, who lives on the Voznessensky Avenue (his surname is lost, and even on his signboard, depicting a gentleman with a lathered face and bearing the inscription: "Also lets blood," no surname appears)—the barber Ivan Yakovlevich woke up rather early and inhaled the smell of hot bread. Raising himself a little in bed, he saw that his wife, a highly respectable lady who was very fond of a cup of coffee, was taking out of the oven some freshly baked bread.

"I won't have coffee today, my dear," said Ivan Yakovlevich. "Instead I'd like some hot bread with onions."

(That is to say, Ivan Yakovlevich would have liked both, but he knew that it was absolutely impossible to ask for two things at once; for his wife disliked such absurd whims.)

"Let the fool eat bread," his wife thought to herself. "All the better for me: there'll be an extra cup of coffee left." And she flung a loaf on the table.

After putting on, for propriety's sake, his frock coat over his shirt, Ivan Yakovlevich sat down at the table, sprinkled some salt, peeled two onions, picked up a knife, and, assuming a solemn expression, began cutting the bread. Having cut it in two, he had a look into the middle of one of the halves and, to his astonishment, noticed some white object there. Ivan Yakovlevich prodded it carefully with the knife and felt it with a finger. "It's solid," he said to himself. "What on earth can it be?"

He dug his fingers into the bread and pulled out—a nose! Ivan Yakovlevich's heart sank: he rubbed his eyes and felt it again: a nose! There could be no doubt about it: it was a nose! And a familiar nose, too, apparently. Ivan Yakovlevich looked horrified. But his horror was nothing compared to the indignation with which his wife was overcome.

"Where have you cut off that nose, you monster?" she screamed angrily. "Blackguard! Drunkard! I shall inform the police against you myself. What a cutthroat! Three gentlemen have told me already that when you are shaving them you pull so violently at their noses that it is a wonder they still remain on their faces!"

But Ivan Yakovlevich was more dead than alive. He recognized the nose as belonging to no other person than the Collegiate Assessor Kovalyov, whom he shaved every Wednesday and every Sunday.

"Wait, my dear, I'll wrap it in a rag and put it in a corner: let it stay there for a bit and then I'll take it out."

"I won't hear of it! What do you take me for? Keep a cut-off nose in my room? You heartless villain, you! All you know is to strop your razor. Soon you won't be fit to carry out your duties at all, you whoremonger, you scoundrel, you! You don't expect me to answer to the police for you, do you? Oh, you filthy wretch, you blockhead, you! Out with it! Out! Take it where you like, only don't let me see it here again!"

Ivan Yakovlevich stood there looking utterly crushed. He thought and thought and did not know what to think.

"Damned if I know how it happened," he said at last, scratching behind his ear. "Did I come home drunk last night? I'm sure I don't know. And yet the whole thing is quite impossible—it can't be true however you look at it: for bread is something you bake, and a nose is something quite different. Can't make head or tail of it!"

Ivan Yakovlevich fell silent. The thought that the police might find the nose at his place and charge him with having cut it off made him feel utterly dejected. He could already see the scarlet collar, beautifully embroidered with silver, the saber—and he trembled all over. At last he got his trousers and boots, pulled on these sorry objects, and, accompanied by his wife's execrations, wrapped the nose in a rag and went out into the street.

He wanted to shove it under something, either under the seat by the gates or drop it, as it were, by accident and then turn off into a side street. But as ill luck would have it, he kept coming across people he knew, who at once addressed him with the question: "Where are you off to?" or "Who are you going to shave so early in the morning?"—so that he could not find a right moment for getting rid of it. On one occasion he did succeed in dropping it, but a policeman shouted to him from the distance, pointing to it with his halberd: "Hey, you, pick it up! You've dropped something!" And Ivan Yakovlevich had to pick up the nose and put it in his pocket. He was overcome by despair, particularly as the number of people in the streets was continually increasing with the opening of the stores and the small shops.

He decided to go to the Issakiyevsky Bridge, for it occurred to him that he might be able to throw it into the Neva. But I'm afraid I am perhaps a little to blame for not having so far said something more about Ivan Yakovlevich, an estimable man in many respects.

Ivan Yakovlevich, like every other Russian working man, was a terrible drunkard. And though every day he shaved other people's chins, he never bothered to shave his own. Ivan Yakovlevich's frock coat (he never wore an ordinary coat) was piebald; that is to say, it was black, but covered all over with large brown, yellow, and gray spots; his collar was shiny; and instead of three buttons only bits of thread dangled from his coat. Ivan Yakovlevich was a great cynic, and every time the Collegiate Assessor Kovalyov said to him: "Your hands always stink, Ivan Yakovlevich," he would reply with the question: "Why should they stink, sir?" "I don't know why, my dear fellow," the Collegiate Assessor would say, "only they do stink." And after taking a pinch of snuff, Ivan Yakovlevich would lather him for that all over his cheeks, under the nose, behind his ears, and under his beard, in short, wherever he fancied.

This worthy citizen had in the meantime reached Issakiyevsky Bridge. First of all he looked round cautiously, then he leaned over the parapet, as though anxious to see whether there were a great many fishes swimming by, and as he did so he stealthily threw the rag with the nose into the river. He felt as though a heavy weight had been lifted from his shoulders: Ivan Yakovlevich even grinned. Instead of going to shave the chins of civil servants, he set off towards an establishment which bore the inscription: "Tea and Victuals," intending to ask for a glass of punch, when he suddenly noticed at the end of the bridge a police inspector of noble exterior, with large whiskers, with a three-cornered hat, and with a saber. He stood rooted to the spot; meanwhile the police officer beckoned to him and said: "Come here, my man!"

Knowing the rules, Ivan Yakovlevich took off his cap some way off and, coming up promptly, said: "I hope your honor is well."

"No, no, my good man, not 'your honor.' Tell me, what were you doing there on the bridge?"

"Why, sir, I was going to shave one of my customers and I just stopped to have a look how fast the current was running."

"You're lying, sir, you're lying! You won't get off with that. Answer my question, please!"

"I'm ready to shave you two or even three times a week, sir, with no conditions attached," replied Ivan Yakovlevich.

"No, my dear sir, that's nothing! I have three barbers who shave me and they consider it a great honor, too. You'd better tell me what you were doing there!"

Ivan Yakovlevich turned pale.... But here the incident is completely shrouded in a fog and absolutely nothing is known of what happened next.

2.

Collegiate Assessor Kovalyov woke up fairly early and muttered, "Brr..." with his lips, which he always did when he woke up, though he could not say himself why he did so. Kovalyov stretched and asked for the little looking glass standing on the table. He wanted to look at the pimple which had appeared on his nose the previous evening, but to his great astonishment, instead of his nose, he saw a completely empty, flat place! Frightened, Kovalyov asked for some water and rubbed his eyes with a towel: there was no nose! He began feeling with his hand and pinched himself to see whether he was still asleep: no, he did not appear to be asleep. The Collegiate Assessor Kovalyov jumped out of bed and shook himself: he had no nose! He immediately told his servant to help him dress and rushed off straight to the Commissioner of Police.

Meanwhile we had better say something about Kovalyov so that the reader may see what sort of a person this Collegiate Assessor was. Collegiate Assessors who receive that title in consequence of their learned diplomas cannot be compared with those Collegiate Assessors who obtain this rank in the Caucasus. They are two quite different species. Learned Collegiate Assessors ... But Russia is such a wonderful country that if you say something about one Collegiate Assessor, all the Collegiate Assessors, from Riga to Kamchatka, will most certainly think that you are referring to them. The same, of course, applies to all other callings and ranks. Kovalyov was a Caucasian Collegiate Assessor. He had obtained that rank only two years earlier and that was why he could not forget it for a moment; and to add to his own importance and dignity, he never described himself as a Collegiate Assessor, that is to say, a civil servant of the eighth rank, but always as a major, that is to say, by the corresponding rank in the army. "Look here, my good woman," he used to say when he met a peasant woman selling shirt fronts in the street, "you go to my house—I live on Sadovaya Street—and just ask: Does Major Kovalyov live here? Anyone will show you." But if he met some pretty little minx, he'd give her besides a secret instruction, adding: "You just ask for Major Kovalyov's apartment, darling." And that is why we, too, will in future refer to this Collegiate Assessor as Major Kovalyov.

Major Kovalyov was in the habit of taking a stroll on Nevsky Avenue every day. The collar of his shirt front was always extremely clean and well starched. His whiskers were such as one can still see nowadays on provincial district surveyors, architects, and army doctors, as well as on police officers performing various duties and, in general, on all gallant gentlemen who have full, ruddy cheeks and are very good at a game of boston: these whiskers go right across the middle of the cheek and straight up to the nose. Major Kovalyov wore a great number of cornelian seals, some with crests and others which had engraved on them: Wednesday, Thursday, Monday, and so on. Major Kovalyov came to Petersburg on business, to wit, to look for a post befitting his rank: if he were lucky, the post of a vice-governor, if not, one of an administrative clerk in some important department. Major Kovalyov was not averse to matrimony, either, but only if he could find a girl with a fortune of two hundred thousand. The reader can, therefore, judge for himself the state in which the major was when he saw, instead of a fairly handsome nose of moderate size, a most idiotic, flat, smooth place.

As misfortune would have it, there was not a single cab to be seen in the street and he had to walk, wrapping himself in his cloak and covering his face with a handkerchief, as though his nose were bleeding. "But perhaps I imagined it all," he thought. "It's impossible that I could have lost my nose without noticing it!" He went into a pastry cook's for the sole purpose of having a look at himself in a mirror. Fortunately, there was no one in the shop: the boys were sweeping the rooms and arranging the chairs; some of them, sleepy-eyed, were bringing in hot cream puffs on trays; yesterday's papers, stained with coffee, were lying about on tables and chairs. "Well, thank God, there's nobody here," he said. "Now I can have a look." He went timidly up to the mirror and looked. "Damn it," he said, disgusted, "the whole thing is too ridiculous for words! If only there'd be something instead of a nose, but there's just nothing!"

Biting his lips with vexation, Kovalyov went out of the pastry cook's and made up his mind, contrary to his usual practice, not to look or smile at anyone. Suddenly he stopped dead in his tracks at the front doors of a house; a most inexplicable thing happened before his very eyes: a carriage drew up before the entrance, the carriage door opened, and a gentleman in uniform jumped out and, stooping, rushed up the steps. Imagine the horror and, at the same time, amazement of Kovalyov when he recognized that this was his own nose! At this extraordinary sight everything went swimming before his eyes. He felt that he could hardly stand on his feet; but he made up his mind that, come what may, he would wait for the gentleman's return to the carriage. He was trembling all over as though in a fever. Two minutes later the nose really did come out. He wore a gold-embroidered uniform with a large stand-up collar, chamois-leather breeches, and a sword at his side. From his plumed hat it could be inferred that he was a State Councillor, a civil servant of the fifth rank. Everything showed that he was going somewhere to pay a visit. He looked round to the right and to the left, shouted to his driver, who had driven off a short distance, to come back, got into the carriage, and drove off.

Poor Kovalyov nearly went out of his mind. He did not know what to think of such a strange occurrence. And, indeed, how was it possible for a nose which had only the day before been on his face and which could neither walk nor drive—to be in a uniform! He ran after the carriage which, luckily, did not go far, stopping before the Kazan Cathedral.

He hastened into the cathedral, pushing his way through the crowd of beggarwomen with bandaged faces and only two slits for the eyes, at whom he used to laugh so much before, and went into the church. There were only a few worshippers inside the church; they were all standing near the entrance. Kovalyov felt so distraught that he was unable to pray and he kept searching with his eyes for the gentleman in the State Councillor's uniform. At last he saw him standing apart from the other worshippers. The nose was hiding his face completely in his large stand-up collar and was saying his prayers with the expression of the utmost piety.

"How am I to approach him?" thought Kovalyov. "It is clear from everything, from his uniform, from his hat, that he is a State Councillor. I'm damned if I know how to do it!"

He went up to him and began clearing his throat; but the nose did not change his devout attitude for a moment and carried on with his genuflections.

"Sir," said Kovalyov, inwardly forcing himself to take courage, "Sir——"

"What do you want?" answered the nose, turning round.

"I find it strange, sir, I—I believe you ought to know your proper place. And all of a sudden I find you in church of all places! You—you must admit that——"

"I'm sorry but I can't understand what you are talking about. . . . Explain yourself."

"How can I explain it to him?" thought Kovalyov and,

plucking up courage, began: "Of course—er—you see—I—I am a major and—and you must admit that it isn't right for —er—a man of my rank to walk about without a nose. I mean—er—a tradeswoman selling peeled oranges on Voskressensky Bridge can sit there without a nose; but for a man like me who expects to obtain the post of a governor, which without a doubt he will obtain and—er—besides, being received in many houses by ladies of good position, such as Mrs. Chekhtaryov, the widow of a State Councillor, sir, and many others—er——Judge for yourself, sir, I mean, I—I don't know"—Major Kovalyov shrugged his shoulders—"I am sorry but if one were to look upon it according to the rules of honor and duty—er—you can understand yourself, sir——"

"I don't understand anything, sir," replied the nose. "Please explain yourself more clearly."

"Sir," said Kovalyov with a consciousness of his own dignity, "I don't know how to understand your words. It seems to me the whole thing is perfectly obvious. Or do you wish— I mean, you are my own nose, sir!"

The nose looked at the major and frowned slightly.

"You are mistaken, sir. I am *myself*. Besides, there can be no question of any intimate relationship between us. I see, sir, from the buttons of your uniform that you are serving in a different department."

Having said this, the nose turned away and went on praying.

Kovalyov was utterly confounded, not knowing what to do or even what to think. At that moment he heard the agreeable rustle of a lady's dress; an elderly lady, her dress richly trimmed with lace, walked up to them, accompanied by a slim girl in a white dress, which looked very charming on her slender figure, and in a straw-colored hat, as light as a pastry puff. Behind them, opening a snuffbox, stood a tall flunkey with enormous whiskers and quite a dozen collars on his Cossack coat.

Kovalyov came nearer, pulled out the cambric collar of his shirt front, straightened the seals hanging on his gold watch chain and, turning his head this way and that and smiling, turned his attention to the ethereal young lady who, like a spring flower, bent forward a little, as she prayed, and put her little white hand with its semi-transparent fingers to her forehead to cross herself. The smile on Kovalyov's face distended a little more when he caught sight under her pretty hat of a chin of dazzling whiteness and part of her cheek, suffused with the color of the first spring rose. But suddenly he sprang back as though he had burnt himself. He recollected that, instead of a nose, he had absolutely nothing on his face, and tears started to his eyes. He turned round, intending to tell the gentleman in uniform plainly that he was merely pretending to be a State Councillor, that he was a rogue and an impostor and nothing else than his own nose. . . . But the nose was no longer there: he had managed to gallop off, no doubt to pay another visit. . . .

That plunged Kovalyov into despair. He left the church and stopped for a moment under the colonnade, carefully looking in all directions to see whether he could catch sight of the nose anywhere. He remembered very well that he wore a hat with a plume and a gold-embroidered uniform; but he had not noticed his cloak, nor the color of his carriage, nor his horses, nor even whether he had a footman behind him and, if so, in what livery. Besides, there were so many carriages careering backwards and forwards that it was difficult to distinguish one from another. But even if he had been able to distinguish any of them, there was no way of stopping it. It was a lovely, sunny day. There were hundreds of people on Nevsky Avenue. A whole flowery cascade of ladies was pouring all over the pavement from the Police Bridge to the Anichkin Bridge. There he saw coming a good acquaintance of his, a civil servant of the seventh rank, whom he always addressed as lieutenant colonel, especially in the presence of strangers. And there was Yaryzhkin, the head clerk in the Senate, a great friend of his, who always lost points when he went eight at boston. And here was another major, who had received the eighth rank of Collegiate Assessor in the Caucasus, waving to him to come up....

"Oh, hell!" said Kovalyov. "Hey, cabby, take me straight to the Commissioner of Police!"

Kovalyov got into the cab and kept shouting to the driver: "Faster! Faster!"

"Is the Police Commissioner at home?" he asked, entering the hall.

"No, sir," replied the janitor. "He's just gone out."

"Well, of all things!"

"Yes, sir," the janitor added, "he's not been gone so long, but he's gone all right. If you'd come a minute earlier, you'd probably have found him at home."

Without taking his handkerchief off his face, Kovalyov got into the cab and shouted in an anguished voice:

"Drive on!"

"Where to, sir?" asked the cabman.

"Straight ahead!"

"Straight ahead, sir? But there's a turning here: to right or to left?"

This question stumped Kovalyov and made him think again. A man in his position ought first of all apply to the City Police Headquarters, not because they dealt with matters of this kind there, but because instructions coming from there might be complied with much more quickly than those coming from any other place; to seek satisfaction from the authorities of the department in which the nose claimed to be serving would have been unreasonable, for from the nose's replies he perceived that nothing was sacred to that individual and that he was quite capable of telling a lie just as he had lied in denying that he had ever seen him. Kovalyov was, therefore, about to tell the cabman to drive him to Police

Headquarters, when it again occurred to him that this rogue
and impostor, who had treated him in such a contumelious
way, might take advantage of the first favorable opportunity
and slip out of town, and then all his searches would be in
vain or, which God forbid, might go on for a whole month.
At last it seemed that Heaven itself had suggested a plan
of action to him. He decided to go straight to a newspaper
office and, while there was still time, put in an advertisement
with a circumstantial description of the nose so that anyone
meeting it might bring it to him at once or, at any rate, let
him know where it was. And so, having made up his mind,
he told the cabman to drive him to the nearest newspaper office and all the way there he kept hitting the cabman on the
back with his fist, repeating, "Faster, you rogue! Faster, you
scoundrel!" "Good Lord, sir, what are you hitting me for?"
said the cabman, shaking his head and flicking with the rein
at the horse, whose coat was as long as a lap dog's. At last the
cab came to a stop and Kovalyov ran panting into a small reception room where a gray-haired clerk, in an old frock coat
and wearing spectacles, sat at a table, with a pen between his
teeth, counting some coppers.

"Who receives advertisements here?" cried Kovalyov.
"Oh, good morning!"

"How do you do?" said the clerk, raising his eyes for a moment and dropping them again on the carefully laid out heaps
of coppers before him.

"I should like to insert——"

"One moment, sir, I must ask you to wait a little," said
the clerk, writing down a figure on a piece of paper with one
hand and moving two beads on his abacus with the other.

A footman with galloons on his livery and a personal appearance which showed that he came from an aristocratic
house, was standing beside the clerk with a note in his
hand. He thought it an opportune moment for displaying his
knowledge of the world.

"Would you believe it, sir," he said, "the little bitch isn't worth eighty kopecks, and indeed I shouldn't give even eight kopecks for her, but the countess dotes on her, sir, she simply dotes on her, and that's why she's offering a hundred rubles to anyone who finds her! Now, to put it politely, sir, just as you and me are speaking now, you can never tell what people's tastes may be. What I mean is that if you are a sportsman, then keep a pointer or a poodle, don't mind spending five hundred or even a thousand rubles, so long as your dog is a good one."

The worthy clerk listened to this with a grave air and at the same time kept counting the number of letters in the advertisement the footman had brought. The room was full of old women, shop assistants, and house porters—all with bits of paper in their hands. In one a coachman of sober habits was advertised as being let out on hire; in another an almost new, secondhand carriage, brought from Paris in 1814, was offered for sale; in still others were offered for sale: a serf girl of nineteen, experienced in laundry work and suitable for other work, a well-built open carriage with only one spring broken, a young, dappled-gray, mettlesome horse of seventeen years of age, a new consignment of turnip and radish seed from London, a summer residence with all the conveniences, including two boxes for horses and a piece of land on which an excellent birchwood or pinewood could be planted; there was also an advertisement containing a challenge to those who wished to purchase old boot soles with an invitation to come to the auction rooms every day from eight o'clock in the morning to three o'clock in the afternoon. The room, in which all these people were crowded, was very small and the air extremely thick; but the Collegiate Assessor Kovalyov did not notice the bad smell because he kept the handkerchief over his face and also because his nose was at the time goodness knows where.

"Excuse me, sir," he said at last with impatience, "it's very urgent...."

"Presently, presently," said the gray-haired gentleman, flinging their notes back to the old women and the house porters. "Two rubles forty kopecks! One moment, sir! One ruble sixty-four kopecks! What can I do for you?" he said at last, turning to Kovalyov.

"Thank you, sir," said Kovalyov. "You see, I've been robbed or swindled, I can't so far say which, but I should like you to put in an advertisement that anyone who brings the scoundrel to me will receive a handsome reward."

"What is your name, sir?"

"What do you want my name for? I'm sorry I can't give it to you. I have a large circle of friends: Mrs. Chekhtaryov, the widow of a State Councillor, Pelageya Grigoryevna Podtochin, the widow of a first lieutenant.... God forbid that they should suddenly find out! You can simply say: a Collegiate Assessor or, better still, a gentleman of the rank of major."

"And is the runaway your house serf?"

"My house serf? Good Lord, no! That wouldn't have been so bad! You see, it's my—er—nose that has run away from me...."

"Dear me, what a strange name! And has this Mr. Nosov robbed you of a large sum of money?"

"I said nose, sir, nose! You're thinking of something else! It is my nose, my own nose that has disappeared I don't know where. The devil himself must have played a joke on me!"

"But how did it disappear? I'm afraid I don't quite understand it."

"I can't tell you how it happened. The worst of it is that now it is driving about all over the town under the guise of a State Councillor. That's why I should like you to insert an advertisement that anyone who catches him should bring him at once to me. You can see for yourself, sir, that I cannot possibly carry on without such a conspicuous part of myself. It's not like some little toe which no one can see whether it is missing or not once I'm wearing my boots. I call on Thursdays on Mrs. Chekhtaryov, the widow of a State Councillor. Mrs. Podtochin, the widow of a first lieutenant, and her pretty daughter are also good friends of mine, and you can judge for yourself the position I am in now. I can't go and see them now, can I?"

The clerk pursed his lips tightly which meant that he was thinking hard.

"I'm sorry, sir," he said at last, after a long pause, "but I can't possibly insert such an advertisement in the paper."

"What? Why not?"

"Well, you see, sir, the paper might lose its reputation. If everyone were to write that his nose had run away, why—— As it is, people are already saying that we are publishing a lot of absurd stories and false rumors."

"But why is it so absurd? I don't see anything absurd in it."

"It only seems so to you. Last week, for instance, a similar thing happened. A civil servant came to see me just as you have now. He brought an advertisement, it came to two rubles and seventy-three kopecks, but all it was about was that a poodle with a black coat had run away. You wouldn't think there was anything in that, would you? And yet it turned out to be a libelous statement. You see, the poodle was the treasurer of some institution or other. I don't remember which."

"But I am not asking you to publish an advertisement about a poodle, but about my own nose, which is the same as about myself."

"No, sir, I cannot possibly insert such an advertisement."

"Not even if my own nose really has disappeared?"

"If it's lost, then it's a matter for a doctor. I'm told there are people who can fit you with a nose of any shape you like. But I can't help observing, sir, that you are a gentleman of a merry disposition and are fond of pulling a person's leg."

"I swear to you by all that is holy! Why, if it has come to that, I don't mind showing you."

"Don't bother, sir," said the clerk, taking a pinch of snuff. "Still," he added, unable to suppress his curiosity, "if it's no bother, I'd like to have a look."

The Collegiate Assessor removed the handkerchief from his face.

"It is very strange, indeed!" said the clerk. "The place is perfectly flat, just like a pancake from a frying pan. Yes, quite incredibly flat."

"Well, you won't dispute it now, will you? You can see for yourself that you simply must insert it. I shall be infinitely grateful to you and very glad this incident has given me the pleasure of making your acquaintance...."

It may be seen from that that the major decided to lay it on a bit thick this time.

"Well, of course, it's easy enough to insert an advertisement," said the clerk, "but I don't see that it will do you any good. If you really want to publish a thing like that, you'd better put it in the hands of someone skillful with his pen and let him describe it as a rare natural phenomenon and publish it in *The Northern Bee*"—here he took another pinch of snuff—"for the benefit of youth"—here he wiped his nose—"or just as a matter of general interest."

The Collegiate Assessor was utterly discouraged. He dropped his eyes and glanced at the bottom of the newspaper where the theatrical announcements were published; his face was ready to break into a smile as he read the name of a very pretty actress, and his hand went automatically to his pocket to feel whether he had a five-ruble note there, for, in Kovalyov's opinion, officers of the higher ranks ought to have a seat in the stalls—but the thought of his nose spoilt it all!

The clerk himself appeared to be touched by Kovalyov's embarrassing position. Wishing to relieve his distress a little, he thought it proper to express his sympathy in a few words.

"I'm very sorry indeed, sir," he said, "that such a thing should have happened to you. Would you like a pinch of snuff? It relieves headaches, dispels melancholy moods, and it is even a good remedy against hemorrhoids."

Saying this, the clerk offered his snuffbox to Kovalyov, very deftly opening the lid with the portrait of a lady in a hat on it.

This unintentional action made Kovalyov lose his patience.

"I can't understand, sir," he said angrily, "how you can joke in a matter like this! Don't you see I haven't got the thing with which to take a pinch of snuff? To hell with your snuff! I can't bear the sight of it now, and not only your rotten beresina brand, but even if you were to offer me rappee itself!"

Having said this, he walked out of the newspaper office, greatly vexed, and went to see the police inspector of his district, a man who had a great liking for sugar. At his home, the entire hall, which was also the dining room, was stacked with sugar loaves with which local tradesmen had presented him out of friendship. When Kovalyov arrived, the police inspector's cook was helping him off with his regulation top boots; his saber and the rest of his martial armor were already hung peaceably in the corners of the room, and his three-year-old son was playing with his awe-inspiring three-cornered hat. He himself was getting ready to partake of the pleasures of peace after his gallant, warlike exploits.

Kovalyov walked in at the time when he stretched, cleared his throat, and said: "Oh, for a couple of hours of sleep!" It could, therefore, be foreseen that the Collegiate Assessor could have hardly chosen a worse time to arrive; indeed, I am not sure whether he would have got a more cordial reception even if he had brought the police inspector several pounds of sugar or a piece of cloth. The inspector was a great patron of the arts and manufactures, but he preferred a bank note to everything else. "This is something," he used to say. "There is nothing better than that: it doesn't ask for food, it doesn't take up a lot of space, there's always room for it in the pocket, and when you drop it, it doesn't break."

The inspector received Kovalyov rather coldly and said that after dinner was not the time to carry out investigations and that nature herself had fixed it so that after a good meal a man had to take a nap (from which the Collegiate Assessor could deduce that the inspector was not unfamiliar with the sayings of the ancient sages), and that a respectable man would not have his nose pulled off.

A bull's eye! . . . It must be observed that Kovalyov was extremely quick to take offense. He could forgive anything people said about himself, but he could never forgive an insult to his rank or his calling. He was even of the opinion that any reference in plays to army officers or civil servants of low rank was admissible, but that the censorship ought not to pass any attack on persons of higher rank. The reception given him by the police inspector disconcerted him so much that he tossed his head and said with an air of dignity, with his hands slightly parted in a gesture of surprise: "I must say that after such offensive remarks, I have nothing more to say. . . ." and went out.

He arrived home hardly able to stand on his feet. By now it was dusk. After all these unsuccessful quests his rooms looked melancholy or rather extremely disgusting to him. On entering the hall, he saw his valet Ivan lying on his back on the dirty leather sofa and spitting on the ceiling and rather successfully aiming at the same spot. Such an indifference on the part of his servant maddened him; he hit him on the forehead with his hat, saying: "You pig, you're always doing something stupid!"

Ivan jumped up and rushed to help him off with his cloak.

On entering his room, the major, tired and dejected, threw himself into an armchair and, at last, after several sighs, said:

"Lord, oh Lord, why should I have such bad luck? If I had lost an arm or a leg, it would not be so bad; if I had lost my ears, it would be bad enough, but still bearable; but without a nose a man is goodness knows what, neither fish, nor flesh, nor good red herring—he isn't a respectable citizen at all! He is simply something to take and chuck out of the window! If I had had it cut off in battle or in a duel or had been the cause of its loss myself, but to lose it without any reason whatever, for nothing, for absolutely nothing! . . . But no," he added after a brief reflection, "it can't be. It's inconceivable that a nose should be lost, absolutely inconceivable. I must be simply dreaming or just imagining it all. Perhaps by some mistake I drank, instead of water, the spirits which I rub on my face after shaving. Ivan, the blithering fool, did not take it away and I must have swallowed it by mistake."

To convince himself that he was not drunk, the major pinched himself so painfully that he cried out. The pain completely convinced him that he was fully awake and that everything had actually happened to him. He went up slowly to the looking glass and at first screwed up his eyes with the idea that perhaps he would see his nose in its proper place; but almost at the same moment he jumped back, saying: "What a horrible sight!"

And, indeed, the whole thing was quite inexplicable. If he had lost a button, a silver spoon, his watch, or something of the kind, but to lose—and in his own apartment, too! Taking all the circumstances into consideration, Major Kovalyov decided that he would not be far wrong in assuming that the whole thing was the fault of no other person than Mrs. Podtochin, who wanted him to marry her daughter. He was not himself averse to flirting with her, but he avoided a final decision. But when Mrs. Podtochin told him plainly that she would like her daughter to marry him, he quietly hung back with his compliments, declaring that he was still too young, that he had to serve another five years, as he had decided not to marry till he was exactly forty-two. That was why Mrs. Podtochin, out of revenge no doubt, had made up her mind to disfigure him and engaged some old witch to do the foul deed, for he simply refused to believe that his nose had been cut off;

no one had entered his room, and his barber, Ivan Yakovlevich, had shaved him on Wednesday, and during the whole
of that day and even on Thursday his nose was intact—he remembered that, he knew that for certain; besides, he would
have felt pain and the wound could not possibly have healed
so quickly and become as smooth as a pancake. He made all
sorts of plans in his head: to issue a court summons against
her or to go to see her and confront her with the undeniable
proof of her crime. His thoughts were interrupted by a gleam of
light through all the cracks of the door, which let him know
that Ivan had lighted a candle in the hall. Soon Ivan himself
appeared, carrying the candle in front of him and lighting the
whole room brightly. Kovalyov instinctively seized his handkerchief and covered the place where his nose had been only
the day before so that the stupid fellow should not stand
there gaping, seeing his master so strangely transformed.

Ivan had scarcely had time to go back to his cubbyhole
when an unfamiliar voice was heard in the hall, saying:

"Does the Collegiate Assessor Kovalyov live here?"

"Come in," said Kovalyov, jumping up quickly and opening the door. "Major Kovalyov is here."

A police officer of a handsome appearance, with whiskers
that were neither too dark nor too light and with fairly full
cheeks, came in. It was, in fact, the same police officer who,
at the beginning of this story, had been standing at the end of
Issakiyevsky Bridge.

"Did you lose your nose, sir?"

"That's right."

"It's been found now."

"What are you saying?" cried Major Kovalyov.

He was bereft of speech with joy. He stared fixedly at the
police officer who was standing before him and whose full
lips and cheeks reflected the flickering light of the candle.

"How was it found?"

"By a most extraordinary piece of luck, sir. It was intercepted just before he was leaving town. It was about to get into the stagecoach and leave for Riga. He even had a passport made out in the name of a certain civil servant. And the funny thing is that at first I was myself inclined to take him for a gentleman. But luckily I was wearing my glasses at the time and I saw at once that it was a nose. You see, sir, I am shortsighted, and if you were to stand in front of me I would just see that you have a face, but would not be able to make out either your nose or your beard or anything else for that matter. My mother-in-law, that is to say, my wife's mother, can't see anything, either."

Kovalyov was beside himself with excitement.

"Where is it? Where? I'll go at once!"

"Don't trouble, sir. Realizing how much you must want it, I brought it with me. And the funny part about it is that the chief accomplice in this affair is the scoundrel of a barber on Voznessensky Avenue, who is now locked up in a cell at the police station. I've suspected him for a long time of theft and drunkenness and, as a matter of fact, he stole a dozen buttons from a shop only the other day. Your nose, sir, is just as it was."

At these words, the police officer put his hand in his pocket and pulled out the nose wrapped in a piece of paper.

"Yes, yes, it's my nose!" cried Kovalyov. "It's my nose all right! Won't you have a cup of tea with me, sir?"

"I'd be very glad to, sir, but I'm afraid I'm rather in a hurry. I have to go to the House of Correction from here. Food prices have risen a great deal, sir. . . . I have my mother-in-law, that is to say, my wife's mother, living with me and, of course, there are the children. My eldest, in particular, is a very promising lad, sir. A very clever boy he is, sir, but I haven't the means to provide a good education for him—none at all. . . ."

Kovalyov took the hint and, snatching up a ten-ruble note from the table, thrust it into the hand of the police officer, who bowed and left the room, and almost at the same moment Kovalyov heard his voice raised in the street, where he was boxing the ears of a foolish peasant who had happened to drive with his cart on to the boulevard.

After the departure of the police officer, the Collegiate Assessor remained for a time in a sort of daze, and it was only after several minutes that he was able to recover his senses, so overwhelmed was he by his joy at the unexpected recovery of his nose. He took the newly found nose very carefully in both his cupped hands and examined it attentively once more.

"Yes, it's my nose all right!" said Major Kovalyov. "There's the pimple on the left side which I only got the other day."

The major almost laughed with joy. But nothing lasts very long in the world, and that is why even joy is not so poignant after the first moment. A moment later it grows weaker still and at last it merges imperceptibly into one's ordinary mood, just as a circle made in the water by a pebble at last merges into its smooth surface. Kovalyov began to ponder and he realized that the matter was not at an end: the nose had been found, but it had still to be affixed, to be put back in its place.

"And what if it doesn't stick?"

At this question that he had put to himself the major turned pale.

With a feeling of indescribable panic he rushed up to the table and drew the looking glass closer to make sure that he did not stick his nose on crookedly. His hands trembled. Carefully and with the utmost circumspection he put it back on its former place. Oh horror! The nose did not stick! . . . He put it to his mouth, breathed on it to warm it a little, and once more put it back on the smooth place between his two cheeks; but, try as he might, the nose refused to stick.

"Come on, come on! Stick, you idiot!" he kept saying to it.

But the nose, as though made of wood, kept falling down on the table with so strange a sound that it might have been cork. The major's face contorted spasmodically. "Won't it adhere?" he asked himself in a panic. But though he kept putting it back on its own place a great many times, his efforts were as unavailing as ever.

He called Ivan and sent him for the doctor, who occupied the best flat on the ground floor of the same house. The doctor was a fine figure of a man; he had wonderful pitch-black whiskers, a fresh, healthy wife, he ate fresh apples in the morning and kept his mouth quite extraordinarily clean, rinsing it every morning for nearly three quarters of an hour and brushing his teeth with five different kinds of tooth-brushes. The doctor came at once. After asking how long it was since the accident, he lifted up Major Kovalyov's face by the chin and gave a fillip with his thumb, on the spot where the nose had been, with such force that the major threw back his head so violently that he hit the wall. The doctor said that it was nothing and, after advising him to move away from the wall a little, told him to bend his head to the right. After feeling the place where the nose had been, he said: "H'm!" Then he told him to bend his head to the left, and again said: "H'm!" In conclusion he gave him another fillip with the thumb so that the major tossed his head like a horse whose teeth are being examined. Having carried out this experiment, the doctor shook his head and said:

"No, I'm afraid it can't be done! You'd better remain like this, for it might be much worse. It is, of course, quite possible to affix your nose. In fact, I could do it right now. But I assure you that it might be the worse for you."

"How do you like that! How am I to remain without a nose?" said Kovalyov. "It can't possibly be worse than now. It's—it's goodness only knows what! How can I show myself with such a horrible face? I know lots of people of good social position. Why, today I have been invited to two parties. I have a large circle of friends: Mrs. Chekhtaryov, the widow of a State Councillor, Mrs. Podtochin, the widow of an army officer—though after what she did to me now I shall have no further dealings with her except through the police. Do me a favor, Doctor," said Kovalyov in an imploring voice. "Is there no way at all? Stick it on somehow. It may not be quite satisfactory, but so long as it sticks I don't mind. I could even support it with a hand in an emergency. Besides, I don't dance, so that I could hardly do any harm to it by some inadvertent movement. As for my gratitude for your visits, you may be sure that I will recompense you as much as I can...."

"Believe me, sir," said the doctor neither in too loud nor in too soft a voice, but in a very persuasive and magnetic one, "I never allow any selfish motives to interfere with the treatment of my patients. This is against my principles and my art. It is true I charge for my visits, but that is only because I hate to offend by my refusal. Of course, I could put your nose back, but I assure you on my honor, if you won't believe my words, that it will be much worse. You'd better leave it to nature. Wash it often with cold water, and I assure you that without a nose you will be as healthy as with one. As for your nose, I'd advise you to put it in a bottle of spirits or, better still, pour two spoonfuls of aqua fortis and warmed-up vinegar into the bottle, and you'd be able to get a lot of money for it. I might take it myself even, if you won't ask too much for it."

"No, no," cried the desperate Major Kovalyov, "I'd rather it rotted away!"

"I'm sorry," said the doctor, taking his leave, "I wish I could be of some help to you, but there's nothing I can do! At least you saw how anxious I was to help you."

Having said this, the doctor left the room with a dignified air. Kovalyov did not even notice his face, and in his profound impassivity only caught sight of the cuffs of his spotlessly clean white shirt peeping out of his black frock coat.

On the following day he decided, before lodging his complaint, to write to Mrs. Podtochin a letter with a request to return to him without a fight what she had taken away from him. The letter was as follows:

Dear Mrs. Podtochin,

I cannot understand your strange treatment of me. I assure you that, by acting like this, you will gain nothing and will certainly not force me to marry your daughter. Believe me, I know perfectly well what happened to my nose and that you, and no one else, are the chief instigator of this affair. Its sudden detachment from its place, its flight, and its disguise, first in the shape of a civil servant and then in its own shape, is nothing more than the result of witchcraft employed by you or by those who engage in the same honorable occupations as yourself. For my part, I deem it my duty to warn you that if the aforementioned nose is not back in its usual place today, I shall be forced to have recourse to the protection and the safeguard of the law.

However, I have the honor of remaining, madam, with the utmost respect

Your obedient servant,
Platon Kovalyov

Dear Platon Kuzmich,

Your letter has greatly surprised me. To be quite frank, I never expected it, particularly as regards your unjust reproaches. I wish to inform you that I have never received the civil servant you mention, neither in disguise nor in his own shape. It is true, Filipp Ivanovich Potachkin used to come to see me. And though he did ask me for my daughter's hand and is a man of good and sober habits and of great learning, I have never held out any hopes to him. You also mention your nose. If you mean by that that I wished to put your nose out of joint, that is, to give you a formal refusal, I am surprised that you should speak of such a thing when, as you know perfectly well, I was quite of the contrary opinion and if you should now make a formal proposal to my daughter, I should be ready to satisfy you immediately, for that has always been my dearest wish, in the hope of which I remain always at your service,

Pelageya Podtochin

"No," said Kovalyov, after he had read the letter, "she had certainly nothing to do with it. It's impossible! The letter is not written as a guilty person would have written it." The Collegiate Assessor was an expert on such things, for, while serving in the Caucasus, he had several times been under judicial examination. "How then, in what way, did it happen? The devil alone can sort it out!" he said at last, utterly discouraged.

Meanwhile the rumors about this extraordinary affair spread all over the town and, as usually happens, not without all sorts of embellishments. At that time people's minds were particularly susceptible to anything of an extraordinary nature: only a short time before everybody had shown a great interest in the experiments of magnetism. Besides, the story of the dancing chairs in Konyushennaya Street was still fresh in people's minds, and it is therefore not surprising that people soon began talking about the Collegiate Assessor Kovalyov's nose which, it was alleged, was taking a walk on Nevsky Avenue at precisely three o'clock in the afternoon. Thousands of curious people thronged Nevsky Avenue every day. Someone said that the nose was in Junker's Stores, and such a crowd of people collected at the stores that the police had to be called to restore order. One enterprising, bewhiskered businessman of respectable appearance, who was selling all sorts of dry pasties at the entrance to the theatre, had purposely made beautiful wooden benches on which it was perfectly safe to stand and invited people to use them for eighty kopecks each. One highly estimable colonel, who had left his home earlier than usual so that he could see the nose, pushed his way through the crowd with great difficulty; but, to his great indignation, he saw in the window of the stores, instead of the nose, an ordinary woolen sweater and a lithograph of a girl pulling up her stocking and a dandy, with a small beard and an open waistcoat, peeping at her from behind a tree—a picture that had hung in the same place for over ten years. On stepping back from the window, he said with vexation: "One should not be allowed to create a disturbance among the common people by such stupid and improbable stories."

Then the rumor spread that Major Kovalyov's nose was not taking a walk on Nevsky Avenue but in Tavrichesky Gardens and that he had been there for a long time; in fact, that when the Persian Prince Khozrev Mirza had lived there he had greatly marveled at that curious freak of nature. A few students of the Surgical Academy set off there. One highly aristocratic lady wrote a letter to the head keeper of the gardens specially to ask him to show that rare phenomenon to her children and, if possible, with instructive and edifying explanations for young boys.

All men about town, without whom no important social gathering is complete, who liked to amuse the ladies and whose stock of amusing stories had been entirely used up at the time, were extremely glad of all this affair. A small section of respectable and well-meaning people were highly dissatisfied. One gentleman declared indignantly that he failed to understand how in our enlightened age such absurd stories could be spread abroad and that he was surprised the government paid no attention to it. This gentleman evidently was one of those gentlemen who would like to involve the government in everything, even in his daily tiffs with his wife. After that —but here again a thick fog descends on the whole incident, and what happened afterwards is completely unknown.

3.

The world is full of all sorts of absurdities. Sometimes there is not even a semblance of truth: suddenly the very same nose, which had been driving about disguised as a State Councillor and had created such an uproar in town, found itself, as if nothing had happened, on its accustomed place again, namely, between the two cheeks of Major Kovalyov. This happened on the seventh of April. Waking up and looking quite accidentally into the mirror, he saw—his nose! He grabbed it with his hand—it was his nose all right! . . ."Aha!" said Kovalyov, and nearly went leaping barefoot all over the room in a roisterous dance in his joy. But Ivan, who entered just then, prevented him. He told Ivan to bring in some water for washing at once and, while washing, glanced once again into the mirror: he had a nose! While wiping himself with a towel, he again glanced into the mirror: he had a nose!

"Have a look, Ivan, there seems to be a pimple on my nose," he said, thinking to himself: "Won't it be awful if Ivan were to say, No, sir, there's no pimple and no nose, either!"

But Ivan said: "There's nothing, sir. I can't see no pimple. Nothing at all on your nose, sir."

"That's good, damn it!" said the major to himself, snapping his fingers.

At that moment the barber Ivan Yakovlevich poked his head through the door, but as timidly as a cat which had just been thrashed for the theft of suet.

"Tell me first of all—are your hands clean?" Kovalyov shouted to him from the other end of the room.

"They are clean, sir."

"You're lying!"

"I swear they are clean, sir!"

"Very well, they'd better be!"

Kovalyov sat down. Ivan Yakovlevich put a napkin round him and in a twinkling, with the aid of his brush alone, transformed his whole beard and part of his cheek into the sort of cream that is served in a merchant's home at a name-day party.

"Well, I never!" said Ivan Yakovlevich to himself as he glanced at the nose. Then he bent his head to the other side and looked at the nose sideways. "Well, I'm damned," he went on, looking at the nose for some considerable time. "Dear, oh dear, just think of it!" At last, gently and as cautiously as can only be imagined, he raised two fingers to grasp it by its end. Such was Ivan Yakovlevich's system.

"Mind, mind what you're doing!" cried Kovalyov.

Ivan Yakovlevich was utterly discouraged, perplexed, and confused as he had never been confused before. At last he began carefully titillating him with the razor under the beard, and though he found it difficult and not at all convenient to shave without holding on to the olfactory organ, he did at last overcome all the obstacles by pressing his rough thumb against the cheek and the lower jaw and finished shaving him.

When everything was ready, Kovalyov hastened to dress at once, took a cab, and drove straight to the nearest pastry cook's. On entering, he at once shouted to the boy at the other end of the shop: "Boy, a cup of chocolate!" and immediately went up to the looking glass: he had a nose all right! He turned round gaily and glanced ironically, screwing up one eye a little, at two military gentlemen, one of whom had a nose no bigger than a waistcoat button. After that he set off for the office of the department where he was trying to obtain the post of vice-governor or, if unsuccessful, of an administrative clerk. On passing through the reception room, he glanced into the looking glass: he had a nose all right! Then he went to see another Collegiate Assessor, a man who was very fond of sneering at people, to whom he often used to say in reply to his biting remarks: "Oh, away with you! I know you, Mr. Pinprick!" On the way he thought: "If the major does not split his sides with laughter when he sees me, it's a sure sign that everything is in its proper place." But the Collegiate Assessor showed no signs of merriment. "It's perfect, perfect, damn it!" thought Kovalyov to himself. On the way back he met Mrs. Podtochin and her daughter, greeted them, and was met with joyful exclamations, which again proved to him that there was nothing wrong with him. He talked a long time with them and, taking out his snuffbox deliberately, kept stuffing his nose with snuff at both entrances for a great while, saying to himself: "There, I'm putting on this show specially for you, stupid females! And I won't marry your daughter all the same. Flirt with her—by all means, but nothing more!" And Major Kovalyov took his walks after that as if nothing had happened. He was to be seen on Nevsky Avenue, in the theatres—everywhere. And his nose, too, just as if nothing had happened, remained on his face, without as much as a hint that he had been playing truant. And after that Major Kovalyov was always seen in the best of humor, smiling, running after all the pretty ladies, and once even stopping before a little shop in the Arcade and buying himself a ribbon of some order for some mysterious reason, for he had never been a member of any order.

So that is the sort of thing that happened in the northern capital of our far-flung Empire. Only now, on thinking it all over, we can see that there is a great deal that is improbable in it. Quite apart from the really strange fact of the supernatural displacement of the nose and its appearance in various parts of the town in the guise of a State Councillor, how did Kovalyov fail to realize that he could not advertise about his nose in a newspaper? I am not saying that because I think that advertisement rates are too high—that's nonsense, and I am not at all a mercenary person. But it's improper, awkward, not nice! And again—how did the nose come to be in a loaf of bread and what about Ivan Yakovlevich? No, that I cannot understand, I simply cannot understand it! But what is even stranger and more incomprehensible than anything is that authors should choose such subjects. I confess that is entirely beyond my comprehension. It's like—no, I simply don't understand it. In the first place it's of no benefit whatever to our country, and in the second place—but even in the second place there's no benefit whatever. I simply don't know what to make of it. . . .

And yet, in spite of it all, though, of course, we may take for granted this and that and the other—may even—— But then where do you not find all sorts of absurdities? All the same, on second thought, there really is something in it. Say what you like, but such things do happen—not often, but they do happen.

Translated by David Magarshack

ELIZABETH BOWEN

HER TABLE SPREAD

ALBAN HAD few opinions on the subject of marriage; his attitude to women was negative, but in particular he was not attracted to Miss Cuffe. Coming down early for dinner, red satin dress cut low, she attacked the silence with loud laughter before he had spoken. He recollected having heard that she was abnormal—at twenty-five, of statuesque development, still detained in childhood. The two other ladies, in beaded satins, made entrances of a surprising formality. It occurred to him, his presence must constitute an occasion: they certainly sparkled. Old Mr. Rossiter, uncle to Mrs. Treye, came last, more sourly. They sat for some time without the addition of lamplight. Dinner was not announced; the ladies, by remaining on guard, seemed to deprecate any question of its appearance. No sound came from other parts of the Castle.

Miss Cuffe was an heiress to whom the Castle belonged and whose guests they all were. But she carefully followed the movements of her aunt, Mrs. Treye; her ox-eyes moved from face to face in happy submission rather than expectancy. She was continually preoccupied with attempts at gravity, as though holding down her skirts in a high wind. Mrs. Treye and Miss Carbin combined to cover her excitement; still, their looks frequently stole from the company to the windows, of which there were too many. He received a strong impression someone outside was waiting to come in. At last, with a sigh, they got up: dinner had been announced.

The Castle was built on high ground, commanding the

85

estuary; a steep hill, with trees, continued above it. On fine days the view was remarkable, of almost Italian brilliance, with that constant reflection up from the water that even now prolonged the too-long day. Now, in continuous evening rain, the winding wooded line of the further shore could be seen and, nearer the windows, a smothered island with the stump of a watch-tower. Where the Castle stood, a higher tower had answered the island's. Later a keep, then wings, had been added; now the fine peaceful residence had French windows opening on to the terrace. Invasions from the water would henceforth be social, perhaps amorous. On the slope down from the terrace, trees began again; almost, but not quite, concealing the destroyer. Alban, who knew nothing, had not yet looked down.

It was Mr. Rossiter who first spoke of the destroyer—Alban meanwhile glancing along the table; the preparations had been stupendous. The destroyer had come today. The ladies all turned to Alban: the beads on their bosoms sparkled. So this was what they had here, under their trees. Engulfed by their pleasure, from now on he disappeared personally. Mr. Rossiter, rising a note, continued. The estuary, it appeared, was deep, with a channel buoyed up it. By a term of the Treaty, English ships were permitted to anchor in these waters.

"But they've been afraid of the rain!" chimed in Valeria Cuffe.

"Hush," said her aunt, "that's silly. Sailors would be accustomed to getting wet."

But, Miss Carbin reported, that spring there *had* already been one destroyer. Two of the officers had been seen dancing at the hotel at the head of the estuary.

"So," said Alban, "you are quite in the world." He adjusted his glasses in her direction.

Miss Carbin—blonde, not forty, and an attachment of Mrs. Treye's—shook her head despondently. "We were all away at Easter. Wasn't it curious they should have come then? The sailors walked in the demesne but never touched the daffodils."

"As though I should have cared!" exclaimed Valeria passionately.

"Morale too good," stated Mr. Rossiter.

"But next evening," continued Miss Carbin, "the officers did not go to the hotel. They climbed up here through the trees to the terrace—you see, they had no idea. Friends of ours were staying here at the Castle, and they apologized. Our friends invited them in to supper. . . ."

"Did they accept?"

The three ladies said in a breath: "Yes, they came."

Valeria added urgently, "So don't you *think*—?"

"So to-night we have a destroyer to greet you," Mrs. Treye said quickly to Alban. "It is quite an event; the country people are coming down from the mountains. These waters are very lonely; the steamers have given up since the bad times; there is hardly a pleasure-boat. The weather this year has driven visitors right away."

"You are beautifully remote."

"Yes," agreed Miss Carbin. "Do you know much about the Navy? Do you think, for instance, that this is likely to be the same destroyer?"

"*Will they remember?*" Valeria's bust was almost on the table. But with a rustle Mrs. Treye pressed Valeria's toe. For the dining-room also looked out across the estuary, and the great girl had not once taken her eyes from the window. Perhaps it was unfortunate that Mr. Alban should have coincided with the destroyer. Perhaps it was unfortunate for Mr. Alban too.

For he saw now he was less than half the feast; unappeased, the party sat looking through him, all grouped at an end of the table—to the other, chairs had been pulled up. Dinner was being served very slowly. Candles—possible to see from the water—were lit now; some wet peonies glistened.

Outside, day still lingered hopefully. The bushes over the edge of the terrace were like heads—you could have sworn sometimes you saw them mounting, swaying in manly talk. Once, wound up in the rain, a bird whistled, seeming hardly a bird.

"Perhaps since then they have been to Greece, or Malta?"

"That would be the Mediterranean fleet," said Mr. Rossiter.

They were sorry to think of anything out in the rain tonight.

"The decks must be streaming," said Miss Carbin.

Then Valeria, exclaiming, "Please excuse me!" pushed her chair in and ran from the room.

"She is impulsive," explained Mrs. Treye. "Have *you* been to Malta, Mr. Alban?"

In the drawing-room, empty of Valeria, the standard lamps had been lit. Through their ballet-skirt shades, rose and lemon, they gave out a deep, welcoming light. Alban, at the ladies' invitation, undraped the piano. He played, but they could see he was not pleased. It was obvious he had always been a civilian, and when he had taken his place on the piano-stool—which he twirled round three times, rather fussily—his dinner-jacket wrinkled across the shoulders. It was sad they should feel so indifferent, for he came from London. Mendelssohn was exasperating to them—they opened all four windows to let the music downhill. They preferred not to draw the curtains; the air, though damp, being pleasant tonight, they said.

The piano was damp, but Alban played almost all his heart out. He played out the indignation of years his mild manner concealed. He had failed to love; nobody did anything about this; partners at dinner gave him less than half their attention. He knew some spring had dried up at the root of the world. He was fixed in the dark rain, by an indifferent shore. He played badly, but they were unmusical. Old Mr. Rossiter, who was not what he seemed, went back to the dining-room to talk to the parlormaid.

Valeria, glittering vastly, appeared in a window.

"Come *in*!" her aunt cried in indignation. She would die of a chill, childless, in fact unwedded; the Castle would have to be sold and where would they all be?

But—"Lights down there!" Valeria shouted above the music.

They had to run out for a moment, laughing and holding cushions over their bare shoulders. Alban left the piano: they looked boldly down from the terrace. Indeed, there they were: two lights like arc-lamps, blurred by rain and drawn down deep in reflection into the steady water. There were, too, ever so many portholes, all lit up.

"Perhaps they are playing bridge," said Miss Carbin.

"Now I wonder if Uncle Robert ought to have called," said Mrs. Treye. "Perhaps we have seemed remiss—one calls on a regiment."

"Patrick could row him out to-morrow."

"He hates the water." She sighed. "Perhaps they will be gone."

"Let's go for a row now—let's go for a row with a lantern," besought Valeria, jumping and pulling her aunt's elbow. They produced such indignation she disappeared again—wet satin skirts and all—into the bushes. The ladies could do no more: Alban suggested the rain might spot their dresses.

"They must lose a great deal, playing cards throughout an evening for high stakes," Miss Carbin said with concern as they all sat down again.

"Yet, if you come to think of it, somebody must win."

But the naval officers who so joyfully supped at Easter had been, Miss Carbin knew, a Mr. Graves and a Mr. Garrett: *they* would certainly lose. "At all events, it is better than dancing at the hotel; there would be nobody of their type."

"There is nobody there at all."

"I expect they are best where they are.... Mr. Alban, a Viennese waltz?"

He played while the ladies whispered, waving the waltz time a little distractedly. Mr. Rossiter, coming back, momentously stood: they turned in hope: even the waltz halted. But he brought no news. "You should call Valeria in. You can't tell who may be round the place. She's not fit to be out to-night."

"Perhaps she's not out."

"She is," said Mr. Rossiter crossly. "I just saw her racing past the window with a lantern."

Valeria's mind was made up: she was a princess. Not for nothing had she had the dining-room silver polished and all set out. She would pace around in red satin that swished behind, while Mr. Alban kept on playing a loud waltz. They would be dazed at all she had to offer—also her two new statues and the leopard-skin from the auction.

When he and she were married (she inclined a little to Mr. Garrett) they would invite all the Navy up the estuary and give them tea. Her estuary would be filled up, like a regatta, with loud excited battleships tooting to one another and flags flying. The terrace would be covered with grateful sailors, leaving room for the band. She would keep the peacocks her aunt did not allow. His friends would be surprised to notice that Mr. Garrett had meanwhile become an admiral, all gold. He would lead the other admirals into the Castle and say, while they wiped their feet respectfully: "These are my wife's statues; she has given them to me. One is Mars, one is Mercury. We have a Venus, but she is not dressed. And wait till I show you our silver and gold plates . . ." The Navy would be unable to tear itself away.

She had been excited for some weeks at the idea of marrying Mr. Alban, but now the lovely appearance of the destroyer put him out of her mind. He would not have done; he was not handsome. But she could keep him to play the piano on quiet afternoons.

Her friends had told her Mr. Garrett was quite a Viking.

She was so very familiar with his appearance that she felt sometimes they had already been married for years—though still, sometimes, he could not realize his good luck. She still had to remind him the island was hers too. . . . To-night, Aunt and darling Miss Carbin had so fallen in with her plans, putting on their satins and decorating the drawing-room, that the dinner became a betrothal feast. There was some little hitch about the arrival of Mr. Garrett—she had heard that gentlemen sometimes could not tie their ties. And now he was late and would be discouraged. So she must now go halfway down to the water and wave a lantern.

But she put her two hands over the lantern, then smothered it in her dress. She had a panic. Supposing she should prefer Mr. Graves?

She had heard Mr. Graves was stocky, but very merry; when he came to supper at Easter he slid in the gallery. He would teach her to dance, and take her to Naples and Paris. . . . Oh, dear, oh, dear, then they must fight for her; that was all there was to it. . . . She let the lantern out of her skirts and waved. Her fine arm with bangles went up and down, up and down, with the staggering light; the trees one by one jumped up from the dark, like savages.

Inconceivably, the destroyer took no notice.

Undisturbed by oars, the rain stood up from the waters; not a light rose to peer, and the gramophone, though it remained very faint, did not cease or alter.

In mackintoshes, Mr. Rossiter and Alban meanwhile made their way to the boat-house, Alban did not know why. "If that goes on," said Mr. Rossiter, nodding towards Valeria's lantern, "they'll fire one of their guns at us."

"Oh, no. Why?" said Alban. He buttoned up, however, the collar of his mackintosh.

"Nervous as cats. It's high time that girl was married. She's a nice girl in many ways, too."

"Couldn't we get the lantern away from her?" They

stepped on a paved causeway and heard the water nibble the rocks.

"She'd scream the place down. She's of age now, you see."

"But if—"

"Oh, she won't do that; I was having a bit of fun with you." Chuckling equably, Mrs. Treye's uncle unlocked and pulled open the boat-house door. A bat whistled out.

"Why are we here?"

"She might come for the boat; she's a fine oar," said Mr. Rossiter wisely. The place was familiar to him; he lit an oil-lamp and, sitting down on a trestle with a staunch air of having done what he could, reached a bottle of whisky out of the boat. He motioned the bottle to Alban. "It's a wild night," he said. "Ah, well, we don't have these destroyers every day."

"That seems fortunate."

"Well, it is and it isn't." Restoring the bottle to the vertical, Mr. Rossiter continued: "It's a pity you don't want a wife. You'd be the better for a wife, d'you see, a young fellow like you. She's got a nice character; she's a girl you could shape. She's got a nice income." The bat returned from the rain and knocked round the lamp. Lowering the bottle frequently, Mr. Rossiter talked to Alban (whose attitude remained negative) of women in general and the parlormaid in particular. . . .

"*Bat!*" Alban squealed irrepressibly, and with his hand to his ear—where he still felt it—fled from the boat-house. Mr. Rossiter's conversation continued. Alban's pumps squelched as he ran; he skidded along the causeway and balked at the upward steps. His soul squelched equally: he had been warned; he had been warned. He had heard they were all mad; he had erred out of headiness and curiosity. A degree of terror was agreeable to his vanity: by express wish he had occupied haunted rooms. Now he had no other pumps in this country, no idea where to buy them, and a ducal visit ahead. Also, wandering as it were among the apples and amphoras of an art school, he had blundered into the life room: woman revolved gravely.

"Hell," he said to the steps, mounting, his mind blank to the outcome.

He was nerved for the jumping lantern, but half-way up to the Castle darkness was once more absolute. Her lantern had gone out; he could orientate himself—in spite of himself—by her sobbing. Absolute desperation. He pulled up so short that, for balance, he had to cling to a creaking tree.

"Hi!" she croaked. Then: "You *are* there! I hear you!"

"Miss Cuffe—"

"How too bad you are! I never heard you rowing. I thought you were never coming—"

"Quietly, my dear girl."

"Come up quickly. I haven't even seen you. Come up to the windows—"

"Miss Cuffe—"

"Don't you remember the way?" As sure but not so noiseless as a cat in the dark, Valeria hurried to him.

"Mr. Garrett—" she panted. "I'm Miss Cuffe. Where have you been? I've destroyed my beautiful red dress and they've eaten up your dinner. But we're still waiting. Don't be afraid; you'll soon be there now. I'm Miss Cuffe; this is my Castle—"

"Listen, it's I, Mr. Alban—"

"Ssh, ssh, Mr. Alban: *Mr. Garrett has landed.*"

Her cry, his voice, some breath of the joyful intelligence, brought the others on to the terrace, blind with lamplight.

"Valeria?"

"Mr. Garrett has landed!"

Mrs. Treye said to Miss Carbin under her breath, "Mr. Garrett has come."

Miss Carbin, half weeping with agitation, replied, "We must go in." But uncertain who was to speak next, or how to speak, they remained leaning over the darkness. Behind, through the windows, lamps spread great skirts of light, and Mars and Mercury, unable to contain themselves, stooped from their pedestals. The dumb keyboard shone like a ball-room floor.

Alban, looking up, saw their arms and shoulders under the bright rain. Close by, Valeria's fingers creaked on her warm wet satin. She laughed like a princess, magnificently justified. Their unseen faces were all three lovely, and, in the silence after the laughter, such a strong tenderness reached him that, standing there in full manhood, he was for a moment not exiled. For the moment, without moving or speaking, he stood, in the dark, in a flame, as though all three said: "My darling..."

Perhaps it was best for them all that early, when next day first lightened the rain, the destroyer steamed out—below the extinguished Castle where Valeria lay with her arms wide, past the boat-house where Mr. Rossiter lay insensible and the bat hung masked in its wings—down the estuary into the open sea.

LUDWIG TIECK

FAIR ECKBERT

In a region of the Harz Mountains there lived a knight whom people generally called simply Fair Eckbert. He was about forty years old, scarcely of medium height, and short, very fair hair fell thick and straight over his pale, sunken face. He lived very quietly unto himself, and was never implicated in the feuds of his neighbors; people saw him but rarely outside the encircling wall of his little castle. His wife loved solitude quite as much as he, and both seemed to love each other from the heart; only they were wont to complain because Heaven seemed unwilling to bless their marriage with children.

Very seldom was Eckbert visited by guests, and even when he was, almost no change on their account was made in the ordinary routine of his life. Frugality dwelt there, and Economy herself seemed to regulate everything. Eckbert was then cheerful and gay—only when he was alone one noticed in him a certain reserve, a quiet distant melancholy.

Nobody came so often to the castle as did Philip Walther, a man to whom Eckbert had become greatly attached, because he found in him very much his own way of thinking. His home was really in Franconia, but he often spent more than half a year at a time in the vicinity of Eckbert's castle, where he busied himself gathering herbs and stones and arranging them in order. He had a small income, and was therefore dependent upon no one. Eckbert often accompanied him on his lonely rambles, and thus a closer friendship developed between the two men with each succeeding year.

There are hours in which it worries a man to keep from a friend a secret, which hitherto he has often taken great pains to conceal. The soul then feeds an irresistible impulse to impart itself completely, and reveal its innermost self to the friend, in order to make him so much the more a friend. At these moments delicate souls disclose themselves to each other, and it doubtless sometimes happens that the one shrinks back in fright from its acquaintance with the other.

One foggy evening in early autumn Eckbert was sitting with his friend and his wife, Bertha, around the hearth-fire. The flames threw a bright glow into the room and played on the ceiling above. The night looked in darkly through the windows, and the trees outside were shivering in the damp cold. Walther was lamenting that he had so far to go to get back home, and Eckbert proposed that he remain there and spend half the night in familiar talk, and then sleep until morning in one of the rooms of the castle. Walther accepted the proposal, whereupon wine and supper were brought in, the fire was replenished with wood, and the conversation of the two friends became more cheery and confidential.

After the dishes had been cleared off, and the servants had gone out, Eckbert took Walther's hand and said:

"Friend, you ought once to let my wife tell you the story of her youth, which is indeed strange enough."

"Gladly," replied Walther, and they all sat down again around the hearth. It was now exactly midnight, and the moon shone intermittently through the passing clouds.

"You must forgive me," began Bertha, "but my husband says your thoughts are so noble that it is not right to conceal anything from you. Only you must not regard my story as a fairy-tale, no matter how strange it may sound.

"I was born in a village, my father was a poor shepherd. The household economy of my parents was on a humble plane—often they did not know where they were going to get their bread. But what grieved me far more than that was the fact that my father and mother often quarreled over their poverty, and cast bitter reproaches at each other. Furthermore I was constantly hearing about myself, that I was a simple, stupid child, who could not perform even the most trifling task. And I was indeed extremely awkward and clumsy; I let everything drop from my hands, I learned neither to sew nor to spin, I could do nothing to help around the house. The misery of my parents, however, I understood extremely well. I often used to sit in the corner and fill my head with notions —how I would help them if I suddenly became rich, how I would shower them with gold and silver and take delight in their astonishment. Then I would see spirits come floating up, who would reveal subterranean treasures to me or give me pebbles which afterward turned into gems. In short, the most wonderful fantasies would occupy my mind, and when I had to get up and help or carry something, I would show myself far more awkward than ever, for the reason that my head would be giddy with all the strange notions.

"My father was always very cross with me, because I was such an absolutely useless burden on the household; so he often treated me with great cruelty, and I seldom heard him say a kind word to me. Thus it went along until I was about eight years old, when serious steps were taken to get me to do and to learn something. My father believed that it was sheer obstinacy and indolence on my part, so that I might spend my days in idleness. Enough—he threatened me unspeakably, and when this turned out to be of no avail, he chastised me most barbarously, adding that this punishment was to be repeated every day because I was an absolutely useless creature.

"All night long I cried bitterly—I felt so entirely forsaken, and I pitied myself so that I wanted to die. I dreaded the break of day, and did not know what to do. I longed for any possible kind of ability, and could not understand at all why I was more stupid than the other children of my acquaintance. I was on the verge of despair.

"When the day dawned, I got up, and, scarcely realizing what I was doing, opened the door of our little cabin. I found myself in the open field, soon afterward in a forest, into which the daylight had hardly yet shone. I ran on without looking back; but I did not get tired, for I thought all the time that my father would surely overtake me and treat me even more cruelly on account of my running away.

"When I emerged from the forest again the sun was already fairly high, and I saw, lying ahead of me, something dark, over which a thick mist was resting. One moment I was obliged to scramble over hills, the next to follow a winding path between rocks. I now guessed that I must be in the neighboring mountains, and the mere word mountains, whenever I heard them talked about, had an extremely terrible sound to my childish ear. I hadn't the heart to turn back —it was indeed precisely my fear which drove me onwards. I often looked around me in terror when the wind rustled through the leaves above me, or when a distant sound of chopping rang out through the quiet morning. Finally, when I began to meet colliers and miners and heard a strange pronunciation, I nearly fainted with fright.

"You must forgive my prolixity. As often as I tell this story I involuntarily become garrulous, and Eckbert, the only person to whom I have told it, has spoiled me by his attention.

"I passed through several villages and begged, for I now felt hungry and thirsty. I helped myself along very well with the answers I gave to questions asked me. I had wandered along in this way for about four days, when I came to a small footpath which led me farther from the highway. The rocks around me now assumed a different, far stranger shape. They were cliffs, and were piled up on one another in such a way that they looked as if the first gust of wind would hurl them all together into a heap. I did not know whether to go on or not. I had always slept overnight either in out-of-the-way shepherds' huts, or else in the open woods, for it was just then the most beautiful season of the year. Here I came across no human habitations whatever, nor could I expect to meet with any in the wilderness. The rocks became more and more terrible—I often had to pass close by dizzy precipices, and finally even the path under my feet came to an end. I was absolutely wretched; I wept and screamed, and my voice echoed horribly in the rocky glens. And now night set in; first I thought it was wild beasts, then the wind moaning through the rocks, then again strange birds. I prayed, and not until toward morning did I fall asleep.

"I woke up when the daylight shone in my face. In front of me there was a rock. I climbed up on it, hoping to find a way out of the wilderness, and perhaps see some houses or people. But when I reached the top, everything as far as my eye could see, was like night about me—all over-cast with a gloomy mist. The day was dark and dismal, and not a tree, not a meadow, not even a thicket could my eye discern, with the exception of a few bushes which, in solitary sadness, had shot up through the crevices in the rocks. It is impossible to describe the longing I felt merely to see a human being, even had it been the most strange-looking person before whom I should inevitably have taken fright. At the same time I was ravenously hungry. I sat down and resolved to die. But after a while the desire to live came off victorious; I got up quickly and walked on all day long, occasionally crying out. At last I was scarcely conscious of what I was doing; I was tired and exhausted, had hardly any desire to live, and yet was afraid to die.

"Toward evening the region around me began to assume a somewhat more friendly aspect. My thoughts and wishes took new life, and the desire to live awakened in all my veins. I now thought I heard the swishing of a mill in the distance; I redoubled my steps, and how relieved, how joyous I felt when at last I actually reached the end of the dreary rocks! Woods and meadows and, far ahead, pleasant mountains lay before me again. I felt as if I had stepped out of hell into paradise; the solitude and my helplessness did not seem to me at all terrible now.

"Instead of the hoped-for mill, I came upon a water-fall, which, to be sure, considerably diminished my joy. I dished up some water from the river with my hand and drank. Suddenly I thought I heard a low cough a short distance away. Never have I experienced so pleasant a surprise as at that moment; I went nearer and saw, on the edge of the forest, an old woman, apparently resting. She was dressed almost entirely in black; a black hood covered her head and a large part of her face. In her hand she held a walking stick.

"I approached her and asked for help; she had me sit down beside her and gave me bread and some wine. While I was eating she sang a hymn in a shrill voice, and when she had finished she said that I might follow her.

"I was delighted with this proposal, strange as the voice and the personality of the old woman seemed to me. She walked rather fast with her cane, and at every step she distorted her face, which at first made me laugh. The wild rocks steadily receded behind us—we crossed a pleasant meadow, and then passed through a fairly long forest. When we emerged from this, the sun was just setting, and I shall never forget the view and the feelings of that evening. Everything was fused in the most delicate red and gold; the tree-tops stood forth in the red glow of evening, the charming light was spread out over the fields, the forest and the leaves of the trees were motionless, the clear sky looked like an open paradise, and the evening bells of the villages rang out with a strange mournfulness across the lea. My young soul now got its first presentiment of the world and its events. I forgot myself and my guide; my spirit and my eyes were wandering among golden clouds.

"We now climbed a hill, which was planted with birch-trees, and from its summit looked down into a little valley,

likewise full of birches. In the midst of the trees stood a little
hut. A lively barking came to our ears, and presently a spry
little dog was dancing around the old woman and wagging its
tail. Presently he came to me, examined me from all sides,
and then returned with friendly actions to the old woman.

"When we were descending the hill I heard some wonderful singing, which seemed to come from the hut. It sounded
like a bird, and ran:

> O solitude
> Of lonely wood
> Where none intrude,
> Thou bringest good
> For every mood,
> O solitude!

"These few words were repeated over and over; if I were
to attempt to describe the effect, it was somewhat like the
blended notes of a bugle and a shawm.

"My curiosity was strained to the utmost. Without waiting for the old woman's invitation, I walked into the hut with
her. Dusk had already set in. Everything was in proper order;
a few goblets stood in a cupboard, some strange-looking vessels lay on a table, and a bird was hanging in a small, shiny
cage by the window. And he, indeed, it was that I had heard
singing. The old woman gasped and coughed, seemingly as if
she would never get over it. Now she stroked the little dog,
now talked to the bird, which only answered her with its
usual words. Furthermore, she acted in no way as if I were
present. While I was thus watching her, a series of shudders
passed through my body; for her face was constantly twitching and her head shaking, as if with age, and in such a way
that it was impossible for me to tell how she really looked.

"When she finally ceased coughing she lighted a candle,
set a very small table, and laid the supper on it. Then she

looked around at me and told me to take one of the woven cane chairs. I sat down directly opposite her, and the candle stood between us. She folded her bony hands and prayed aloud, all the time twitching her face in such a way that it almost made me laugh. I was very careful, however, not to do anything to make her angry.

"After supper she prayed again, and then showed me to a bed in a tiny little side-room—she herself slept in the main room. I did not stay awake long, for I was half dazed. I woke up several times during the night, however, and heard the old woman coughing and talking to the dog, and occasionally I heard the bird, which seemed to be dreaming and sang only a few isolated words of its song. These stray notes, united with the rustling of the birches directly in front of the window, and also with the song of the far-off nightingale, made such a strange combination that I felt all the time, not as if I were awake, but as if I were lapsing into another, still stranger, dream.

"In the morning the old woman woke me up and soon afterward gave me some work to do; I had, namely, to spin, and I soon learned how to do it; in addition I had to take care of the dog and the bird. I was not long in getting acquainted with the housekeeping, and came to know all the objects around. I now began to feel that everything was as it should be; I no longer thought that there was anything strange about the old woman, or romantic about the location of her home, or that the bird was in any way extraordinary. To be sure, I was all the time struck by his beauty; for his feathers displayed every possible color, varying from a most beautiful light blue to a glowing red, and when he sang he puffed himself out proudly, so that his feathers shone even more gorgeously.

"The old woman often went out and did not return until evening. Then I would go with the dog to meet her and she would call me child and daughter. Finally I came to like her heartily; for our minds, especially in childhood, quickly accustom themselves to everything. In the evening hours she taught me to read; I soon learned the art, and afterward it was a source of endless pleasure to me in my solitude, for she had a few old, hand-written books which contained wonderful stories.

"The memory of the life I led at that time still gives me a strange feeling even now. I was never visited by any human being, and felt at home only in that little family circle; for the dog and the bird made the same impression on me which ordinarily only old and intimate friends create. Often as I used it at that time, I have never been able to recall the dog's strange name.

"In this way I had lived with the old woman for four years, and I must have been at any rate about twelve years old when she finally began to grow more confidential and revealed a secret to me. It was this: every day the bird laid one egg, and in this egg there was always a pearl or a gem. I had already noticed that she often did something in the cage secretly, but had never particularly concerned myself about it. She now charged me with the task of taking out these eggs during her absence, and of carefully preserving them in the vessels. She would leave food for me and stay away quite a long time— weeks and months. My little spinning-wheel hummed, the dog barked, the wonderful bird sang, and meanwhile everything was so quiet in the region round about that I cannot recall a single high wind or a thunder-storm during the entire time. Not a human being strayed thither, not a wild animal came near our habitation. I was happy, and sang and worked away from one day to the next. Man would perhaps be right happy if he could thus spend his entire life, unseen by others.

"From the little reading that I did I formed quite wonderful impressions of the world and mankind. They were all drawn from myself and the company I lived in; thus, if whimsical people were spoken of I could not imagine them other than the little dog, beautiful women always looked like the bird, and all old women were as my wonderful old friend. I had also read a little about love, and in my imagination I figured in strange tales. I formed a mental picture of the most beautiful knight in the world and adorned him with all sorts of excellences, without really knowing, after all my trouble, what he looked like. But I could feel genuine pity for myself if he did not return my love, and then I would make long, emotional speeches to him, sometimes aloud, in order to win him. You smile—we are all now past this period of youth.

"I now liked it rather better when I was alone, for I was then myself mistress of the house. The dog was very fond of me and did everything I wanted him to do, the bird answered all my questions with his song, my wheel was always spinning merrily, and so in the bottom of my heart I never felt any desire for a change. When the old woman returned from her wanderings she would praise my diligence, and say that her household was conducted in a much more orderly manner since I belonged to it. She was delighted with my development and my healthy look. In short, she treated me in every way as if I were a daughter.

" 'You are a good child,' she once said to me in a squeaky voice. 'If you continue thus, it will always go well with you. It never pays to swerve from the right course—the penalty is sure to follow, though it may be a long time coming.' While she was saying this I did not give a great deal of heed to it, for I was very lively in all my movements. But in the night it occurred to me again, and I could not understand what she meant by it. I thought her words over carefully—I had read about riches, and it finally dawned on me that her pearls and gems might perhaps be valuable. This idea presently became still clearer to me—but what could she have meant by the right course? I was still unable to understand fully the meaning of her words.

"I was now fourteen years old. It is indeed a misfortune

that human beings acquire reason, only to lose, in so doing, the innocence of their souls. In other words I now began to realize the fact that it depended only upon me to take the bird and the gems in the old woman's absence, and go out into the world of which I had read. At the same time it was perhaps possible that I might meet my wonderfully beautiful knight, who still held a place in my imagination.

"At first this thought went no further than any other, but when I would sit there spinning constantly, it always came back against my will and I became so deeply absorbed in it that I already saw myself dressed up and surrounded by knights and princes. And whenever I would thus lose myself, I easily grew very sad when I glanced up and found myself in my little, narrow home. When I was about my business, the old woman paid no further attention to me.

"One day my hostess went away and told me that she would be gone longer this time than usual—I should pay strict attention to everything, and not let the time drag on my hands. I took leave of her with a certain uneasiness, for I somehow felt that I should never see her again. I looked after her for a long time, and did not myself know why I was so uneasy; it seemed almost as if my intention were already standing before me, without my being distinctly conscious of it.

"I had never taken such diligent care of the dog and the bird before—they lay closer to my heart than ever now. The old woman had been away when I arose with the firm purpose of abandoning the hut with the bird and going out into the so-called world. My mind was narrow and limited; I wanted again to remain there, and yet the thought was repugnant to me. One moment the quiet solitude would seem so beautiful to me, and then again I would be charmed by the vision of a new world with its manifold wonders.

"I did not know what to do with myself. The dog was continually dancing around me with friendly advances, the sunlight was spread out cheerfully over the fields, and the green birch-trees shone brightly. I had a feeling as if I had something to do requiring haste. Accordingly, I caught the little dog, tied him fast in the room, and took the cage, with the bird in it, under my arm. The dog cringed and whined over this unusual treatment; he looked at me with imploring eyes but I was afraid to take him with me. I also took one of the vessels, which was filled with gems, and concealed it about me. The others I left there. The bird twisted its head around in a singular manner when I walked out of the door with him; the dog strained hard to follow me, but was obliged to remain behind.

"I avoided the road leading toward the wild rocks, and walked in the opposite direction. The dog continued to bark and whine, and I was deeply touched by it. Several times the bird started to sing, but, as he was being carried, it was necessarily rather difficult for him. As I walked along the barking grew fainter and fainter, and, finally, ceased altogether. I cried and was on the point of turning back, but the longing to see something new drove me on.

"I had already traversed mountains and several forests when evening came, and I was obliged to pass the night in a village. I was very timid when I entered the public-house; they showed me to a room and a bed, and I slept fairly well, except that I dreamt of the old woman, who was threatening me.

"My journey was rather monotonous; but the further I went the more the picture of the old woman and the little dog worried me. I thought how he would probably starve to death without my help, and in the forest I often thought I would suddenly meet the old woman. Thus, crying and sighing, I wandered along, and as often as I rested and put the cage on the ground, the bird sang its wonderful song, and reminded me vividly of the beautiful home I had deserted. As human nature is prone to forget, I now thought that the journey I had made as a child was not as dismal as the one I was now making, and I wished that I were back in the same situation.

"I had sold a few gems, and now, after wandering many days, I arrived in a village. Even as I was entering it, a strange feeling came over me—I was frightened and did not know why. But soon I discovered why—it was the very same village in which I was born. How astonished I was! How the tears of joy ran down my cheeks as a thousand strange memories came back to me! There were a great many changes; new houses had been built, others, which had then only recently been erected, were now in a state of dilapidation. I came across places where there had been a fire. Everything was a great deal smaller and more crowded than I had expected. I took infinite delight in the thought of seeing my parents again after so many years. I found the little house and the well-known threshold—the handle on the door was just as it used to be. I felt as if I had only yesterday left it ajar. My heart throbbed vehemently. I quickly opened the door—but faces entirely strange to me stared at me from around the room. I inquired after the shepherd, Martin, and was told that both he and his wife had died three years before. I hurried out and, crying aloud, left the village.

"I had looked forward with such pleasure to surprising them with my riches, and as a result of a remarkable accident the dream of my childhood had really come true. And now it was all in vain—they could no longer rejoice with me—the fondest hope of my life was lost to me forever.

"I rented a small house with a garden in a pleasant city, and engaged a waiting-maid. The world did not appear to be such a wonderful place as I had expected, but the old woman and my former home dropped more and more out of my memory, so that, upon the whole, I lived quite contentedly.

"The bird had not sung for a long time, so that I was not a little frightened one night when he suddenly began again. The song he sang, however, was different—it was:

O solitude
Of lonely wood,
A vanished good
In dreams pursued,
In absence rued,
O solitude!

"I could not sleep through the night; everything came back to my mind, and I felt more than ever that I had done wrong. When I got up the sight of the bird was positively repugnant to me; he was constantly staring at me, and his presence worried me. He never ceased singing now, and sang more loudly and shrilly than he used to. The more I looked at him the more uneasiness I felt. Finally, I opened the cage, stuck my hand in, seized him by the neck and squeezed my fingers together forcibly. He looked at me imploringly, and I relaxed my grip—but he was already dead. I buried him in the garden.

"And now I was often seized with fear of my waiting-maid. My own past came back to me, and I thought that she too might rob me some day, or perhaps even murder me. For a long time I had known a young knight whom I liked very much—I gave him my hand, and with that, Mr. Walther, my story ends."

"You should have seen her then," broke in Eckbert quickly. "Her youth, her innocence, her beauty—and what an incomprehensible charm her solitary breeding had given her! To me she seemed like a wonder, and I loved her inexpressibly. I had no property, but with the help of her love I attained my present condition of comfortable prosperity. We moved to this place, and our union thus far has never brought us a single moment of remorse."

"But while I have been chattering," began Bertha again, "the night has grown late. Let us go to bed."

She rose to go to her room. Walther kissed her hand and wished her a good-night, adding:

"Noble woman, I thank you. I can readily imagine you with the strange bird, and how you fed the little Strohmi."

Without answering she left the room. Walther also lay down to sleep, but Eckbert continued to walk up and down the room.

"Aren't human beings fools?" he finally asked himself. "I myself induced my wife to tell her story, and now I regret this confidence! Will he not perhaps misuse it? Will he not impart it to others? Will he not perhaps—for it is human nature—come to feel a miserable longing for our gems and devise plans to get them and dissemble his nature?"

It occurred to him that Walther had not taken leave of him as cordially as would perhaps have been natural after so confidential a talk. When the soul is once led to suspect, it finds confirmations of its suspicions in every little thing. Then again Eckbert reproached himself for his ignoble distrust of his loyal friend, but he was unable to get the notion entirely out of his mind. All night long he tossed about with these thoughts and slept but little.

Bertha was sick and could not appear for breakfast. Walther seemed little concerned about it, and furthermore he left the knight in a rather indifferent manner. Eckbert could not understand his conduct. He went in to see his wife—she lay in a severe fever and said that her story the night before must have excited her in this manner.

After that evening Walther visited his friend's castle but rarely, and even when he did come he went away again after a few trivial words. Eckbert was exceedingly troubled by this behavior; to be sure, he tried not to let either Bertha or Walther notice it, but both of them must surely have been aware of his inward uneasiness.

Bertha's sickness grew worse and worse. The doctor shook

his head—the color in her cheeks disappeared, and her eyes became more and more brilliant.

One morning she summoned her husband to her bedside and told the maids to withdraw.

"Dear husband," she began, "I must disclose to you something which has almost deprived me of my reason and has ruined my health, however trivial it may seem to be. Often as I have told my story to you, you will remember that I have never been able, despite all the efforts I have made, to recall the name of the little dog with which I lived so long. That evening when I told the story to Walther he suddenly said to me when we separated: 'I can readily imagine how you fed the little Strohmi.' Was that an accident? Did he guess the name, or did he mention it designedly? And what, then, is this man's connection with my lot? The idea has occurred to me now and then that I merely imagine this accident—but it is certain, only too certain. It sent a feeling of horror through me to have a strange person like that assist my memory. What do you say, Eckbert?"

Eckbert looked at his suffering wife with deep tenderness. He kept silent, but was meditating. Then he said a few comforting words to her and left the room. In an isolated room he walked back and forth with indescribable restlessness— Walther for many years had been his sole male comrade, and yet this man was now the only person in the world whose existence oppressed and harassed him. It seemed to him that his heart would be light and happy if only this one person might be put out of the way. He took down his cross-bow with a view to distracting his thoughts by going hunting.

It was a raw and stormy day in the winter; deep snow lay on the mountains and bent down the branches of the trees. He wandered about, with the sweat oozing from his forehead. He came across no game, and that increased his ill-humor. Suddenly he saw something move in the distance—it was Walther gathering moss from the trees. Without knowing what he was doing he took aim—Walther looked around and motioned to him with a threatening gesture. But as he did so the arrow sped, and Walther fell headlong.

Eckbert felt relieved and calm, and yet a feeling of horror drove him back to his castle. He had a long distance to go, for he had wandered far into the forest. When he arrived home, Bertha had already died—before her death she had spoken a great deal about Walther and the old woman.

For a long time Eckbert lived in greatest seclusion. He had always been somewhat melancholy because the strange story of his wife rather worried him; he had always lived in fear of an unfortunate event that might take place, but now he was completely at variance with himself. The murder of his friend stood constantly before his eyes—he spent his life reproaching himself.

In order to divert his thoughts, he occasionally betook himself to the nearest large city, where he attended parties and banquets. He wished to have a friend to fill the vacancy in his soul, and then again, when he thought of Walther, the very word friend made him shudder. He was convinced that he would necessarily be unhappy with all his friends. He had lived so long in beautiful harmony with Bertha, and Walther's friendship had made him happy for so many years, and now both of them had been so suddenly taken from him that his life seemed at times more like a strange fairy-tale than an actual mortal existence.

A knight, Hugo von Wolfsberg, became attached to the quiet, melancholy Eckbert, and seemed to cherish a genuine fondness for him. Eckbert was strangely surprised; he met the knight's friendly advances more quickly than the other expected. They were now frequently together, the stranger did Eckbert all sorts of favors, scarcely ever did either of them ride without the other, they met each other at the parties—in short, they seemed to be inseparable.

Eckbert was, nevertheless, happy only for short moments

at a time, for he felt quite sure that Hugo loved him only by mistake—he did not know him, nor his history, and he felt the same impulse again to unfold his soul to him in order to ascertain for sure how staunch a friend Hugo was. Then again doubts and the fear of being detested restrained him. There were many hours in which he felt so convinced of his own unworthiness as to believe that no person, who knew him at all intimately, could hold him worthy of esteem. But he could not resist the impulse; in the course of a long walk he revealed his entire history to his friend, and asked him if he could possibly love a murderer. Hugo was touched and tried to comfort him. Eckbert followed him back to the city with a lighter heart.

However, it seemed to be his damnation that his suspicions should awaken just at the time when he grew confidential; for they had no more than entered the hall when the glow of the many lights revealed an expression in his friend's features which he did not like. He thought he detected a malicious smile, and it seemed to him that he, Hugo, said very little to him, that he talked a great deal with the other people present, and seemed to pay absolutely no attention to him. There was an old knight in the company who had always shown himself as Eckbert's rival, and had often inquired in a peculiar way about his riches and his wife. Hugo now approached this man, and they talked together a long time secretly, while every now and then they glanced toward Eckbert. He, Eckbert, saw in this a confirmation of his suspicions; he believed that he had been betrayed, and a terrible rage overcame him. As he continued to stare in that direction, he suddenly saw Walther's head, all his features, and his entire figure, so familiar to him. Still looking, he became convinced that it was nobody but Walther himself who was talking with the old man. His terror was indescribable; completely beside himself, he rushed out, left the city that night, and, after losing his way many times, returned to his castle.

Like a restless spirit he hurried from room to room. No

thought could he hold fast; the pictures in his mind grew more and more terrible, and he did not sleep a wink. The idea often occurred to him that he was crazy and that all these notions were merely the product of his own imagination. Then again he remembered Walther's features, and it was all more puzzling to him than ever. He resolved to go on a journey in order to compose his thoughts; he had long since given up the idea of a friend and the wish for a companion.

Without any definite destination in view, he set out, nor did he pay much attention to the country that lay before him. After he had trotted along several days on his horse, he suddenly lost his way in a maze of rocks, from which he was unable to discover any egress. Finally he met an old peasant who showed him a way out, leading past a water-fall. He started to give him a few coins by way of thanks, but the peasant refused them.

"What can it mean?" he said to himself. "I could easily imagine that that man was no other than Walther." He looked back once more—it was indeed no one else but Walther!

Eckbert spurred on his horse as fast as it could run—through meadows and forests, until, completely exhausted, it collapsed beneath him. Unconcerned, he continued his journey on foot.

Dreamily he ascended a hill. There he seemed to hear a dog barking cheerily close by—birch-trees rustled about him—he heard the notes of a wonderful song:

> O solitude
> Of lonely wood,
> Thou chiefest good,
> Where thou dost brood
> Is joy renewed,
> O solitude!

Now it was all up with Eckbert's consciousness and his senses; he could not solve the mystery whether he was now dreaming or had formerly dreamt of a woman Bertha. The most marvelous was confused with the most ordinary—the world around him bewitched—no thought, no memory was under his control.

An old crook-backed woman with a cane came creeping up the hill, coughing.

"Are you bringing back my bird, my pearls, my dog?" she cried out to him. "Look—wrong punishes itself. I and no other was your friend Walther, your Hugo."

"God in Heaven!" said Eckbert softly to himself. "In what terrible solitude have I spent my life."

"And Bertha was your sister."

Eckbert fell to the ground.

"Why did she desert me so deceitfully? Otherwise everything would have ended beautifully—her probation time was already over. She was the daughter of a knight, who had a shepherd bring her up—the daughter of your father."

"Why have I always had a presentiment of these facts?" cried Eckbert.

"Because in your early youth you heard your father tell of them. On his wife's account he could not bring up this daughter himself, for she was the child of another woman."

Eckbert was delirious as he breathed his last; dazed and confused he heard the old woman talking, the dog barking, and the bird repeating its song.

BERTOLT BRECHT

CONCERNING THE INFANTICIDE, MARIE FARRAR

MARIE FARRAR, born in April,
No marks, a minor, rachitic, both parents dead,
Allegedly, up to now without police record,
Committed infanticide, it is said,
As follows: in her second month, she says,
With the aid of a barmaid she did her best
To get rid of her child with two douches,
Allegedly painful but without success.
But you, I beg you, check your wrath and scorn
For man needs help from every creature born.

She then paid out, she says, what was agreed
And continued to lace herself up tight.
She also drank liquor with pepper mixed in it
Which purged her but did not cure her plight.
Her body distressed her as she washed the dishes,
It was swollen now quite visibly.
She herself says, for she was still a child,
She prayed to Mary most earnestly.
But you, I beg you, check your wrath and scorn
For man needs help from every creature born.

Her prayers, it seemed, helped her not at all.
She longed for help. Her trouble made her falter
And faint at early mass. Often drops of sweat
Broke out in anguish as she knelt at the altar.

Yet until her time had come upon her
She still kept secret her condition.
For no one believed such a thing had happened,
That she, so unenticing, had yielded to temptation.
But you, I beg you, check your wrath and scorn
For man needs help from every creature born.

And on that day, she says, when it was dawn,
As she washed the stairs it seemed a nail
Was driven into her belly. She was wrung with pain.
But still she secretly endured her travail.
All day long while hanging out the laundry
She racked her brains till she got it through her head
She had to bear the child and her heart was heavy.
It was very late when she went up to bed.
But you, I beg you, check your wrath and scorn
For man needs help from every creature born.

She was sent for again as soon as she lay down:
Snow had fallen and she had to go downstairs.
It went on till eleven. It was a long day.
Only at night did she have time to bear.
And so, she says, she gave birth to a son.
The son she bore was just like all the others.
She was unlike the others but for this
There is no reason to despise this mother.
You too, I beg you, check your wrath and scorn
For man needs help from every creature born.

Accordingly I will go on with the story
Of what happened to the son that came to be.
(She says she will hide nothing that befell)
So let it be a judgment upon both you and me.
She says she had scarcely gone to bed when she

Was overcome with sickness and she was alone,
Not knowing what would happen, yet she still
Contrived to stifle all her moans.
And you, I beg you, check your wrath and scorn
For man needs help from every creature born.

With her last strength, she says, because
Her room had now grown icy cold, she then
Dragged herself to the latrine and there
Gave birth as best she could (not knowing when)
But toward morning. She says she was already
Quite distracted and could barely hold
The child, for snow came into the latrine
And her fingers were half numb with cold.
You too, I beg you, check your wrath and scorn
For man needs help from every creature born.

Between the latrine and her room, she says,
Not earlier, the child began to cry until
It drove her mad so that she says
She did not cease to beat it with her fists
Blindly for some time till it was still.
And then she took the body to her bed
And kept it with her there all through the night:
When morning came she hid it in the shed.
But you, I beg you, check your wrath and scorn
For man needs help from every creature born.

Marie Farrar, born in April,
An unmarried mother, convicted, died in
The Meissen penitentiary,
She brings home to you all men's sin.
You who bear pleasantly between clean sheets
And give the name "blessed" to your womb's weight

Must not damn the weakness of the outcast,
For her sin was black but her pain was great.
Therefore, I beg you, check your wrath and scorn
For man needs help from every creature born.

Translated by H. R. Hays

LEO TOLSTOY

THE THREE HERMITS

An Old Legend Current in the Volga District

And in praying use not vain repetitions as the Gentiles do:
for they think that they shall be heard for their much speaking.
Be not therefore like unto them: for your Father knoweth what
things ye have need of, before ye ask Him.

MATT. VI. 7, 8.

A BISHOP was sailing from Archangel to the Solovétsk Monastery, and on the same vessel were a number of pilgrims on their way to visit the shrines at that place. The voyage was a smooth one. The wind favorable and the weather fair. The pilgrims lay on deck, eating, or sat in groups talking to one another. The Bishop, too, came on deck, and as he was pacing up and down he noticed a group of men standing near the prow and listening to a fisherman, who was pointing to the sea and telling them something. The Bishop stopped, and looked in the direction in which the man was pointing. He could see nothing, however, but the sea glistening in the sunshine. He drew nearer to listen, but when the man saw him, he took off his cap and was silent. The rest of the people also took off their caps and bowed.

"Do not let me disturb you, friends," said the Bishop. "I came to hear what this good man was saying."

"The fisherman was telling us about the hermits," replied one, a tradesman, rather bolder than the rest.

"What hermits?" asked the Bishop, going to the side of the vessel and seating himself on a box. "Tell me about them. I should like to hear. What were you pointing at?"

"Why, that little island you can just see over there," answered the man, pointing to a spot ahead and a little to the right. "That is the island where the hermits live for the salvation of their souls."

"Where is the island?" asked the Bishop. "I see nothing."

"There, in the distance, if you will please look along my hand. Do you see that little cloud? Below it, and a bit to the left, there is just a faint streak. That is the island."

The Bishop looked carefully, but his unaccustomed eyes could make out nothing but the water shimmering in the sun.

"I cannot see it," he said. "But who are the hermits that live there?"

"They are holy men," answered the fisherman. "I had long heard tell of them, but never chanced to see them myself till the year before last."

And the fisherman related how once, when he was out fishing, he had been stranded at night upon that island, not knowing where he was. In the morning, as he wandered about the island, he came across an earth hut, and met an old man standing near it. Presently two others came out, and after having fed him and dried his things, they helped him mend his boat.

"And what are they like?" asked the Bishop.

"One is a small man and his back is bent. He wears a priest's cassock and is very old; he must be more than a hundred, I should say. He is so old that the white of his beard is taking a greenish tinge, but he is always smiling, and his face is as bright as an angel's from heaven. The second is taller, but he also is very old. He wears a tattered peasant coat. His beard is broad, and of a yellowish gray color. He is a strong man. Before I had time to help him, he turned my boat over as if it were only a pail. He too is kindly and cheerful. The third is tall, and has a beard as white as snow and reaching to his knees. He is stern, with overhanging eyebrows; and he wears nothing but a piece of matting tied round his waist."

"And did they speak to you?" asked the Bishop.

"For the most part they did everything in silence, and spoke but little even to one another. One of them would just give a glance, and the others would understand him. I asked the tallest whether they had lived there long. He frowned, and muttered something as if he were angry; but the oldest one took his hand and smiled, and then the tall one was quiet. The oldest one only said: 'Have mercy upon us,' and smiled."

While the fisherman was talking, the ship had drawn nearer to the island.

"There, now you can see it plainly, if your Lordship will please to look," said the tradesman, pointing with his hand.

The Bishop looked, and now he really saw a dark streak—which was the island. Having looked at it a while, he left the prow of the vessel, and going to the stern, asked the helmsman:

"What island is that?"

"That one," replied the man, "has no name. There are many such in this sea."

"Is it true that there are hermits who live there for the salvation of their souls?"

"So it is said, your Lordship, but I don't know if it's true. Fishermen say they have seen them; but of course they may only be spinning yarns."

"I should like to land on the island and see these men," said the Bishop. "How could I manage it?"

"The ship cannot get close to the island," replied the helmsman, "but you might be rowed there in a boat. You had better speak to the captain."

The captain was sent for and came.

"I should like to see these hermits," said the Bishop. "Could I not be rowed ashore?"

The captain tried to dissuade him.

"Of course it could be done," said he, "but we should lose

much time. And if I might venture to say so to your Lordship, the old men are not worth your pains. I have heard say that they are foolish old fellows, who understand nothing, and never speak a word, any more than the fish in the sea."

"I wish to see them," said the Bishop, "and I will pay you for your trouble and loss of time. Please let me have a boat."

There was no help for it; so the order was given. The sailors trimmed the sails, the steersman put up the helm, and the ship's course was set for the island. A chair was placed at the prow for the Bishop, and he sat there, looking ahead. The passengers all collected at the prow, and gazed at the island. Those who had the sharpest eyes could presently make out the rocks on it, and then a mud hut was seen. At last one man saw the hermits themselves. The captain brought a telescope and, after looking through it, handed it to the Bishop.

"It's right enough. There are three men standing on the shore. There, a little to the right of that big rock."

The Bishop took the telescope, got it into position, and he saw the three men: a tall one, a shorter one, and one very small and bent, standing on the shore and holding each other by the hand.

The captain turned to the Bishop.

"The vessel can get no nearer in than this, your Lordship. If you wish to go ashore, we must ask you to go in the boat, while we anchor here."

The cable was quickly let out; the anchor cast, and the sails furled. There was a jerk, and the vessel shook. Then, a boat having been lowered, the oarsmen jumped in, and the Bishop descended the ladder and took his seat. The men pulled at their oars and the boat moved rapidly towards the island. When they came within a stone's throw, they saw three old men: a tall one with only a piece of matting tied round his waist: a shorter one in a tattered peasant coat, and a very old one bent with age and wearing an old cassock—all three standing hand in hand.

The oarsmen pulled in to the shore, and held on with the boathook while the Bishop got out.

The old men bowed to him, and he gave them his blessing, at which they bowed still lower. Then the Bishop began to speak to them.

"I have heard," he said, "that you, godly men, live here saving your own souls and praying to our Lord Christ for your fellow men. I, an unworthy servant of Christ, am called, by God's mercy, to keep and teach His flock. I wished to see you, servants of God, and to do what I can to teach you, also."

The old men looked at each other smiling, but remained silent.

"Tell me," said the Bishop, "what you are doing to save your souls, and how you serve God on this island."

The second hermit sighed, and looked at the oldest, the very ancient one. The latter smiled, and said:

"We do not know how to serve God. We only serve and support ourselves, servant of God."

"But how do you pray to God?" asked the Bishop.

"We pray in this way," replied the hermit. "Three are ye, three are we, have mercy upon us."

And when the old man said this, all three raised their eyes to heaven, and repeated:

"Three are ye, three are we, have mercy upon us!"

The Bishop smiled.

"You have evidently heard something about the Holy Trinity," said he. "But you do not pray aright. You have won my affection, godly men. I see you wish to please the Lord, but you do not know how to serve Him. That is not the way to pray; but listen to me, and I will teach you. I will teach you, not a way of my own, but the way in which God in the Holy Scriptures has commanded all men to pray to Him."

And the Bishop began explaining to the hermits how God had revealed Himself to men; telling them of God the Father, and God the Son, and God the Holy Ghost.

"God the Son came down on earth," said he, "to save men, and this is how He taught us all to pray. Listen, and repeat after me: 'Our Father.' "

And the first old man repeated after him, "Our Father," and the second said, "Our Father," and the third said, "Our Father."

"Which art in heaven," continued the Bishop.

The first hermit repeated, "Which art in heaven," but the second blundered over the words, and the tall hermit could not say them properly. His hair had grown over his mouth so that he could not speak plainly. The very old hermit, having no teeth, also mumbled indistinctly.

The Bishop repeated the words again, and the old men repeated them after him. The Bishop sat down on a stone, and the old men stood before him, watching his mouth, and repeating the words as he uttered them. And all day long the Bishop labored, saying a word twenty, thirty, a hundred times over, and the old men repeated it after him. They blundered, and he corrected them, and made them begin again.

The Bishop did not leave off till he had taught them the whole of the Lord's Prayer so that they could not only repeat it after him, but could say it by themselves. The middle one was the first to know it, and to repeat the whole of it alone. The Bishop made him say it again and again, and at last the others could say it too.

It was getting dark and the moon was appearing over the water, before the Bishop rose to return to the vessel. When he took leave of the old men they all bowed down to the ground before him. He raised them, and kissed each of them, telling them to pray as he had taught them. Then he got into the boat and returned to the ship.

And as he sat in the boat and was rowed to the ship he could hear the three voices of the hermits loudly repeating the Lord's Prayer. As the boat drew near the vessel their voices could no longer be heard, but they could still be seen in the moonlight, standing as he had left them on the shore, the shortest in the middle, the tallest on the right, the middle one on the left. As soon as the Bishop had reached the vessel and got on board, the anchor was weighed and the sails unfurled. The wind filled them and the ship sailed away, and the Bishop took a seat in the stern and watched the island they had left. For a time he could still see the hermits, but presently they disappeared from sight, though the island was still visible. At last it too vanished, and only the sea was to be seen, rippling in the moonlight.

The pilgrims lay down to sleep, and all was quiet on deck. The Bishop did not wish to sleep, but sat alone at the stern, gazing at the sea where the island was no longer visible, and thinking of the good old men. He thought how pleased they had been to learn the Lord's Prayer; and he thanked God for having sent him to teach and help such godly men.

So the Bishop sat, thinking, and gazing at the sea where the island had disappeared. And the moonlight flickered before his eyes, sparkling, now here, now there, upon the waves. Suddenly he saw something white and shining, on the bright path which the moon cast across the sea. Was it a seagull, or the little gleaming sail of some small boat? The Bishop fixed his eyes on it, wondering.

"It must be a boat sailing after us," thought he, "but it is overtaking us very rapidly. It was far, far away a minute ago, but now it is much nearer. It cannot be a boat, for I can see no sail; but whatever it may be, it is following us and catching us up."

And he could not make out what it was. Not a boat, nor a bird, nor a fish! It was too large for a man, and besides a man could not be out there in the midst of the sea. The Bishop rose, and said to the helmsman:

"Look there, what is that, my friend? What is it?" the Bishop repeated, though he could now see plainly what it was—the three hermits running upon the water, all gleaming white, their gray beards shining, and approaching the ship as quickly as though it were not moving.

The steersman looked, and let go the helm in terror.

"Oh Lord! The hermits are running after us on the water as though it were dry land!"

The passengers, hearing him, jumped up and crowded to the stern. They saw the hermits coming along hand in hand, and the two outer ones beckoning the ship to stop. All three were gliding along upon the water without moving their feet. Before the ship could be stopped, the hermits had reached it, and raising their heads, all three as with one voice, began to say:

"We have forgotten your teaching, servant of God. As long as we kept repeating it we remembered, but when we stopped saying it for a time, a word dropped out, and now it has all gone to pieces. We can remember nothing of it. Teach us again."

The Bishop crossed himself, and leaning over the ship's side, said:

"Your own prayer will reach the Lord, men of God. It is not for me to teach you. Pray for us sinners."

And the Bishop bowed low before the old men; and they turned and went back across the sea. And a light shone until daybreak on the spot where they were lost to sight.

Translated by Aylmer Maude

PETER TAYLOR

WHAT YOU HEAR FROM 'EM?

SOMETIMES people misunderstood Aunt Munsie's question, but she wouldn't bother to clarify it. She might repeat it two or three times, in order to drown out some fool answer she was getting from some fool white woman, or man, either. "What you hear from 'em?" she would ask. And, then, louder and louder: "What you hear from 'em? *What you hear from 'em?*" She was so deaf that anyone whom she thoroughly drowned out only laughed and said Aunt Munsie had got so deaf she couldn't hear it thunder.

It was, of course, only the most utterly fool answers that ever received Aunt Munsie's drowning-out treatment. She was, for a number of years at least, willing to listen to those who mistook her "'em" to mean any and all of the Dr. Tolliver children. And for more years than that she was willing to listen to those who thought she wanted just *any* news of her two favorites among the Tolliver children—Thad and Will. But later on she stopped putting the question to all insensitive and frivolous souls who didn't understand that what she was interested in hearing—and *all* she was interested in hearing—was when Mr. Thad Tolliver and Mr. Will Tolliver were going to pack up their families and come back to Thornton for good.

They had always promised her to come back—to come back sure enough, once and for all. On separate occasions, both Thad and Will had actually given her their word. She had not seen them together for ten years, but each of them

127

had made visits to Thornton now and then with his own family. She would see a big car stopping in front of her house on a Sunday afternoon and see either Will or Thad with his wife and children piling out into the dusty street—it was nearly always summer when they came—and then see them filing across the street, jumping the ditch, and unlatching the gate to her yard. She always met them in that pen of a yard, but long before they had jumped the ditch she was clapping her hands and calling out, "Hai-ee! Hai-ee, now! Look-a-here! Whee! Whee! Look-a-here!" She had got so blind that she was never sure whether it was Mr. Thad or Mr. Will until she had her arms around his waist. They had always looked a good deal alike, and their city clothes made them look even more alike nowadays. Aunt Munsie's eyes were so bad, besides being so full of moisture on those occasions, that she really recognized them by their girth. Will had grown a regular wash pot of a stomach and Thad was still thin as a rail. They would sit on her porch for twenty or thirty minutes—whichever one it was and his family—and then they would be gone again.

Aunt Munsie would never try to detain them—not seriously. Those short little old visits didn't mean a thing to her. He—Thad or Will—would lean against the banister rail and tell her how well his children were doing in school or college, and she would make each child in turn come and sit beside her on the swing for a minute and receive a hug around the waist or shoulders. They were timid with her, not seeing her any more than they did, but she could tell from their big Tolliver smiles that they liked her to hug them and make over them. Usually, she would lead them all out to her back yard and show them her pigs and dogs and chickens. (She always had at least one frizzly chicken to show the children.) They would traipse through her house to the back yard and then traipse through again to the front porch. It would be time for them to go when they came back, and Aunt Munsie would look up at *him*—Mr. Thad or Mr. Will (she had begun calling them "Mr." the day they married)—and say, "Now, look-a-here. When you comin' back?"

Both Thad and Will knew what she meant, of course, and whichever it was would tell her he was making definite plans to wind up his business and that he was going to buy a certain piece of property, "a mile north of town" or "on the old River Road," and build a jim-dandy house there. He would say, too, how good Aunt Munsie's own house was looking, and his wife would say how grand the zinnias and cannas looked in the yard. (The yard was all flowers—not a blade of grass, and the ground packed hard in little paths between the flower beds.) The visit was almost over then. There remained only the exchange of presents. One of the children would hand Aunt Munsie a paper bag containing a pint of whisky or a carton of cigarettes. Aunt Munsie would go to her back porch or to the pit in the yard and get a fern or a wandering Jew, potted in a rusty lard bucket, and make Mrs. Thad or Mrs. Will take it along. Then the visit was over, and they would leave. From the porch Aunt Munsie would wave good-by with one hand and lay the other hand, trembling slightly, on the banister rail. And sometimes her departing guests, looking back from the yard, would observe that the banisters themselves were trembling under her hand—so insecurely were those knobby banisters attached to the knobby porch pillars. Often as not Thad or Will, observing this, would remind his wife that Aunt Munsie's porch banisters and pillars had come off a porch of the house where he had grown up. (Their father, Dr. Tolliver, had been one of the first to widen his porches and remove the gingerbread from his house.) The children and their mother would wave to Aunt Munsie from the street. Their father would close the gate, resting his hand a moment on its familiar wrought-iron frame, and wave to her before he jumped the ditch. If the children had not gone too far ahead, he might even draw their attention to the iron fence which, with its iron gate, had been around the yard at the Tolliver place till Dr. Tolliver took it down and set out a hedge, just a few weeks before he died.

But such paltry little visits meant nothing to Aunt Munsie. No more did the letters that came with "her things" at Christmas. She was supposed to get her daughter, Lucrecie, who lived next door, to read the letters, but in late years she had taken to putting them away unopened, and some of the presents, too. All she wanted to hear from *them* was when they were coming back for good, and she had learned that the Christmas letters never told her that. On her daily route with her slop wagon through the Square, up Jackson Street, and down Jefferson, there were only four or five houses left where she asked her question. These were houses where the amount of pig slop was not worth stopping for, houses where one old maid, or maybe two, lived, or a widow with one old bachelor son who had never amounted to anything and ate no more than a woman. And so—in the summertime, anyway—she took to calling out at the top of her lungs, when she approached the house of one of the elect, "What you hear from 'em?" Sometimes a Miss Patty or a Miss Lucille or a Mr. Ralph would get up out of a porch chair and come down the brick walk to converse with Aunt Munsie. Or sometimes one of them would just lean out over the shrubbery planted around the porch and call, "Not a thing, Munsie. Not a thing lately."

She would shake her head and call back, "Naw. Naw. Not a thing. Nobody don't hear from 'em. Too busy, they be."

Aunt Munsie's skin was the color of a faded tow sack. She was hardly four feet tall. She was generally believed to be totally bald, and on her head she always wore a white dust cap with an elastic band. She wore an apron, too, while making her rounds with her slop wagon. Even when the weather got bad and she tied a wool scarf about her head and wore an overcoat, she put on an apron over the coat. Her hands and feet were delicately small, which made the old-timers sure she was of Guinea stock that had come to Tennessee out of South Carolina. What most touched the hearts of old ladies on Jackson and Jefferson Streets were her little feet. The sight of her feet "took them back to the old days," they said, because Aunt Munsie still wore flat-heeled, high button shoes. Where ever did Munsie find such shoes any more?

She walked down the street, down the very center of the street, with a spry step, and she was continually turning her head from side to side, as though looking at the old houses and trees for the first time. If her sight was as bad as she sometimes let on it was, she probably recognized the houses only by their roof lines against the Thornton sky. Since this was nearly thirty years ago, most of the big Victorian and ante-bellum houses were still standing, though with their lovely gingerbread work beginning to go. (It went first from houses where there was someone, like Dr. Tolliver, with a special eye for style and for keeping up with the times.) The streets hadn't yet been broadened—or only Nashville Street had—and the maples and elms met above the streets. In the autumn, their leaves covered the high banks and filled the deep ditches on either side. The dark macadam surfacing itself was barely wide enough for two automobiles to pass. Aunt Munsie, pulling her slop wagon, which was a long, low, four-wheeled vehicle about the size and shape of a coffin, paraded down the center of the street without any regard for, if with any awareness of, the traffic problems she sometimes made. Seizing the wagon's heavy, sawed-off-looking tongue, she hauled it after her with a series of impatient jerks, just as though that tongue were the arm of some very stubborn, overgrown white child she had to nurse in her old age. Strangers in town or trifling high-school boys would blow their horns at her, but she was never known to so much as glance over her shoulder at the sound of a horn. Now and then a pedestrian on the sidewalk would call out to the driver of an automobile, "She's so deaf she can't hear it thunder."

It wouldn't have occurred to anyone in Thornton—not in those days—that something ought to be done about Aunt Munsie and her wagon for the sake of the public good. In those days, everyone had equal rights on the streets of Thornton. A vehicle was a vehicle, and a person was a person, each with the right to move as slowly as he pleased and to stop where and as often as he pleased. In the Thornton mind, there was no imaginary line down the middle of the street, and, indeed, no one there at that time had heard of drawing a real line on *any* street. It was merely out of politeness that you made room for others to pass. Nobody would have blown a horn at an old colored woman with her slop wagon—nobody but some Yankee stranger or a trifling high-school boy or maybe old Mr. Ralph Hadley in a special fit of temper. When citizens of Thornton were in a particular hurry and got caught behind Aunt Munsie, they leaned out their car windows and shouted: "Aunt Munsie, can you make a little room?" And Aunt Munsie didn't fail to hear *them*. She would holler, "Hai-ee, now! Whee! Look-a-here!" and jerk her wagon to one side. As they passed her, she would wave her little hand and grin a toothless, pink-gummed grin.

Yet, without any concern for the public good, Aunt Munsie's friends and connections among the white women began to worry more and more about the danger of her being run down by an automobile. They talked among themselves and they talked to her about it. They wanted her to give up collecting slop, now she had got so blind and deaf. "Pshaw," said Aunt Munsie, closing her eyes contemptuously. "Not me." She meant by that that no one would dare run into her or her wagon. Sometimes when she crossed the Square on a busy Saturday morning or on a first Monday, she would hold up one hand with the palm turned outward and stop all traffic until she was safely across and in the alley beside the hotel.

Thornton wasn't even then what it had been before the Great World War. In every other house there was a stranger or a mill hand who had moved up from Factory Town. Some of the biggest old places stood empty, the way Dr. Tolliver's had until it burned. They stood empty not because nobody wanted to rent them or buy them but because the heirs who had gone off somewhere making money could never be got to part with "the home place." The story was that Thad Tolliver nearly went crazy when he heard their old house had burned, and wanted to sue the town, and even said he was going to help get the Republicans into office. Yet Thad had hardly put foot in the house since the day his daddy died. It was said the Tolliver house had caught fire from the Major Pettigru house, which had burned two nights before. And no doubt it had. Sparks could have smoldered in that roof of rotten shingles for a long time before bursting into flame. Some even said the Pettigru house might have caught from the Johnston house, which had burned earlier that same fall. But Thad knew and Will knew and everybody knew the town wasn't to blame, and knew there was no firebug. Why, those old houses stood there empty year after year, and in the fall the leaves fell from the trees and settled around the porches and stoops, and who was there to rake the leaves? Maybe it was a good thing those houses burned, and maybe it would have been as well if some of the houses that still had people in them burned, too. There were houses in Thornton the heirs had never left that looked far worse than the Tolliver or the Pettigru or the Johnston house ever had. The people who lived in them were the ones who gave Aunt Munsie the biggest fool answers to her question, the people whom she soon quit asking her question of or even passing the time of day with, except when she couldn't help it, out of politeness. For, truly, to Aunt Munsie there were things under the sun worse than going off and getting rich in Nashville or in Memphis or even in Washington, D.C. It was a subject she and her daughter Lucrecie some-times mouthed at each other about across their back fence. Lucrecie was shiftless, and she liked shiftless white people like the ones who didn't have the ambition to leave Thorn-ton. She thought their shiftlessness showed they were *quality*. "Quality?" Aunt Munsie would echo, her voice full of sarcasm. "Whee! Hai-ee! You talk like *you* was *my* mammy, Crecie. Well, if there be quality, there be quality *and* quality. There's quality and there's *has-been* quality, Crecie." There was no end to that argument Aunt Munsie had with Crecie, and it wasn't at all important to Aunt Munsie. The people who still lived in those houses—the ones she called has-been quality—meant little more to her than the mill hands, or the strangers from up North who ran the Piggly Wiggly, the five-and-ten-cent store, and the roller-skating rink.

There was this to be said, though, for the has-been quality: They knew *who* Aunt Munsie was, and in a limited, literal way they understood what she said. But those *others*—why, they thought Aunt Munsie a beggar, and she knew they did. They spoke of her as Old What You Have for Mom, because that's what they thought she was saying when she called out, "What you hear from 'em?" Their ears were not attuned to that soft "r" she put in "from" or the elision that made "from 'em" sound to them like "for Mom." Many's the time Aunt Munsie had seen or sensed the presence of one of those *other* people, watching from next door, when Miss Leonora Lovell, say, came down her front walk and handed her a little parcel of scraps across the ditch. Aunt Munsie knew what they thought of her—how they laughed at her and felt sorry for her and despised her all at once. But, like the has-been quality, they didn't matter, never had, never would. Not ever.

Oh, they mattered in a way to Lucrecie. Lucrecie thought

about them and talked about them a lot. She called them "white trash" and even "radical Republicans." It made Aunt Munsie grin to hear Crecie go on, because she knew Crecie got all her notions from her own has-been-quality people. And so it didn't matter, except that Aunt Munsie knew that Crecie truly had all sorts of good sense and had only been carried away and spoiled by such folks as she had worked for, such folks as had really raised Crecie from the time she was big enough to run errands for them, fifty years back. In her heart, Aunt Munsie knew that even Lucrecie didn't matter to her the way a daughter might. It was because while Aunt Munsie had been raising a family of white children, a different sort of white people from hers had been raising her own child, Crecie. Sometimes, if Aunt Munsie was in her chicken yard or out in her little patch of cotton when Mr. Thad or Mr. Will arrived, Crecie would come out to the fence and say, "Mama, some of your chillun's out front."

Miss Leonora Lovell and Miss Patty Bean, and especially Miss Lucille Satterfield, were all the time after Aunt Munsie to give up collecting slop. "You're going to get run over by one of those crazy drivers, Munsie," they said. Miss Lucille was the widow of old Judge Satterfield. "If the Judge were alive, Munsie," she said, "I'd make him find a way to stop you. But the men down at the courthouse don't listen to the women in this town any more. Not since we got the vote. And I think they'd be most too scared of you to do what I want them to do." Aunt Munsie wouldn't listen to any of that. She knew that if Miss Lucille had come out there to her gate, she must have *something* she was going to say about Mr. Thad or Mr. Will. Miss Lucille had two brothers and a son of her own who were lawyers in Memphis, and who lived in style down there and kept Miss Lucille in style here in Thornton. Memphis was where Thad Tolliver had his Ford and Lincoln agency, and so Miss Lucille always had news about Thad, and indirectly about Will, too.

———

"Is they doin' any good? What you hear from 'em?" Aunt Munsie asked Miss Lucille one afternoon in early spring. She had come along just when Miss Lucille was out picking some of the jonquils that grew in profusion on the steep bank between the sidewalk and the ditch in front of her house.

"Mr. Thad and his folks will be up one day in April, Munsie," Miss Lucille said in her pleasantly hoarse voice. "I understand Mr. Will and his crowd may come for Easter Sunday."

"One day, and gone again!" said Aunt Munsie.

"We always try to get them to stay at least one night, but they're busy folks, Munsie."

"When they comin' back sure enough, Miss Lucille?"

"Goodness knows, Munsie. Goodness knows. Goodness knows when any of them are coming back to stay." Miss Lucille took three quick little steps down the bank and hopped lightly across the ditch. "They're prospering so, Munsie," she said, throwing her chin up and smiling proudly. This fragile lady, this daughter, wife, sister, mother of lawyers (and, of course, the darling of all their hearts), stood there in the street with her pretty little feet and shapely ankles close together, and holding a handful of jonquils before her as if it were her bridal bouquet. "They're *all* prospering so, Munsie. Mine *and* yours. You ought to go down to Memphis to see them now and then, the way I do. Or go up to Nashville to see Mr. Will. I understand he's got an even finer establishment than Thad. They've done well, Munsie—yours *and* mine—and we can be proud of them. You owe it to yourself to go and see how well they're fixed. They're rich men by our standards in Thornton, and they're going farther—*all* of them."

Aunt Munsie dropped the tongue of her wagon noisily on the pavement. "What I want to go see 'em for?" she said angrily and with a lowering brow. Then she stooped and, picking up the wagon tongue again, she wheeled her vehicle toward the middle of the street, to get by Miss Lucille, and started off toward the Square. As she turned out into the street, the brakes of a car, as so often, screeched behind her. Presently everyone in the neighborhood could hear Mr. Ralph Hadley tooting the insignificant little horn on his mama's coupé and shouting at Aunt Munsie in his own tooty voice, above the sound of the horn. Aunt Munsie pulled over, making just enough room to let poor old Mr. Ralph get by but without once looking back at him. Then, before Mr. Ralph could get his car started again, Miss Lucille was running along beside Aunt Munsie, saying, "Munsie, you be careful! You're going to meet your death on the streets of Thornton, Tennessee!"

"Let 'em," said Aunt Munsie.

Miss Lucille didn't know whether Munsie meant "Let 'em run over me; I don't care" or meant "Let 'em just dare!" Miss Lucille soon turned back, without Aunt Munsie's ever looking at her. And when Mr. Ralph Hadley did get his motor started, and sailed past in his mama's coupé, Aunt Munsie didn't give him a look, either. Nor did Mr. Ralph bother to turn his face to look at Aunt Munsie. He was on his way to the drugstore, to pick up his mama's prescriptions, and he was too entirely put out, peeved, and upset to endure even the briefest exchange with that ugly, uppity old Munsie of the Tollivers.

Aunt Munsie continued to tug her slop wagon on toward the Square. There was a more animated expression on her face than usual, and every so often her lips would move rapidly and emphatically over a phrase or sentence. Why should she go to Memphis and Nashville and see how rich they were? No matter how rich they were, what difference did it make; they didn't own any land, did they? Or at least none in Cameron County. She had heard the old Doctor tell them—tell his boys and tell his girls, and tell the old lady, too, in her day—

137

that nobody was rich who didn't own land, and nobody stayed rich who didn't see after his land firsthand. But of course Aunt Munsie had herself mocked the old Doctor to his face for going on about land so much. She knew it was only something he had heard his own daddy go on about. She would say right to his face that she hadn't ever seen *him* behind a plow. And was there ever anybody more scared of a mule than Dr. Tolliver was? Mules or horses, either? Aunt Munsie had heard him say that the happiest day of his life was the day he first learned that the horseless carriage was a reality.

No, it was not really to own land that Thad and Will ought to come back to Thornton. It was more that if they were going to be rich, they ought to come home, where their granddaddy had owned land and where their money counted for something. How could they ever be rich anywhere else? They could have a lot of money in the bank and a fine house, that was all—like that mill manager from Chi. The mill manager could have a yard full of big cars and a stucco house as big as you like, but who would ever take him for rich? Aunt Munsie would sometimes say all these things to Crecie, or something as nearly like them as she could find words for. Crecie might nod her head in agreement or she might be in a mood to say being rich wasn't any good for anybody and didn't matter, and that you could live on just being quality better than on being rich in Thornton. "Quality's better than land or better than money in the bank here," Crecie would say.

Aunt Munsie would sneer at her and say, "It never were."

Lucrecie could talk all she wanted about the old times! Aunt Munsie knew too much about what they were like, for both the richest white folks and the blackest field hands. Nothing about the old times was as good as these days, and there were going to be better times yet when Mr. Thad and Mr. Will Tolliver came back. Everybody lived easier now than they

used to, and were better off. She could never be got to reminisce about her childhood in slavery, or her life with her husband, or even about those halcyon days after the old Mizziz
had died and Aunt Munsie's word had become law in the
Tolliver household. Without being able to book-read or even
to make numbers, she had finished raising the whole pack of
towheaded Tollivers just as the Mizziz would have wanted it
done. The Doctor told her she *had* to—he didn't ever once
think about getting another wife, or taking in some cousin,
not after his "Molly darling"—and Aunt Munsie *did*. But, as
Crecie said, when a time was past in her mama's life, it
seemed to be gone and done with in her head, too.

Lucrecie would say frankly she thought her mama was
"hard about people and things in the world." She talked
about her mama not only to the Blalocks, for whom she had
worked all her life, but to anybody else who gave her an
opening. It wasn't just about her mama, though, that she
would talk to anybody. She liked to talk, and she talked about
Aunt Munsie not in any ugly, resentful way but as she would
about when the sheep-rains would begin or where the fire
was last night. (Crecie was twice the size of her mama, and
black the way her old daddy had been, and loud and good-
natured the way he was—or at least the way Aunt Munsie
wasn't. You wouldn't have known they were mother and
daughter, and not many of the young people in town did realize it. Only by accident did they live next door to each other;
Mr. Thad and Mr. Will had bought Munsie her house, and
Crecie had heired hers from her second husband.) *That* was
how she talked about her mama—as she would have about
any lonely, eccentric, harmless neighbor. "I may be dead
wrong, but I think Mama's kind of hardhearted," she would
say. "Mama's a good old soul, I reckon, but when something's
past, it's gone and done with for Mama. She don't think about
day before yestiddy—yestiddy, either. I don't know, maybe
that's the way to be. Maybe that's why the old soul's gonna

outlive us all." Then, obviously thinking about what a picture of health she herself was at sixty, Crecie would toss her head about and laugh so loud you might hear her all the way out to the fair grounds.

Crecie, however, knew her mama was not honest-to-God mean and hadn't ever been mean to the Tolliver children, the way the Blalocks liked to make out she had. All the Tolliver children but Mr. Thad and Mr. Will had quarreled with her for good by the time they were grown, but they had quarreled with the old Doctor, too (and as if they were the only ones who shook off their old folks this day and time). When Crecie talked about her mama, she didn't spare her anything, but she was fair to her, too. And it was in no hateful or disloyal spirit that she took part in the conspiracy that finally got Aunt Munsie and her slop wagon off the streets of Thornton. Crecie would have done the same for any neighbor. She had small part enough, actually, in that conspiracy. Her part was merely to break the news to Aunt Munsie that there was now a law against keeping pigs within the city limits. It was a small part but one that no one else quite dared to take.

"They ain't no such law!" Aunt Munsie roared back at Crecie. She was slopping her pigs when Crecie came to the fence and told her about the law. It had seemed the most appropriate time to Lucrecie. "They ain't never been such a law, Crecie," Aunt Munsie said. "Every house on Jackson and Jefferson used to keep pigs."

"It's a brand-new law, Mama."

Aunt Munsie finished bailing out the last of the slop from her wagon. It was just before twilight. The last, weak rays of the sun colored the clouds behind the mock orange tree in Crecie's yard. When Aunt Munsie turned around from the sty, she pretended that that little bit of light in the clouds hurt her eyes, and turned away her head. And when Lucrecie said that everybody had until the first of the year to get rid of their pigs, Aunt Munsie was in a spell of deafness. She headed out toward the crib to get some corn for the chickens. She was trying to think whether anybody else inside the town still kept pigs. Herb Mallory did—two doors beyond Crecie. Then Aunt Munsie remembered Herb didn't pay town taxes. The town line ran between him and Shad Willis.

That was sometime in June, and before July came, Aunt Munsie knew all there was worth knowing about the conspiracy. Mr. Thad and Mr. Will had each been in town for a day during the spring. They and their families had been to her house and sat on the porch; the children had gone back to look at her half-grown collie dog and the two hounds, at the old sow and her farrow of new pigs, and at the frizzliest frizzly chicken Aunt Munsie had ever had. And on those visits to Thornton, Mr. Thad and Mr. Will had also made their usual round among their distant kin and close friends. Everywhere they went, they had heard of the near-accidents Aunt Munsie was causing with her slop wagon and the real danger there was of her being run over. Miss Lucille Satterfield and Miss Patty Bean had both been to the mayor's office and also to see Judge Lawrence to try to get Aunt Munsie "ruled" off the streets, but the men in the courthouse and in the mayor's office didn't listen to the women in Thornton any more. And so either Mr. Thad or Mr. Will—how would which one of them it was matter to Munsie?—had been prevailed upon to stop by Mayor Lunt's office, and in a few seconds' time had set the wheels of conspiracy in motion. Soon a general inquiry had been made in the town as to how many citizens still kept pigs. Only two property owners besides Aunt Munsie had been found to have pigs on their premises, and they, being men, had been docile and reasonable enough to sell what they had on hand to Mr. Will or Mr. Thad Tolliver. Immediately afterward—within a matter of weeks, that is—a town ordinance had been passed forbidding the possession of swine within the corporate limits of Thornton. Aunt Munsie had got the story bit by bit from Miss Leonora and Miss Patty and Miss Lucille and others, including the constable himself, whom she did not hesitate to stop right in the middle of the Square on a Saturday noon. Whether it was Mr. Thad or Mr. Will who had been prevailed upon by the ladies she never ferreted out, but that was only because she did not wish to do so.

The constable's word was the last word for her. The constable said yes, it was the law, and he admitted yes, he had sold his own pigs—for the constable was one of those two reasonable souls—to Mr. Thad or Mr. Will. He didn't say which of them it was, or if he did, Aunt Munsie didn't bother to remember it. And after her interview with the constable, Aunt Munsie never again exchanged words with any human being about the ordinance against pigs. That afternoon, she took a fishing pole from under her house and drove the old sow and the nine shoats down to Herb Mallory's, on the outside of town. They were his, she said, if he wanted them, and he could pay her at killing time.

It was literally true that Aunt Munsie never again exchanged words with anyone about the ordinance against pigs or about the conspiracy she had discovered against herself. But her daughter Lucrecie had a tale to tell about what Aunt Munsie did that afternoon after she had seen the constable and before she drove the pigs over to Herb Mallory's. It was mostly a tale of what Aunt Munsie said to her pigs and to her dogs and her chickens.

Crecie was in her own back yard washing her hair when her mama came down the rickety porch steps and into the yard next door. Crecie had her head in the pot of suds, and so she couldn't look up, but she knew by the way Mama flew down the steps that there was trouble. "She come down them steps like she was wasp-nest bit, or like some youngon who's got hisself wasp-nest bit—and her all of eighty, I reckon!" Then, as Crecie told it, her mama scurried around in the yard for a minute or so like she thought Judgment was about to catch up with her, and pretty soon she commenced slamming at something. Crecie wrapped a towel about her soapy head, squatted low, and edged over toward the plank fence. She peered between the planks and saw what her mama was up to. Since there never had been a gate to the fence around the pigsty, Mama had taken the wood ax and was knocking a hole in it. But directly, just after Crecie had taken her place by the plank fence, her mama had left off her slamming at the sty and turned about so quickly and so exactly toward Crecie that Crecie thought the poor, blind old soul had managed to spy her squatting there. Right away, though, Crecie realized it was not *her* that Mama was staring at. She saw that all Aunt Munsie's chickens and those three dogs of hers had come up behind her, and were all clucking and whining to know why she didn't stop that infernal racket and put out some feed for them.

Crecie's mama set one hand on her hip and rested the ax on the ground. "Just look at yuh!" she said, and then she let the chickens and the dogs—and the pigs, too—have it. She told them what a miserable bunch of creatures they were, and asked them what right they had to always be looking for handouts from her. She sounded like the bossman who's caught all his pickers laying off before sundown, and she sounded, too, like the preacher giving his sinners Hail Columbia at camp meeting. Finally, shouting at the top of her voice and swinging the ax wide and broad above their heads, she sent the dogs howling under the house and the chickens scattering in every direction. "Now, g'wine! G'wine widja!" she shouted after them. Only the collie pup, of the three dogs, didn't scamper to the farthest corner underneath the house. He stopped under the porch steps, and not two seconds later he was poking his long head out again and showing the whites of his doleful brown eyes. Crecie's mama took a step toward him and then she halted. "You want to know what's the commotion about? I reckoned you would," she said with profound contempt, as though the collie were a more reasonable soul than the other animals, and as though there were nothing she held in such thorough disrespect as reason. "I tell you what the commotion's about," she said. "They *ain't* comin' back. They ain't never comin' back. They ain't never had no notion of comin' back." She turned her head to one side, and the only explanation Crecie could find for her mama's next words was that that collie pup did look so much like Miss Lucille Satterfield.

"Why don't I go down to Memphis or up to Nashville and see 'em sometime, like *you* does?" Aunt Munsie asked the collie. "I tell you why. Becaze I ain't nothin' to 'em in Memphis, and they ain't nothin' to me in Nashville. *You* can go!" she said, advancing and shaking the big ax at the dog. "A collie dog's a collie dog anywhar. But Aunt Munsie, she's just their Aunt Munsie here in Thornton. I got mind enough to see *that*." The collie slowly pulled his head back under the steps, and Aunt Munsie watched for a minute to see if he would show himself again. When he didn't, she went and jerked the fishing pole out from under the house and headed toward the pigsty. Crecie remained squatting beside the fence until her mama and the pigs were out in the street and on their way to Herb Mallory's.

That was the end of Aunt Munsie's keeping pigs and the end of her daily rounds with her slop wagon, but it was not the end of Aunt Munsie. She lived on for nearly twenty years after that, till long after Lucrecie had been put away, in fine style, by the Blalocks. Ever afterward, though, Aunt Munsie seemed different to people. They said she softened, and every-

body said it was a change for the better. She would take paper
money from under her carpet, or out of the chinks in her
walls, and buy things for up at the church, or buy her own
whisky when she got sick, instead of making somebody bring
her a nip. On the Square she would laugh and holler with the
white folks the way they liked her to and the way Crecie and
all the other old-timers did, and she even took to tying a ban-
danna about her head—took to talking old-nigger foolishness,
too, about the Bell Witch, and claiming she remembered
the day General N. B. Forrest rode into town and saved all the
cotton from the Yankees at the depot. When Mr. Will and Mr.
Thad came to see her with their families, she got so she
would reminisce with them about their daddy and tease them
about all the silly little things they had done when they were
growing up: "Mr. Thad—him still in kilts, too—he says, 'Aunt
Munsie, reach down in yo' stockin' and git me a copper cent.
I want some store candy.' " She told them about how Miss
Yola Ewing, the sewing woman, heard her threatening to bust
Will's back wide open when he broke the lamp chimney, and
how Miss Yola went to the Doctor and told him he ought to
run Aunt Munsie off. Then Aunt Munsie and the Doctor had
had a big laugh about it out in the kitchen, and Miss Yola
must have eavesdropped on them, because she left without
finishing the girls' Easter dresses.

Indeed, these visits from Mr. Thad and Mr. Will continued
as long as Aunt Munsie lived, but she never asked them
any more about when they were sure enough coming back.
And the children, though she hugged them more than ever—
and, toward the last, there were the children's children to be
hugged—never again set foot in her back yard. Aunt Munsie
lived on for nearly twenty years, and when they finally buried
her, they put on her tombstone that she was aged one hundred years, though nobody knew how old she was. There was
no record of when she was born. All anyone knew was that
in her last years she had said she was a girl helping about the

big house when freedom came. That would have made her probably about twelve years old in 1865, according to her statements and depictions. But all agreed that in her extreme old age Aunt Munsie, like other old darkies, was not very reliable about dates and such things. Her spirit softened, even her voice lost some of the rasping quality that it had always had, and in general she became not very reliable about facts.

HANS CHRISTIAN ANDERSEN

THE FIR TREE

OUT IN THE forest stood a pretty little fir tree. It had a good place; it could have sunlight, air there was in plenty, and all around grew many larger comrades—pines as well as firs. But the little fir tree was in such a hurry to grow. It did not care for the warm sun and the fresh air; it took no notice of the peasant children, who went about talking together, when they had come out to look for strawberries and raspberries. Often they came with a whole pot full, or had strung berries on a straw; then they would sit down by the little fir tree and say, "How pretty and small that one is!" and the tree did not like to hear that at all.

Next year it had grown a great joint, and the following year it was longer still, for in fir trees one can always tell by the number of joints they have how many years they have been growing.

"Oh, if I were only as great a tree as the others!" sighed the little fir, "then I would spread my branches far around, and look out from my crown into the wide world. The birds would then build nests in my boughs, and when the wind blew I could nod just as grandly as the others yonder."

It took no pleasure in the sunshine, in the birds, and in the red clouds that went sailing over it morning and evening.

When it was winter, and the snow lay all around, white and sparkling, a hare would often come jumping along, and spring right over the little fir tree. Oh! this made it so angry. But two winters went by, and when the third came the little tree had grown so tall that the hare was obliged to run round it.

"Oh! to grow, to grow, and become old; that's the only fine thing in the world," thought the tree.

In the autumn woodcutters always came and felled a few of the largest trees; that happened every year, and the little fir tree, that was now quite well grown, shuddered with fear, for the great stately trees fell to the ground with a crash, and their branches were cut off, so that the trees looked quite naked, long, and slender—they could hardly be recognized. But then they were laid upon wagons, and horses dragged them away out of the wood. Where were they going? What destiny awaited them?

In the spring, when the swallows and the stork came, the tree asked them, "Do you know where they were taken? Did you not meet them?"

The swallows knew nothing about it, but the stork looked thoughtful, nodded his head, and said,

"Yes, I think so. I met many new ships when I flew out of Egypt; on the ships were stately masts; I fancy that these were the trees. They smelt like fir. I can assure you they're stately—very stately."

"Oh that I were only big enough to go over the sea! What kind of thing is this sea, and how does it look?"

"It would take too long to explain all that," said the stork, and he went away.

"Rejoice in thy youth," said the sunbeams; "rejoice in thy fresh growth, and in the young life that is within thee."

And the wind kissed the tree, and the dew wept tears upon it; but the fir tree did not understand that.

When Christmas time approached, quite young trees were felled, sometimes trees which were neither so old nor so large as this fir tree, that never rested but always wanted to go away. These young trees, which were just the most beautiful, kept all their branches; they were put upon wagons, and horses dragged them away out of the wood.

"Where are they all going?" asked the fir tree. "They are not greater than I—indeed, one of them was much smaller. Why do they keep all their branches? Whither are they taken?"

"We know that! We know that!" chirped the sparrows. "Yonder in the town we looked in at the windows. We know where they go. Oh! they are dressed up in the greatest pomp and splendor that can be imagined. We have looked in at the windows, and have perceived that they are planted in the middle of the warm room, and adorned with the most beautiful things—gilt apples, honey cakes, playthings, and many hundreds of candles."

"And then?" asked the fir tree, and trembled through all its branches. "And then? What happens then?"

"Why, we have not seen anything more. But it was incomparable."

"Perhaps I may be destined to tread this glorious path one day!" cried the fir tree rejoicingly. "That is even better than traveling across the sea. How painfully I long for it! If it were only Christmas now! Now I am great and grown up, like the rest who were led away last year. Oh, if I were only on the carriage! If I were only in the warm room, among all the pomp and splendor! And then? Yes, then something even better will come, something far more charming, or else why should they adorn me so? There must be something grander, something greater still to come, but what? Oh! I'm suffering, I'm longing! I don't know myself what is the matter with me!"

"Rejoice in us," said air and sunshine. "Rejoice in thy fresh youth here in the woodland."

But the fir tree did not rejoice at all, but it grew and grew; winter and summer it stood there, green, dark green. The people who saw it said, "That's a handsome tree!" and at Christmas time it was felled before any one of the others. The ax cut deep into its marrow, and the tree fell to the ground with a sigh; it felt a pain, a sensation of faintness, and could not think at all of happiness, for it was sad at parting from its home, from the place where it had grown up; it knew that it should never again see the dear old companions, the little bushes and flowers all around—perhaps not even the birds. The parting was not at all agreeable.

The tree only came to itself when it was unloaded in a yard, with other trees, and heard a man say,

"This one is famous; we only want this one!"

Now two servants came in gay liveries, and carried the fir tree into a large beautiful salon. All around the walls hung pictures, and by the great stove stood large Chinese vases with lions on the covers; there were rocking chairs, silken sofas, great tables covered with picture books, and toys worth a hundred times a hundred dollars, at least the children said so. And the fir tree was put into a great tub filled with sand; but no one could see that it was a tub, for it was hung round with green cloth, and stood on a large many-colored carpet. Oh, how the tree trembled! What was to happen now? The servants, and the young ladies also, decked it out. On one branch they hung little nets, cut out of colored paper; every net was filled with sweetmeats; golden apples and walnuts hung down as if they grew there, and more than a hundred little candles, red, white, and blue, were fastened to the different boughs. Dolls that looked exactly like real people—the tree had never seen such before—swung among the foliage, and high on the summit of the tree was fixed a tinsel star. It was splendid, particularly splendid.

"This evening," said all, "this evening it will shine."

"Oh," thought the tree, "that it were evening already! Oh that the lights may be soon lit up! What will happen then? I wonder if trees will come out of the forest to look at me? Will the sparrows fly against the panes? Shall I grow fast here, and stand adorned in summer and winter?"

THE FIR TREE

Yes, it knew all about it. But it had a regular bark ache from mere longing, and the bark ache is just as bad for a tree as the headache for a person.

At last the candles were lighted. What a brilliance, what splendor! The tree trembled so in all its branches that one of the candles set fire to a green twig, and it was really painful.

"Heaven preserve us!" cried the young ladies; and they hastily put the fire out.

Now the tree might not even tremble. Oh, that was terrible! It was so afraid of losing any of its ornaments, and it was quite bewildered with all the brilliance. And now the folding doors were thrown open, and a number of children rushed in as if they would have overturned the whole tree; the older people followed more deliberately. The little ones stood quite silent, but only for a minute; then they shouted till the room rang; they danced gleefully round the tree, and one present after another was plucked from it.

"What are they about?" thought the tree. "What's going to be done?"

And the candles burned down to the twigs, and as they burned down they were extinguished, and then the children received permission to plunder the tree. Oh! they rushed in upon it, so that every branch cracked again: if it had not been fastened by the top and by the golden star to the ceiling, it would have fallen down.

The children danced about with their pretty toys. No one looked at the tree except the old nursemaid, who came up and peeped among the branches, but only to see if a fig or an apple had not been forgotten.

"A story! a story!" shouted the children: and they drew a little fat man toward the tree; and he sat down just beneath it—"for then we shall be in the green wood," said he, "and the tree may have the advantage of listening to my tale. But I can only tell one. Will you hear the story of Ivede-Avede, or of

151

Humpty-Dumpty, who fell downstairs, and still was raised up to honor and married the princess?"

"Ivede-Avede!" cried some, "Humpty-Dumpty!" cried others, and there was a great crying and shouting. Only the fir tree was quite silent, and thought, "Shall I not be in it? Shall I have nothing to do in it?" But it had been in the evening's amusement, and had done what was required of it.

And the fat man told about Humpty-Dumpty, who fell downstairs, and yet was raised to honor and married the princess. And the children clapped their hands, and cried, "Tell another! tell another!" for they wanted to hear about Ivede-Avede; but they only got the story of Humpty-Dumpty. The fir tree stood quite silent and thoughtful; never had the birds in the wood told such a story as that. Humpty-Dumpty fell downstairs, and yet came to honor and married the princess!

"Yes, so it happens in the world!" thought the fir tree, and believed it must be true, because that was such a nice man who told it. "Well, who can know? Perhaps I shall fall downstairs too, and marry a princess!" And it looked forward with pleasure to being adorned again, the next evening, with candles and toys, gold and fruit. "Tomorrow I shall not tremble," it thought. "I will rejoice in all my splendor. Tomorrow I shall hear the story of Humpty-Dumpty again, and perhaps, that of Ivede-Avede too."

And the tree stood all night quiet and thoughtful.

In the morning the servants and the chambermaid came in.

"Now my splendor will begin afresh," thought the tree. But they dragged it out of the room, and upstairs to the garret, and here they put it in a dark corner where no daylight shone.

"What's the meaning of this?" thought the tree. "What am I to do here? What am I to get to know here?"

And he leaned against the wall, and thought, and thought. And he had time enough, for days and nights went by, and nobody came up; and when at length some one came, it was only to put some great boxes in a corner. Now the tree stood quite hidden away, and one would think that it was quite forgotten.

"Now it's winter outside," thought the tree. "The earth is hard and covered with snow, and people cannot plant me; therefore I suppose I'm to be sheltered here until spring comes. How considerate that is! How good people are! If it were only not so dark here, and so terribly solitary!—not even a little hare! It was pretty out there in the wood, when the snow lay thick and the hare sprang past; yes, even when he jumped over me, although I did not like that at the time. It is terribly lonely up here!"

"Piep! piep!" said a little mouse, and crept forward, and then came another little one. They smelt at the fir tree, and then slipped among the branches.

"It's horribly cold," said the two little mice, "or else it would be comfortable here. Don't you think so, you old fir tree?"

"I'm not old at all," said the fir tree. "There are many much older than I."

"Where do you come from?" asked the mice. "And what do you know?" They were dreadfully inquisitive. "Tell us about the most beautiful spot on earth. Have you been there? Have you been in the storeroom, where cheeses lie on the shelves, and hams hang from the ceiling, where one dances on tallow candles, and goes in thin and comes out fat?"

"I don't know that!" replied the tree; "but I know the wood, where the sun shines, and where the birds sing."

And then it told all about its youth.

And the little mice had never heard anything of the kind; and they listened and said,

"What a number of things you have seen! How happy you must have been!"

"I?" said the fir tree; and it thought about what it had told. "Yes, those were really quite happy times." But then it told of

153

the Christmas Eve, when it had been hung with sweetmeats and candles.

"Oh!" said the little mice, "how happy you have been, you old fir tree!"

"I'm not old at all," said the tree. "I only came out of the wood this winter. I'm in my very best years."

"What splendid stories you can tell!" said the little mice.

And next night they came with four other little mice, to hear what the tree had to relate; and the more it said, the more clearly did it remember everything, and thought, "Those were quite merry days! But they may come again. Humpty-Dumpty fell downstairs, and yet he married the princess. Perhaps I may marry a princess too!" And then the fir tree thought of a pretty little birch tree that grew out in the forest: for the fir tree, that birch was a real princess.

"Who's Humpty-Dumpty?" asked the little mice.

And then the fir tree told the whole story. It could remember every single word; and the little mice were ready to leap to the very top of the tree with pleasure. Next night a great many more mice came, and on Sunday two rats even appeared; but these thought the story was not pretty, and the little mice were sorry for that, for now they also did not like it so much as before.

"Do you only know one story?" asked the rats.

"Only that one," replied the tree. "I heard that on the happiest evening of my life; I did not think then how happy I was."

"That's an exceedingly poor story. Don't you know any about bacon and tallow candles—a storeroom story?"

"No," said the tree.

"Then we'd rather not hear you," said the rats.

And they went back to their own people. The little mice at last stayed away also; and then the tree sighed and said,

"It was very nice when they sat round me, the merry little mice, and listened when I spoke to them. Now that's past too. But I shall remember to be pleased when they take me out."

But when did that happen? Why, it was one morning that people came and rummaged in the garret: the boxes were put away, and the tree brought out; they certainly threw it rather roughly on the floor, but a servant dragged it away at once to the stairs, where the daylight shone.

"Now life is beginning again!" thought the tree.

It felt the fresh air and the first sunbeams, and now it was out in the courtyard. Everything passed so quickly that the tree quite forgot to look at itself, there was so much to look at all round. The courtyard was close to a garden, and here everything was blooming; the roses hung fresh and fragrant over the little paling, the linden trees were in blossom, and the swallows cried, "Quirre-virre-vit! my husband's come!" But it was not the fir tree that they meant.

"Now I shall live!" said the tree, rejoicingly, and spread its branches far out; but, alas! they were all withered and yellow; and it lay in the corner among nettles and weeds. The tinsel star was still upon it, and shone in the bright sunshine.

In the courtyard a couple of the merry children were playing, who had danced round the tree at Christmas time, and had rejoiced over it. One of the youngest ran up and tore off the golden star.

"Look what is sticking to the ugly old fir tree," said the child, and he trod upon the branches till they cracked again under his boots.

And the tree looked at all the blooming flowers and the splendor of the garden, and then looked at itself, and wished it had remained in the dark corner of the garret; it thought of its fresh youth in the wood, of the merry Christmas Eve, and of the little mice which had listened so pleasantly to the story of Humpty-Dumpty.

"Past! past!" said the poor tree. "Had I but rejoiced when I could have done so! Past! past!"

And the servant came and chopped the tree into little pieces; a whole bundle lay there: it blazed brightly under the great brewing copper, and it sighed deeply, and each sigh was like a little shot: and the children who were at play there ran up and seated themselves at the fire, looked into it, and cried, "Puff! puff!" But at each explosion, which was a deep sigh, the tree thought of a summer day in the woods, or of a winter night there, when the stars beamed; it thought of Christmas Eve and of Humpty-Dumpty, the only story it had ever heard or knew how to tell; and then the tree was burned.

The boys played in the garden, and the youngest had on his breast a golden star, which the tree had worn on its happiest evening. Now that was past, and the tree's life was past, and the story is past too: past! past!—and that's the way with all stories.

KATHERINE ANNE PORTER

HE

LIFE WAS very hard for the Whipples. It was hard to feed all the hungry mouths, it was hard to keep the children in flannels during the winter, short as it was: "God knows what would become of us if we lived north," they would say: keeping them decently clean was hard. "It looks like our luck won't never let up on us," said Mr. Whipple, but Mrs. Whipple was all for taking what was sent and calling it good, anyhow when the neighbors were in earshot. "Don't ever let a soul hear us complain," she kept saying to her husband. She couldn't stand to be pitied. "No, not if it comes to it that we have to live in a wagon and pick cotton around the country," she said, "nobody's going to get a chance to look down on us."

Mrs. Whipple loved her second son, the simple-minded one, better than she loved the other two children put together. She was forever saying so, and when she talked with certain of her neighbors, she would even throw in her husband and her mother for good measure.

"You needn't keep on saying it around," said Mr. Whipple, "you'll make people think nobody else has any feelings about Him but you."

"It's natural for a mother," Mrs. Whipple would remind him. "You know yourself it's more natural for a mother to be that way. People don't expect so much of fathers, some way."

This didn't keep the neighbors from talking plainly among themselves. "A Lord's pure mercy if He should die," they said. "It's the sins of the fathers," they agreed among themselves.

"There's bad blood and bad doings somewhere, you can bet on that." This behind the Whipples' backs. To their faces everybody said, "He's not so bad off. He'll be all right yet. Look how He grows!"

Mrs. Whipple hated to talk about it, she tried to keep her mind off it, but every time anybody set foot in the house, the subject always came up, and she had to talk about Him first, before she could get on to anything else. It seemed to ease her mind. "I wouldn't have anything happen to Him for all the world, but it just looks like I can't keep Him out of mischief. He's so strong and active, He's always into everything; He was like that since He could walk. It's actually funny sometimes, the way He can do anything; it's laughable to see Him up to His tricks. Emly has more accidents; I'm forever tying up her bruises, and Adna can't fall a foot without cracking a bone. But He can do anything and not get a scratch. The preacher said such a nice thing once when he was here. He said, and I'll remember it to my dying day, 'The innocent walk with God—that's why He don't get hurt.'" Whenever Mrs. Whipple repeated these words, she always felt a warm pool spread in her breast, and the tears would fill her eyes, and then she could talk about something else.

He did grow and He never got hurt. A plank blew off the chicken house and struck Him on the head and He never seemed to know it. He had learned a few words, and after this He forgot them. He didn't whine for food as the other children did, but waited until it was given Him; He ate squatting in the corner, smacking and mumbling. Rolls of fat covered Him like an overcoat, and He could carry twice as much wood and water as Adna. Emly had a cold in the head most of the time—"she takes that after me," said Mrs. Whipple—so in bad weather they gave her the extra blanket off His cot. He never seemed to mind the cold.

Just the same, Mrs. Whipple's life was a torment for fear something might happen to Him. He climbed the peach trees much better than Adna and went skittering along the branches like a monkey, just a regular monkey. "Oh, Mrs. Whipple, you hadn't ought to let Him do that. He'll lose His balance sometime. He can't rightly know what He's doing."

Mrs. Whipple almost screamed out at the neighbor. "He *does* know what He's doing! He's as able as any other child! Come down out of there, you!" When He finally reached the ground she could hardly keep her hands off Him for acting like that before people, a grin all over His face and her worried sick about Him all the time.

"It's the neighbors," said Mrs. Whipple to her husband. "Oh, I do mortally wish they would keep out of our business. I can't afford to let Him do anything for fear they'll come nosing around about it. Look at the bees, now. Adna can't handle them, they sting him up so; I haven't got time to do everything, and now I don't dare let Him. But if He gets a sting He don't really mind."

"It's just because He ain't got sense enough to be scared of anything," said Mr. Whipple.

"You ought to be ashamed of yourself," said Mrs. Whipple, "talking that way about your own child. Who's to take up for Him if we don't, I'd like to know? He sees a lot that goes on, He listens to things all the time. And anything I tell Him to do He does it. Don't never let anybody hear you say such things. They'd think you favored the other children over Him."

"Well, now I don't, and you know it, and what's the use of getting all worked up about it? You always think the worst of everything. Just let Him alone, He'll get along somehow. He gets plenty to eat and wear, don't He?" Mr. Whipple suddenly felt tired out. "Anyhow, it can't be helped now."

Mrs. Whipple felt tired too, she complained in a tired voice. "What's done can't never be undone, I know that good as anybody; but He's my child, and I'm not going to have people say anything. I get sick of people coming around saying things all the time."

In the early fall Mrs. Whipple got a letter from her brother saying he and his wife and two children were coming over for a little visit next Sunday week. "Put the big pot in the little one," he wrote at the end. Mrs. Whipple read this part out loud twice, she was so pleased. Her brother was a great one for saying funny things. "We'll just show him that's no joke," she said, "we'll just butcher one of the sucking pigs."

"It's a waste and I don't hold with waste the way we are now," said Mr. Whipple. "That pig'll be worth money by Christmas."

"It's a shame and a pity we can't have a decent meal's vittles once in a while when my own family comes to see us," said Mrs. Whipple. "I'd hate for his wife to go back and say there wasn't a thing in the house to eat. My God, it's better than buying up a great chance of meat in town. There's where you'd spend the money!"

"All right, do it yourself then," said Mr. Whipple. "Christamighty, no wonder we can't get ahead!"

The question was how to get the little pig away from his ma, a great fighter, worse than a Jersey cow. Adna wouldn't try it: "That sow'd rip my insides out all over the pen." "All right, old fraidy," said Mrs. Whipple, "*He's* not scared. Watch *Him* do it." And she laughed as though it was all a good joke and gave Him a little push towards the pen. He sneaked up and snatched the pig right away from the teat and galloped back and was over the fence with the sow raging at His heels. The little black squirming thing was screeching like a baby in a tantrum, stiffening its back and stretching its mouth to the ears. Mrs. Whipple took the pig with her face stiff and sliced its throat with one stroke. When He saw the blood He gave a great jolting breath and ran away. "But He'll forget and eat plenty, just the same," thought Mrs. Whipple. Whenever she was thinking, her lips moved making words. "He'd eat it all if I didn't stop Him. He'd eat up every mouthful from the other two if I'd let Him."

She felt badly about it. He was ten years old now and a third again as large as Adna, who was going on fourteen. "It's a shame, a shame," she kept saying under her breath, "and Adna with so much brains!"

She kept on feeling badly about all sorts of things. In the first place it was the man's work to butcher; the sight of the pig scraped pink and naked made her sick. He was too fat and soft and pitiful-looking. It was simply a shame the way things had to happen. By the time she had finished it up, she almost wished her brother would stay at home.

Early Sunday morning Mrs. Whipple dropped everything to get Him all cleaned up. In an hour He was dirty again, with crawling under fences after a possum, and straddling along the rafters of the barn looking for eggs in the hayloft. "My Lord, look at you now after all my trying! And here's Adna and Emly staying so quiet. I get tired trying to keep you decent. Get off that shirt and put on another, people will say I don't half dress you!" And she boxed Him on the ears, hard. He blinked and blinked and rubbed His head, and His face hurt Mrs. Whipple's feelings. Her knees began to tremble, she had to sit down while she buttoned His shirt. "I'm just all gone before the day starts."

The brother came with his plump healthy wife and two great roaring hungry boys. They had a grand dinner, with the pig roasted to a crackling in the middle of the table, full of dressing, a pickled peach in his mouth and plenty of gravy for the sweet potatoes.

"This looks like prosperity all right," said the brother; "you're going to have to roll me home like I was a barrel when I'm done."

Everybody laughed out loud; it was fine to hear them laughing all at once around the table. Mrs. Whipple felt warm and good about it. "Oh, we've got six more of these; I say it's as little as we can do when you come to see us so seldom."

He wouldn't come into the dining room, and Mrs. Whipple

passed it off very well. "He's timider than my other two,"
she said, "He'll just have to get used to you. There isn't
everybody He'll make up with, you know how it is with
some children, even cousins." Nobody said anything out of
the way.

"Just like my Alfy here," said the brother's wife. "I sometimes got to lick him to make him shake hands with his own
grand-mammy."

So that was over, and Mrs. Whipple loaded up a big plate
for Him first, before everybody. "I always say He ain't to be
slighted, no matter who else goes without," she said, and carried it to Him herself.

"He can chin Himself on the top of the door," said Emly,
helping along.

"That's fine, He's getting along fine," said the brother.

They went away after supper. Mrs. Whipple rounded
up the dishes, and sent the children to bed and sat down and
unlaced her shoes. "You see?" she said to Mr. Whipple.
"That's the way my whole family is. Nice and considerate
about everything. No out-of-the-way remarks—they *have* got
refinement. I get awfully sick of people's remarks. Wasn't
that pig good?"

Mr. Whipple said, "Yes, we're out three hundred pounds of
pork, that's all. It's easy to be polite when you come to eat.
Who knows what they had in their minds all along?"

"Yes, that's like you," said Mrs. Whipple. "I don't expect
anything else from you. You'll be telling me next that my
own brother will be saying around that we made Him eat in
the kitchen! Oh, my God!" She rocked her head in her hands,
a hard pain started in the very middle of her forehead. "Now
it's all spoiled, and everything was so nice and easy. All right,
you don't like them and you never did—all right, they'll not
come here again soon, never you mind! But they *can't* say He
wasn't dressed every lick as good as Adna—oh, honest, sometimes I wish I was dead!"

"I wish you'd let up," said Mr. Whipple. "It's bad enough as it is."

It was a hard winter. It seemed to Mrs. Whipple that they hadn't ever known anything but hard times, and now to cap it all a winter like this. The crops were about half of what they had a right to expect; after the cotton was in it didn't do much more than cover the grocery bill. They swapped off one of the plow horses, and got cheated, for the new one died of the heaves. Mrs. Whipple kept thinking all the time it was terrible to have a man you couldn't depend on not to get cheated. They cut down on everything, but Mrs. Whipple kept saying there are things you can't cut down on, and they cost money. It took a lot of warm clothes for Adna and Emly, who walked four miles to school during the three-months session. "He sets around the fire a lot, He won't need so much," said Mr. Whipple. "That's so," said Mrs. Whipple, "and when He does the outdoor chores He can wear your tarpaullion coat. I can't do no better, that's all."

In February He was taken sick, and lay curled up under His blanket looking very blue in the face and acting as if He would choke. Mr. and Mrs. Whipple did everything they could for Him for two days, and then they were scared and sent for the doctor. The doctor told them they must keep Him warm and give Him plenty of milk and eggs. "He isn't as stout as He looks, I'm afraid," said the doctor. "You've got to watch them when they're like that. You must put more cover onto Him, too."

"I just took off His big blanket to wash," said Mrs. Whipple, ashamed. "I can't stand dirt."

"Well, you'd better put it back on the minute it's dry," said the doctor, "or He'll have pneumonia."

Mr. and Mrs. Whipple took a blanket off their own bed and put His cot in by the fire. "They can't say we didn't do

everything for Him," she said, "even to sleeping cold ourselves on His account."

When the winter broke He seemed to be well again, but
He walked as if His feet hurt Him. He was able to run a cotton planter during the season.

"I got it all fixed up with Jim Ferguson about breeding the
cow next time," said Mr. Whipple. "I'll pasture the bull this
summer and give Jim some fodder in the fall. That's better
than paying out money when you haven't got it."

"I hope you didn't say such a thing before Jim Ferguson,"
said Mrs. Whipple. "You oughtn't to let him know we're so
down as all that."

"Godamighty, that ain't saying we're down. A man is got
to look ahead sometimes. *He* can lead the bull over today. I
need Adna on the place."

At first Mrs. Whipple felt easy in her mind about sending
Him for the bull. Adna was too jumpy and couldn't be trusted.
You've got to be steady around animals. After He was gone
she started thinking, and after a while she could hardly bear
it any longer. She stood in the lane and watched for Him. It
was nearly three miles to go and a hot day, but He oughtn't to
be so long about it. She shaded her eyes and stared until colored bubbles floated in her eyeballs. It was just like everything else in life, she must always worry and never know a
moment's peace about anything. After a long time she saw
Him turn into the side lane, limping. He came on very slowly,
leading the big hulk of an animal by a ring in the nose, twirling
a little stick in His hand, never looking back or sideways, but
coming on like a sleepwalker with His eyes half shut.

Mrs. Whipple was scared sick of bulls; she had heard awful
stories about how they followed on quietly enough, and then
suddenly pitched on with a bellow and pawed and gored a
body to pieces. Any second now that black monster would
come down on Him, my God, He'd never have sense enough
to run.

She mustn't make a sound nor a move; she mustn't get the bull started. The bull heaved his head aside and horned the air at a fly. Her voice burst out of her in a shriek, and she screamed at Him to come on, for God's sake. He didn't seem to hear her clamor, but kept on twirling His switch and limping on, and the bull lumbered along behind him as gently as a calf. Mrs. Whipple stopped calling and ran towards the house, praying under her breath: "Lord, don't let anything happen to Him. Lord, you *know* people will say we oughtn't to have sent Him. You *know* they'll say we didn't take care of Him. Oh, get Him home, safe home, safe home, and I'll look out for Him better! Amen."

She watched from the window while He led the beast in, and tied him up in the barn. It was no use trying to keep up, Mrs. Whipple couldn't bear another thing. She sat down and rocked and cried with her apron over her head.

From year to year the Whipples were growing poorer and poorer. The place just seemed to run down of itself, no matter how hard they worked. "We're losing our hold," said Mrs. Whipple. "Why can't we do like other people and watch for our best chances? They'll be calling us poor white trash next."

"When I get to be sixteen I'm going to leave," said Adna. "I'm going to get a job in Powell's grocery store. There's money in that. No more farm for me."

"I'm going to be a schoolteacher," said Emly. "But I've got to finish the eighth grade, anyhow. Then I can live in town. I don't see any chances here."

"Emly takes after my family," said Mrs. Whipple. "Ambitious every last one of them, and they don't take second place for anybody."

When fall came Emly got a chance to wait on table in the railroad eating-house in the town near by, and it seemed such a shame not to take it when the wages were good and she could get her food too, that Mrs. Whipple decided to let her take it, and not bother with school until the next session. "You've got plenty of time," she said. "You're young and smart as a whip."

With Adna gone too, Mr. Whipple tried to run the farm with just Him to help. He seemed to get along fine, doing His work and part of Adna's without noticing it. They did well enough until Christmas time, when one morning He slipped on the ice coming up from the barn. Instead of getting up He thrashed round and round, and when Mr. Whipple got to Him, He was having some sort of fit.

They brought Him inside and tried to make Him sit up, but He blubbered and rolled, so they put Him to bed and Mr. Whipple rode to town for the doctor. All the way there and back he worried about where the money was to come from: it sure did look like he had about all the troubles he could carry.

From then on He stayed in bed. His legs swelled up double their size, and the fits kept coming back. After four months, the doctor said, "It's no use, I think you'd better put Him in the County Home for treatment right away. I'll see about it for you. He'll have good care there and be off your hands."

"We don't begrudge Him any care, and I won't let Him out of my sight," said Mrs. Whipple. "I won't have it said I sent my sick child off among strangers."

"I know how you feel," said the doctor. "You can't tell me anything about that, Mrs. Whipple. I've got a boy of my own. But you'd better listen to me. I can't do anything more for Him, that's the truth."

Mr. and Mrs. Whipple talked it over a long time that night after they went to bed. "It's just charity," said Mrs. Whipple, "that's what we've come to, charity! I certainly never looked for this."

"We pay taxes to help support the place just like everybody else," said Mr. Whipple, "and I don't call that taking charity. I think it would be fine to have Him where He'd get the best of everything . . . and besides, I can't keep up with these doctor bills any longer."

"Maybe that's why the doctor wants us to send Him—he's scared he won't get his money," said Mrs. Whipple.

"Don't talk like that," said Mr. Whipple, feeling pretty sick, "or we won't be able to send Him."

"Oh, but we won't keep Him there long," said Mrs. Whipple. "Soon's He's better, we'll bring Him right back home."

"The doctor has told you and told you time and again He can't ever get better, and you might as well stop talking," said Mr. Whipple.

"Doctors don't know everything," said Mrs. Whipple, feeling almost happy. "But anyhow, in the summer Emly can come home for a vacation, and Adna can get down for Sundays: we'll all work together and get on our feet again, and the children will feel they've got a place to come to."

All at once she saw it full summer again, with the garden going fine, and new white roller shades up all over the house, and Adna and Emly home, so full of life, all of them happy together. Oh, it could happen, things would ease up on them.

They didn't talk before Him much, but they never knew just how much He understood. Finally the doctor set the day and a neighbor who owned a double-seated carryall offered to drive them over. The hospital would have sent an ambulance, but Mrs. Whipple couldn't stand to see Him going away looking so sick as all that. They wrapped Him in blankets, and the neighbor and Mr. Whipple lifted Him into the back seat of the carryall beside Mrs. Whipple, who had on her black shirtwaist. She couldn't stand to go looking like charity.

"You'll be all right, I guess I'll stay behind," said Mr. Whipple. "It don't look like everybody ought to leave the place at once."

"Besides, it ain't as if He was going to stay forever," said Mrs. Whipple to the neighbor. "This is only for a little while."

They started away, Mrs. Whipple holding to the edges of

the blankets to keep Him from sagging sideways. He sat there blinking and blinking. He worked His hands out and began rubbing His nose with His knuckles, and then with the end of the blanket. Mrs. Whipple couldn't believe what she saw; He was scrubbing away big tears that rolled out of the corners of His eyes. He sniveled and made a gulping noise. Mrs. Whipple kept saying, "Oh, honey, you don't feel so bad, do you? You don't feel so bad, do you?" for He seemed to be accusing her of something. Maybe He remembered that time she boxed His ears, maybe He had been scared that day with the bull, maybe He had slept cold and couldn't tell her about it; maybe He knew they were sending Him away for good and all because they were too poor to keep Him. Whatever it was, Mrs. Whipple couldn't bear to think of it. She began to cry, frightfully, and wrapped her arms tight around Him. His head rolled on her shoulder: she had loved Him as much as she possibly could, there were Adna and Emly who had to be thought of too, there was nothing she could do to make up to Him for His life. Oh, what a mortal pity He was ever born.

They came in sight of the hospital, with the neighbor driving very fast, not daring to look behind him.

ANONYMOUS

THE RED KING
AND THE WITCH

A Gypsy Folk-tale

It WAS THE Red King, and he bought ten ducats' worth of victuals. He cooked them, and he put them in a press. And he locked the press, and from night to night posted people to guard the victuals.

In the morning, when he looked, he found the platters bare; he did not find anything in them. Then the king said, "I will give the half of my kingdom to whoever shall be found to guard the press, that the victuals may not go amissing from it."

The king had three sons. Then the eldest thought within himself, "God! What, give half the kingdom to a stranger! It were better for me to watch. Be it unto me according to God's will!"

He went to his father. "Father, all hail. What, give the kingdom to a stranger! It were better for me to watch."

And his father said to him, "As God will, only don't be frightened by what you may see."

Then he said, "Be it unto me according to God's will." And he went and lay down in the palace. And he put his head on the pillow, and remained with his head on the pillow till towards dawn. And a warm sleepy breeze came and lulled him to slumber. And his little sister arose. And she turned a somersault, and her nails became like an axe and her teeth like a shovel. And she opened the cupboard and ate up everything. Then she became a child again and returned to her place in the cradle, for she was a babe at the breast. The lad arose and told his father that he had seen nothing. His father looked in the press, found the platters bare—no victuals, no anything. His father said, "It would take a better man than you, and even he might do nothing."

His middle son also said, "Father, all hail. I am going to watch tonight."

"Go, dear, only play the man."

"Be it unto me according to God's will."

And he went into the palace and put his head on a pillow. And at ten o'clock came a warm breeze and sleep seized him. Up rose his sister and unwound herself from her swaddling-bands and turned a somersault, and her teeth became like a shovel and her nails like an axe. And she went to the press and opened it, and ate off the platters what she found. She ate it all, and turned a somersault again and went back to her place in the cradle. Day broke and the lad arose, and his father asked him and said, "It would take a better man than you, and even he might do nought for me if he were as poor a creature as you."

The youngest son arose. "Father, all hail. Give me also leave to watch the cupboard by night."

"Go, dear, only don't be frightened by what you see."

"Be it unto me according to God's will," said the lad.

And he went and took four needles and lay down with his head on the pillow; and he stuck the four needles in four places. When sleep seized him he knocked his head against a needle, so he stayed awake until ten o'clock. And his sister arose from her cradle, and he saw. And she turned a somersault, and he was watching her. And her teeth became like a shovel and her nails like an axe. And she went to the press and ate up everything. She left the platters bare. And she turned a somersault, and became tiny again as she was; went to her cradle. The lad, when he saw that, trembled with fear; it seemed to him ten years till daybreak. And he arose and went to his father. "Father, all hail."

Then his father asked him, "Didst see anything, Peterkin?"

"What did I see? what did I not see? Give me money and a horse, a horse fit to carry the money, for I am away to marry me."

His father gave him a couple of sacks of ducats, and he put them on his horse. The lad went and made a hole on the border of the city. He made a chest of stone, and put all the money there and buried it. He placed a stone cross above and departed. And he journeyed eight years and came to the queen of all the birds that fly.

And the queen of the birds asked him, "Whither away, Peterkin?"

"Thither, where there is neither death nor old age, to marry me."

The queen said to him, "Here is neither death nor old age."

Then Peterkin said to her, "How comes it that here is neither death nor old age?"

Then she said to him, "When I whittle away the wood of all this forest, then death will come and take me and old age."

Then Peterkin said, "One day and one morning death will come and old age, and take me."

And he departed further, and journeyed on eight years and arrived at a palace of copper. And a maiden came forth from that palace and took him and kissed him. She said, "I have waited long for thee."

She took the horse and put him in the stable, and the lad spent the night there. He arose in the morning and placed his saddle on the horse.

Then the maiden began to weep, and asked him, "Whither away, Peterkin?"

"Thither, where there is neither death nor old age."

Then the maiden said to him, "Here is neither death nor old age."

Then he asked her, "How comes it that here is neither death nor old age?"

"Why, when these mountains are leveled, and these forests, then death will come."

"This is no place for me," said the lad to her. And he departed further.

Then what said his horse to him? "Master, whip me four times, and twice yourself, for you are come to the Plain of Regret. And Regret will seize you and cast you down, horse and all. So spur your horse, escape, and tarry not."

He came to a hut. In that hut he beholds a lad, as it were ten years old, who asked him, "What seekest thou, Peterkin, here?"

"I seek the place where there is neither death nor old age."

The lad said, "Here is neither death nor old age. I am the Wind."

Then Peterkin said, "Never, never will I go from here." And he dwelt there a hundred years and grew no older.

There the lad dwelt, and he went out to hunt in the Mountains of Gold and Silver, and he could scarce carry home the game.

Then what said the Wind to him? "Peterkin, go unto all the Mountains of Gold and unto the Mountains of Silver; but go not to the Mountain of Regret or to the Valley of Grief."

He heeded not, but went to the Mountain of Regret and the Valley of Grief. And Grief cast him down; he wept till his eyes were full.

And he went to the Wind. "I am going home to my father, I will not stay longer."

"Go not, for your father is dead, and brothers you have no more left at home. A million years have come and gone since then. The spot is not known where your father's palace stood. They have planted melons on it; it is but an hour since I passed that way."

But the lad departed thence, and arrived at the maiden's

whose was the palace of copper. Only one stick remained, and she cut it and grew old. As he knocked at the door, the stick fell and she died. He buried her, and departed thence. And he came to the queen of the birds in the great forest. Only one branch remained, and that was all but through.

When she saw him she said, "Peterkin, thou art quite young."

Then he said to her, "Dost thou remember telling me to tarry here?"

As she pressed and broke through the branch, she, too, fell and died.

He came where his father's palace stood and looked about him. There was no palace, no anything. And he fell to marveling: "God, Thou art mighty!" He only recognized his father's well, and went to it. His sister, the witch, when she saw him, said to him, "I have waited long for you, dog." She rushed at him to devour him, but he made the sign of the cross and she perished.

And he departed thence, and came on an old man with his beard down to his belt. "Father, where is the palace of the Red King? I am his son."

"What is this," said the old man, "thou tellest me, that thou art his son? My father's father has told me of the Red King. His very city is no more. Dost thou not see it is vanished? And dost thou tell me that thou art the Red King's son?"

"It is not twenty years, old man, since I departed from my father, and dost thou tell me that thou knowest not my father?" (It was a million years since he had left his home.) "Follow me if thou dost not believe me."

And he went to the cross of stone; only a palm's breadth was out of the ground. And it took him two days to get at the chest of money. When he had lifted the chest out and opened it, Death sat in one corner groaning, and Old Age groaning in another corner.

Then what said Old Age? "Lay hold of him, Death."

"Lay hold of him yourself."

Old Age laid hold of him in front, and Death laid hold of him behind.

The old man took and buried him decently, and planted the cross near him. And the old man took the money and also the horse.

ANTON CHEKHOV

ROTHSCHILD'S FIDDLE

THE TOWN was small—no better than a village—and it was inhabited almost entirely by old people who died so seldom that it was positively painful. In the hospital, and even in the prison, coffins were required very seldom. In one word, business was bad. If Yakov Ivanov had been coffin-maker in the government town, he would probably have owned his own house, and called himself Yakov Matveyich; but, as it was, he was known only by the name of Yakov, with the street nickname of "Bronza" given for some obscure reason; and he lived as poorly as a simple muzhik in a little, ancient cabin with only one room; and in this room lived he, Marfa, the stove, a double bed, the coffins, a joiner's bench, and all the domestic utensils.

Yet Yakov made admirable coffins, durable and good. For muzhiks and petty tradespeople he made them all of one size, taking himself as model; and this method never failed him, for though he was seventy years of age, there was not a taller or stouter man in the town, not even in the prison. For women and for men of good birth he made his coffins to measure, using for this purpose an iron yardwand. Orders for children's coffins he accepted very unwillingly, made them without measurement, as if in contempt, and every time when paid for his work exclaimed:

"Thanks. But I confess I don't care much for wasting time on trifles."

In addition to coffin-making Yakov drew a small income

from his skill with the fiddle. At weddings in the town there usually played a Jewish orchestra, the conductor of which was the tinsmith Moses Ilyich Shakhkes, who kept more than half the takings for himself. As Yakov played very well upon the fiddle, being particularly skillful with Russian songs, Shakhkes sometimes employed him in the orchestra, paying him fifty kopecks a day, exclusive of gifts from the guests. When Bronza sat in the orchestra he perspired and his face grew purple; it was always hot, the smell of garlic was suffocating; the fiddle whined, at his right ear snored the double-bass, at his left wept the flute, played by a lanky, red-haired Jew with a whole network of red and blue veins upon his face, who bore the same surname as the famous millionaire Rothschild. And even the merriest tunes this accursed Jew managed to play sadly. Without any tangible cause Yakov had become slowly penetrated with hatred and contempt for Jews, and especially for Rothschild; he began with irritation, then swore at him, and once even was about to hit him; but Rothschild flared up, and, looking at him furiously, said:

"If it were not that I respect you for your talents, I should send you flying out of the window."

Then he began to cry. So Bronza was employed in the orchestra very seldom, and only in cases of extreme need when one of the Jews was absent.

Yakov had never been in a good humor. He was always overwhelmed by the sense of the losses which he suffered. For instance, on Sundays and saints' days it was a sin to work, Monday was a tiresome day—and so on; so that in one way or another, there were about two hundred days in the year when he was compelled to sit with his hands idle. That was one loss. If anyone in town got married without music, or if Shakhkes did not employ Yakov, that was another loss. The Inspector of Police was ill for two years, and Yakov waited with impatience for his death, yet in the end the Inspector transferred himself to the government town for the purpose of treatment, where he got worse and died. There was another loss, a loss at the very least of ten rubles, as the Inspector's coffin would have been an expensive one lined with brocade. Regrets for his losses generally overtook Yakov at night; he lay in bed with the fiddle beside him, and, with his head full of such speculations, would take the bow, the fiddle giving out through the darkness a melancholy sound which made Yakov feel better.

On the sixth of May last year Marfa was suddenly taken ill. She breathed heavily, drank much water, and staggered. Yet next morning she lighted the stove, and even went for water. Towards evening she lay down. All day Yakov had played on the fiddle, and when it grew dark he took the book in which every day he inscribed his losses, and from want of something better to do, began to add them up. The total amounted to more than a thousand rubles. The thought of such losses so horrified him that he threw the book on the floor and stamped his feet. Then he took up the book, snapped his fingers, and sighed heavily. His face was purple, and wet with perspiration. He reflected that if this thousand rubles had been lodged in the bank the interest per annum would have amounted to at least forty rubles. That meant that the forty rubles were also a loss. In one word, wherever you turn, everywhere you meet with loss, and profits none.

"Yakov," cried Marfa unexpectedly, "I am dying."

He glanced at his wife. Her face was red from fever and unusually clear and joyful; and Bronza, who was accustomed to see her pale, timid, and unhappy-looking, felt confused. It seemed as if she were indeed dying, and were happy in the knowledge that she was leaving for ever the cabin, the coffins, and Yakov. And now she looked at the ceiling and twitched her lips, as if she had seen Death her deliverer, and were whispering with him.

Morning came; through the window might be seen the rising of the sun. Looking at his old wife, Yakov somehow remembered that all his life he had never treated her kindly, never caressed her, never pitied her, never thought of buying her a kerchief for her head, never carried away from the weddings a piece of tasty food, but only roared at her, abused her for his losses, and rushed at her with shut fists. True, he had never beaten her, but he had often frightened her out of her life and left her rooted to the ground with terror. Yes, and he had forbidden her to drink tea, as the losses without that were great enough; so she drank always hot water. And now, beginning to understand why she had such a strange, enraptured face, he felt uncomfortable.

When the sun had risen high he borrowed a cart from a neighbor, and brought Marfa to the hospital. There were not many patients there, and he had to wait only three hours. To his joy he was received not by the doctor but by the feldscher, Maksim Nikolaïch, an old man of whom it was said that, although he was drunken and quarrelsome, he knew more than the doctor.

"May your health be good!" said Yakov, leading the old woman into the dispensary. "Forgive me, Maksim Nikolaïch, for troubling you with my empty affairs. But there, you can see for yourself my object is ill. The companion of my life, as they say, excuse the expression . . ."

Contracting his gray brows and smoothing his whiskers, the feldscher began to examine the old woman, who sat on the tabouret, bent, skinny, sharp-nosed, and with open mouth so that she resembled a bird that is about to drink.

"So . . ." said the feldscher slowly, and then sighed. "Influenza and may be a bit of a fever. There is typhus now in the town. . . . What can I do? She is an old woman, glory be to God. . . . How old?"

"Sixty-nine years, Maksim Nikolaïch."

"An old woman. It's high time for her."

"Of course! Your remark is very just," said Yakov, smiling out of politeness. "And I am sincerely grateful for your kindness; but allow me to make one remark; every insect is fond of life."

The feldscher replied in a tone which implied that upon him alone depended her life or death. "I will tell you what you'll do, friend; put on her head a cold compress, and give her these powders twice a day. And good-bye to you."

By the expression of the feldscher's face, Yakov saw that it was a bad business, and that no powders would make it any better; it was quite plain to him that Marfa was beyond repair, and would assuredly die, if not to-day, then to-morrow. He touched the feldscher on the arm, blinked his eyes, and said in a whisper:

"Yes, Maksim Nikolaïch, but you will let her blood."

"I have no time, no time, friend. Take your old woman, and God be with you!"

"Do me this one kindness!" implored Yakov. "You yourself know that if she merely had her stomach out of order, or some internal organ wrong, then powders and mixtures would cure; but she has caught cold. In cases of cold the first thing is to bleed the patient."

But the feldscher had already called for the next patient, and into the dispensary came a peasant woman with a little boy.

"Be off!" he said to Yakov, with a frown.

"At least try the effect of leeches. I will pray God eternally for you."

The feldscher lost his temper, and roared:

"Not another word."

Yakov also lost his temper, and grew purple in the face; but he said nothing more and took Marfa under his arm and led her out of the room. As soon as he had got her into the cart, he looked angrily and contemptuously at the hospital and said:

"What an artist! He will let the blood of a rich man, but for a poor man grudges even a leech. Herod!"

When they arrived home, and entered the cabin, Marfa stood for a moment holding on to the stove. She was afraid that if she were to lie down Yakov would begin to complain about his losses, and abuse her for lying in bed and doing no work. And Yakov looked at her with tedium in his soul and remembered that to-morrow was John the Baptist, and the day after Nikolay the Miracle-worker, and then came Sunday, and after that Monday—another idle day. For four days no work could be done, and Marfa would be sure to die on one of these days. Her coffin must be made to-day. He took the iron yardwand, went up to the old woman and took her measure. After that she lay down, and Yakov crossed himself, and began to make a coffin.

When the work was finished, Bronza put on his spectacles and wrote in his book of losses:

"Marfa Ivanovna's coffin—2 rubles, 40 kopecks."

And he sighed. All the time Marfa had lain silently with her eyes closed. Towards evening, when it was growing dark, she called her husband:

"Rememberest, Yakov?" she said, looking at him joyfully. "Rememberest, fifty years ago God gave us a baby with yellow hair. Thou and I then sat every day by the river . . . under the willow . . . and sang songs." And laughing bitterly she added: "The child died."

"That is all imagination," said Yakov.

Later on came the priest, administered to Marfa the Sacrament and extreme unction. Marfa began to mutter something incomprehensible, and towards morning, died.

The old-women neighbors washed her, wrapped her in her winding sheet, and laid her out. To avoid having to pay the deacon's fee, Yakov himself read the psalms; and escaped a fee also at the graveyard, as the watchman there was his godfather. Four peasants carried the coffin free, out of respect for the deceased. After the coffin walked a procession of old women, beggars, and two cripples. The peasants on the road crossed themselves piously. And Yakov was very satisfied that everything passed off in honor, order, and cheapness, without offense to anyone. When saying good-bye for the last time to Marfa, he tapped the coffin with his fingers, and thought, "An excellent piece of work."

But while he was returning from the graveyard he was overcome with extreme weariness. He felt unwell, he breathed feverishly and heavily, he could hardly stand on his feet. His brain was full of unaccustomed thoughts. He remembered again that he had never taken pity on Marfa and never caressed her. The fifty-two years during which they had lived in the same cabin stretched back to eternity, yet in the whole of that eternity he had never thought of her, never paid any attention to her, but treated her as if she were a cat or a dog. Yet every day she had lighted the stove, boiled and baked, fetched water, chopped wood, slept with him on the same bed; and when he returned drunk from weddings, she had taken his fiddle respectfully, and hung it on the wall, and put him to bed—all this silently with a timid, worried expression on her face. And now he felt that he could take pity on her, and would like to buy her a present, but it was too late. . . .

Towards Yakov, smiling and bowing, came Rothschild.

"I was looking for you, uncle," he said. "Moses Ilyich sends his compliments, and asks you to come across to him at once."

Yakov felt inclined to cry.

"Begone!" he shouted, and continued his path.

"You can't mean that," cried Rothschild in alarm, running after him. "Moses Ilyich will take offense! He wants you at once."

The way in which the Jew puffed and blinked, and the multitude of his red freckles awoke in Yakov disgust. He felt disgust, too, for his green frock-coat, with its black patches, and his whole fragile, delicate figure.

Anton Chekhov

"What do you mean by coming after me, garlic?" he shouted. "Keep off!"

The Jew also grew angry, and cried:

"If you don't take care to be a little politer I will send you flying over the fence."

"Out of my sight!" roared Yakov, rushing on him with clenched fists. "Out of my sight, abortion, or I will beat the soul out of your cursed body! I have no peace with Jews."

Rothschild was frozen with terror; he squatted down and waved his arms above his head, as if warding off blows, and then jumped up and ran for his life. While running he hopped, and flourished his hands; and the twitching of his long, flesh-less spine could plainly be seen. The boys in the street were delighted with the incident, and rushed after him, crying, "Jew! Jew!" The dogs pursued him with loud barks. Someone laughed, then someone whistled, and the dogs barked louder and louder. Then, it must have been, a dog bit Rothschild, for there rang out a sickly, despairing cry.

Yakov walked past the common, and then along the outskirts of the town; and the street boys cried, "Bronza! Bronza!" With a piping note snipe flew around him, and ducks quacked. The sun baked everything, and from the wa-ter came scintillations so bright that it was painful to look at. Yakov walked along the path by the side of the river, and watched a stout, red-cheeked lady come out of the bathing-place. Not far from the bathing-place sat a group of boys catching crabs with meat; and seeing him they cried mali-ciously, "Bronza! Bronza!" And at this moment before him rose a thick old willow with an immense hollow in it, and on it a raven's nest. . . . And suddenly in Yakov's mind awoke the memory of the child with the yellow hair of whom Marfa had spoken. . . . Yes, it was the same willow, green, silent, sad. . . . How it had aged, poor thing!

He sat underneath it, and began to remember. On the other bank, where was now a flooded meadow, there then

182

stood a great birch forest, and farther away, where the now bare hill glimmered on the horizon, was an old pine wood. Up and down the river went barges. But now everything was flat and smooth; on the opposite bank stood only a single birch, young and shapely, like a girl; and on the river were only ducks and geese where once had floated barges. It seemed that since those days even the geese had become smaller. Yakov closed his eyes, and in imagination saw flying towards him an immense flock of white geese.

He began to wonder how it was that in the last forty or fifty years of his life he had never been near the river, or if he had, had never noticed it. Yet it was a respectable river, and by no means contemptible; it would have been possible to fish in it, and the fish might have been sold to tradesmen, officials, and the attendant at the railway station buffet, and the money could have been lodged in the bank; he might have used it for rowing from country-house to country-house and playing on the fiddle, and everyone would have paid him money; he might even have tried to act as bargee —it would have been better than making coffins; he might have kept geese, killed them and sent them to Moscow in the wintertime—from the feathers alone he would have made as much as ten rubles a year. But he had yawned away his life, and done nothing. What losses! Akh, what losses! and if he had done all together—caught fish, played on the fiddle, acted as bargee, and kept geese—what a sum he would have amassed! But he had never even dreamed of this; life had passed without profits, without any satisfaction; everything had passed away unnoticed; before him nothing remained. But look backward—nothing but losses, such losses that to think of them it makes the blood run cold. And why cannot a man live without these losses? Why had the birchwood and the pine forest both been cut down? Why is the common pasture unused? Why do people do exactly what they ought not to do? Why did he all his life scream, roar, clench his fists, insult his wife? For what imaginable purpose did he frighten and insult the Jew? Why, indeed, do people prevent one another living in peace? All these are also losses! Terrible losses! If it were not for hatred and malice people would draw from one another incalculable profits.

Evening and night, twinkled in Yakov's brain the willow, the fish, the dead geese, Marfa with her profile like that of a bird about to drink, the pale, pitiable face of Rothschild, and an army of snouts thrusting themselves out of the darkness and muttering about losses. He shifted from side to side, and five times in the night rose from his bed and played on the fiddle.

In the morning he rose with an effort and went to the hospital. The same Maksim Nikolaïch ordered him to bind his head with a cold compress, and gave him powders; and by the expression of his face, and by his tone Yakov saw that it was a bad business, and that no powders would make it any better. But upon his way home he reflected that from death at least there would be one profit; it would no longer be necessary to eat, to drink, to pay taxes, or to injure others; and as a man lies in his grave not one year, but hundreds and thousands of years, the profit was enormous. The life of man was, in short, a loss, and only his death a profit. Yet this consideration, though entirely just, was offensive and bitter; for why in this world is it so ordered that life, which is given to a man only once, passes by without profit?

He did not regret dying, but as soon as he arrived home and saw his fiddle, his heart fell, and he felt sorry. The fiddle could not be taken to the grave; it must remain an orphan, and the same thing would happen with it as had happened with the birchwood and the pine forest. Everything in this world decayed, and would decay! Yakov went to the door of the hut and sat upon the threshold stone, pressing his fiddle to his shoulder. Still thinking of life, full of decay and full of losses, he began to play, and as the tune poured out plaintively and touchingly, the tears flowed down his cheeks. And the harder he thought, the sadder was the song of the fiddle.

The latch creaked twice, and in the wicket door appeared Rothschild. The first half of the yard he crossed boldly, but seeing Yakov, he stopped short, shriveled up, and apparently from fright began to make signs as if he wished to tell the time with his fingers.

"Come on, don't be afraid," said Yakov kindly, beckoning him. "Come!"

With a look of distrust and terror Rothschild drew near and stopped about two yards away.

"Don't beat me, Yakov, it is not my fault!" he said, with a bow. "Moses Ilyich has sent me again. 'Don't be afraid!' he said, 'go to Yakov again and tell him that without him we cannot possibly get on.' The wedding is on Wednesday. Shapovalov's daughter is marrying a wealthy man. . . . It will be a first-class wedding," added the Jew, blinking one eye.

"I cannot go," answered Yakov, breathing heavily. "I am ill, brother."

And again he took his bow, and the tears burst from his eyes and fell upon the fiddle. Rothschild listened attentively, standing by his side with arms folded upon his chest. The distrustful, terrified expression upon his face little by little changed into a look of suffering and grief, he rolled his eyes as if in ecstasy of torment, and ejaculated "Wachchch!" And the tears slowly rolled down his cheeks and made little black patches on his green frock-coat.

All day long Yakov lay in bed and worried. With evening came the priest, and, confessing him, asked whether he had any particular sin which he would like to confess; and Yakov exerted his fading memory, and remembering Marfa's unhappy face, and the Jew's despairing cry when he was bitten by the dog, said in a hardly audible voice:

"Give the fiddle to Rothschild."

And now in the town everyone asks: Where did Rothschild

Anton Chekhov

get such an excellent fiddle? Did he buy it or steal it . . . or did he get it in pledge? Long ago he abandoned his flute, and now plays on the fiddle only. From beneath his bow issue the same mournful sounds as formerly came from the flute; but when he tries to repeat the tune that Yakov played when he sat on the threshold stone, the fiddle emits sounds so passionately sad and full of grief that the listeners weep; and he himself rolls his eyes and ejaculates "Wachchch!". . . But this new song so pleases everyone in the town that wealthy traders and officials never fail to engage Rothschild for their social gatherings, and even force him to play it as many as ten times.

THE BROTHERS GRIMM

CAT AND MOUSE IN PARTNERSHIP

A CERTAIN cat had made the acquaintance of a mouse, and had said so much to her about the great love and friendship she felt for her, that at length the mouse agreed that they should live and keep house together. "But we must make a provision for winter, or else we shall suffer from hunger," said the cat; "and you, little mouse, cannot venture everywhere, or you will be caught in a trap some day." The good advice was followed, and a pot of fat was bought, but they did not know where to put it. At length, after much consideration, the cat said: "I know no place where it will be better stored up than in the church, for no one dares take anything away from there. We will set it beneath the altar, and not touch it until we are really in need of it." So the pot was placed in safety, but it was not long until the cat had a great yearning for it, and said to the mouse: "I want to tell you something, little mouse; my cousin has brought a little son into the world, and has asked me to be godmother; he is white with brown spots, and I am to hold him over the font at the christening. Let me go out today, and you look after the house by yourself." "Yes, yes," answered the mouse, "by all means go, and if you get anything very good to eat, think of me, I should like a drop of sweet red christening wine myself." All this, however, was untrue; the cat had no cousin, and had not been asked to be godmother. She went straight to the church, stole to the pot of fat, began to lick at it, and licked the top of the fat off. Then she took a walk upon the roofs of the town, looked out for opportunities, and then stretched herself in the sun, and licked her lips whenever she thought of the pot of fat, and not until it was evening did she return home. "Well, here you are again," said the mouse, "no doubt you have had a merry day." "All went off well," answered the cat. "What name did they give the child?" "Top-off!" said the cat quite coolly. "Top-off!" cried the mouse, "that is a very odd and uncommon name, is it a usual one in your family?" "What does that matter," said the cat, "it is no worse than Crumb-stealer, as your godchildren are called."

Before long the cat was seized by another fit of yearning. She said to the mouse: "You must do me a favor, and once more manage the house for a day alone. I am again asked to be godmother, and as the child has a white ring round its neck, I cannot refuse." The good mouse consented, but the cat crept behind the town walls to the church, and devoured half the pot of fat. "Nothing ever seems quite so good as what one keeps to oneself," said she, and was quite satisfied with her day's work. When she went home the mouse inquired: "And what was this child christened?" "Half-done," answered the cat. "Half-done! What are you saying? I never heard the name in my life, I'll wager anything it is not in the calendar!"

The cat's mouth soon began to water for some more licking. "All good things go in threes," said she, "I am asked to stand godmother again. The child is quite black, only it has white paws, but with that exception, it has not a single white hair on its whole body; this only happens once every few years, you will let me go, won't you?" "Top-off! Half-done!" answered the mouse, "they are such odd names, they make me very thoughtful." "You sit at home," said the cat, "in your dark-gray fur coat and long tail, and are filled with fancies, that's because you do not go out in the daytime." During the cat's absence the mouse cleaned the house, and put it in order, but the greedy cat entirely emptied the pot of fat. "When everything is eaten up one has some peace," said she to herself, and well filled and fat she did not return home till night. The mouse at once asked what name had been given to the third child. "It will not please you more than the others," said the cat. "He is called All-gone." "All-gone!" cried the mouse, "that is the most suspicious name of all! I have never seen it in print. All-gone; what can that mean?" and she shook her head, curled herself up, and lay down to sleep.

From this time forth no one invited the cat to be godmother, but when the winter had come and there was no longer anything to be found outside, the mouse thought of their provision, and said: "Come, cat, we will go to our pot of fat which we have stored up for ourselves—we shall enjoy that." "Yes," answered the cat, "you will enjoy it as much as you would enjoy sticking that dainty tongue of yours out of the window." They set out on their way, but when they arrived, the pot of fat certainly was still in its place, but it was empty. "Alas!" said the mouse, "now I see what has happened, now it comes to light! You a true friend! You have devoured all when you were standing godmother. First top-off, then half-done, then—" "Will you hold your tongue," cried the cat, "one word more, and I will eat you too." "All-gone" was already on the poor mouse's lips; scarcely had she spoken it before the cat sprang on her, seized her, and swallowed her down. Verily, that is the way of the world.

E. M. FORSTER

THE STORY OF THE SIREN

FEW THINGS have been more beautiful than my notebook on the Deist Controversy as it fell downward through the waters of the Mediterranean. It dived, like a piece of black slate, but opened soon, disclosing leaves of pale green, which quivered into blue. Now it had vanished, now it was a piece of magical india-rubber stretching out to infinity, now it was a book again, but bigger than the book of all knowledge. It grew more fantastic as it reached the bottom, where a puff of sand welcomed it and obscured it from view. But it reappeared, quite sane though a little tremulous, lying decently open on its back, while unseen fingers fidgeted among its leaves.

"It is such pity," said my aunt, "that you will not finish your work in the hotel. Then you would be free to enjoy yourself and this would never have happened."

"Nothing of it but will change into something rich and strange," warbled the chaplain, while his sister said, "Why, it's gone in the water!" As for the boatmen, one of them laughed, while the other, without a word of warning, stood up and began to take his clothes off.

"Holy Moses," cried the Colonel. "Is the fellow mad?"

"Yes, thank him, dear," said my aunt: "that is to say, tell him he is very kind, but perhaps another time."

"All the same I do want my book back," I complained. "It's for my Fellowship Dissertation. There won't be much left of it by another time."

"I have an idea," said some woman or other through her

parasol. "Let us leave this child of nature to dive for the book while we go on to the other grotto. We can land him either on this rock or on the ledge inside, and he will be ready when we return."

The idea seemed good; and I improved it by saying I would be left behind too, to lighten the boat. So the two of us were deposited outside the little grotto on a great sunlit rock that guarded the harmonies within. Let us call them blue, though they suggest rather the spirit of what is clean—cleanliness passed from the domestic to the sublime, the cleanliness of all the sea gathered together and radiating light. The Blue Grotto at Capri contains only more blue water, not bluer water. That color and that spirit are the heritage of every cave in the Mediterranean into which the sun can shine and the sea flow.

As soon as the boat left I realized how imprudent I had been to trust myself on a sloping rock with an unknown Sicilian. With a jerk he became alive, seizing my arm and saying, "Go to the end of the grotto, and I will show you something beautiful."

He made me jump off the rock on to the ledge over a dazzling crack of sea; he drew me away from the light till I was standing on the tiny beach of sand which emerged like powdered turquoise at the farther end. There he left me with his clothes, and returned swiftly to the summit of the entrance rock. For a moment he stood naked in the brilliant sun, looking down at the spot where the book lay. Then he crossed himself, raised his hands above his head, and dived.

If the book was wonderful, the man is past all description. His effect was that of a silver statue, alive beneath the sea, through whom life throbbed in blue and green. Something infinitely happy, infinitely wise—but it was impossible that it should emerge from the depths sunburned and dripping, holding the notebook on the Deist Controversy between its teeth.

A gratuity is generally expected by those who bathe. Whatever I offered, he was sure to want more, and I was disinclined for an argument in a place so beautiful and also so solitary. It was a relief that he should say in conversational tones, "In a place like this one might see the Siren."

I was delighted with him for thus falling into the key of his surroundings. We had been left together in a magic world, apart from all the commonplaces that are called reality, a world of blue whose floor was the sea and whose walls and roof of rock trembled with the sea's reflections. Here only the fantastic would be tolerable, and it was in that spirit I echoed his words, "One might easily see the Siren."

He watched me curiously while he dressed. I was parting the sticky leaves of the notebook as I sat on the sand.

"Ah," he said at last. "You may have read the little book that was printed last year. Who would have thought that our Siren would have given the foreigners pleasure!"

(I read it afterwards. Its account is, not unnaturally, incomplete, in spite of there being a woodcut of the young person, and the words of her song.)

"She comes out of this blue water, doesn't she," I suggested, "and sits on the rock at the entrance, combing her hair."

I wanted to draw him out, for I was interested in his sudden gravity, and there was a suggestion of irony in his last remark that puzzled me.

"Have you ever seen her?" he asked.

"Often and often."

"I, never."

"But you have heard her sing?"

He put on his coat and said impatiently, "How can she sing under the water? Who could? She sometimes tries, but nothing comes from her but great bubbles."

"She should climb on to the rock."

"How can she?" he cried again, quite angry. "The priests have blessed the air, so she cannot breathe it, and blessed the rocks, so that she cannot sit on them. But the sea no man can bless, because it is too big, and always changing. So she lives in the sea."

I was silent.

At this his face took a gentler expression. He looked at me as though something was on his mind, and going out to the entrance rock gazed at the external blue. Then returning into our twilight he said, "As a rule only good people see the Siren."

I made no comment. There was a pause, and he continued. "That is a very strange thing, and the priests do not know how to account for it; for she of course is wicked. Not only those who fast and go to Mass are in danger, but even those who are merely good in daily life. No one in the village had seen her for two generations. I am not surprised. We all cross ourselves before we enter the water, but it is unnecessary. Giuseppe, we thought, was safer than most. We loved him, and many of us he loved: but that is a different thing from being good."

I asked who Giuseppe was.

"That day—I was seventeen and my brother was twenty and a great deal stronger than I was, and it was the year when the visitors, who have brought such prosperity and so many alterations into the village, first began to come. One English lady in particular, of very high birth, came, and has written a book about the place, and it was through her that the Improvement Syndicate was formed, which is about to connect the hotels with the station by a funicular railway."

"Don't tell me about that lady in here," I observed.

"That day we took her and her friends to see the grottoes. As we rowed close under the cliffs I put out my hand, as one does, and caught a little crab, and having pulled off its claws offered it as a curiosity. The ladies groaned, but a gentleman was pleased, and held out money. Being inexperienced, I refused it, saying that his pleasure was sufficient reward! Giuseppe, who was rowing behind, was very angry with me and reached out with his hand and hit me on the side of the mouth, so that a tooth cut my lip, and I bled. I tried to hit him back, but he always was too quick for me, and as I stretched round he kicked me under the armpit, so that for a moment I could not even row. There was a great noise among the ladies, and I heard afterward that they were planning to take me away from my brother and train me as a waiter. That, at all events, never came to pass.

"When we reached the grotto—not here, but a larger one— the gentleman was very anxious that one of us should dive for money, and the ladies consented, as they sometimes do. Giuseppe, who had discovered how much pleasure it gives foreigners to see us in the water, refused to dive for anything but silver, and the gentleman threw in a two-lira piece.

"Just before my brother sprang off he caught sight of me holding my bruise, and crying, for I could not help it. He laughed and said, 'This time, at all events, I shall not see the Siren!' and went into the water without crossing himself. But he saw her."

He broke off and accepted a cigarette. I watched the golden entrance rock and the quivering walls and the magic water through which great bubbles constantly rose.

At last he dropped his hot ash into the ripples and turned his head away, and said, "He came up without the coin. We pulled him into the boat, and he was so large that he seemed to fill it, and so wet that we could not dress him. I have never seen a man so wet. I and the gentleman rowed back, and we covered Giuseppe with sacking and propped him up in the stern."

"He was drowned, then?" I murmured, supposing that to be the point.

"He was not," he cried angrily. "He saw the Siren. I told you."

I was silenced again.

"We put him to bed, though he was not ill. The doctor came, and took money, and the priest came and spattered him with holy water. But it was no good. He was too big—like a piece of the sea. He kissed the thumb-bones of San Biagio and they never dried till evening."

"What did he look like?" I ventured.

"Like any one who has seen the Siren. If you have seen her 'often and often' how is it you do not know? Unhappy, unhappy because he knew everything. Every living thing made him unhappy because he knew it would die. And all he cared to do was sleep."

I bent over my notebook.

"He did no work, he forgot to eat, he forgot whether he had his clothes on. All the work fell on me, and my sister had to go out to service. We tried to make him into a beggar, but he was too robust to inspire pity, and as for an idiot, he had not the right look in his eyes. He would stand in the street looking at people, and the more he looked at them the more unhappy he became. When a child was born he would cover his face with his hands. If any one was married—he was terrible then, and would frighten them as they came out of church. Who would have believed he would marry himself! I caused that, I. I was reading out of the paper how a girl at Ragusa had 'gone mad through bathing in the sea.' Giuseppe got up, and in a week he and that girl came in.

"He never told me anything, but it seems that he went straight to her house, broke into her room, and carried her off. She was the daughter of a rich mineowner, so you may imagine our peril. Her father came down, with a clever lawyer, but they could do no more than I. They argued and they threatened, but at last they had to go back and we lost nothing—that is to say, no money. We took Giuseppe and Maria to the church and had them married. Ugh! that wedding! The priest made no jokes afterward, and coming out the children threw stones. . . . I think I would have died to make her happy; but as always happens, one could do nothing."

"Were they unhappy together then?"

"They loved each other, but love is not happiness. We can all get love. Love is nothing. I had two people to work for now, for she was like him in everything—one never knew which of them was speaking. I had to sell our own boat and work under the bad old man you have today. Worst of all, people began to hate us. The children first—everything begins with them—and then the women and last of all the men. For the cause of every misfortune was—You will not betray me?"

I promised good faith, and immediately he burst into the frantic blasphemy of one who has escaped from supervision, cursing the priests, who had ruined his life, he said. "Thus are we tricked!" was his cry, and he stood up and kicked at the azure ripples with his feet, till he had obscured them with a cloud of sand.

I too was moved. The story of Giuseppe, for all its absurdity and superstition, came nearer to reality than anything I had known before. I don't know why, but it filled me with desire to help others—the greatest of all our desires, I suppose, and the most fruitless. The desire soon passed.

"She was about to have a child. That was the end of everything. People said to me, 'When will your charming nephew be born? What a cheerful, attractive child he will be, with such a father and mother!' I kept my face steady and replied, 'I think he may be. Out of sadness shall come gladness'—it is one of our proverbs. And my answer frightened them very much, and they told the priests, who were frightened too. Then the whisper started that the child would be Antichrist. You need not be afraid: he was never born.

"An old witch began to prophesy, and no one stopped her. Giuseppe and the girl, she said, had silent devils, who could do little harm. But the child would always be speaking and laughing and perverting, and last of all he would go into the sea and fetch up the Siren into the air and all the world would see her and hear her sing. As soon as she sang, the Seven Vials would be opened and the Pope would die and Mongibello flame, and the veil of Santa Agata would be burned. Then the boy and the Siren would marry, and together they would rule the world, for ever and ever.

"The whole village was in tumult, and the hotel-keepers became alarmed, for the tourist season was just beginning. They met together and decided that Giuseppe and the girl must be sent inland until the child was born, and they subscribed the money. The night before they were to start there was a full moon and wind from the east, and all along the coast the sea shot up over the cliffs in silver clouds. It is a wonderful sight, and Maria said she must see it once more.

" 'Do not go,' I said. 'I saw the priest go by, and some one with him. And the hotel-keepers do not like you to be seen, and if we displease them also we shall starve.'

" 'I want to go,' she replied. 'The sea is stormy, and I may never feel it again.'

" 'No, he is right,' said Giuseppe. 'Do not go—or let one of us go with you.'

" 'I want to go alone,' she said; and she went alone.

"I tied up their luggage in a piece of cloth, and then I was so unhappy at thinking I should lose them that I went and sat down by my brother and put my arm round his neck, and he put his arm round me, which he had not done for more than a year, and we remained thus I don't remember how long.

"Suddenly the door flew open and moonlight and wind came in together, and a child's voice said laughing, 'They have pushed her over the cliffs into the sea.'

"I stepped to the drawer where I keep my knives.

" 'Sit down again,' said Giuseppe—Giuseppe of all people! 'If she is dead, why should others die too?'

" 'I guess who it is,' I cried, 'and I will kill him.'

"I was almost out of the door, and he tripped me up and, kneeling upon me, took hold of both my hands and sprained my wrists; first my right one, then my left. No one but

Giuseppe would have thought of such a thing. It hurt more than you would suppose, and I fainted. When I woke up, he was gone, and I never saw him again."

But Giuseppe disgusted me.

"I told you he was wicked," he said. "No one would have expected him to see the Siren."

"How do you know he did see her?"

"Because he did not see her 'often and often,' but once."

"Why do you love him if he is wicked?"

He laughed for the first time. That was his only reply.

"Is that the end?" I asked.

"I never killed her murderer, for by the time my wrists were well he was in America; and one cannot kill a priest. As for Giuseppe, he went all over the world too, looking for some one else who had seen the Siren—either a man, or, better still, a woman, for then the child might still have been born. At last he came to Liverpool—is the district probable? —and there he began to cough, and spat blood until he died.

"I do not suppose there is any one living now who has seen her. There has seldom been more than one in a generation, and never in my life will there be both a man and a woman from whom that child can be born, who will fetch up the Siren from the sea, and destroy silence, and save the world!"

"Save the world?" I cried. "Did the prophecy end like that?"

He leaned back against the rock, breathing deep. Through all the blue-green reflections I saw him color. I heard him say: "Silence and loneliness cannot last for ever. It may be a hundred or a thousand years, but the sea lasts longer, and she shall come out of it and sing." I would have asked him more, but at that moment the whole cave darkened, and there rode in through its narrow entrance the returning boat.

THE BOOK OF JONAH

Now the word of the Lord came unto Jonah the son of Amittai, saying, "Arise, go to Nineveh, that great city, and cry against it; for their wickedness is come up before me." But Jonah rose up to flee unto Tarshish from the presence of the Lord, and went down to Joppa; and he found a ship going to Tarshish: so he paid the fare thereof, and went down into it, to go with them unto Tarshish from the presence of the Lord.

But the Lord sent out a great wind into the sea, and there was a mighty tempest in the sea, so that the ship was like to be broken. Then the mariners were afraid, and cried every man unto his god, and cast forth the wares that were in the ship into the sea, to lighten it of them. But Jonah was gone down into the sides of the ship; and he lay, and was fast asleep. So the shipmaster came to him, and said unto him, "What meanest thou, O sleeper? arise, call upon thy God, if so be that God will think upon us, that we perish not." And they said every one to his fellow, "Come, and let us cast lots, that we may know for whose cause this evil is upon us." So they cast lots, and the lot fell upon Jonah. Then they said unto him, "Tell us, we pray thee, for whose cause this evil is upon us; What is thine occupation? and whence comest thou? what is thy country? and of what people art thou?" And he said unto them, "I am an Hebrew; and I fear the Lord, the God of heaven, which hath made the sea and the dry land." Then were the men exceedingly afraid, and said unto him, "Why hast thou done this?" For the men knew that he fled from the presence of the Lord, because he had told them.

Then said they unto him, "What shall we do unto thee, that the sea may be calm unto us?" for the sea wrought, and was tempestuous. And he said unto them, "Take me up, and cast me forth into the sea; so shall the sea be calm unto you: for I know that for my sake this great tempest is upon you." Nevertheless the men rowed hard to bring it to the land; but they could not, for the sea wrought, and was tempestuous against them. Wherefore they cried unto the Lord, and said, "We beseech thee, O Lord, we beseech thee, let us not perish for this man's life, and lay not upon us innocent blood: for thou, O Lord, hast done as it pleased thee." So they took up Jonah, and cast him forth into the sea: and the sea ceased from her raging. Then the men feared the Lord exceedingly, and offered a sacrifice unto the Lord, and made vows.

Now the Lord had prepared a great fish to swallow up Jonah. And Jonah was in the belly of the fish three days and three nights. Then Jonah prayed unto the Lord his God out of the fish's belly, and said, "I cried by reason of mine affliction unto the Lord, and he heard me; out of the belly of hell cried I, and thou heardest my voice. For thou hadst cast me into the deep, in the midst of the seas; and the floods compassed me about: all thy billows and thy waves passed over me. Then I said, 'I am cast out of thy sight'; yet I will look again toward thy holy temple. The waters compassed me about, even to the soul: the depth closed me round about, the weeds were wrapped about my head. I went down to the bottoms of the mountains; the earth with her bars was about me for ever: yet hast thou brought up my life from corruption, O Lord my God. When my soul fainted within me I remembered the Lord: and my prayer came in unto thee, into thine holy temple. They that observe lying vanities forsake their own mercy. But I will sacrifice unto thee with the voice of thanksgiving; I will pay that that I have vowed. Salvation is of the Lord."

And the Lord spake unto the fish, and it vomited out Jonah upon the dry land. And the word of the Lord came unto Jonah the second time, saying, "Arise, go unto Nineveh, that great city, and preach unto it the preaching that I bid thee." So Jonah arose, and went unto Nineveh, according to the word of the Lord. Now Nineveh was an exceeding great city of three days' journey. And Jonah began to enter into the city a day's journey, and he cried, and said, "Yet forty days, and Nineveh shall be overthrown."

So the people of Nineveh believed God, and proclaimed a fast, and put on sackcloth, from the greatest of them even to the least of them. For word came unto the king of Nineveh, and he arose from his throne, and he laid his robe from him, and covered him with sackcloth, and sat in ashes. And he caused it to be proclaimed and published throughout Nineveh by the decree of the king and his nobles, saying, "Let neither man nor beast, herd nor flock, taste any thing: let them not feed nor drink water: but let man and beast be covered with sackcloth, and cry mightily unto God: yea, let them turn every one from his evil way, and from the violence that is in their hands. Who can tell if God will turn and repent, and turn away from his fierce anger, that we perish not?"

And God saw their works, that they turned from their evil way; and God repented of the evil, that he had said that he would do unto them; and he did it not. But it displeased Jonah exceedingly, and he was very angry. And he prayed unto the Lord, and said, "I pray thee, O Lord, was not this my saying, when I was yet in my country? Therefore I fled before unto Tarshish: for I knew that thou art a gracious God, and merciful, slow to anger, and of great kindness, and repentest thee of the evil. Therefore now, O Lord, take, I beseech thee, my life from me; for it is better for me to die than to live." Then said the Lord, "Doest thou well to be angry?"

So Jonah went out of the city, and sat on the east side of the city, and there made him a booth, and sat under it in the shadow, till he might see what would become of the city. And the Lord God prepared a gourd, and made it to come up over Jonah, that it might be a shadow over his head, to deliver him from his grief. So Jonah was exceeding glad of the gourd. But God prepared a worm when the morning rose the next day, and it smote the gourd that it withered. And it came to pass, when the sun did arise, that God prepared a vehement east wind; and the sun beat upon the head of Jonah that he fainted, and wished in himself to die, and said, "It is better for me to die than to live." And God said to Jonah, "Doest thou well to be angry for the gourd?" And he said, "I do well to be angry, even unto death." Then said the Lord, "Thou hast had pity on the gourd, for the which thou hast not labored, neither madest it grow; which came up in the night, and perished in a night: and should not I spare Nineveh, that great city, wherein are more than sixscore thousand persons that cannot discern between their right hand and their left hand; and also much cattle?"

FRANZ KAFKA

THE BUCKET-RIDER

COAL ALL spent; the bucket empty; the shovel useless; the stove breathing out cold; the room freezing; the leaves outside the window rigid, covered with rime; the sky a silver shield against anyone who looks for help from it. I must have coal; I cannot freeze to death; behind me is the pitiless stove, before me the pitiless sky, so I must ride out between them and on my journey seek aid from the coal-dealer. But he has already grown deaf to ordinary appeals; I must prove irrefutably to him that I have not a single grain of coal left, and that he means to me the very sun in the firmament. I must approach like a beggar who, with the death-rattle already in his throat, insists on dying on the doorstep, and to whom the grand people's cook accordingly decides to give the dregs of the coffee-pot; just so must the coal-dealer, filled with rage, but acknowledging the command, "Thou shalt not kill," fling a shovelful of coal into my bucket.

My mode of arrival must decide the matter; so I ride off on the bucket. Seated on the bucket, my hands on the handle, the simplest kind of bridle, I propel myself with difficulty down the stairs; but once down below my bucket ascends, superbly, superbly; camels humbly squatting on the ground do not rise with more dignity, shaking themselves under the sticks of their drivers. Through the hard frozen streets we go at a regular canter; often I am upraised as high as the first story of a house; never do I sink as low as the house doors. And at last I float at an extraordinary height above the vaulted cellar of the dealer, whom I see far below crouching over his table, where he is writing; he has opened the door to let out the excessive heat.

"Coal-dealer!" I cry in a voice burned hollow by the frost and muffled in the cloud made by my breath, "please, coal-dealer, give me a little coal. My bucket is so light that I can ride on it. Be kind. When I can I'll pay you."

The dealer puts his hand to his ear. "Do I hear rightly?" He throws the question over his shoulder to his wife. "Do I hear rightly? A customer."

"I hear nothing," says his wife, breathing in and out peacefully while she knits on, her back pleasantly warmed by the heat.

"Oh, yes, you must hear," I cry. "It's me; an old customer; faithful and true; only without means at the moment."

"Wife," says the dealer, "it's some one, it must be; my ears can't have deceived me so much as that; it must be an old, a very old customer, that can move me so deeply."

"What ails you, man?" says his wife, ceasing from her work for a moment and pressing her knitting to her bosom. "It's nobody, the street is empty, all our customers are provided for; we could close down the shop for several days and take a rest."

"But I'm sitting up here on the bucket," I cry, and unfeeling frozen tears dim my eyes, "please look up here, just once; you'll see me directly; I beg you, just a shovelful; and if you give me more it'll make me so happy that I won't know what to do. All the other customers are provided for. Oh, if I could only hear the coal clattering into the bucket!"

"I'm coming," says the coal-dealer, and on his short legs he makes to climb the steps of the cellar, but his wife is already beside him, holds him back by the arm and says: "You stay here; seeing you persist in your fancies I'll go myself. Think of the bad fit of coughing you had during the night. But for a piece of business, even if it's one you've only fancied in your head, you're prepared to forget your wife and child and sacrifice your lungs. I'll go."

"Then be sure to tell him all the kinds of coal we have in stock; I'll shout out the prices after you."

"Right," says his wife, climbing up to the street. Naturally she sees me at once. "Frau Coal-dealer," I cry, "my humblest greetings; just one shovelful of coal; here in my bucket; I'll carry it home myself. One shovelful of the worst you have. I'll pay you in full for it, of course, but not just now, not just now." What a knell-like sound the words "not just now" have, and how bewilderingly they mingle with the evening chimes that fall from the church steeple nearby!

"Well, what does he want?" shouts the dealer. "Nothing," his wife shouts back, "there's nothing here; I see nothing, I hear nothing; only six striking, and now we must shut up the shop. The cold is terrible; tomorrow we'll likely have lots to do again."

She sees nothing and hears nothing; but all the same she loosens her apron-strings and waves her apron to waft me away. She succeeds, unluckily. My bucket has all the virtues of a good steed except powers of resistance, which it has not; it is too light; a woman's apron can make it fly through the air.

"You bad woman!" I shout back, while she, turning into the shop, half-contemptuous, half-reassured, flourishes her fist in the air. "You bad woman! I begged you for a shovelful of the worst coal and you would not give me it." And with that I ascend into the regions of the ice mountains and am lost forever.

Translated by Willa and Edwin Muir

SAINT-SIMON

THE DEATH OF
MONSEIGNEUR*

ON SATURDAY, the 11th of the month, and the day before
Quasimodo, I had been walking all the morning, and I had
entered all alone into my cabinet a little before dinner, when
a courier sent by Madame de Saint-Simon, gave me a letter
from her, in which I was informed that Monseigneur was ill.

I learned afterward that this Prince, while on his way
to Meudon for the Easter *fêtes*, met at Chaville a priest, who
was carrying Our Lord to a sick person. Monseigneur, and
Madame de Bourgogne, who was with him, knelt down to
adore the host, and then Monseigneur inquired what was the
malady of the patient. "The smallpox," he was told. That
disease was very prevalent just then. Monseigneur had had it,
but very lightly, and when young. He feared it very much,
and was struck with the answer he now received. In the
evening he said to Boudin, his chief doctor, "I should not
be surprised if I were to have the smallpox." The day, however, passed over as usual.

On the morrow, Thursday, the 9th, Monseigneur rose, and
meant to go out wolf hunting; but as he was dressing, such a
fit of weakness seized him, that he fell into his chair. Boudin
made him get into bed again; but all the day his pulse was in
an alarming state. The King, only half informed by Fagon of

---

*Monseigneur was the Dauphin, the son of Louis XIV. At his death his older son, the
Duc de Bourgogne, became heir to the throne.

what had taken place, believed there was nothing the matter, and went out walking at Marly after dinner, receiving news from time to time. Monseigneur le Duc de Bourgogne and Madame de Bourgogne dined at Meudon, and they would not quit Monseigneur for one moment. The Princess added to the strict duties of a daughter-in-law all that her gracefulness could suggest, and gave everything to Monseigneur with her own hand. Her heart could not have been troubled by what her reason foresaw; but, nevertheless, her care and attention were extreme, without any airs of affectation or acting. The Duc de Bourgogne, simple and holy as he was, and full of the idea of his duty, exaggerated his attention; and although there was a strong suspicion of the smallpox, neither quitted Monseigneur, except for the King's supper.

The next day, Friday, the 10th, in reply to his express demands, the King was informed of the extremely dangerous state of Monseigneur. He had said on the previous evening that he would go on the following morning to Meudon, and remain there during all the illness of Monseigneur whatever its nature might be. He was now as good as his word. Immediately after mass he set out for Meudon. Before doing so, he forbade his children, and all who had not had the smallpox, to go there, which was suggested by a motive of kindness. With Madame de Maintenon and a small suite, he had just taken up his abode in Meudon, when Madame de Saint-Simon sent me the letter of which I have just made mention.

I will continue to speak of myself with the same truthfulness I speak of others, and with as much exactness as possible. According to the terms on which I was with Monseigneur and his intimates, may be imagined the impression made upon me by this news. I felt that one way or other, well or ill, the malady of Monseigneur would soon terminate. I was quite at my ease at La Ferté. I resolved therefore to wait there until I received fresh particulars. I dispatched a courier to Madame de Saint-Simon, requesting her to send me another the next day, and I passed the rest of this day, in an ebb and flow of feelings; the man and the Christian struggling against the man and the courtier, and in the midst of a crowd of vague fancies catching glimpses of the future, painted in the most agreeable colors.

The courier I expected so impatiently arrived the next day, Sunday, after dinner. The smallpox had declared itself, I learned, and was going on as well as could be wished. I believed Monseigneur saved, and wished to remain at my own house; nevertheless I took advice, as I have done all my life, and with great regret set out the next morning. At La Queue, about six leagues from Versailles, I met a financier of the name of La Fontaine, whom I knew well. He was coming from Paris and Versailles, and came up to me as I changed horses. Monseigneur, he said, was going on admirably; and he added details which convinced me he was out of all danger. I arrived at Versailles, full of this opinion, which was confirmed by Madame de Saint-Simon and everybody I met, so that nobody any longer feared, except on account of the treacherous nature of this disease in a very fat man of fifty.

The King held his Council, and worked in the evening with his ministers as usual. He saw Monseigneur morning and evening, oftentimes in the afternoon, and always remained long by the bedside. On the Monday I arrived he had dined early, and had driven to Marly, where the Duchesse de Bourgogne joined him. He saw in passing on the outskirts of the garden of Versailles his grandchildren, who had come out to meet him, but he would not let them come near, and said "good day" from a distance. The Duchesse de Bourgogne had had the smallpox, but no trace was left.

The King only liked his own houses, and could not bear to be anywhere else. This was why his visits to Meudon were few and short, and only made from complaisance. Madame de Maintenon was still more out of her element there. Although her chamber was everywhere a sanctuary, where only ladies entitled to the most extreme familiarity entered, she always wanted another retreat near at hand entirely inaccessible except to the Duchesse de Bourgogne alone, and that only for a few instants at a time. Thus she had Saint Cyr for Versailles and for Marly; and at Marly also a particular retiring place; at Fontainebleau she had her town house. Seeing therefore that Monseigneur was getting on well, and that a long sojourn at Meudon would be necessary, the upholsterers of the King were ordered to furnish a house in the park which once belonged to the Chancellor le Tellier, but which Monseigneur had bought.

When I arrived at Versailles, I wrote to M. de Beauvilliers at Meudon praying him to apprise the King that I had returned on account of the illness of Monseigneur, and that I would have gone to see him, but that, never having had the smallpox, I was included in the prohibition. M. de Beauvilliers did as I asked, and sent word back to me that my return had been very well timed, and that the King still forbade me as well as Madame de Saint-Simon to go to Meudon. This fresh prohibition did not distress me in the least. I was informed of all that was passing there, and that satisfied me.

There were yet contrasts at Meudon worth noticing. Mademoiselle Choin never appeared while the King was with Monseigneur, but kept close in her loft. When the coast was clear she came out, and took up her position at the sick man's bedside. All sorts of compliments passed between her and Madame de Maintenon, yet the two ladies never met. The King asked Madame de Maintenon if she had seen Mademoiselle Choin, and upon learning that she had not, was but ill pleased. Therefore Madame de Maintenon sent excuses and apologies to Mademoiselle Choin, and hoped, she said, to see her soon,—strange compliments from one chamber to another under the same roof. They never saw each other afterward.

It should be observed, that Père Tellier was also incognito

at Meudon, and dwelt in a retired room from which he issued to see the King, but never approached the apartments of Monseigneur.

Versailles presented another scene. Monseigneur le Duc and Madame la Duchesse de Bourgogne held their Court openly there; and this Court resembled the first gleamings of the dawn. All the Court assembled there; all Paris also; and as discretion and precaution were never French virtues, all Meudon came as well. People were believed when they declared that they had not entered the apartments of Monseigneur that day, and consequently could not bring the infection. When the Prince and Princess rose, when they went to bed, when they dined and supped with the ladies,—all public conversations—all meals—all assemblies—were opportunities of paying court to them. The apartments could not contain the crowd. The characteristic features of the room were many. Couriers arrived every quarter of an hour, and reminded people of the illness of Monseigneur—he was going on as well as could be expected; confidence and hope were easily felt; but there was an extreme desire to please at the new Court. The young Prince and Princess exhibited majesty and gravity, mixed with gayety; obligingly received all, continually spoke to every one; the crowd wore an air of complaisance; reciprocal satisfaction showed in every face, the Duc and Duchesse de Berry were treated almost as nobody. Thus five days fled away in increasing thought of future events—in preparation to be ready for whatever might happen.

On Tuesday, the 14th of April, I went to see the Chancellor, and asked for information upon the state of Monseigneur. He assured me it was good, and repeated to me the words Fagon had spoken to him, "that things were going on according to their wishes, and beyond their hopes." The Chancellor appeared to me very confident, and I had faith in him, so much the more, because he was on an extremely good footing with Monseigneur. The Prince, indeed, had so much recovered, that the fish women came in a body the self-same day to congratulate him, as they did after his attack of indigestion. They threw themselves at the foot of his bed, which they kissed several times, and in their joy said they would go back to Paris and have a *Te Deum* sung. But Monseigneur, who was not insensible to these marks of popular affection, told them it was not yet time, thanked them, and gave them a dinner, and some money.

As I was going home, I saw the Duchesse d'Orléans walking on a terrace. She called to me; but I pretended not to notice her, because La Montauban was with her, and hastened home, my mind filled with this news, and withdrew to my cabinet. Almost immediately afterward Madame la Duchesse d'Orléans joined me there. We were bursting to speak to each other alone, upon a point on which our thoughts were alike. She had left Meudon not an hour before, and she had the same tale to tell as the Chancellor. Everybody was at ease there, she said; and then she extolled the care and capacities of the doctors, exaggerating their success; and, to speak frankly and to our shame, she and I lamented together to see Monseigneur, in spite of his age and his fat, escape from so dangerous an illness. She reflected seriously but wittily, that after an illness of this sort, apoplexy was not to be looked for; that an attack of indigestion was equally unlikely to arise, considering the care Monseigneur had taken not to over-gorge himself since his recent danger; and we concluded more than dolefully, that henceforth we must make up our minds that the Prince would live and reign for a long time. In a word, we let ourselves loose in this rare conversation, although not without an occasional scruple of conscience which disturbed it. Madame de Saint-Simon all-devoutly tried what she could to put a drag upon our tongues, but the drag broke, so to speak, and we continued our free discourse, which was humanly speaking very reasonable on our parts, but which we felt, nevertheless, was not according to religion. Thus two hours passed, seemingly very short. Madame d'Orléans went away, and I repaired with Madame de Saint-Simon to receive a numerous company.

While thus all was tranquillity at Versailles, and even at Meudon, everything had changed its aspect at the *château*. The King had seen Monseigneur several times during the day; but in his after-dinner visit he was so much struck with the extraordinary swelling of the face and of the head, that he shortened his stay, and on leaving the *château* shed tears. He was reassured as much as possible, and after the council he took a walk in the garden.

Nevertheless Monseigneur had already mistaken Madame la Princesse de Conti for some one else; and Boudin, the doctor, was alarmed. Monseigneur himself had been so from the first, and he admitted that, for a long time before being attacked, he had been very unwell, and so much on Good Friday, that he had been unable to read his prayer book at chapel.

Toward four o'clock he grew worse, so much so that Boudin proposed to Fagon to call in other doctors, more familiar with the disease than they were. But Fagon flew into a rage at this, and would call in nobody. He declared that it would be better to act for themselves, and to keep Monseigneur's state secret, although it was hourly growing worse, and toward seven o'clock was perceived by several valets and courtiers. But nobody dared to open his mouth before Fagon, and the King was actually allowed to go to supper and to finish it without interruption, believing on the faith of Fagon that Monseigneur was going on well.

While the King supped thus tranquilly, all those who were in the sick chamber began to lose their wits. Fagon and the others poured down physic on physic, without leaving time for any to work. The *curé*, who was accustomed to go and learn the news every evening, found, against all custom, the doors thrown wide open, and the valets in confusion. He entered the chamber, and perceiving what was the matter, ran to the bedside, took the hand of Monseigneur, spoke to him of God, and seeing him full of consciousness, but scarcely able to speak, drew from him a sort of confession, of which nobody had hitherto thought, and suggested some acts of contrition. The poor Prince repeated distinctly several words suggested to him, and confusedly answered others, struck his breast, squeezed the *curé*'s hand, appeared penetrated with the best sentiments, and received with a contrite and willing air the absolution of the *curé*.

As the King rose from the supper table, he well nigh fell backward when Fagon, coming forward, cried in great trouble that all was lost. It may be imagined what terror seized all the company at this abrupt passage from perfect security to hopeless despair. The King, scarcely master of himself, at once began to go toward the apartment of Monseigneur, and repelled very stiffly the indiscreet eagerness of some courtiers who wished to prevent him, saying that he would see his son again, and be quite certain that nothing could be done. As he was about to enter the chamber, Madame la Princesse de Conti presented herself before him, and prevented him from going in. She pushed him back with her hands, and said that henceforth he had only to think of himself. Then the King, nearly fainting from a shock so complete and so sudden, fell upon a sofa that stood near. He asked unceasingly for news of all who passed, but scarce anybody dared to reply to him. He had sent for Père Tellier who went into Monseigneur's room; but it was no longer time. It is true the Jesuit, perhaps to console the King, said that he gave him a well-founded absolution. Madame de Maintenon hastened after the King, and sitting down beside him on the same sofa, tried to cry. She endeavored to lead away the King into the carriage already waiting for him in the courtyard, but he would not go, and sat thus outside the door until Monseigneur had expired.

The agony, without consciousness, of Monseigneur lasted

more than an hour after the King had come into the cabinet. Madame la Duchesse and Madame la Princesse de Conti divided their cares between the dying man and the King, to whom they constantly came back; while the faculty confounded, the valets bewildered, the courtiers hurrying and murmuring, hustled against each other, and moved unceasingly to and fro, backward and forward, in the same narrow space. At last the fatal moment arrived. Fagon came out, and allowed so much to be understood.

The King, much afflicted, and very grieved that Monseigneur's confession had been so tardily made, abused Fagon a little; and went away led by Madame de Maintenon and the two Princesses. He was somewhat struck by finding the vehicle of Monseigneur outside; and made a sign that he would have another coach, for that one made him suffer, and left the *château*. He was not, however, so much occupied with his grief that he could not call Pontchartrain to arrange the hour of the council of the next day. I will not comment on this coolness, and shall merely say it surprised extremely all present; and that if Pontchartrain had not said the council could be put off, no interruption to business would have taken place. The King got into his coach with difficulty, supported on both sides. Madame de Maintenon seated herself beside him. A crowd of officers of Monseigneur lined both sides of the court on their knees, as he passed out, crying to him with strange howlings to have compassion on them, for they had lost all, and must die of hunger.

While Meudon was filled with horror, all was tranquil at Versailles, without the least suspicion. We had supped. The company some time after had retired, and I was talking with Madame de Saint-Simon, who had nearly finished undressing herself to go to bed, when a servant of Madame la Duchesse de Berry, who had formerly belonged to us, entered, all terrified. He said that there must be some bad news from Meudon, since Monseigneur le Duc de Bourgogne had just whispered in the ear of M. le Duc de Berry, whose eyes had at once become red, that he left the table, and that all the company shortly after him rose with precipitation. So sudden a change rendered my surprise extreme. I ran in hot haste to Madame la Duchesse de Berry's. Nobody was there. Everybody had gone to Madame la Duchesse de Bourgogne. I followed on with all speed.

I found all Versailles assembled on arriving, all the ladies hastily dressed—the majority having been on the point of going to bed—all the doors open, and all in trouble. I learned that Monseigneur had received extreme unction, that he was without consciousness and beyond hope, and that the King had sent word to Madame de Bourgogne that he was going to Marly, and that she was to meet him as he passed through the avenue between the two stables.

The spectacle before me attracted all the attention I could bestow. The two Princes and the two Princesses were in the little cabinet behind the bed. The bed toilet was as usual in the chamber of the Duchesse de Bourgogne, which was filled with all the Court in confusion. She came and went from the cabinet to the chamber, waiting for the moment when she was to meet the King; and her demeanor, always distinguished by the same graces, was one of trouble and compassion, which the trouble and compassion of others induced them to take for grief. Now and then, in passing, she said a few rare words. All present were in truth expressive personages. Whoever had eyes, without any knowledge of the Court, could see the interests of all who were interested painted on their faces, and the indifference of the indifferent; these tranquil, the former penetrated with grief, or gravely attentive to themselves to hide their emancipation and their joy.

For my part, my first care was to inform myself thoroughly of the state of affairs, fearing lest there might be too much alarm for too trifling a cause; then, recovering myself, I reflected upon the misery common to all men, and that I myself should find myself some day at the gates of death. Joy nevertheless found its way through the momentary reflections of religion and of humanity, by which I tried to master myself. My own private deliverance seemed so great and so unhoped for, that it appeared to me that the State must gain everything by such a loss. And with these thoughts I felt, in spite of myself, a lingering fear lest the sick man should recover, and was extremely ashamed of it.

Wrapped up thus in myself, I did not fail, nevertheless, to cast clandestine looks upon each face, to see what was passing there. I saw Madame la Duchesse d'Orléans arrive, but her countenance, majestic and constrained, said nothing. She went into the little cabinet, whence she presently issued with the Duc d'Orléans, whose activity and turbulent air marked his emotion at the spectacle more than any other sentiment. They went away, and I noticed this expressly, on account of what happened afterward in my presence.

Soon afterward I caught a distinct glimpse of the Duc de Bourgogne, who seemed much moved and troubled; but the glance with which I probed him rapidly, revealed nothing tender, and told merely of a mind profoundly occupied with the bearings of what had taken place.

Valets and chamber-women were already indiscreetly crying out; and THEIR grief showed well that they were about to lose something.

Toward half past twelve we had news of the King, and immediately after Madame de Bourgogne came out of the little cabinet with the Duke, who seemed more touched than when I first saw him. The Princess took her scarf and her coifs from the toilet, standing with a deliberate air, her eyes scarcely wet—a fact betrayed by inquisitive glances cast rapidly to the right and left—and, followed only by her ladies, went to her coach by the great staircase.

I took the opportunity to go to the Duchesse d'Orléans, where I found many people. Their presence made me very impatient; the Duchess, who was equally impatient, took a light and went in. I whispered in the ear of the Duchesse de Villeroy, who thought as I thought of this event. She nudged me, and said in a very low voice that I must contain myself. I was smothered with silence, amid the complaints and the narrative surprises of these ladies; but at last M. le Duc d'Orléans appeared at the door of his cabinet, and beckoned me to come to him.

I followed him into the cabinet where we were alone. What was my surprise, remembering the terms on which he was with Monseigneur, to see the tears streaming from his eyes.

"Sir!" exclaimed I, rising. He understood me at once; and answered in a broken voice, really crying: "You are right to be surprised—I am surprised myself; but such a spectacle touches. He was a man with whom I passed much of my life, and who treated me well when he was uninfluenced. I feel very well that my grief won't last long; in a few days I shall discover motives of joy; at present, blood, relationship, humanity,—all work; and my entrails are moved." I praised his sentiments, but repeated my surprise. He rose, thrust his head into a corner, and with his nose there, wept bitterly and sobbed, which if I had not seen I could not have believed.

After a little silence, however, I exhorted him to calm himself. I represented to him that, everybody knowing on what terms he had been with Monseigneur, he would be laughed at, as playing a part, if his eyes showed that he had been weeping. He did what he could to remove the marks of his tears, and we then went back into the other room.

The interview of the Duchesse de Bourgogne with the King had not been long. She met him in the avenue between the two stables, got down, and went to the door of the carriage. Madame de Maintenon cried out, "Where are you going? We bear the plague about with us." I do not know what the King said or did. The Princess returned to her carriage, and came back to Versailles, bringing in reality the first news of the actual death of Monseigneur.

Acting upon the advice of M. de Beauvilliers, all the company had gone into the *salon*. The two Princes, Monseigneur de Bourgogne and M. de Berry, were there, seated on one sofa, their Princesses at their side; all the rest of the company were scattered about in confusion, seated or standing, some of the ladies being on the floor, near the sofa. There could be no doubt of what had happened. It was plainly written on every face in the chamber and throughout the apartment. Monseigneur was no more: it was known: it was spoken of: constraint with respect to him no longer existed. Amid the surprise, the confusion, and the movements that prevailed, the sentiments of all were painted to the life in looks and gestures.

In the outside rooms were heard the constrained groans and sighs of the valets—grieving for the master they had lost as well as for the master that had succeeded. Farther on began the crowd of courtiers of all kinds. The greater number— that is to say the fools—pumped up sighs as well as they could, and with wandering but dry eyes, sung the praises of Monseigneur—insisting especially on his goodness. They pitied the King for the loss of so good a son. The keener began already to be uneasy about the health of the King; and admired themselves for preserving so much judgment amid so much trouble, which could be perceived by the frequency of their repetitions. Others, really afflicted—the discomfited Cabal—wept bitterly, and kept themselves under with an effort as easy to notice as sobs. The most strong-minded or the wisest, with eyes fixed on the ground, in corners, meditated on the consequences of such an event—and especially on their own interests. Few words passed in conversation—here and there an exclamation wrung from grief was answered by some neighboring grief—a word every quarter of an hour— somber and haggard eyes—movements quite involuntary of the hands—immobility of all other parts of the body. Those who already looked upon the event as favorable in vain exaggerated their gravity so as to make it resemble chagrin and severity; the veil over their faces was transparent and hid not a single feature. They remained as motionless as those who grieved most, fearing opinion, curiosity, their own satisfaction, their every movement; but their eyes made up for their immobility. Indeed they could not refrain from repeatedly changing their attitude like people ill at ease, sitting or standing, from avoiding each other too carefully, even from allowing their eyes to meet—nor repress a manifest air of liberty —nor conceal their increased liveliness—nor put out a sort of brilliancy which distinguished them in spite of themselves.

The two Princes, and the two Princesses who sat by their sides, were more exposed to view than any other. The Duc de Bourgogne wept with tenderness, sincerity, and gentleness, the tears of nature, of religion, and of patience. M. le Duc de Berry also sincerely shed abundance of tears, but bloody tears, so to speak, so great appeared their bitterness; and he uttered not only sobs, but cries, nay, even yells. He was silent sometimes, but from suffocation, and then would burst out again with such a noise, such a trumpet sound of despair, that the majority present burst out also at these dolorous repetitions, either impelled by affliction or decorum. He became so bad, in fact, that his people were forced to undress him then and there, put him to bed, and call in the doctor. Madame la Duchesse de Berry was beside herself, and we shall soon see why. The most bitter despair was painted with horror on her face. There was seen written, as it were, a sort of furious grief, based on interest, not affection; now and then came dry lulls deep and sullen, then a torrent of tears and involuntary gestures, yet restrained, which showed extreme bitterness of mind, fruit of the profound meditation that had preceded. Often aroused by the cries of her husband, prompt to assist him, to support him, to embrace him, to give her smelling bottle, her care for him was evident; but soon came another profound reverie—then a gush of tears assisted to suppress her cries. As for Madame la Duchesse de Bourgogne, she consoled her husband with less trouble than she had to appear herself in want of consolation. Without attempting to play a part, it was evident that she did her best to acquit herself of a pressing duty of decorum. But she found extreme difficulty in keeping up appearances. When the Prince her brother-in-law howled, she blew her nose. She had brought some tears along with her and kept them up with care; and these combined with the art of the handkerchief, enabled her to redden her eyes, and make them swell, and smudge her face; but her glances often wandered on the sly to the countenances of all present.

Madame arrived, in full dress she knew not why, and howling she knew not why, inundated everybody with her tears in embracing them, making the *château* echo with renewed cries, and furnished the odd spectacle of a princess putting on her robes of ceremony in the dead of night to come and cry among a crowd of women with but little on except their nightdresses,—almost as masqueraders.

In the gallery several ladies, Madame la Duchesse d'Orléans, Madame de Castries, and Madame de Saint-Simon among the rest, finding no one close by, drew near each other by the side of a tent bedstead, and began to open their hearts to each other, which they did with the more freedom, inasmuch as they had but one sentiment in common upon what had occurred. In this gallery, and in the *salon*, there were always during the night several beds in which, for security's sake, certain Swiss guards and servants slept. These beds had been put in their usual place this evening before the bad news came from Meudon. In the midst of the conversation of the ladies, Madame de Castries touched the bed, felt something move, and was much terrified. A moment after they saw a sturdy arm, nearly naked, raise on a sudden the curtains, and thus show them a great brawny Swiss under the sheets, half awake, and wholly amazed. The fellow was a long time in making out his position, fixing his eyes upon every face one after the other; but at last, not judging it advisable to get up in the midst of such a grand company, he reburied himself in his bed, and closed the curtains. Apparently the good man had gone to bed before anything had been known, and had slept so soundly ever since that he had not been aroused until then. The saddest sights have often the most ridiculous contrasts. This caused some of the ladies to laugh, and made Madame d'Orléans fear lest the conversation should have been overheard. But after reflection, the sleep and the stupidity of the sleeper reassured her.

I had some doubts yet as to the event that had taken place; for I did not like to abandon myself to belief, until the word was pronounced by some one in whom I could have faith. By chance I met D'O, and I asked him. He answered me clearly that Monseigneur was no more. Thus answered, I tried not to be glad. I know not if I succeeded well, but at least it is certain, that neither joy nor sorrow blunted my curiosity, and that while taking due care to preserve all decorum, I did not consider myself in any way forced to play the doleful. I no longer feared any fresh attack from the citadel of Meudon, nor any cruel charges from its implacable garrison. I felt, therefore, under no constraint, and followed every face with my glances, and tried to scrutinize them unobserved. It must be admitted, that for him who is well acquainted with the privacies of a Court, the first sight of rare events of this nature, so interesting in so many different respects, is extremely satisfactory. Every countenance recalls the cares, the intrigues, the labors employed in the advancement of fortunes—in the overthrow of rivals; the relations, the coldness, the hatreds, the evil offices done, the baseness of all; hope, despair, rage, satisfaction, express themselves in the features. See how all eyes wander to and fro examining what passes around—how some are astonished to find others more mean, or less mean than was expected! Thus this spectacle produced a pleasure, which, hollow as it may be, is one of the greatest a Court can bestow.

The turmoil in this vast apartment lasted about an hour, at the end of which M. de Beauvilliers thought it was high time to deliver the Princes of their company. The rooms were cleared. M. le Duc de Berry went away to his rooms, partly supported by his wife. All through the night he asked, amid tears and cries, for news from Meudon; he would not understand the cause of the King's departure to Marly. When at length the mournful curtain was drawn from before his eyes, the state he fell into cannot be described. The night of Monseigneur and Madame de Bourgogne was more tranquil. Some one having said to the Princess, that having no real cause to be affected, it would be terrible to play a part, she replied, quite naturally, that without feigning, pity touched her and decorum controlled her; and indeed she kept herself within these bounds with truth and decency. Their chamber, in which they invited several ladies to pass the night in armchairs, became immediately a palace of Morpheus. All quietly fell asleep. The curtains were left open, so that the Prince and Princess could be seen sleeping profoundly. They woke up once or twice for a moment. In the morning the Duke and Duchess rose early, their tears quite dried up. They shed no more for this cause, except on special and rare occasions. The ladies who had watched and slept in their chamber, told their friends how tranquil the night had been. But nobody was surprised, and as there was no longer a Monseigneur, nobody was scandalized. Madame de Saint-Simon and I remained up two hours before going to bed, and then went there without feeling any want of rest. In fact, I slept so little that at seven in the morning I was up; but it must be admitted that such restlessness is sweet, and such reawakenings are savory.

Horror reigned at Meudon. As soon as the King left, all the courtiers left also, crowding into the first carriages that came. In an instant Meudon was empty. Mademoiselle Choin remained alone in her garret, and unaware of what had taken place. She learned it only by the cry raised. Nobody thought of telling her. At last some friends went up to her, hurried her into a hired coach, and took her to Paris. The dispersion was general. One or two valets, at the most, remained near the body. La Vrillière, to his praise be it said, was the only courtier who, not having abandoned Monseigneur during life, did not abandon him after his death. He had some difficulty to find somebody to go in search of Capuchins to pray over the corpse. The decomposition became so rapid and so great, that the opening of windows was not enough; the Capuchins, La Vrillière, and the valets, were compelled to pass the night outside.

ISAAC BABEL

AWAKENING

ALL THE folk in our circle—brokers, shopkeepers, clerks in banks and steamship offices—used to have their children taught music. Our fathers, seeing no other escape from their lot, had thought up a lottery, building it on the bones of little children. Odessa more than other towns was seized by the craze. And in fact, in the course of ten years or so our town supplied the concert platforms of the world with infant prodigies. From Odessa came Mischa Elman, Zimbalist, Gabrilowitsch. Odessa witnessed the first steps of Jascha Heifetz.

When a lad was four or five, his mother took the puny creature to Zagursky's. Mr. Zagursky ran a factory of infant prodigies, a factory of Jewish dwarfs in lace collars and patent-leather pumps. He hunted them out in the slums of the Moldavanka, in the evil-smelling courtyards of the Old Market. Mr. Zagursky charted the first course, then the children were shipped off to Professor Auer in St. Petersburg. A wonderful harmony dwelt in the souls of those wizened creatures with their swollen blue hands. They became famous virtuosi. My father decided that I should emulate them. Though I had, as a matter of fact, passed the age limit set for infant prodigies, being now in my fourteenth year, my shortness and lack of strength made it possible to pass me off as an eight-year-old. Herein lay father's hope.

I was taken to Zagursky's. Out of respect for my grandfather, Mr. Zagursky agreed to take me on at the cut rate of a ruble a lesson. My grandfather Leivi-Itzkhok was the laughingstock of the town, and its chief adornment. He used to walk about the streets in a top hat and old boots, dissipating doubt in the darkest of cases. He would be asked what a Gobelin was, why the Jacobins betrayed Robespierre, how you made artificial silk, what a Caesarean section was. And my grandfather could answer these questions. Out of respect for his learning and craziness, Mr. Zagursky only charged us a ruble a lesson. And he had the devil of a time with me, fearing my grandfather, for with me there was nothing to be done. The sounds dripped from my fiddle like iron filings, causing even me excruciating agony, but father wouldn't give in. At home there was no talk save of Mischa Elman, exempted by the Tsar himself from military service. Zimbalist, father would have us know, had been presented to the King of England and had played at Buckingham Palace. The parents of Gabrilowitsch had bought two houses in St. Petersburg. Infant prodigies brought wealth to their parents, but though my father could have reconciled himself to poverty, fame he must have.

"It's not possible," people feeding at his expense would insinuate, "it's just not possible that the grandson of such a grandfather..."

But what went on in my head was quite different. Scraping my way through the violin exercises, I would have books by Turgenev or Dumas on my music stand. Page after page I devoured as I deedled away. In the daytime I would relate impossible happenings to the kids next door; at night I would commit them to paper. In our family, composition was a hereditary occupation. Grandfather Leivi-Itzkhok, who went cracked as he grew old, spent his whole life writing a tale entitled "The Headless Man." I took after him.

Three times a week, laden with violin case and music, I made my reluctant way to Zagursky's place on Witte (formerly Dvoryanskaya) Street. There Jewish girls aflame with hysteria sat along the wall awaiting their turn, pressing to their feeble knees violins exceeding in dimensions the exalted persons they were to play to at Buckingham Palace.

The door to the sanctum would open, and from Mr. Zagursky's study there would stagger big-headed, freckled children with necks as thin as flower stalks and an epileptic flush on their cheeks. The door would bang to, swallowing up the next dwarf. Behind the wall, straining his throat, the teacher sang and waved his baton. He had ginger curls and frail legs, and sported a big bow tie. Manager of a monstrous lottery, he populated the Moldavanka and the dark culs-de-sac of the Old Market with the ghosts of pizzicato and cantilena. Afterward old Professor Auer lent these strings a diabolical brilliance.

In this crew I was quite out of place. Though like them in my dwarfishness, in the voice of my forebears I perceived inspiration of another sort.

The first step was difficult. One day I left home laden like a beast of burden with violin case, violin, music, and twelve rubles in cash—payment for a month's tuition. I was going along Nezhin Street; to get to Zagursky's I should have turned into Dvoryanskaya, but instead of that I went up Tiraspolskaya and found myself at the harbor. The alloted time flew past in the part of the port where ships went after quarantine. So began my liberation. Zagursky's saw me no more: affairs of greater moment occupied my thoughts. My pal Nemanov and I got into the habit of slipping aboard the S.S. *Kensington* to see an old salt named Trottyburn. Nemanov was a year younger than I. From the age of eight onward he had been doing the most ingenious business deals you can imagine. He had a wonderful head for that kind of thing, and later on amply fulfilled his youthful promise. Now he is a New York millionaire, director of General Motors, a company no less powerful than Ford. Nemanov took me along with him because I silently obeyed all his orders. He used to buy pipes smuggled in by Mr. Trottyburn. They were made in Lincoln by the old sailor's brother.

"Gen'lemen," Mr. Trottyburn would say to us, "take my

word, the pets must be made with your own hands. Smoking a factory-made pipe—might as well shove an enema in your mouth. D'you know who Benvenuto Cellini was? He was a grand lad. My brother in Lincoln could tell you about him. Live and let live is my brother's motto. He's got it into his head that you just has to make the pets with your own hands, and not with no one else's. And who are we to say him no, gen'lemen?"

Nemanov used to sell Trottyburn's pipes to bank-managers, foreign consuls, well-to-do Greeks. He made a hundred percent on them.

The pipes of the Lincolnshire master breathed poetry. In each one of them thought was invested, a drop of eternity. A little yellow eye gleamed in their mouthpieces, and their cases were lined with satin. I tried to picture the life in Old England of Matthew Trottyburn, the last master-pipemaker, who refused to swim with the tide.

"We can't but agree, gen'lemen, that the pets has to be made with your own hands."

The heavy waves by the sea wall swept me further and further away from our house, impregnated with the smell of leeks and Jewish destiny. From the harbor I migrated to the other side of the breakwater. There on a scrap of sand-spit dwelt the boys from Primorskaya Street. Trouserless from morn till eve, they dived under wherries, sneaked coconuts for dinner, and awaited the time when boats would arrive from Kherson and Kamenka laden with watermelons, which melons it would be possible to break open against moorings.

To learn to swim was my dream. I was ashamed to confess to those bronzed lads that, born in Odessa, I had not seen the sea till I was ten, and at fourteen didn't know how to swim.

How slow was my acquisition of the things one needs to know! In my childhood, chained to the Gemara, I had led the life of a sage. When I grew up I started climbing trees.

But swimming proved beyond me. The hydrophobia of my

ancestors—Spanish rabbis and Frankfurt moneychangers—
dragged me to the bottom. The waves refused to support me.
I would struggle to the shore pumped full of salt water and
feeling as though I had been flayed, and return to where my
fiddle and music lay. I was fettered to the instruments of
my torture, and dragged them about with me. The struggle
of rabbis versus Neptune continued till such time as the local
water-god took pity on me. This was Yefim Nikitich Smo-
lich, proofreader of the *Odessa News*. In his athletic breast
there dwelt compassion for Jewish children, and he was the
god of a rabble of rickety starvelings. He used to collect them
from the bug-infested joints on the Moldavanka, take them
down to the sea, bury them in the sand, do gym with them,
dive with them, teach them songs. Roasting in the perpendi-
cular sunrays, he would tell them tales about fishermen and
wild beasts. To grownups Nikitich would explain that he was
a natural philosopher. The Jewish kids used to roar with
laughter at his tales, squealing and snuggling up to him like
so many puppies. The sun would sprinkle them with creeping freckles, freckles of the same color as lizards.

Silently, out of the corner of his eye, the old man had been
watching my duel with the waves. Seeing that the thing was
hopeless, that I should simply never learn to swim, he included
me among the permanent occupants of his heart. That cheerful heart of his was with us there all the time; it never went
careering off anywhere else, never knew covetousness and
never grew disturbed. With his sunburned shoulders, his su-
perannuated gladiator's head, his bronzed and slightly bandy
legs, he would lie among us on the other side of the mole, lord
and master of those melon-sprinkled, paraffin-stained waters.
I came to love that man, with the love that only a lad suffering from hysteria and headaches can feel for a real man. I was
always at his side, always trying to be of service to him.

He said to me:

"Don't you get all worked up. You just strengthen your

nerves. The swimming will come of itself. How d'you mean, the water won't hold you? Why shouldn't it hold you?"

Seeing how drawn I was to him, Nikitich made an exception of me alone of all his disciples. He invited me to visit the clean and spacious attic where he lived in an ambience of straw mats, showed me his dogs, his hedgehog, his tortoise, and his pigeons. In return for this wealth I showed him a tragedy I had written the day before.

"I was sure you did a bit of scribbling," said Nikitich. "You've the look. You're looking in *that* direction all the time; no eyes for anywhere else."

He read my writings, shrugged a shoulder, passed a hand through his stiff gray curls, paced up and down the attic.

"One must suppose," he said slowly, pausing after each word, "one must suppose that there's a spark of the divine fire in you."

We went out into the street. The old man halted, struck the pavement with his stick, and fastened his gaze upon me.

"Now what is it you lack? Youth's no matter—it'll pass with the years. What you lack is a feeling for nature."

He pointed with his stick at a tree with a reddish trunk and a low crown.

"What's that tree?"

I didn't know.

"What's growing on that bush?"

I didn't know this either. We walked together across the little square on the Alexandrovsky Prospect. The old man kept poking his stick at trees; he would seize me by the shoulder when a bird flew past, and he made me listen to the various kinds of singing.

"What bird is that singing?"

I knew none of the answers. The names of trees and birds, their division into species, where birds fly away to, on which side the sun rises, when the dew falls thickest—all these things were unknown to me.

"And you dare to write! A man who doesn't live in nature, as a stone does or an animal, will never in all his life write two worthwhile lines. Your landscapes are like descriptions of stage props. In heaven's name, what have your parents been thinking of for fourteen years?"

What *had* they been thinking of? Of protested bills of exchange, of Mischa Elman's mansions. I didn't say anything to Nikitich about that, but just kept mum.

At home, over dinner, I couldn't touch my food. It just wouldn't go down.

"A feeling for nature," I thought to myself. "Goodness, why did that never enter my head? Where am I to find someone who will tell me about the way birds sing and what trees are called? What do *I* know about such things? I might perhaps recognize lilac, at any rate when it's in bloom. Lilac and acacia—there are acacias along De Ribas and Greek Streets."

At dinner father told a new story about Jascha Heifetz. Just before he got to Robinat's he had met Mendelssohn, Jascha's uncle. It appeared that the lad was getting eight hundred rubles a performance. Just work out how much that comes to at fifteen concerts a month!

I did, and the answer was twelve thousand a month. Multiplying and carrying four in my head, I glanced out of the window. Across the cement courtyard, his cloak swaying in the breeze, his ginger curls poking out from under his soft hat, leaning on his cane, Mr. Zagursky, my music teacher, was advancing. It must be admitted he had taken his time in spotting my truancy. More than three months had elapsed since the day when my violin had grounded on the sand by the breakwater.

Mr. Zagursky was approaching the main entrance. I dashed to the back door, but the day before it had been nailed up for fear of burglars. Then I locked myself in the privy. In half an hour the whole family had assembled outside the door. The women were weeping. Aunt Bobka, exploding with sobs, was rubbing her fat shoulder against the door. Father was silent.

Finally he started speaking, quietly and distinctly as he had never before spoken in his life.

"I am an officer," said my father. "I own real estate. I go hunting. Peasants pay me rent. I have entered my son in the Cadet Corps. I have no need to worry about my son."

He was silent again. The women were sniffling. Then a terrible blow descended on the privy door. My father was hurling his whole body against it, stepping back and then throwing himself forward.

"I am an officer," he kept wailing. "I go hunting. I'll kill him. This is the end."

The hook sprang from the door, but there was still a bolt hanging onto a single nail. The women were rolling about on the floor, grasping father by the legs. Crazy, he was trying to break loose. Father's mother came over, alerted by the hubbub.

"My child," she said to him in Hebrew, "our grief is great. It has no bounds. Only blood was lacking in our house. I do not wish to see blood in our house."

Father gave a groan. I heard his footsteps retreating. The bolt still hung by its last nail.

I sat it out in my fortress till nightfall. When all had gone to bed, Aunt Bobka took me to grandmother's. We had a long way to go. The moonlight congealed on bushes unknown to me, on trees that had no name. Some anonymous bird emitted a whistle and was extinguished, perhaps by sleep. What bird was it? What was it called? Does dew fall in the evening? Where is the constellation of the Great Bear? On what side does the sun rise?

We were going along Post Office Street. Aunt Bobka held me firmly by the hand so that I shouldn't run away. She was right to. I was thinking of running away.

1930

CHUANG T'ZU

FIVE ANECDOTES

1.
LIEH TZU AND THE SKULL

Lieh tzu, being on a journey, was eating by the roadside, when he saw an old skull. Plucking a blade of grass, he pointed to it and said, "Only you and I know that there is no such thing as life and no such thing as death."

2.
THE GRAND AUGUR AND THE PIGS

The Grand Augur, in his ceremonial robes, approached the shambles and thus addressed the pigs:—

"How can you object to die? I shall fatten you for three months. I shall discipline myself for ten days and fast for three. I shall strew fine grass, and place you bodily upon a carved sacrificial dish. Does not this satisfy you?"

Then speaking from the pigs' point of view, he continued: "It is better perhaps after all to live on bran and escape the shambles. . . ."

"But then," added he, speaking from his own point of view, "to enjoy honor when alive one would readily die on a war-shield or in the headsman's basket."

So he rejected the pigs' point of view and adopted his own point of view. In what sense then was he different from the pigs?

3.

THE WISE COOK

Prince Hui's cook was cutting up a bullock. Every blow of his hand, every heave of his shoulders, every tread of his foot, every thrust of his knee, every *whshh* of rent flesh, every *chhk* of the chopper, was in perfect harmony,—rhythmical like the dance of the Mulberry Grove, simultaneous like the chords of the Ching Shou.

"Well done!" cried the Prince. "Yours is skill indeed."

"Sire," replied the cook; "I have always devoted myself to TAO. It is better than skill. When I first began to cut up bullocks, I saw before me simply whole bullocks. After three years' practice, I saw no more whole animals. And now I work with my mind and not with my eye. When my senses bid me stop, but my mind urges me on, I fall back upon eternal principles. I follow such openings or cavities as there may be, according to the natural constitution of the animal. I do not attempt to cut through joints: still less through large bones.

"A good cook changes his chopper once a year,—because he cuts. An ordinary cook, once a month,—because he hacks. But I have had this chopper nineteen years, and although I have cut up many thousand bullocks, its edge is as if fresh from the whetstone. For at the joints there are always interstices, and the edge of a chopper being without thickness, it remains only to insert that which is without thickness into such an interstice. By these means the interstices will be enlarged, and the blade will find plenty of room. It is thus that I have kept my chopper for nineteen years as though fresh from the whetstone.

"Nevertheless, when I come upon a hard part where the blade meets with a difficulty, I am all caution. I fix my eye on it. I stay my hand, and gently apply my blade, until with a *hwah* the part yields like earth crumbling to the ground. Then I take out my chopper, and stand up, and look around, and pause, until with an air of triumph I wipe my chopper and put it carefully away."

"Bravo!" cried the Prince. "From the words of this cook I have learnt how to take care of my life."

4.

WHY FEAR DEATH?

Four men were conversing together, when the following resolution was suggested: "Whosoever can make inaction the head, life the backbone, and death the tail, of his existence,—that man shall be admitted to friendship with us." The four looked at each other and smiled; and tacitly accepting the conditions, became friends forthwith.

By and by, one of them, named Tze Yu, fell ill, and another, Tze Ssu, went to see him. "Verily God is great!" said the sick man. "See how he has doubled me up. My back is so hunched that my viscera are at the top of my body. My cheeks are level with my navel. My shoulders are higher than my neck. My hair grows up towards the sky. The whole economy of my organism is deranged. Nevertheless, my mental equilibrium is not disturbed." So saying, he dragged himself painfully to a well, where he could see himself, and continued, "Alas, that God should have doubled me up like this!"

"Are you afraid?" asked Tze Ssu.

"I am not," replied Tze Yu. "What have I to fear? Ere long I shall be decomposed. My left shoulder will become a cock, and I shall herald the approach of morn. My right shoulder will become a crossbow, and I shall be able to get broiled duck. My buttocks will become wheels; and with my soul for a horse, I shall be able to ride in my own chariot. I obtained life because it was my time: I am now parting with it in accordance with the same law. Content with the natural sequence of these states, joy and sorrow touch me not. I am simply, as the ancients expressed it, hanging in the air, unable to cut myself down, bound with the trammels of material existence. But man has ever given way before God: why, then, should I be afraid?"

By and by, another of the four, named Tze Lai, fell ill, and lay gasping for breath, while his family stood weeping around. The fourth friend, Tze Li, went to see him. "Chut!" cried he to the wife and children; "begone! you balk his decomposition." Then, leaning against the door, he said, "Verily, God is great! I wonder what he will make of you now. I wonder whither you will be sent. Do you think he will make you into rat's liver or into the shoulders of a snake?"

"A son," answered Tze Lai, "must go whithersoever his parents bid him. Nature is no other than a man's parents. If she bid me die quickly, and I demur, then I am an unfilial son. She can do me no wrong. TAO gives me this form, this toil in manhood, this repose in old age, this rest in death. And surely that which is such a kind arbiter of my life is the best arbiter of my death.

"Suppose that the boiling metal in a smelting-pot were to bubble up and say, 'Make of me an Excalibur'; I think the caster would reject that metal as uncanny. And if a sinner like myself were to say to God, 'Make of me a man, make of me a man'; I think he too would reject me as uncanny. The universe is the smelting-pot, and God is the caster. I shall go whithersoever I am sent, to wake unconscious of the past, as a man wakes from a dreamless sleep."

5.

ON LETTING ALONE

The Spirit of the Clouds when passing eastwards through the expanse of Air happened to fall in with the Vital Principle. The latter was slapping his thighs and hopping about; whereupon the Spirit of the Clouds said, "Who are you, old man, and what are you doing here?"

"Strolling!" replied the Vital Principle, without stopping.

"I want to *know* something," continued the Spirit of the Clouds.

"Ah!" uttered the Vital Principle, in a tone of disapprobation.

"The relationship of heaven and earth is out of harmony," said the Spirit of the Clouds; "the six influences do not combine, and the four seasons are no longer regular. I desire to blend the six influences so as to nourish all living beings. What am I to do?"

"I do not know!" cried the Vital Principle, shaking his head, while still slapping his ribs and hopping about; "I do not know!"

So the Spirit of the Clouds did not press the question; but three years later, when passing eastwards through the Yu-Sung territory, he again fell in with the Vital Principle. The former was overjoyed, and hurrying up, said, "Has your Highness forgotten me?"

He then prostrated himself, and desired to be allowed to interrogate the Vital Principle; but the latter said, "I wander on without knowing what I want. I roam about without knowing where I am going. I stroll in this ecstatic manner, simply awaiting events. What should I know?"

"I too roam about," answered the Spirit of the Clouds, "but the people depend upon my movements. I am thus unavoidably summoned to power; and under these circumstances I would gladly receive some advice."

"That the scheme of empire is in confusion," said the Vital Principle, "that the conditions of life are violated, that the will of God does not triumph, that the beasts of the field are disorganized, that the birds of the air cry at night, that blight reaches the trees and herbs, that destruction spreads among creeping things,—this, alas! is the fault of *government*."

"True," replied the Spirit of the Clouds, "but what am I to do?"

"It is here," cried the Vital Principle, "that the poison lurks! Go back!"

"It is not often," urged the Spirit of the Clouds, "that I meet your Holiness. I would gladly receive some advice."

"Feed then your people," said the Vital Principle, "with your heart. Rest in inaction, and the world will be good of itself. Cast your slough. Spit forth intelligence. Ignore all differences. Become one with the infinite. Release your mind. Free your soul. Be vacuous. Be Nothing!

"Let all things revert to their original constitution. If they do this, without knowledge, the result will be a simple purity which they will never lose; but knowledge will bring with it a divergence therefrom. Seek not the names nor the relations of things, and all things will flourish of themselves."

"Your Holiness," said the Spirit of the Clouds, as he prostrated himself and took leave, "has informed me with power and filled me with mysteries. What I had long sought, I have now found."

HUGO VON HOFMANNSTHAL

A TALE OF THE CAVALRY

ON JULY 22, 1848, before six o'clock in the morning, the second squadron of Wallmoden cuirassiers, a troop of cavalry a hundred and seven strong under Captain Baron Rofrano, left the Casino San Alessandro and took the road to Milan. The wide, sunny landscape lay in untroubled peace; from distant mountain peaks, morning clouds rose like steady plumes of smoke into the radiant sky. Not a breath of air stirred the corn. Here and there, between clumps of trees fresh-bathed in the morning air, there was a bright gleam of a house or a church. Hardly had the troop left the foremost outposts of its own army about a mile behind them when they caught sight of a glint of weapons in the corn-fields, and the vanguard reported enemy infantry. The squadron drew up for the attack by the side of the highroad; over their heads cannon-balls flew, whizzing with a strangely loud, mewing noise; they attacked across country, driving before them like quails a troop of men irregularly armed. They belonged to the Manara Legion, and wore strange headgear. The prisoners were sent back in charge of a corporal and eight men. Outside a beautiful villa approached by an avenue of ancient cypresses, the vanguard reported suspicious figures. Anton Lerch, the sergeant, dismounted, took twelve men armed with carbines, whom he posted at the windows, and captured eighteen students of the Pisan Legion, well-bred, handsome young men with white hands and long hair. Half-an-hour later the squadron stopped a wayfarer in the Bergamasque costume whose very guilelessness and insignificance aroused suspicion. Sewn into the lining of his coat he was carrying detailed plans of the greatest importance relating to the formation of irregular corps in the Giudicaria and their liaison with the Piedmontese army. About ten o'clock, a herd of cows fell into the squadron's hands. Immediately afterwards, they encountered a strong enemy detachment which fired on the vanguard from a cemetery wall. The front line, under Lieutenant Count Trautsohn, vaulted over the low wall and laid about them among the graves on the enemy, most of whom escaped in wild confusion into the church and through the vestry door into a dense thicket. The twenty-seven new prisoners reported themselves as Neapolitan irregulars under Papal officers. The squadron had lost one man. Corporal Wotrubek, with two men, Dragoons Holl and Haindl, riding round the thicket, captured a light howitzer drawn by two farm-horses by knocking the guard senseless, taking the horses by the bridles, and turning them round. Corporal Wotrubek was sent back to headquarters, slightly wounded, to report these skirmishes and the other successes of the day, the prisoners were also sent back, while the howitzer was taken on by the squadron which, deducting the escort, now numbered seventy-eight men.

Since the prisoners declared with one voice that the city of Milan had been abandoned by the enemy troops, regular and irregular, and stripped of artillery and ammunition, the captain could not deny himself and his men the pleasure of riding into the great, beautiful, defenseless city. Amid the ringing of noonday bells, under the march trumpeted into the steely, glittering sky by the four buglers, to rattle against a thousand windows and re-echo on seventy-eight cuirasses and seventy-eight upright, naked swords, with streets to right and left swarming like a broken anthill with gaping faces, watching pallid, cursing figures slipping into housedoors, drowsy windows flung wide open by the bare arms of unknown beauty, past Santa Babila, San Fedele, San Carlo, past the famous white marble cathedral, San Satiro, San Giorgio, San Lorenzo, San Eustorgio, their ancient bronze doors all opening wide on silvery saints and brocade-clad women with shining eyes, on candle-light and fumes of incense, on the alert for shots from a thousand attics, dark archways, and low shop-stalls, yet seeing at every turn mere half-grown girls and boys with flashing teeth and black hair, looking down on it all from their trotting horses, their eyes glittering in masks of blood-spattered dust, in at the Porta Venezia, out at the Porta Ticinese—thus the splendid squadron rode through Milan.

Not far from the Porta Ticinese, on a rampart set with fine plane-trees, it seemed to Sergeant Anton Lerch that he saw, at the ground-floor window of a new, bright-yellow house, a woman's face he knew. Curious to know more, he turned in his saddle; a slight stiffness in his horse's gait made him suspect a stone in one of its foreshoes, and as he was riding in the rear of the squadron, and could break file without disturbance, he made up his mind to dismount, even going so far as to back his horse into the entry of the house. Hardly had he raised the second white-socked hoof of his bay to inspect the shoe when a door leading straight into the front of the entry actually opened to show a woman, sensual-looking and still not quite past her youth, in a somewhat disheveled bedgown, and behind her a sunny room with a few pots of basil and red pelargonium in the windows, while his sharp eyes caught in a pier-glass the reflection of the other side of the room, which was filled with a large white bed and a papered door, through which a stout, clean-shaven, elderly man was just withdrawing.

As there struggled back into the sergeant's mind the woman's name and a great many other things besides—that she was the widow or divorced wife of a Croat paymaster, that, nine or ten years before, he had on occasion spent the evening or half the night in Vienna with her and her accredited lover of the moment—he tried to distinguish, under her present stoutness, the full yet slender figure of those days.

243

But standing there, she gave him a fawning Slav smile which sent the blood pulsing into his thick neck and under his eyes, and he was daunted by a certain archness in the way she spoke to him, by her bedgown and the furniture in the room behind. At the very moment, however, when with heavy eyes he was watching a big fly crawl over the woman's comb, when he had no thought in mind but of his hand on the warm, cool neck, brushing it away, the memory of the skirmishes and other lucky chances of the day came flooding back upon him, and he pressed her head forward with a heavy hand, saying: "Vuic"—he had not pronounced her name for ten years at least, and had completely forgotten her first name—"a week from now we shall occupy the town and these shall be my quarters," and he pointed to the half-open door of the room. Meanwhile he heard door after door slam in the house, felt his horse urging him to be gone, first by a dumb dragging at the bridle, then by loud neighing after the others. He mounted and trotted off after the squadron with no answer from Vuic save an evasive laugh and a toss of the head. But the word, once spoken, made him feel its power within him. Riding beside the main column of the squadron, his bay a little jaded, under the heavy, metallic glow of the sky, half blinded by the cloud of dust that moved with the riders, the sergeant, in his imagination, slowly took possession of the room with the mahogany furniture and the pots of basil, and at the same time entered into a life of peace still irradiated by war, an atmosphere of comfort and pleasant brutality with no officer to give him orders, a slippered life with the hilt of his saber sticking through the left-hand pocket of his dressing-gown. And the stout, clean-shaven man who had vanished through the papered door, something between a priest and a pensioned footman, played an important part in it all, more important, even, than the fine, broad bed and Vuic's white skin. The clean-shaven man was now a somewhat servile companion who told court gossip and brought presents of tobacco and capons, now he was hard pressed and had to pay black-mail, was involved in many intrigues, was in the confidence of the Piedmontese, was the Pope's cook, procurer, owner of suspect houses with gloomy pavilions for political meetings, and swelled up into a huge, bloated figure from which, if it were tapped in twenty places, gold, not blood would pour.

There were no further surprises for the squadron that afternoon, and there was nothing to check the sergeant's musings. But there had awakened in him a craving for strokes of luck, for prize moneys, for ducats suddenly falling into his pockets. And the thorn which festered in his flesh, round which all wishes and desires clustered, was the anticipation of his first entrance into the room with the mahogany furniture.

When the squadron, its horses fed and half-rested, attempted towards evening to advance by a detour on Lodi and the Adda bridge, where there was every prospect of an encounter with the enemy, a village lying in a dark hollow off the highroad with a half-ruined church spire looked enticing and suspicious enough to attract the sergeant's attention. Beckoning to two dragoons, Holl and Scarmolin, he broke away from the squadron's route with them, and, so inflamed was his imagination that it swelled to the hope of surprising in the village some ill-defended enemy general, or of winning some other great prize. Having arrived at the wretched and seemingly deserted place, he ordered Scarmolin to reconnoitre the houses from the outside to the left, Holl to the right, while he himself, pistol in hand, set off at the gallop through the village. Soon, feeling under his feet hard flagstones which were coated with some slippery kind of grease, he had to put his horse to the walk. Deathly silence reigned in the village—not a child, not a bird, not a breath of air. To right and left there stood foul hovels, the mortar scaling from their walls, with obscene drawings in charcoal here and there on the bare bricks. Between the naked doorposts the sergeant caught sight from time to time of a dirty, half-naked figure lounging on a bed or hobbling through the room as if on broken hips. His horse advanced painfully, pushing its haunches leadenly forward. As he turned and bent to look at its hind shoe, shuffling footsteps issued from a house; he sat upright, and a woman whose face he could not see passed close in front of his mount. She was only half-dressed, her ragged, filthy gown of flowered silk, half torn off her shoulders, trailed in the gutter, there were dirty slippers on her feet. She passed so close in front of his horse that the breath from its nostrils stirred the bunch of greasy curls that hung down her bare neck under an old straw hat, yet she made no move to hurry, nor did she make way for the rider. From a doorstep to the left, two rats, bleeding in their death-agony, rolled into the middle of the street, the under one screaming so desperately that the sergeant's horse stopped, staring at the ground, its head averted and its breathing audible. A pressure on its flank sent it forward again, the woman having disappeared in an entry before the sergeant could see her face. A dog ran out busily with upraised head, dropped a bone in the middle of the street and set about burying it between the paving-stones. It was a dirty white bitch with trailing teats; she scraped with fiendish intentness, then took the bone between her teeth and carried it away. As she began to dig again, three dogs ran up, two of them mere puppies with soft bones and loose skin; unable to bark or bite, they pulled at each other's muzzles with blunt teeth. The dog which had come with them was a pale yellow greyhound, its body so bloated that it could only drag itself along on its four skinny legs. The body was taut as a drum, so that its head looked far too small; there was a dreadful look of pain and fear in its restless little eyes. Two other dogs ran up at once, one thin and white, with black furrows running from its reddened eyes, and hideous in its avidity, the other a vile dachshund with long legs. This dog raised its head towards the sergeant and looked at him. It must have been very old. Its eyes were fathomlessly weary and sad. But the bitch ran to and fro in silly haste before the rider, the two puppies snapped soundlessly with their muzzles round the horse's fetlocks, and the greyhound dragged its hideous body close in front of the horse's hoofs. The bay could not advance a step. But when, having drawn his pistol to shoot one of the dogs, it misfired, the sergeant spurred his horse on both flanks and thundered away over the paving-stones. After a few bounds he was brought up short by a cow which a lad was dragging to the shambles at the end of a tight-stretched rope. But the cow, shrinking from the smell of blood and the fresh hide of a calf nailed to the doorpost, planted its hoofs firm on the ground, drew the reddish haze of the sunset in through dilated nostrils and, before the lad could drag her across the road with stick and rope, tore away with piteous eyes a mouthful of the hay which the sergeant had tied on the front of his saddle.

He had now left the last house of the village behind him and, riding between two low and crumbling walls, could see his way ahead on the farther side of an old single-span bridge over an apparently dry ditch. He felt in his horse's step such an unutterable heaviness that every foot of the walls to right and left, and even every single one of the centipedes and wood-lice which housed in them, passed toilsomely before his eyes, and it seemed to him that he had spent eternity riding through the hideous village. But as, at the same time, he heard a great rasping breath from his horse's chest without at once realizing what it was, he looked above and beside him, and then ahead to see whence it came, and in doing so became aware, on the farther side of the bridge and at the same distance from it as himself, of a man of his own regiment, a sergeant riding a bay with white-socked forefeet. But as he knew that there was no other horse of the kind in the whole squadron but the one on which he was at that moment mounted, and as he still could not recognize the face of the other rider, he impatiently spurred his horse into a very lively trot, whereupon the other mended his pace in exactly the same way till there was only a stone's throw between them. And now, as the two horses, each from its own side, placed the same white-socked forefoot on the bridge, the sergeant, recognizing with starting eyes his own wraith, reined in his horse aghast, and stretched his right hand with stiffened fingers towards the being, while the wraith, also reining in its horse and raising its right hand, was suddenly there no longer; Holl and Scarmolin appeared from the dry ditch to left and right quite unperturbed, while loud and near at hand the bugles of the squadron sounded the attack.

Taking a rise in the ground at full speed, the sergeant saw the squadron already galloping towards a thicket from which enemy cavalry, armed with pikes, were pouring, and as he gathered the four loose reins in his left hand and wound the hand-strap round his right, he saw the fourth rank leave the squadron and slacken its pace, was already on the thundering earth, now in the thick smell of dust, now in the midst of the enemy, struck at a blue arm wielding a pike, saw close at hand the captain's face with starting eyes and savagely bared teeth, was suddenly wedged in among enemy faces and foreign colors, dived below whirling blades, lunged at the next man's neck and unseated him, saw Scarmolin beside him, laughing, hew off the fingers of a man's bridle hand and strike deep into the horse's neck, felt the thick of battle slacken, and was suddenly alone on the bank of a brook behind an enemy officer on an iron-gray horse. The officer put his horse to the jump across the brook, the horse refused. The officer pulled it round, turning towards the sergeant a young, very pale face and the mouth of a pistol, then a saber was driven into his mouth with the full force of a galloping horse in its tiny point. The sergeant snatched back his saber, and at the very spot where the fingers of the fallen rider had opened, laid hold of the snaffle of the iron-gray, which, light and airy as a fawn, lifted its hoofs across its dying master.

As the sergeant rode back with his splendid prize, the sun,

setting in a thick mist, cast a vast crimson haze over the fields. Even on untrodden ground there seemed to lie whole pools of blood. A crimson glow lay on white uniforms and laughing faces, cuirasses and saddle-cloths sparkled and shone, and three little fig trees on which the men had wiped the grooves in their sabers glowed deepest of all. The captain came to a halt by the blood-stained trees, beside the bugler of the squadron, who raised his crimson-dripping bugle to his lips and blew. The sergeant rode from line to line and saw that the squadron had not lost a man, but had taken nine horses. He rode up to the captain to report, the iron-gray still beside him, capering with upraised head and wide nostrils, like the young, vain, beautiful horse it was. The captain hardly listened to the report. He made a sign to Lieutenant Count Trautsohn, who at once dismounted, unharnessed the captured light howitzer, ordered the gun to be dragged away by a detachment of six men and sunk in a swamp formed by the brook, having driven away the now useless draught-horses with a blow from the flat of his saber, and silently resumed his place at the head of the first rank. During this time, the squadron, drawn up in two ranks, was not really restless, yet there was a strange feeling in the air; the elation of four successful skirmishes in one day found vent in outbursts of suppressed laughter and smothered shouts to each other. Even the horses were restless, especially those flanking the prizes. What with all these windfalls, the parade-ground seemed too small to hold them; in the pride of victory, the men felt they must scatter, swarm in upon a new enemy, fling themselves upon him, and carry off yet more horses.

At that moment Captain Baron Rofrano rode up to the front rank of his squadron and, raising his big eyelids from his rather sleepy blue eyes, gave, audibly but without raising his voice, the command "Release led horses." The squadron stood still as death. Only the iron-gray beside the sergeant stretched its neck, almost touching with its nostrils the forehead of the captain's mount. The captain sheathed his saber, drew a pistol from its holster and, wiping a little dust from its shining barrel with the back of his bridlehand, repeated the command, raising his voice slightly and beginning to count, "One . . . two . . . ." When he had counted "two," he fixed his veiled eyes on the sergeant, who sat motionless in his saddle, staring him full in the face. While Anton Lerch's steady, unflinching gaze, flashing now and then an oppressed, doglike look, seemed to express a kind of servile trust born of many years of service, his mind was almost unaware of the huge tension of the moment, but was flooded with visions of an alien ease, and from depths in him unknown to himself there rose a bestial anger against the man before him who was taking away his horse, a dreadful rage against the face, the voice, the bearing, the whole being of the man, such as can only arise, in some mysterious fashion, through years of close companionship. Whether something of the same sort was going on in the captain's mind too, or whether he felt the silently spreading danger of critical situations coming to a head in this moment of mute insubordination, we cannot know. Raising his arm with a negligent, almost graceful gesture, he counted "three" with a contemptuous curl of his upper lip, the shot cracked, and the sergeant, hit in the forehead, reeled, his body across his horse's neck, then fell between the iron-gray and the bay. He had not reached the ground, however, before all the other non-commissioned officers and men had driven off their captured horses with a twist of the rein or a kick, and the captain quietly putting away his pistol, was able to rally his squadron, still twitching from the lightning stroke, against the enemy, who seemed to be gathering in the distant, shadowy dusk. The enemy, however, did not engage the new attack, and not long after, the squadron arrived unmolested at the southern outposts of its own army.

WILLIAM BLAKE

THE MENTAL TRAVELLER

I TRAVEL'D thro' a Land of Men,
A Land of Men and Women too,
And heard and saw such dreadful things
As cold Earth-wanderers never knew.

For there the Babe is born in joy
That was begotten in dire woe;
Just as we reap in joy the fruit
Which we in bitter tears did sow.

And if the Babe is born a Boy
He's given to a Woman Old,
Who nails him down upon a rock,
Catches his Shrieks in Cups of gold.

She binds iron thorns around his head,
She pierces both his hands and feet,
She cuts his heart out at his side
To make it feel both cold and heat.

Her fingers number every Nerve,
Just as a Miser counts his gold;
She lives upon his shrieks and cries,
And she grows young as he grows old.

Till he becomes a bleeding youth,
And she becomes a Virgin bright;
Then he rends up his Manacles
And binds her down for his delight.

He plants himself in all her Nerves,
Just as a Husbandman his mould;
And she becomes his dwelling-place
And Garden fruitful seventy-fold.

An Agèd Shadow, soon he fades,
Wand'ring round an Earthly Cot,
Full-fillèd all with gems and gold
Which he by industry had got.

And these are the gems of the Human Soul,
The rubies and pearls of a love-sick eye,
The countless gold of the akeing heart,
The martyr's groan and the lover's sigh.

They are his meat, they are his drink;
He feeds the Beggar and the Poor
And the wayfaring Traveller:
For ever open is his door.

His grief is their eternal joy;
They make the roofs and walls to ring.
Till from the fire on the hearth
A little Female Babe does spring;

And she is all of solid fire
And gems and gold, that none his hand
Dares stretch to touch her Baby form,
Or wrap her in his swaddling band.

But She comes to the Man she loves,
If young or old, or rich or poor;
They soon drive out the agèd Host,
A Beggar at another's door.

He wanders weeping far away,
Until some other take him in;
Oft blind and age-bent, sore distrest,
Until he can a Maiden win.

And to allay his freezing Age,
The Poor Man takes her in his arms;
The Cottage fades before his sight,
The Garden and its lovely Charms.

The Guests are scatter'd thro' the land,
For the Eye altering alters all;
The Senses roll themselves in fear,
And the flat Earth becomes a Ball;

The Stars, Sun, Moon, all shrink away,
A desart vast without a bound,
And nothing left to eat or drink,
And a dark desart all around.

The honey of her Infant lips,
The bread and wine of her sweet smile,
The wild game of her roving Eye,
Does him to Infancy beguile;

For as he eats and drinks he grows
Younger and younger every day;
And on the desart wild they both
Wander in terror and dismay.

Like the wild Stag she flees away,
Her fear plants many a thicket wild;
While he pursues her night and day,
By various arts of love beguil'd,

By various arts of Love and Hate,
Till the wide desart planted o'er
With Labyrinths of wayward Love,
Where roam the Lion, Wolf, and Boar,

Till he becomes a wayward Babe,
And she a weeping Woman Old.
Then many a Lover wanders here;
The Sun and Stars are nearer roll'd;

The trees bring forth sweet extacy
To all who in the desert roam;
Till many a City there is Built,
And many a pleasant Shepherd's home.

But when they find the frowning Babe,
Terror strikes thro' the region wide:
They cry "The Babe! the Babe is Born!"
And flee away on Every side.

For who dare touch the frowning form,
His arm is wither'd to its root;
Lions, Boars, Wolves, all howling flee,
And every Tree does shed its fruit.

And none can touch that frowning form,
Except it be a Woman Old;
She nails him down upon the Rock,
And all is done as I have told.

D. H. LAWRENCE

SAMSON AND DELILAH

A MAN GOT down from the motor-omnibus that runs from Penzance to St. Just-in-Penwith, and turned northwards, up-hill towards the Polestar. It was only half-past six, but already the stars were out, a cold little wind was blowing from the sea, and the crystalline, three-pulse flash of the lighthouse below the cliffs beat rhythmically in the first darkness.

The man was alone. He went his way unhesitating, but looked from side to side with cautious curiosity. Tall, ruined power-houses of tin-mines loomed in the darkness from time to time, like remnants of some by-gone civilization. The lights of many miners' cottages scattered on the hilly dark-ness twinkled desolate in their disorder, yet twinkled with the lonely homeliness of the Celtic night.

He tramped steadily on, always watchful with curiosity. He was a tall, well-built man, apparently in the prime of life. His shoulders were square and rather stiff, he leaned forwards a little as he went, from the hips, like a man who must stoop to lower his height. But he did not stoop his shoulders: he bent his straight back from the hips.

Now and again short, stump, thick-legged figures of Cor-nish miners passed him, and he invariably gave them good night, as if to insist that he was on his own ground. He spoke with the West Cornish intonation. And as he went along the dreary road, looking now at the lights of the dwellings on land, now at the lights away to sea, vessels veering round in sight of the Longships Lighthouse, the whole of the Atlantic

Ocean in darkness and space between him and America, he seemed a little excited and pleased with himself, watchful, thrilled, veering along in a sense of mastery and of power in conflict.

The houses began to close on the road, he was entering the straggling, formless, desolate mining village, that he knew of old. On the left was a little space set back from the road, and cozy lights of an inn. There it was. He peered up at the sign: 'The Tinners' Rest.' But he could not make out the name of the proprietor. He listened. There was excited talking and laughing, a woman's voice laughing shrilly among the men's.

Stooping a little, he entered the warmly-lit bar. The lamp was burning, a buxom woman rose from the white-scrubbed deal table where the black and white and red cards were scattered, and several men, miners, lifted their faces from the game.

The stranger went to the counter, averting his face. His cap was pulled down over his brow.

"Good evening!" said the landlady, in her rather ingratiating voice.

"Good evening. A glass of ale."

"A glass of ale," repeated the landlady suavely. "Cold night—but bright."

"Yes," the man assented, laconically. Then he added, when nobody expected him to say any more: "Seasonable weather."

"Quite seasonable, quite," said the landlady. "Thank you."

The man lifted his glass straight to his lips, and emptied it. He put it down again on the zinc counter with a click.

"Let's have another," he said.

The woman drew the ale, and the man went away with his glass to the second table, near the fire. The woman, after a moment's hesitation, took her seat again at the table with the card-players. She had noticed the man: a big fine fellow, well dressed, a stranger.

But he spoke with that Cornish-Yankee accent she accepted as the natural twang among the miners.

The stranger put his foot on the fender and looked into the fire. He was handsome, well colored, with well-drawn Cornish eyebrows, and the usual dark, bright, mindless Cornish eyes. He seemed abstracted in thought. Then he watched the card-party. The woman was buxom and healthy, with dark hair and small, quick brown eyes. She was bursting with life and vigor, the energy she threw into the game of cards excited all the men, they shouted, and laughed, and the woman held her breast, shrieking with laughter.

"Oh, my, it'll be the death o' me," she panted. "Now, come on, Mr. Trevorrow, play fair. Play fair, I say, or I s'll put the cards down."

"Play fair! Why, who's played unfair?" ejaculated Mr. Trevorrow. "Do you mean t' accuse me, as I haven't played fair, Mrs. Nankervis?"

"I do. I say it, and I mean it. Haven't you got the Queen of Spades? Now, come on, no dodging round me. I know you've got that Queen, as well as I know my name's Alice."

"Well—if your name's Alice, you'll have to have it——"

"Ay, now—what did I say? Did ever you see such a man? My word, but your missus must be easy took in, by the looks of things."

And off she went into peals of laughter. She was interrupted by the entrance of four men in khaki, a short stumpy sergeant of middle age, a young corporal, and two young privates. The woman leaned back in her chair.

"Oh, my!" she cried. "If there isn't the boys back: looking perished, I believe——"

"Perished, Ma!" exclaimed the sergeant. "Not yet."

"Near enough," said a young private uncouthly.

The woman got up.

"I'm sure you are, my dears. You'll be wanting your suppers, I'll be bound."

"We could do with 'em."

"Let's have a wet first," said the sergeant.

The woman bustled about getting the drinks. The soldiers moved to the fire, spreading out their hands.

"Have your suppers in here, will you?" she said. "Or in the kitchen?"

"Let's have it here," said the sergeant. "More cosier—if you don't mind."

"You shall have it where you like, boys, where you like."

She disappeared. In a minute a girl of about sixteen came in. She was tall and fresh, with dark, young, expressionless eyes, and well-drawn brows, and the immature softness and mindlessness of the sensuous Celtic type.

"Ho, Maryann! Evenin', Maryann! How's Maryann, now?" came the multiple greeting.

She replied to everybody in a soft voice, a strange, soft aplomb that was very attractive. And she moved round with rather mechanical, attractive movements, as if her thoughts were elsewhere. But she had always this dim far-awayness in her bearing: a sort of modesty. The strange man by the fire watched her curiously. There was an alert, inquisitive, mindless curiosity on his well-colored face.

"I'll have a bit of supper with you, if I might," he said.

She looked at him with her clear, unreasoning eyes, just like the eyes of some non-human creature.

"I'll ask mother," she said. Her voice was soft-breathing, gently sing-song.

When she came in again:

"Yes," she said, almost whispering. "What will you have?"

"What have you got?" he said, looking up into her face.

"There's cold meat——"

"That's for me, then."

The stranger sat at the end of the table, and ate with the tired, quiet soldiers. Now the landlady was interested in him. Her brow was knit rather tense, there was a look of panic in her large, healthy face, but her small brown eyes were fixed most dangerously. She was a big woman, but her eyes were small and tense. She drew near the stranger. She wore a rather loud-patterned flannelette blouse and a dark skirt.

"What will you have to drink with your supper?" she asked, and there was a new, dangerous note in her voice.

He moved uneasily.

"Oh, I'll go on with ale."

She drew him another glass. Then she sat down on the bench at the table with him and the soldiers, and fixed him with her attention.

"You've come from St. Just, have you?" she said.

He looked at her with those clear, dark, inscrutable Cornish eyes, and answered at length:

"No, from Penzance."

"Penzance!—but you're not thinking of going back there to-night?"

"No—no."

He still looked at her with those wide, clear eyes that seemed like very bright agate. Her anger began to rise. It was seen on her brow. Yet her voice was still suave and deprecating.

"I thought not—but you're not living in these parts, are you?"

"No—no, I'm not living here." He was always slow in answering, as if something intervened between him and any outside question.

"Oh, I see," she said. "You've got relations down here."

Again he looked straight into her eyes, as if looking her into silence.

"Yes," he said.

He did not say any more. She rose with a flounce. The anger was tight on her brow. There was no more laughing and card-playing that evening, though she kept up her motherly, suave, good-humored way with the men. But they knew her, they were all afraid of her.

The supper was finished, the table cleared, the stranger did not go. Two of the young soldiers went off to bed, with their cheery:

"Good night, Ma. Good night, Maryann."

The stranger talked a little to the sergeant about the war, which was in its first year, about the new army, a fragment of which was quartered in this district, about America.

The landlady darted looks at him from her small eyes, minute by minute the electric storm welled in her bosom, as still he did not go. She was quivering with suppressed, violent passion, something frightening and abnormal. She could not sit still for a moment. Her heavy form seemed to flash with sudden, involuntary movements as the minutes passed by, and still he sat there, and the tension on her heart grew unbearable. She watched the hands of the clock move on. Three of the soldiers had gone to bed, only the crop-headed, terrier-like old sergeant remained.

The landlady sat behind the bar fidgeting spasmodically with the newspaper. She looked again at the clock. At last it was five minutes to ten.

"Gentlemen—the enemy!" she said in her diminished, furious voice. "Time, please. Time, my dears. And good night, all!"

The men began to drop out, with a brief good night. It was a minute to ten. The landlady rose.

"Come," she said. "I'm shutting the door."

The last of the miners passed out. She stood, stout and menacing, holding the door. Still the stranger sat on by the fire, his black overcoat opened, smoking.

"We're closed now, sir," came the perilous, narrowed voice of the landlady.

The little, dog-like, hard-headed sergeant touched the arm of the stranger.

"Closing time," he said.

The stranger turned round in his seat, and his quick-moving dark, jewel-like eyes went from the sergeant to the landlady.

"I'm stopping here to-night," he said, in his laconic Cornish-Yankee accent.

The landlady seemed to tower. Her eyes lifted strangely, frightening.

"Oh, indeed!" she cried. "Oh, indeed! And whose orders are those, may I ask?"

He looked at her again.

"My orders," he said.

Involuntarily she shut the door, and advanced like a great, dangerous bird. Her voice rose, there was a touch of hoarseness in it.

"And what might your orders be, if you please?" she cried. "Who might you be, to give orders, in the house?"

He sat still, watching her.

"You know who I am," he said. "At least, I know who you are."

"Oh, do you? Oh, do you? And who am I then, if you'll be so good as to tell me?"

He stared at her with his bright, dark eyes.

"You're my Missis, you are," he said. "And you know it, as well as I do."

She started as if something had exploded in her.

Her eyes lifted and flared madly.

"Do I know it, indeed!" she cried. "I know no such thing! I know no such thing! Do you think a man's going to walk into this bar, and tell me off-hand I'm his Missis, and I'm going to believe him? I say to you, whoever you may be, you're mistaken. I know myself for no Missis of yours, and I'll thank you to go out of this house, this minute, before I get those that will put you out."

The man rose to his feet, stretching his head towards her a little. He was a handsomely built Cornishman in the prime of life.

"What you say, eh? You don't know me?" he said in his sing-song voice, emotionless, but rather smothered and pressing: it reminded one of the girl's. "I should know you anywhere, you see. I should! I shouldn't have to look twice to know you, you see. You see, now, don't you?"

The woman was baffled.

"So you may say," she replied, staccato. "So you may say. That's easy enough. My name's known, and respected, by most people for ten miles round. But I don't know you."

Her voice ran to sarcasm. "I can't say I know you. You're a perfect stranger to me, and I don't believe I've ever set eyes on you before to-night."

Her voice was very flexible and sarcastic.

"Yes, you have," replied the man, in his reasonable way. "Yes, you have. Your name's my name, and that girl Maryann is my girl; she's my daughter. You're my Missis right enough. As sure as I'm Willie Nankervis."

He spoke as if it were an accepted fact. His face was handsome, with a strange, watchful alertness and a fundamental fixity of intention that maddened her.

"You villain!" she cried. "You villain, to come to this house and dare to speak to me. You villain, you downright rascal!"

He looked at her.

"Ay," he said, unmoved. "All that." He was uneasy before her. Only he was not afraid of her. There was something impenetrable about him, like his eyes, which were as bright as agate.

She towered, and drew near to him menacingly.

"You're going out of this house, aren't you?" She stamped her foot in sudden madness. "This minute!"

He watched her. He knew she wanted to strike him.

"No," he said, with suppressed emphasis. "I've told you, I'm stopping here."

He was afraid of her personality, but it did not alter him. She wavered. Her small, tawny-brown eyes concentrated in a point of vivid, sightless fury, like a tiger's. The man was wincing, but he stood his ground. Then she bethought herself. She would gather her forces.

"We'll see whether you're stopping here," she said. And she turned, with a curious, frightening lifting of her eyes, and surged out of the room. The man, listening, heard her go upstairs, heard her tapping at a bedroom door, heard her saying: "Do you mind coming down a minute, boys? I want you. I'm in trouble."

The man in the bar took off his cap and his black overcoat, and threw them on the seat behind him. His black hair was short and touched with gray at the temples. He wore a well-cut, well-fitting suit of dark gray, American in style, and a turn-down collar. He looked well-to-do, a fine, solid figure of a man. The rather rigid look of the shoulders came from his having had his collar-bone twice broken in the mines.

The little terrier of a sergeant, in dirty khaki, looked at him furtively.

"She's your Missis?" he asked, jerking his head in the direction of the departed woman.

"Yes, she is," barked the man. "She's that, sure enough."

"Not seen her for a long time, haven't ye?"

"Sixteen years come March month."

"Hm!"

And the sergeant laconically resumed his smoking.

The landlady was coming back, followed by the three young soldiers, who entered rather sheepishly, in trousers and shirt and stocking-feet. The woman stood histrionically at the end of the bar, and exclaimed:

"That man refuses to leave the house, claims he's stopping the night here. You know very well I have no bed, don't you? And this house doesn't accommodate travelers. Yet he's going to stop in spite of all! But not while I've a drop of blood in my body, that I declare with my dying breath. And not if you men are worth the name of men, and will help a woman as has no one to help her."

Her eyes sparkled, her face was flushed pink. She was drawn up like an Amazon.

The young soldiers did not quite know what to do. They looked at the man, they looked at the sergeant, one of them looked down and fastened his braces on the second button.

"What say, sergeant?" asked one whose face twinkled for a little devilment.

"Man says he's husband to Mrs. Nankervis," said the sergeant.

"He's no husband of mine. I declare I never set eyes on him before this night. It's a dirty trick, nothing else, it's a dirty trick."

"Why, you're a liar, saying you never set eyes on me before," barked the man near the hearth. "You're married to me, and that girl Maryann you had by me—well enough you know it."

The young soldiers looked on in delight, the sergeant smoked imperturbed.

"Yes," sang the landlady, slowly shaking her head in supreme sarcasm, "it sounds very pretty, doesn't it? But you see we don't believe a word of it, and how are you going to prove it?" She smiled nastily.

The man watched in silence for a moment, then he said:

"It wants no proof."

"Oh yes, but it does! Oh, yes, but it does, sir, it wants a lot of proving!" sang the lady's sarcasm. "We're not such gulls as all that, to swallow your words whole."

But he stood unmoved near the fire. She stood with one hand resting on the zinc-covered bar, the sergeant sat with legs crossed, smoking, on the seat half-way between them, the three young soldiers in their shirts and braces stood wavering in the gloom behind the bar. There was silence.

"Do you know anything of the whereabouts of your husband, Mrs. Nankervis? Is he still living?" asked the sergeant, in his judicious fashion.

Suddenly the landlady began to cry, great scalding tears, that left the young men aghast.

"I know nothing of him," she sobbed, feeling for her pocket handkerchief. "He left me when Maryann was a baby, went mining to America, and after about six months never wrote a line nor sent me a penny bit. I can't say whether he's alive or dead, the villain. All I've heard of him's the bad —and I've heard nothing for years an' all, now." She sobbed violently.

The golden-skinned, handsome man near the fire watched her as she wept. He was frightened, he was troubled, he was bewildered, but none of his emotions altered him underneath.

There was no sound in the room but the violent sobbing of the landlady. The men, one and all, were overcome.

"Don't you think as you'd better go, for to-night?" said the sergeant to the man, with sweet reasonableness. "You'd better leave it a bit, and arrange something between you. You can't have much claim on a woman, I should imagine, if it's how she says. And you've come down on her a bit too sudden-like."

The landlady sobbed heart-brokenly. The man watched her large breasts shaken. They seemed to cast a spell over his mind.

"How I've treated her, that's no matter," he replied. "I've come back, and I'm going to stop in my own home—for a bit, anyhow. There you've got it."

"A dirty action," said the sergeant, his face flushing dark. "A dirty action, to come, after deserting a woman for that number of years, and want to force yourself on her! A dirty action—as isn't allowed by the law."

The landlady wiped her eyes.

"Never you mind about law nor nothing," cried the man, in a strange, strong voice. "I'm not moving out of this public to-night."

The woman turned to the soldiers behind her, and said in a wheedling, sarcastic tone:

"Are we going to stand it, boys? Are we going to be done like this, Sergeant Thomas, by a scoundrel and a bully as has led a life beyond mention in those American mining-camps, and then wants to come back and make havoc of a poor woman's life and savings, after having left her with a baby in arms to struggle as best she might? It's a crying shame if no-body will stand up for me—a crying shame——!"

The soldiers and the little sergeant were bristling. The woman stooped and rummaged under the counter for a minute. Then, unseen to the man away near the fire, she threw out a plaited grass rope, such as is used for binding bales, and left it lying near the feet of the young soldiers, in the gloom at the back of the bar.

Then she rose and fronted the situation.

"Come now," she said to the man, in a reasonable, coldly-coaxing tone, "put your coat on and leave us alone. Be a man, and not worse than a brute of a German. You can get a bed easy enough in St. Just, and if you've nothing to pay for it, sergeant would lend you a couple of shillings, I'm sure he would."

All eyes were fixed on the man. He was looking down at the woman like a creature spell-bound or possessed by some devil's own intention.

"I've got money of my own," he said. "Don't you be fright-ened for your money, I've plenty of that, for the time."

"Well, then," she coaxed, in a cold, almost sneering propi-tiation, "put your coat on and go where you're wanted—be a man, not a brute of a German."

She had drawn quite near to him, in her challenging coaxing intentness. He looked down at her with his be-witched face.

"No, I shan't," he said. "I shan't do no such thing. You'll put me up for to-night."

"Shall I?" she cried. And suddenly she flung her arms round him, hung on to him with all her powerful weight, calling to the soldiers: "Get the rope, boys, and fasten him up. Alfred—John, quick now——"

The man reared, looked round with maddened eyes, and heaved his powerful body. But the woman was powerful also, and very heavy, and was clenched with the determination of death. Her face, with its exulting, horribly vindictive look, was turned up to him from his own breast; he reached back his head frantically, to get away from it. Meanwhile the young soldiers, after having watched this frightful Laocoön swaying for a moment, stirred, and the malicious one darted swiftly with the rope. It was tangled a little.

"Give me the end here," cried the sergeant.

Meanwhile the big man heaved and struggled, swung them round against the seat and the table, in his convulsive effort to get free. But she pinned down his arms like a cuttlefish wreathed heavily upon him. And he heaved and swayed, and they crashed about the room, the soldiers hopping, the furniture bumping.

The young soldier had got the rope once round, the brisk sergeant helping him. The woman sank heavily lower, they got the rope round several times. In the struggle the victim fell over against the table. The ropes tightened till they cut his arms. The woman clung to his knees. Another soldier ran in a flash of genius, and fastened the strange man's feet with the pair of braces. Seats had crashed over, the table was thrown against the wall, but the man was bound, his arms pinned against his sides, his feet tied. He lay half-fallen, sunk against the table, still for a moment.

The woman rose, and sank, faint, on to the seat against the wall. Her breast heaved, she could not speak, she thought she was going to die. The bound man lay against the overturned table, his coat all twisted and pulled up beneath the ropes, leaving the loins exposed. The soldiers stood around, a little dazed, but excited with the row.

The man began to struggle again, heaving instinctively

against the ropes, taking great, deep breaths. His face, with its golden skin, flushed dark and surcharged. He heaved again. The great veins in his neck stood out. But it was no good, he went relaxed. Then again, suddenly, he jerked his feet.

"Another pair of braces, William," cried the excited soldier. He threw himself on the legs of the bound man, and managed to fasten the knees. Then again there was stillness. They could hear the clock tick.

The woman looked at the prostrate figure, the strong straight limbs, the strong back bound in subjection, the wide-eyed face that reminded her of a calf tied in a sack in a cart, only its head stretched dumbly backwards. And she triumphed.

The bound-up body began to struggle again. She watched fascinated the muscles working, the shoulders, the hips, the large, clean thighs. Even now he might break the ropes. She was afraid. But the lively young soldier sat on the shoulders of the bound man, and after a few perilous moments, there was stillness again.

"Now," said the judicious sergeant to the bound man, "if we untie you, will you promise to go off and make no more trouble?"

"You'll not untie him in here," cried the woman. "I wouldn't trust him as far as I could blow him."

There was silence.

"We might carry him outside, and undo him there," said the soldier. "Then we could get the policeman, if he made any more bother."

"Yes," said the sergeant. "We could do that." Then again, in an altered, almost severe tone, to the prisoner: "If we undo you outside, will you take your coat and go without creating any more disturbance?"

But the prisoner would not answer, he only lay with wide, dark, bright eyes, like a bound animal. There was a space of perplexed silence.

"Well, then, do as you say," said the woman irritably. "Carry him out amongst you, and let us shut up the house."

They did so. Picking up the bound man, the four soldiers staggered clumsily into the silent square in front of the inn, the woman following with the cap and the overcoat. The young soldiers quickly unfastened the braces from the prisoner's legs, and they hopped indoors. They were in their stocking-feet, and outside the stars flashed cold. They stood in the doorway watching. The man lay quite still on the cold ground.

"Now," said the sergeant, in a subdued voice, "I'll loosen the knot, and he can work himself free, if you go in, Missis."

She gave a last look at the disheveled, bound man, as he sat on the ground. Then she went indoors, followed quickly by the sergeant. They were heard locking and barring the door.

The man seated on the ground outside worked and strained at the rope. But it was not so easy to undo himself even now. So, with hands bound, making an effort, he got on his feet, and went and worked the cord against the rough edge of an old wall. The rope, being of a kind of plaited grass, soon frayed and broke, and he freed himself. He had various contusions. His arms were hurt and bruised from the bonds. He rubbed them slowly. Then he pulled his clothes straight, stooped, put on his cap, struggled into his overcoat, and walked away.

The stars were very brilliant. Clear as crystal, the beam from the lighthouse under the cliffs struck rhythmically on the night. Dazed, the man walked along the road past the churchyard. Then he stood leaning up against a wall, for a long time.

He was roused because his feet were so cold. So he pulled himself together, and turned again in the silent night, back towards the inn.

The bar was in darkness. But there was a light in the kitchen. He hesitated. Then very quietly he tried the door.

He was surprised to find it open. He entered, and quietly

closed it behind him. Then he went down the step past the bar-counter, and through to the lighted doorway of the kitchen. There sat his wife, planted in front of the range, where a furze fire was burning. She sat in a chair full in front of the range, her knees wide apart on the fender. She looked over her shoulder at him as he entered, but she did not speak. Then she stared in the fire again.

It was a small, narrow kitchen. He dropped his cap on the table that was covered with yellowish American cloth, and took a seat with his back to the wall, near the oven. His wife still sat with her knees apart, her feet on the steel fender and stared into the fire, motionless. Her skin was smooth and rosy in the firelight. Everything in the house was very clean and bright. The man sat silent, too, his head dropped. And thus they remained.

It was a question who would speak first. The woman leaned forward and poked the ends of the sticks in between the bars of the range. He lifted his head and looked at her.

"Others gone to bed, have they?" he asked.

But she remained closed in silence.

"'S a cold night, out," he said, as if to himself.

And he laid his large, yet well-shapen workman's hand on the top of the stove, that was polished black and smooth as velvet. She would not look at him, yet she glanced out of the corners of her eyes.

His eyes were fixed brightly on her, the pupils large and electric like those of a cat.

"I should have picked you out among thousands," he said. "Though you're bigger than I'd have believed. Fine flesh you've made."

She was silent for some time. Then she turned in her chair upon him.

"What do you think of yourself," she said, "coming back on me like this after over fifteen year? You don't think I've not heard of you, neither, in Butte City and elsewhere?"

He was watching her with his clear, translucent, unchallenged eyes.

"Yes," he said. "Chaps comes an' goes—I've heard tell of you from time to time."

She drew herself up.

"And what lies have you heard about me?" she demanded superbly.

"I dunno as I've heard any lies at all—'cept as you was getting on very well, like."

His voice ran warily and detached. Her anger stirred again in her violently. But she subdued it, because of the danger there was in him, and more, perhaps, because of the beauty of his head and his level drawn brows, which she could not bear to forfeit.

"That's more than I can say of you," she said. "I've heard more harm than good about you."

"Ay, I dessay," he said looking into the fire. It was a long time since he had seen the furze burning, he said to himself. There was a silence, during which she watched his face.

"Do you call yourself a man?" she said, more in contemptuous reproach than in anger. "Leave a woman as you've left me, you don't care to what!—and then to turn up in this fashion, without a word to say for yourself."

He stirred in his chair, planted his feet apart, and resting his arms on his knees, looked steadily into the fire without answering. So near to her was his head, and the close black hair, she could scarcely refrain from starting away, as if it would bite her.

"Do you call that the action of a man?" she repeated.

"No," he said, reaching and poling the bits of wood into the fire with his fingers. "I don't call it anything, as I know of. It's no good calling things by any names whatsoever, as I know of."

She watched him in his actions. There was a longer and longer pause between each speech, though neither knew it.

D. H. Lawrence

"I wonder what you think of yourself!" she exclaimed, with vexed emphasis. "I wonder what sort of a fellow you take yourself to be!" She was really perplexed as well as angry.

"Well," he said, lifting his head to look at her, "I guess I'll answer for my own faults, if everybody else'll answer for theirs."

Her heart beat fiery hot as he lifted his face to her. She breathed heavily, averting her face, almost losing her self-control.

"And what do you take me to be?" she cried, in real helplessness. His face was lifted, watching her soft, averted face. And the softly heaving mass of her breasts.

"I take you," he said, with that laconic truthfulness which exercised such power over her, "to be the deuce of a fine woman—darn me if you're not as fine a built woman as I've seen, handsome with it as well. I shouldn't have expected you to put on such handsome flesh: 'struth I shouldn't."

Her heart beat fiery hot, as he watched her with those bright agate eyes, fixedly.

"Been very handsome to you, for fifteen years, my sakes!" she replied.

He made no answer to this, but sat with his bright, quick eyes upon her.

Then he rose. She started involuntarily. But he only said, in his laconic, measured way:

"It's warm in here now."

And he pulled off his overcoat, throwing it on the table. She sat as if slightly cowed, whilst he did so.

"Them ropes has given my arms something, by Ga-ard," he drawled, feeling his arms with his hands.

Still she sat in her chair before him, slightly cowed.

"You was sharp, wasn't you, to catch me like that, eh?" he smiled slowly. "By Ga-ard, you had me fixed proper, proper you had. Darn me, you fixed me up proper—proper, you did."

He leaned forwards in his chair towards her.

"I don't think no worse of you for it, no, darned if I do. Fine pluck in a woman's what I admire. That I do, indeed."

She only gazed into the fire.

"We fet from the start, we did. And, my word, you begin again quick the minute you see me, you did. Darn me, you was too sharp for me. A darn fine woman, puts up a darn good fight. Darn me if I could find a woman in all the darn States as could get me down like that. Wonderful fine woman you be, truth to say, at this minute."

She only sat glowering into the fire.

"As grand a pluck as a man could wish to find in a woman, true as I'm here," he said, reaching forward his hand and tentatively touching her between her full, warm breasts, quietly.

She started, and seemed to shudder. But his hand insinuated itself between her breasts, as she continued to gaze into the fire.

"And don't you think I've come back here a-begging," he said. "I've more than one thousand pounds to my name, I have. And a bit of a fight for a how-de-do pleases me, that it do. But that doesn't mean as you're going to deny as you're my Missis . . ."

LEO TOLSTOY

THE PORCELAIN DOLL

A letter written six months after his marriage by Tolstoy to his wife's younger sister, the Natasha of War and Peace. *The first few lines are in his wife's handwriting, the rest in his own.*

21ST MARCH 1863

WHY, TANYA, have you dried up? . . . You don't write to me at all and I so love receiving letters from you, and you have not yet replied to Levochka's [Tolstoy's] crazy epistle, of which I did not understand a word.

23RD MARCH

There, she began to write and suddenly stopped, because she could not continue. And do you know why, Tanya dear? A strange thing has befallen her and a still stranger thing has befallen me. As you know, like the rest of us she has always been made of flesh and blood, with all the advantages and disadvantages of that condition: she breathed, was warm and sometimes hot, blew her nose (and how loud!) and so on, and above all she had control of her limbs, which—both arms and legs—could assume different positions: in a word she was corporeal like all of us. Suddenly on March 21st 1863, at ten o'clock in the evening, this extraordinary thing befell her and me. Tanya! I know you always loved her (I do not know what feeling she will arouse in you now); I know you felt a sympathetic interest in me, and I know your reasonableness, your sane view of the important affairs of life, and your love of your parents (please prepare them and inform them of this event), and so I write to tell you just how it happened.

I got up early that day and walked and rode a great deal. We lunched and dined together and had been reading (she was still able to read) and I felt tranquil and happy. At ten o'clock I said goodnight to Auntie (Sonya was still then as usual and said she would follow me) and I went off to bed. Through my sleep I heard her open the door and heard her breathe as she undressed . . . I heard how she came out from behind the screen and approached the bed. I opened my eyes . . . and saw —not the Sonya you and I have known—but a porcelain Sonya! Made of that very porcelain about which your parents had a dispute. You know those porcelain dolls with bare cold shoulders, and necks and arms bent forward, but made of the same lump of porcelain as the body. They have black painted hair arranged in large waves, the paint of which gets rubbed off at the top, and protruding porcelain eyes that are too wide and are also painted black at the corners, and the stiff porcelain folds of their skirts are made of the same one piece of porcelain as the rest. And Sonya was like that! I touched her arm—she was smooth, pleasant to feel, and cold porcelain. I thought I was asleep and gave myself a shake, but she remained like that and stood before me immovable. I said: Are you porcelain? And without opening her mouth (which remained as it was, with curved lips painted bright red) she replied: Yes, I am porcelain. A shiver ran down my back. I looked at her legs: they also were porcelain and (you can imagine my horror) fixed on a porcelain stand, made of one piece with herself, representing the ground and painted green to depict grass. By her left leg, a little above and at the back of the knee, there was a porcelain column, colored brown and probably representing the stump of a tree. This too was in one piece with her. I understood that without this stump she could not remain erect, and I became very sad, as you who loved her can imagine. I still did not believe my senses

and began to call her. She could not move without that
stump and its base, and only rocked a little—together with
the base—to fall in my direction. I heard how the porcelain
base knocked against the floor. I touched her again, and she
was all smooth, pleasant, and cold porcelain. I tried to lift her
hand, but could not. I tried to pass a finger, or even a nail,
between her elbow and her side—but it was impossible.
The obstacle was the same porcelain mass, such as is made
at Auerbach's, and of which sauce-boats are made. She was
planned for external appearance only. I began to examine her
chemise, it was all of one piece with the body, above and below. I looked more closely, and noticed that at the bottom a
bit of the fold of her chemise was broken off and it showed
brown. At the top of her head it showed white where the
paint had come off a little. The paint had also come off a lip
in one place, and a bit was chipped off one shoulder. But it
was all so well made and so natural that it was still our same
Sonya. And the chemise was one I knew, with lace, and there
was a knot of black hair behind, but of porcelain, and the fine
slender hands, and large eyes, and the lips—all were the same,
but of porcelain. And the dimple in her chin and the small
bones in front of her shoulders were there too, but of porcelain. I was in a terrible state and did not know what to say or
do or think. She would have been glad to help me, but what
could a porcelain creature do? The half-closed eyes, the eye-
lashes and eyebrows, were all like her living self when looked
at from a distance. She did not look at me, but past me at her
bed. She evidently wanted to lie down, and rocked on her
pedestal all the time. I quite lost control of myself, seized her,
and tried to take her to her bed. My fingers made no impression on her cold porcelain body, and what surprised me yet
more was that she had become as light as an empty flask.
And suddenly she seemed to shrink, and became quite small,
smaller than the palm of my hand, although she still looked
just the same. I seized a pillow, put her in a corner of it,

pressed down another corner with my fist, and placed her
there, then I took her nightcap, folded it in four, and covered
her up to the head with it. She lay there still just the same.
Then I extinguished the candle and placed her under my
beard. Suddenly I heard her voice from the corner of the pillow: "Leva, why have I become porcelain?" I did not know
what to reply. She said again: "Does it make any difference
that I am porcelain?" I did not want to grieve her, and said
that it did not matter. I felt her again in the dark—she was
still as before, cold and porcelain. And her stomach was the
same as when she was alive, protruding upwards—rather unnatural for a porcelain doll. Then I experienced a strange feeling. I suddenly felt it pleasant that she should be as she was,
and ceased to feel surprised—it all seemed natural. I took her
out, passed her from one hand to the other, and tucked her
under my head. She liked it all. We fell asleep. In the morning
I got up and went out without looking at her. All that had
happened the day before seemed so terrible. When I returned
for lunch she had again become such as she always was. I did
not remind her of what had happened the day before, fearing
to grieve her and Auntie. I have not yet told anyone but you
about it. I thought it had all passed off, but all these days,
every time we are alone together, the same thing happens.
She suddenly becomes small and porcelain. In the presence of
others she is just as she used to be. She is not oppressed by
this, nor am I. Strange as it may seem, I frankly confess that I
am glad of it, and though she is porcelain we are very happy.

I write to you of all this, dear Tanya, only that you should
prepare her parents for the news, and through papa should
find out from the doctors what this occurrence means, and
whether it will not be bad for our expected child. Now we are
alone, and she is sitting under my necktie and I feel how her
sharp little nose cuts into my neck. Yesterday she had been
left in a room by herself. I went in and saw that Dora (our little dog) had dragged her into a corner, was playing with her,

and nearly broke her. I whipped Dora, put Sonya in my waist-coat pocket and took her to my study. Today however I am expecting from Tula a small wooden box I have ordered, covered outside with morocco and lined inside with raspberry-colored velvet, with a place arranged in it for her so that she can be laid in it with her elbows, head, and back all supported evenly so that she cannot break. I shall also cover it completely with chamois leather.

I had written this letter when suddenly a terrible misfortune occurred. She was standing on the table, when Natalya Petrovna pushed against her in passing, and she fell and broke off a leg above the knee with the stump. Alexey says that it can be mended with a cement made of the white of eggs. If such a recipe is known in Moscow please send me it.

Translated by Aylmer Maude

IVAN TURGENEV

BYEZHIN PRAIRIE

It was a glorious July day, one of those days which only come after many days of fine weather. From earliest morning the sky is clear; the sunrise does not glow with fire; it is suffused with a soft roseate flush. The sun, not fiery, not red-hot as in time of stifling drought, not dull purple as before a storm, but with a bright and genial radiance, rises peacefully behind a long and narrow cloud, shines out freshly, and plunges again into its lilac mist. The delicate upper edge of the strip of cloud flashes in little gleaming snakes; their brilliance is like polished silver. But, lo! the dancing rays flash forth again, and in solemn joy, as though flying upward, rises the mighty orb. About mid-day there is wont to be, high up in the sky, a multitude of rounded clouds, golden-gray, with soft white edges. Like islands scattered over an overflowing river, that bathes them in its unbroken reaches of deep transparent blue, they scarcely stir; farther down the heavens they are in movement, packing closer; now there is no blue to be seen between them, but they are themselves almost as blue as the sky, filled full with light and heat. The color of the horizon, a faint pale lilac, does not change all day, and is the same all round; nowhere is there storm gathering and darkening; only somewhere rays of bluish color stretch down from the sky; it is a sprinkling of scarce-perceptible rain. In the evening these clouds disappear; the last of them, blackish and undefined as smoke, lie streaked with pink, facing the setting sun; in the place where it has gone down, as calmly as it rose, a crimson glow lingers long over the darkening earth, and, softly flashing like a candle carried carelessly, the evening star flickers in the sky. On such days all the colors are softened, bright but not glaring; everything is suffused with a kind of touching tenderness. On such days the heat is sometimes very great; often it is even "steaming" on the slopes of the fields, but a wind dispels this growing sultriness, and whirling eddies of dust—sure sign of settled, fine weather—move along the roads and across the fields in high white columns. In the pure dry air there is a scent of wormwood, rye in blossom, and buckwheat; even an hour before nightfall there is no moisture in the air. It is for such weather that the farmer longs, for harvesting his wheat. . . .

On just such a day I was once out grouse-shooting in the Tchern district of the province of Tula. I started and shot a fair amount of game; my full game-bag cut my shoulder mercilessly; but already the evening glow had faded, and the cool shades of twilight were beginning to grow thicker, and to spread across the sky, which was still bright, though no longer lighted up by the rays of the setting sun, when I at last decided to turn back homewards. With swift steps I passed through the long "square" of underwoods, clambered up a hill, and instead of the familiar plain I expected to see, with the oakwood on the right and the little white church in the distance, I saw before me a scene completely different, and quite new to me. A narrow valley lay at my feet, and directly facing me a dense wood of aspen-trees rose up like a thick wall. I stood still in perplexity, looked round me. . . . "Aha!" I thought, "I have somehow come wrong; I kept too much to the right," and surprised at my own mistake, I rapidly descended the hill. I was at once plunged into a disagreeable clinging mist, exactly as though I had gone down into a cellar; the thick high grass at the bottom of the valley, all drenched with dew, was white like a smooth tablecloth; one felt afraid somehow to walk on it. I made haste to get on the other side, and walked along beside the aspen-wood, bearing to the left. Bats were already hovering over its slumbering tree-tops, mysteriously flitting and quivering across the clear obscure of the sky; a young belated hawk flew in swift, straight course upwards, hastening to its nest. "Here, directly I get to this corner," I thought to myself, "I shall find the road at once; but I have come a mile out of my way!"

I did at last reach the end of the wood, but there was no road of any sort there; some kind of low bushes overgrown with long grass extended far and wide before me; behind them in the far, far distance could be discerned a tract of waste land. I stopped again. "Well? Where am I?" I began ransacking my brain to recall how and where I had been walking during the day. . . . "Ah! but these are the bushes at Parahin," I cried at last; "of course! then this must be Sindyev wood. But how did I get here? So far? . . . Strange! Now I must bear to the right again."

I went to the right through the bushes. Meantime the night had crept close and grown up like a storm-cloud; it seemed as though, with the mists of evening, darkness was rising up on all sides and flowing down from overhead. I had come upon some sort of little, untrodden, overgrown path; I walked along it, gazing intently before me. Soon all was blackness and silence around—only the quail's cry was heard from time to time. Some small night-bird, flitting noiselessly near the ground on its soft wings, almost flapped against me and scurried away in alarm. I came out on the further side of the bushes, and made my way along a field by the hedge. By now I could hardly make out distant objects; the field showed dimly white around; beyond it rose up a sullen darkness, which seemed moving up closer in huge masses every instant. My steps gave a muffled sound in the air that grew colder and colder. The pale sky began again to grow blue—but it was the blue of night. The tiny stars glimmered and twinkled in it.

What I had been taking for a wood turned out to be a dark round hillock. "But where am I, then?" I repeated again aloud, standing still for the third time and looking inquiringly at my spot and tan English dog, Dianka by name, certainly the most intelligent of four-footed creatures. But the most intelligent of four-footed creatures only wagged her tail, blinked her weary eyes dejectedly, and gave me no sensible advice. I felt myself disgraced in her eyes and pushed desperately forward, as though I had suddenly guessed which way I ought to go; I scaled the hill, and found myself in a hollow of no great depth, ploughed round.

A strange sensation came over me at once. This hollow had the form of an almost perfect cauldron, with sloping sides; at the bottom of it were some great white stones standing upright—it seemed as though they had crept there for some secret council—and it was so still and dark in it, so dreary and weird seemed the sky, overhanging it, that my heart sank. Some little animal was whining feebly and piteously among the stones. I made haste to get out again on to the hillock. Till then I had not quite given up all hope of finding the way home; but at this point I finally decided that I was utterly lost, and without any further attempt to make out the surrounding objects, which were almost completely plunged in darkness, I walked straight forward, by the aid of the stars, at random.... For about half-an-hour I walked on in this way, though I could hardly move one leg before the other. It seemed as if I had never been in such a deserted country in my life; nowhere was there the glimmer of a fire, nowhere a sound to be heard. One sloping hillside followed another; fields stretched endlessly upon fields; bushes seemed to spring up out of the earth under my very nose. I kept walking and was just making up my mind to lie down somewhere till morning, when suddenly I found myself on the edge of a horrible precipice.

I quickly drew back my lifted foot, and through the almost

opaque darkness I saw far below me a vast plain. A long river skirted it in a semicircle, turned away from me; its course was marked by the steely reflection of the water still faintly glimmering here and there. The hill on which I found myself terminated abruptly in an almost overhanging precipice, whose gigantic profile stood out black against the dark-blue waste of sky, and directly below me, in the corner formed by this precipice and the plain near the river, which was there a dark, motionless mirror, under the lee of the hill, two fires side by side were smoking and throwing up red flames. People were stirring round them, shadows hovered, and sometimes the front of a little curly head was lighted up by the glow.

I found out at last where I had got to. This plain was well known in our parts under the name of Byezhin Prairie.... But there was no possibility of returning home, especially at night; my legs were sinking under me from weariness. I decided to get down to the fires and to wait for the dawn in the company of these men, whom I took for drovers. I got down successfully, but I had hardly let go of the last branch I had grasped, when suddenly two large shaggy white dogs rushed angrily barking upon me. The sound of ringing boyish voices came from round the fires; two or three boys quickly got up from the ground. I called back in response to their shouts of inquiry. They ran up to me, and at once called off the dogs, who were specially struck by the appearance of my Dianka. I came down to them.

I had been mistaken in taking the figures sitting round the fires for drovers. They were simply peasant boys from a neighboring village, who were in charge of a drove of horses. In hot summer weather with us they drive the horses out at night to graze in the open country: the flies and gnats would give them no peace in the daytime; they drive out the drove towards evening, and drive them back in the early morning: it's a great treat for the peasant boys. Bareheaded, in old fur-capes, they bestride the most spirited nags, and scurry along with merry cries and hooting and ringing laughter, swinging their arms and legs, and leaping into the air. The fine dust is stirred up in yellow clouds and moves along the road; the tramp of hoofs in unison resounds afar; the horses race along, pricking up their ears; in front of all, with his tail in the air and thistles in his tangled mane, prances some shaggy chestnut, constantly shifting his paces as he goes.

I told the boys I had lost my way, and sat down with them. They asked me where I came from, and then were silent for a little and turned away. Then we talked a little again. I lay down under a bush, whose shoots had been nibbled off, and began to look round. It was a marvelous picture; about the fire a red ring of light quivered and seemed to swoon away in the embrace of a background of darkness; the flame flaring up from time to time cast swift flashes of light beyond the boundary of this circle; a fine tongue of light licked the dry twigs and died away at once; long thin shadows, in their turn breaking in for an instant, danced right up to the very fires; darkness was struggling with light. Sometimes, when the fire burnt low and the circle of light shrank together, suddenly out of the encroaching darkness a horse's head was thrust in, bay, with striped markings or all white, stared with intent blank eyes upon us, nipped hastily the long grass, and drawing back again, vanished instantly. One could only hear it still munching and snorting. From the circle of light it was hard to make out what was going on in the darkness; everything close at hand seemed shut off by an almost black curtain; but farther away hills and forests were dimly visible in long blurs upon the horizon.

The dark unclouded sky stood, inconceivably immense, triumphant, above us in all its mysterious majesty. One felt a sweet oppression at one's heart, breathing in that peculiar, overpowering, yet fresh fragrance—the fragrance of a summer night in Russia. Scarcely a sound was to be heard around. . . . Only at times, in the river near, the sudden splash of a big

fish leaping, and the faint rustle of a reed on the bank, swaying lightly as the ripples reached it . . . the fires alone kept up
a subdued crackling.

The boys sat round them: there too sat the two dogs, who
had been so eager to devour me. They could not for long after
reconcile themselves to my presence, and, drowsily blinking
and staring into the fire, they growled now and then with an
unwonted sense of their own dignity; first they growled, and
then whined a little, as though deploring the impossibility of
carrying out their desires. There were altogether five boys:
Fedya, Pavlusha, Ilyusha, Kostya and Vanya. (From their talk
I learnt their names, and I intend now to introduce them to
the reader.)

The first and eldest of all, Fedya, one would take to be
about fourteen. He was a well-made boy, with good-looking,
delicate, rather small features, curly fair hair, bright eyes, and
a perpetual half-merry, half-careless smile. He belonged, by
all appearances, to a well-to-do family, and had ridden out to
the prairie, not through necessity, but for amusement. He
wore a gay print shirt, with a yellow border; a short new overcoat slung round his neck was almost slipping off his narrow
shoulders; a comb hung from his blue belt. His boots, coming
a little way up the leg, were certainly his own—not his father's. The second boy, Pavlusha, had tangled black hair, gray
eyes, broad cheek-bones, a pale face pitted with small-pox,
a large but well-cut mouth; his head altogether was large—"a
beer-barrel head," as they say—and his figure was square and
clumsy. He was not a good-looking boy—there's no denying
it!—and yet I liked him; he looked very sensible and straight-
forward, and there was a vigorous ring in his voice. He had
nothing to boast of in his attire; it consisted simply of a
homespun shirt and patched trousers. The face of the third,
Ilyusha, was rather uninteresting; it was a long face, with
short-sighted eyes and a hook nose; it expressed a kind of
dull, fretful uneasiness; his tightly-drawn lips seemed rigid;

his contracted brow never relaxed; he seemed continually blinking from the firelight. His flaxen—almost white—hair hung out in thin wisps under his low felt hat, which he kept pulling down with both hands over his ears. He had on new bast-shoes and leggings; a thick string, wound three times round his figure, carefully held together his neat black smock. Neither he nor Pavlusha looked more than twelve years old. The fourth, Kostya, a boy of ten, aroused my curiosity by his thoughtful and sorrowful look. His whole face was small, thin, freckled, pointed at the chin like a squirrel's; his lips were barely perceptible; but his great black eyes, that shone with liquid brilliance, produced a strange impression; they seemed trying to express something for which the tongue— his tongue, at least—had no words. He was undersized and weakly, and dressed rather poorly. The remaining boy, Vanya, I had not noticed at first; he was lying on the ground, peace- fully curled up under a square rug, and only occasionally thrust his curly brown head out from under it: this boy was seven years old at the most.

So I lay under the bush at one side and looked at the boys. A small pot was hanging over one of the fires; in it potatoes were cooking. Pavlusha was looking after them, and on his knees he was trying them by poking a splinter of wood into the boiling water. Fedya was lying leaning on his elbow, and smoothing out the skirts of his coat. Ilyusha was sitting be- side Kostya, and still kept blinking constrainedly. Kostya's head drooped despondently, and he looked away into the dis- tance. Vanya did not stir under his rug. I pretended to be asleep. Little by little, the boys began talking again.

At first they gossiped of one thing and another, the work of to-morrow, the horses; but suddenly Fedya turned to Ilyusha, and, as though taking up again an interrupted con- versation, asked him:

"Come then, so you've seen the domovoy?"

"No, I didn't see him, and no one ever can see him," an-

swered Ilyusha, in a weak hoarse voice, the sound of which
was wonderfully in keeping with the expression of his face; "I
heard him. . . . Yes, and not I alone."

"Where does he live—in your place?" asked Pavlusha.

"In the old paper-mill."

"Why, do you go to the factory?"

"Of course we do. My brother Avdushka and I, we are
paper-glazers."

"I say—factory-hands!"

"Well, how did you hear it, then?" asked Fedya.

"It was like this. It happened that I and my brother
Avdushka, with Fyodor of Mihyevska, and Ivashka the Squint-
eyed, and the other Ivashka who comes from the Red Hills,
and Ivashka of Suhorukov too—and there were some other
boys there as well—there were ten of us boys there altogether
—the whole shift, that is—it happened that we spent the
night at the paper-mill; that's to say, it didn't happen, but
Nazarov, the overseer, kept us. 'Why,' said he, 'should you
waste time going home, boys; there's a lot of work to-morrow,
so don't go home, boys.' So we stopped, and were all lying
down together, and Avdushka had just begun to say, 'I say,
boys, suppose the domovoy were to come?' And before he'd
finished saying so, some one suddenly began walking over
our heads; we were lying down below, and he began walking
upstairs overhead, where the wheel is. We listened: he walked;
the boards seemed to be bending under him, they creaked so;
then he crossed over, above our heads; all of a sudden the water began to drip and drip over the wheel; the wheel rattled
and rattled and again began to turn, though the sluices of the
conduit above had been let down. We wondered who could
have lifted them up so that the water could run; any way, the
wheel turned and turned a little, and then stopped. Then he
went to the door overhead and began coming down-stairs,
and came down like this, not hurrying himself; the stairs
seemed to groan under him too. . . . Well, he came right down

to our door, and waited and waited . . . and all of a sudden the door simply flew open. We were in a fright; we looked—there was nothing. . . . Suddenly what if the net on one of the vats didn't begin moving; it got up, and went rising and ducking and moving in the air as though some one were stirring with it, and then it was in its place again. Then, at another vat, a hook came off its nail, and then was on its nail again; and then it seemed as if some one came to the door, and suddenly coughed and choked like a sheep, but so loudly! . . . We all fell down in a heap and huddled against one another. . . . Just weren't we in a fright that night!"

"I say!" murmured Pavel, "what did he cough for?"

"I don't know; perhaps it was the damp."

All were silent for a little.

"Well," inquired Fedya, "are the potatoes done?"

Pavlusha tried them.

"No, they are raw. . . . My, what a splash!" he added, turning his face in the direction of the river; "that must be a pike. . . . And there's a star falling."

"I say, I can tell you something, brothers," began Kostya, in a shrill little voice; "listen what my dad told me the other day."

"Well, we are listening," said Fedya with a patronizing air.

"You know Gavrila, I suppose, the carpenter up in the big village?"

"Yes, we know him."

"And do you know why he is so sorrowful always, never speaks? do you know? I'll tell you why he's so sorrowful; he went one day, daddy said, he went, brothers, into the forest nutting. So he went nutting into the forest and lost his way; he went on—God only can tell where he got to. So he went on and on, brothers—but 'twas no good!—he could not find the way; and so night came on out of doors. So he sat down under a tree. 'I'll wait till morning,' thought he. He sat down and began to drop asleep. So as he was falling asleep, suddenly he heard some one call him. He looked up; there was no one. He fell asleep again; again he was called. He looked and looked again; and in front of him there sat a russalka on a branch, swinging herself and calling him to her, and simply dying with laughing; she laughed so.... And the moon was shining bright, so bright, the moon shone so clear—everything could be seen plain, brothers. So she called him, and she herself was as bright and as white sitting on the branch as some dace or a roach, or like some little carp so white and silvery.... Gavrila the carpenter almost fainted, brothers, but she laughed without stopping, and kept beckoning him to her like this. Then Gavrila was just getting up; he was just going to yield to the russalka, brothers, but—the Lord put it into his heart, doubtless—he crossed himself like this.... And it was so hard for him to make that cross, brothers; he said, 'My hand was simply like a stone; it would not move.' ... Ugh! the horrid witch.... So when he made the cross, brothers, the russalka, she left off laughing, and all at once how she did cry.... She cried, brothers, and wiped her eyes with her hair, and her hair was green as any hemp. So Gavrila looked and looked at her, and at last he fell to questioning her. 'Why are you weeping, wild thing of the woods?' And the russalka began to speak to him like this: 'If you had not crossed yourself, man,' she says, 'you should have lived with me in gladness of heart to the end of your days; and I weep, I am grieved at heart because you crossed yourself; but I will not grieve alone; you too shall grieve at heart to the end of your days.' Then she vanished, brothers, and at once it was plain to Gavrila how to get out of the forest.... Only since then he goes always sorrowful, as you see."

"Ugh!" said Fedya after a brief silence; "but how can such an evil thing of the woods ruin a Christian soul—he did not listen to her?"

"And I say!" said Kostya. "Gavrila said that her voice was as shrill and plaintive as a toad's."

"Did your father tell you that himself?" Fedya went on.

"Yes. I was lying in the loft; I heard it all."

"It's a strange thing. Why should he be sorrowful? . . . But I suppose she liked him, since she called him."

"Ay, she liked him!" put in Ilyusha. "Yes, indeed! she wanted to tickle him to death, that's what she wanted. That's what they do, those russalkas."

"There ought to be russalkas here too, I suppose," observed Fedya.

"No," answered Kostya, "this is a holy open place. There's one thing, though: the river's near."

All were silent. Suddenly from out of the distance came a prolonged, resonant, almost wailing sound, one of those inexplicable sounds of the night, which break upon a profound stillness, rise upon the air, linger, and slowly die away at last. You listen: it is as though there were nothing, yet it echoes still. It is as though some one had uttered a long, long cry upon the very horizon, as though some other had answered him with shrill harsh laughter in the forest, and a faint, hoarse hissing hovers over the river. The boys looked round about shivering. . . .

"Christ's aid be with us!" whispered Ilyusha.

"Ah, you craven crows!" cried Pavel, "what are you frightened of? Look, the potatoes are done." (They all came up to the pot and began to eat the smoking potatoes; only Vanya did not stir.) "Well, aren't you coming?" said Pavel.

But he did not creep out from under his rug. The pot was soon completely emptied.

"Have you heard, boys," began Ilyusha, "what happened with us at Varnavitsi?"

"Near the dam?" asked Fedya.

"Yes, yes, near the dam, the broken-down dam. That is a haunted place, such a haunted place, and so lonely. All round there are pits and quarries, and there are always snakes in pits."

"Well, what did happen? Tell us."

"Well, this is what happened. You don't know, perhaps,

Fedya, but there a drowned man was buried; he was drowned long, long ago, when the water was still deep; only his grave can still be seen, though it can only just be seen . . . like this —a little mound. . . . So one day the bailiff called the hunts-man Yermil, and says to him, 'Go to the post, Yermil.' Yermil always goes to the post for us; he has let all his dogs die; they never will live with him, for some reason, and they have never lived with him, though he's a good huntsman, and everyone liked him. So Yermil went to the post, and he stayed a bit in the town, and when he rode back, he was a little tipsy. It was night, a fine night; the moon was shining. . . . So Yermil rode across the dam; his way lay there. So, as he rode along, he saw, on the drowned man's grave, a little lamb, so white and curly and pretty, running about. So Yermil thought, 'I will take him,' and he got down and took him in his arms. But the little lamb didn't take any notice. So Yermil goes back to his horse, and the horse stares at him, and snorts and shakes his head; however, he said 'wo' to him and sat on him with the lamb, and rode on again; he held the lamb in front of him. He looks at him, and the lamb looks him straight in the face, like this. Yermil the huntsman felt upset. 'I don't remember,' he said, 'that lambs ever look at any one like that'; however, he began to stroke it like this on its wool, and to say, 'Chucky! chucky!' And the lamb suddenly showed its teeth and said too, 'Chucky! chucky!'"

The boy who was telling the story had hardly uttered this last word, when suddenly both dogs got up at once, and, bark-ing convulsively, rushed away from the fire and disappeared in the darkness. All the boys were alarmed. Vanya jumped up from under his rug. Pavlusha ran shouting after the dogs. Their barking quickly grew fainter in the distance. . . . There was the noise of the uneasy tramp of the frightened drove of horses. Pavlusha shouted aloud: "Hey Gray! Beetle!" . . . In a few minutes the barking ceased; Pavel's voice sounded still in the distance. . . . A little time more passed; the boys kept looking about in perplexity, as though expecting something to happen.... Suddenly the tramp of a galloping horse was heard; it stopped short at the pile of wood, and, hanging on to the mane, Pavel sprang nimbly off it. Both the dogs also leaped into the circle of light and at once sat down, their red tongues hanging out.

"What was it? what was it?" asked the boys.

"Nothing," answered Pavel, waving his hand to his horse; "I suppose the dogs scented something. I thought it was a wolf," he added, calmly drawing deep breaths into his chest.

I could not help admiring Pavel. He was very fine at that moment. His ugly face, animated by his swift ride, glowed with hardihood and determination. Without even a switch in his hand, he had, without the slightest hesitation, rushed out into the night alone to face a wolf.... "What a splendid fellow!" I thought, looking at him.

"Have you seen any wolves, then?" asked the trembling Kostya.

"There are always a good many of them here," answered Pavel; "but they are only troublesome in the winter."

He crouched down again before the fire. As he sat down on the ground, he laid his hand on the shaggy head of one of the dogs. For a long while the flattered brute did not turn his head, gazing sidewise with grateful pride at Pavlusha.

Vanya lay down under his rug again.

"What dreadful things you were telling us, Ilyusha!" began Fedya, whose part it was, as the son of a well-to-do peasant, to lead the conversation. (He spoke little himself, apparently afraid of lowering his dignity.) "And then some evil spirit set the dogs barking.... Certainly I have heard that place was haunted."

"Varnavitsi?...I should think it was haunted! More than once, they say, they have seen the old master there—the late master. He wears, they say, a long skirted coat, and keeps groaning like this, and looking for something on the ground.

Once grandfather Trofimitch met him. 'What,' says he, 'your honor, Ivan Ivanitch, are you pleased to look for on the ground?'"

"He asked him?" put in Fedya in amazement.

"Yes, he asked him."

"Well, I call Trofimitch a brave fellow after that.... Well, what did he say?"

"'I am looking for the herb that cleaves all things,' says he. But he speaks so thickly, so thickly. 'And what, your honor, Ivan Ivanitch, do you want with the herb that cleaves all things?' 'The tomb weighs on me; it weighs on me, Trofimitch: I want to get away—away.'"

"My word!" observed Fedya, "he didn't enjoy his life enough, I suppose."

"What a marvel!" said Kostya. "I thought one could only see the departed on All Hallows' day."

"One can see the departed any time," Ilyusha interposed with conviction. From what I could observe, I judged he knew the village superstitions better than the others.... "But on All Hallows' day you can see the living too; those, that is, whose turn it is to die that year. You need only sit in the church porch, and keep looking at the road. They will come by you along the road; those, that is, who will die that year. Last year old Ulyana went to the porch."

"Well, did she see anyone?" asked Kostya inquisitively.

"To be sure she did. At first she sat a long, long while, and saw no one and heard nothing...only it seemed as if some dog kept whining and whining like this somewhere.... Suddenly she looks up: a boy comes along the road with only a shirt on. She looked at him. It was Ivashka Fedosyev."

"He who died in the spring?" put in Fedya.

"Yes, he. He came along and never lifted up his head. But Ulyana knew him. And then she looks again: a woman came along. She stared and stared at her.... Ah, God Almighty!... it was herself coming along the road; Ulyana herself."

"Could it be herself?" asked Fedya.

"Yes, by God, herself."

"Well, but she is not dead yet, you know?"

"But the year is not over yet. And only look at her; her life hangs on a thread."

All were still again. Pavel threw a handful of dry twigs on to the fire. They were soon charred by the suddenly leaping flame; they cracked and smoked, and began to contract, curling up their burning ends. Gleams of light in broken flashes glanced in all directions, especially upwards. Suddenly a white dove flew straight into the bright light, fluttered round and round in terror, bathed in the red glow, and disappeared with a whirr of its wings.

"It's lost its home, I suppose," remarked Pavel. "Now it will fly till it gets somewhere, where it can rest till dawn."

"Why, Pavlusha," said Kostya, "might it not be a just soul flying to heaven?"

Pavel threw another handful of twigs on to the fire.

"Perhaps," he said at last.

"But tell us, please, Pavlusha," began Fedya, "what was seen in your parts at Shalamovy at the heavenly portent?"*

"When the sun could not be seen? Yes, indeed."

"Were you frightened then?"

"Yes; and we weren't the only ones. Our master, though he talked to us beforehand, and said there would be a heavenly portent, yet when it got dark, they say he himself was frightened out of his wits. And in the house-serfs' cottage the old woman, directly it grew dark, broke all the dishes in the oven with the poker. 'Who will eat now?' she said; 'the last day has come.' So the soup was all running about the place. And in the village there were such tales about among us: that white wolves would run over the earth, and would eat men, that a

---

*This is what the peasants call an eclipse.

bird of prey would pounce down on us, and that they would even see Trishka."*

"What is Trishka?" asked Kostya.

"Why, don't you know?" interrupted Ilyusha warmly. "Why, brother, where have you been brought up, not to know Trishka? You're a stay-at-home, one-eyed lot in your village, really! Trishka will be a marvelous man, who will come one day, and he will be such a marvelous man that they will never be able to catch him, and never be able to do anything with him; he will be such a marvelous man. The people will try to take him; for example, they will come after him with sticks, they will surround him, but he will blind their eyes so that they fall upon one another. They will put him in prison, for example; he will ask for a little water to drink in a bowl; they will bring him the bowl, and he will plunge into it and vanish from their sight. They will put chains on him, but he will only clap his hands—they will fall off him. So this Trishka will go through villages and towns; and this Trishka will be a wily man; he will lead astray Christ's people ... and they will be able to do nothing to him.... He will be such a marvelous, wily man."

"Well, then," continued Pavel, in his deliberate voice, "that's what he's like. And so they expected him in our parts. The old man declared that directly the heavenly portent began, Trishka would come. So the heavenly portent began. All the people were scattered over the street, in the fields, waiting to see what would happen. Our place, you know, is open country. They look; and suddenly down the mountain-side from the big village comes a man of some sort; such a strange man, with such a wonderful head ... that all scream: 'Oy, Trishka is coming! Oy, Trishka is coming!' and all run in

*The popular belief in Trishka is probably derived from some tradition of the Antichrist.

all directions! Our elder crawled into a ditch; his wife stumbled on the door-board and screamed with all her might; she terrified her yard-dog, so that he broke away from his chain and over the hedge and into the forest; and Kuzka's father, Dorofyitch, ran into the oats, lay down there, and began to cry like a quail. 'Perhaps,' says he, 'the Enemy, the Destroyer of Souls, will spare the birds, at least.' So they were all in such a scare! But he that was coming was our cooper Vavila; he had bought himself a new pitcher, and had put the empty pitcher over his head."

All the boys laughed; and again there was a silence for a while, as often happens when people are talking in the open air. I looked out into the solemn, majestic stillness of the night; the dewy freshness of late evening had been succeeded by the dry heat of midnight; the darkness still had long to lie in a soft curtain over the slumbering fields; there was still a long while left before the first whisperings, the first dewdrops of dawn. There was no moon in the heavens; it rose late at that time. Countless golden stars, twinkling in rivalry, seemed all running softly towards the Milky Way, and truly, looking at them, you were almost conscious of the whirling, never-resting motion of the earth.... A strange, harsh, painful cry sounded twice together over the river, and a few moments later, was repeated farther down....

Kostya shuddered. "What was that?"

"That was a heron's cry," replied Pavel tranquilly.

"A heron," repeated Kostya.... "And what was it, Pavlusha, I heard yesterday evening," he added, after a short pause; "you perhaps will know."

"What did you hear?"

"I will tell you what I heard. I was going from Stony Ridge to Shashkino; I went first through our walnut wood, and then passed by a little pool—you know where there's a sharp turn down to the ravine—there is a water-pit there, you know; it is quite overgrown with reeds; so I went near this pit, brothers, and suddenly from this came a sound of some one groaning, and piteously, so piteously; oo-oo, oo-oo! I was in such a fright, my brothers; it was late, and the voice was so miserable. I felt as if I should cry myself. . . . What could that have been, eh?"

"It was in that pit the thieves drowned Akim the forester, last summer," observed Pavel; "so perhaps it was his soul lamenting."

"Oh, dear, really, brothers," replied Kostya, opening wide his eyes, which were round enough before, "I did not know they had drowned Akim in that pit. Shouldn't I have been frightened if I'd known!"

"But they say there are little, tiny frogs," continued Pavel, "who cry piteously like that."

"Frogs? Oh, no, it was not frogs, certainly not. [A heron again uttered a cry above the river.] Ugh, there it is!" Kostya cried involuntarily; "it is just like a wood-spirit shrieking."

"The wood-spirit does not shriek; it is dumb," put in Ilyusha; "it only claps its hands and rattles."

"And have you seen it then, the wood-spirit?" Fedya asked him ironically.

"No, I have not seen it, and God preserve me from seeing it; but others have seen it. Why, one day it misled a peasant in our parts, and led him through the woods and all in a circle in one field. . . . He scarcely got home till daylight."

"Well, and did he see it?"

"Yes. He says it was a big, big creature, dark, wrapped up, just like a tree; you could not make it out well; it seemed to hide away from the moon, and kept staring and staring with its great eyes, and winking and winking with them. . . ."

"Ugh!" exclaimed Fedya with a slight shiver, and a shrug of the shoulders; "pfoo."

"And how does such an unclean brood come to exist in the world?" said Pavel; "it's a wonder."

"Don't speak ill of it; take care, it will hear you," said Ilyusha.

Again there was a silence.

"Look, look, brothers," suddenly came Vanya's childish voice; "look at God's little stars; they are swarming like bees!"

He put his fresh little face out from under his rug, leaned on his little fist, and slowly lifted up his large soft eyes. The eyes of all the boys were raised to the sky, and they were not lowered quickly.

"Well, Vanya," began Fedya caressingly, "is your sister Anyutka well?"

"Yes, she is very well," replied Vanya with a slight lisp.

"You ask her, why doesn't she come to see us?"

"I don't know."

"You tell her to come."

"Very well."

"Tell her I have a present for her."

"And a present for me too?"

"Yes, you too."

Vanya sighed.

"No; I don't want one. Better give it to her; she is so kind to us at home."

And Vanya laid his head down again on the ground. Pavel got up and took the empty pot in his hand.

"Where are you going?" Fedya asked him.

"To the river, to get water; I want some water to drink."

The dogs got up and followed him.

"Take care you don't fall into the river!" Ilyusha cried after him.

"Why should he fall in?" said Fedya. "He will be careful."

"Yes, he will be careful. But all kinds of things happen; he will stoop over, perhaps, to draw the water, and the water-spirit will clutch him by the hand, and drag him to him. Then they will say, 'The boy fell into the water.'... Fell in, indeed! ... There, he has crept in among the reeds," he added, listening.

The reeds certainly "shished," as they call it among us, as they were parted.

"But is it true," asked Kostya, "that crazy Akulina has been mad ever since she fell into the water?"

"Yes, ever since. . . . How dreadful she is now! But they say she was a beauty before then. The water-spirit bewitched her. I suppose he did not expect they would get her out so soon. So down there at the bottom he bewitched her."

(I had met this Akulina more than once. Covered with rags, fearfully thin, with face as black as a coal, blear-eyed and for ever grinning, she would stay whole hours in one place in the road, stamping with her feet, pressing her flesh-less hands to her breast, and slowly shifting from one leg to the other, like a wild beast in a cage. She understood nothing that was said to her, and only chuckled spasmodically from time to time.)

"But they say," continued Kostya, "that Akulina threw herself into the river because her lover had deceived her."

"Yes, that was it."

"And do you remember Vasya?" added Kostya, mournfully.

"What Vasya?" asked Fedya.

"Why, the one who was drowned," replied Kostya, "in this very river. Ah, what a boy he was! What a boy he was! His mother, Feklista, how she loved him, her Vasya! And she seemed to have a foreboding, Feklista did, that harm would come to him from the water. Sometimes, when Vasya went with us boys in the summer to bathe in the river, she used to be trembling all over. The other women did not mind; they passed by with the pails, and went on, but Feklista put her pail down on the ground, and set to calling him, "Come back, come back, my little joy; come back, my darling!" And no one knows how he was drowned. He was playing on the bank, and his mother was there hay-making; suddenly she hears, as though some one was blowing bubbles through the water, and behold! there was only Vasya's little cap to be seen swimming on the water. You know since then Feklista has not been right in her mind: she goes and lies down at the place where he was drowned; she lies down, brothers, and sings a song—you remember Vasya was always singing a song like that—so she sings it too, and weeps and weeps, and bitterly rails against God."

"Here is Pavlusha coming," said Fedya.

Pavel came up to the fire with a full pot in his hand.

"Boys," he began, after a short silence, "something bad happened."

"Oh, what?" asked Kostya hurriedly.

"I heard Vasya's voice."

They all seemed to shudder.

"What do you mean? what do you mean?" stammered Kostya.

"I don"t know. Only I went to stoop down to the water; suddenly I hear my name called in Vasya's voice, as though it came from below water: 'Pavlusha, Pavlusha, come here.' I came away. But I fetched the water, though."

"Ah, God have mercy upon us!" said the boys, crossing themselves.

"It was the water-spirit calling you, Pavel," said Fedya; "we were just talking of Vasya."

"Ah, it's a bad omen," said Ilyusha, deliberately.

"Well, never mind, don't bother about it," Pavel declared stoutly, and he sat down again; "no one can escape his fate."

The boys were still. It was clear that Pavel's words had produced a strong impression on them. They began to lie down before the fire as though preparing to go to sleep.

"What is that?" asked Kostya, suddenly lifting his head.

Pavel listened.

"It's the curlews flying and whistling."

"Where are they flying to?"

"To a land where, they say, there is no winter."

"But is there such a land?"

"Yes."

"Is it far away?"

"Far, far away, beyond the warm seas."

Kostya sighed and shut his eyes.

More than three hours had passed since I first came across the boys. The moon at last had risen; I did not notice it at first; it was such a tiny crescent. This moonless night was as solemn and hushed as it had been at first.... But already many stars, that not long before had been high up in the heavens, were setting over the earth's dark rim; everything around was perfectly still, as it is only still towards morning; all was sleeping the deep unbroken sleep that comes before daybreak. Already the fragrance in the air was fainter; once more a dew seemed falling.... How short are nights in summer!... The boys' talk died down when the fires did. The dogs even were dozing; the horses, so far as I could make out, in the hardly-perceptible, faintly shining light of the stars, were asleep with downcast heads.... I fell into a state of weary unconsciousness, which passed into sleep.

A fresh breeze passed over my face. I opened my eyes; the morning was beginning. The dawn had not yet flushed the sky, but already it was growing light in the east. Everything had become visible, though dimly visible, around. The pale gray sky was growing light and cold and bluish; the stars twinkled with a dimmer light, or disappeared; the earth was wet, the leaves covered with dew, and from the distance came sounds of life and voices, and a light morning breeze went fluttering over the earth. My body responded to it with a faint shudder of delight. I got up quickly and went to the boys. They were all sleeping, as though they were tired out, round the smoldering fire; only Pavel half rose and gazed intently at me.

I nodded to him, and walked homewards beside the misty river. Before I had walked two miles, already all around me, over the wide dew-drenched prairie, and in front from forest to forest, where the hills were growing green again, and behind, over the long dusty road and the sparkling bushes, flushed with the red glow, and the river faintly blue now under the lifting mist, flowed fresh streams of burning light, first pink, then red and golden. . . . All things began to stir, to awaken, to sing, to flutter, to speak. On all sides thick drops of dew sparkled in glittering diamonds; to welcome me, pure and clear as though bathed in the freshness of morning, came the notes of a bell, and suddenly there rushed by me, driven by the boys I had parted from, the drove of horses, refreshed and rested. . . .

Sad to say, I must add that in that year Pavel met his end. He was not drowned; he was killed by a fall from his horse. Pity! he was a splendid fellow!

WILLIAM WORDSWORTH

THE RUINED COTTAGE

. . . . SUPINE the Wanderer lay,
His eyes as if in drowsiness half shut,
The shadows of the breezy elms above
Dappling his face. He had not heard the sound
Of my approaching steps, and in the shade
Unnoticed did I stand some minutes' space.
At length I hailed him, seeing that his hat
Was moist with water-drops, as if the brim
Had newly scooped a running stream. He rose,
And ere our lively greeting into peace
Had settled, "'Tis," said I, "a burning day:
My lips are parched with thirst, but you, it seems,
Have somewhere found relief." He, at the word,
Pointing towards a sweet-briar, bade me climb
The fence where that aspiring shrub looked out
Upon the public way. It was a plot
Of garden ground run wild, its matted weeds
Marked with the steps of those, whom, as they passed,
The gooseberry trees that shot in long lank slips,
Or currants, hanging from their leafless stems,
In scanty strings, had tempted to o'erleap
The broken wall. I looked around, and there,
Where two tall hedge-rows of thick alder boughs
Joined in a cold damp nook, espied a well
Shrouded with willow-flowers and plum fern.
My thirst I slaked, and, from the cheerless spot

Withdrawing, straightway to the shade returned
Where sate the old Man on the cottage-bench;
And, while, beside him, with uncovered head,
I yet was standing, freely to respire,
And cool my temples in the fanning air,
Thus did he speak. "I see around me here
Things which you cannot see: we die, my Friend,
Nor we alone, but that which each man loved
And prized in his peculiar nook of earth
Dies with him, or is changed; and very soon
Even of the good is no memorial left.
—The poets, in their elegies and songs
Lamenting the departed, call the groves,
They call upon the hills and streams to mourn,
And senseless rocks; nor idly; for they speak,
In these their invocations, with a voice
Obedient to the strong creative power
Of human passion. Sympathies there are
More tranquil, yet perhaps of kindred birth,
That steal upon the meditative mind,
And grow with thought. Beside yon spring I stood,
And eyed its waters till we seemed to feel
One sadness, they and I. For them a bond
Of brotherhood is broken: time has been
When, everyday, the touch of human hand
Dislodged the natural sleep that binds them up
In mortal stillness; and they ministered
To human comfort. Stooping down to drink,
Upon the slimy foot-stone I espied
The useless fragment of a wooden bowl,
Green with the moss of years, and subject only
To the soft handling of the elements:
There let it lie—how foolish are such thoughts!
Forgive them;—never—never did my steps
Approach this door but she who dwelt within

A daughter's welcome gave me, and I loved her
As my own child. Oh, Sir! the good die first,
And they whose hearts are dry as summer dust
Burn to the socket. Many a passenger
Hath blessed poor Margaret for her gentle looks
When she upheld the cool refreshment drawn
From that forsaken spring; and no one came
But he was welcome; no one went away
But that it seemed she loved him. She is dead,
The light extinguished of her lonely hut,
The hut itself abandoned to decay,
And she forgotten in the quiet grave.

   "I speak," continued he, "of One whose stock
Of virtues bloomed beneath this lowly roof.
She was a Woman of a steady mind,
Tender and deep in her excess of love;
Not speaking much, pleased rather with the joy
Of her own thoughts: by some especial care
Her temper had been framed, as if to make
A Being, who by adding love to peace
Might live on earth a life of happiness.
Her wedded Partner lacked not on his side
The humble worth that satisfied her heart:
Frugal, affectionate, sober, and withal
Keenly industrious. She with pride would tell
That he was often seated at his loom,
In summer, ere the mower was abroad
Among the dewy grass,—in early spring,
Ere the last star had vanished.—They who passed
At evening, from behind the garden fence
Might hear his busy spade, which he would ply,
After his daily work, until the light
Had failed, and every leaf and flower were lost
In the dark hedges. So their days were spent

In peace and comfort; and a pretty boy
Was their best hope, next to the God in heaven.

   "Not twenty years ago, but you I think
Can scarcely bear it now in mind, there came
Two blighting seasons, when the fields were left
With half a harvest. It pleased Heaven to add
A worse affliction in the plague of war:
This happy Land was stricken to the heart!
A Wanderer then among the cottages,
I, with my freight of winter raiment, saw
The hardships of that season: many rich
Sank down, as in a dream, among the poor;
And of the poor did many cease to be,
And their place knew them not. Meanwhile, abridged
Of daily comforts, gladly reconciled
To numerous self-denials, Margaret
Went struggling on through those calamitous years
With cheerful hope, until the second autumn,
When her life's Helpmate on a sick-bed lay,
Smitten with perilous fever. In disease
He lingered long; and, when his strength returned,
He found the little he had stored, to meet
The hour of accident or crippling age,
Was all consumed. A second infant now
Was added to the troubles of a time
Laden, for them and all of their degree,
With care and sorrow: shoals of artisans
From ill-requited labour turned adrift
Sought daily bread from public charity,
They, and their wives and children—happier far
Could they have lived as do the little birds
That peck along the hedge-rows, or the kite
That makes her dwelling on the mountain rocks!

"A sad reverse it was for him who long
Had filled with plenty, and possessed in peace,
This lonely Cottage. At the door he stood,
And whistled many a snatch of merry tunes
That had no mirth in them; or with his knife
Carved uncouth figures on the heads of sticks—
Then, not less idly, sought, through every nook
In house or garden, any casual work
Of use or ornament; and with a strange,
Amusing, yet uneasy, novelty,
He mingled, where he might, the various tasks
Of summer, autumn, winter, and of spring.
But this endured not; his good humour soon
Became a weight in which no pleasure was:
And poverty brought on a petted mood
And a sore temper: day by day he drooped,
And he would leave his work—and to the town
Would turn without an errand his slack steps;
Or wander here and there among the fields.
One while he would speak lightly of his babes,
And with a cruel tongue: at other times
He tossed them with a false unnatural joy:
And 'twas a rueful thing to see the looks
Of the poor innocent children. 'Every smile,'
Said Margaret to me, here beneath these trees,
"Made my heart bleed.'"

                         At this the Wanderer paused;
And, looking up to those enormous elms,
He said, "'Tis now the hour of deepest noon.
At this still season of repose and peace,
This hour when all things which are not at rest
Are cheerful; while this multitude of flies
With tuneful hum is filling all the air;
Why should a tear be on an old Man's cheek?

Why should we thus, with an untoward mind,
And in the weakness of humanity,
From natural wisdom turn our hearts away;
To natural comfort shut our eyes and ears;
And, feeding on disquiet, thus disturb
The calm of nature with our restless thoughts?"

———

He spake with somewhat of a solemn tone:
But, when he ended, there was in his face
Such easy cheerfulness, a look so mild,
That for a little time it stole away
All recollection; and that simple tale
Passed from my mind like a forgotten sound.
A while on trivial things we held discourse,
To me soon tasteless. In my own despite,
I thought of that poor Woman as of one
Whom I had known and loved. He had rehearsed
Her homely tale with such familiar power,
With such an active countenance, an eye
So busy, that the things of which he spake
Seemed present; and, attention now relaxed,
A heart-felt chillness crept along my veins.
I rose; and, having left the breezy shade,
Stood drinking comfort from the warmer sun,
That had not cheered me long—ere, looking round
Upon that tranquil Ruin, I returned,
And begged of the old Man that, for my sake,
He would resume his story.
                              He replied,
"It were a wantonness, and would demand
Severe reproof, if we were men whose hearts
Could hold vain dalliance with the misery
Even of the dead; contented thence to draw

A momentary pleasure, never marked
By reason, barren of all future good.
But we have known that there is often found
In mournful thoughts, and always might be found,
A power to virtue friendly; were't not so,
I am a dreamer among men, indeed
An idle dreamer! 'Tis a common tale,
An ordinary sorrow of man's life,
A tale of silent suffering, hardly clothed
In bodily form.—But without further bidding
I will proceed.

       While thus it fared with them,
To whom this cottage, till those hapless years,
Had been a blessed home, it was my chance
To travel in a country far remote;
And when these lofty elms once more appeared
What pleasant expectations lured me on
O'er the flat Common!—With quick step I reached
The threshold, lifted with light hand the latch;
But, when I entered, Margaret looked at me
A little while; then turned her head away
Speechless,—and, sitting down upon a chair,
Wept bitterly. I wist not what to do,
Nor how to speak to her. Poor Wretch! at last
She rose from off her seat, and then,—O Sir!
I cannot *tell* how she pronounced my name:—
With fervent love, and with a face of grief
Unutterably helpless, and a look
That seemed to cling upon me, she enquired
If I had seen her husband. As she spake
A strange surprise and fear came to my heart,
Nor had I power to answer ere she told
That he had disappeared—not two months gone.
He left his house: two wretched days had past,
And on the third, as wistfully she raised

Her head from off her pillow, to look forth,
Like one in trouble, for returning light,
Within her chamber-casement she espied
A folded paper, lying as if placed
To meet her waking eyes. This tremblingly
She opened—found no writing, but beheld
Pieces of money carefully enclosed,
Silver and gold. 'I shuddered at the sight,'
Said Margaret, 'for I knew it was his hand
That must have placed it there; and ere that day
Was ended, that long anxious day, I learned,
From one who by my husband had been sent
With the sad news, that he had joined a troop
Of soldiers, going to a distant land.
—He left me thus—he could not gather heart
To take a farewell of me; for he feared
That I should follow with my babes, and sink
Beneath the misery of that wandering life.'

    "This tale did Margaret tell with many tears:
And, when she ended, I had little power
To give her comfort, and was glad to take
Such words of hope from her own mouth as served
To cheer us both. But long we had not talked
Ere we built up a pile of better thoughts,
And with a brighter eye she looked around
As if she had been shedding tears of joy.
We parted.—'Twas the time of early spring;
I left her busy with her garden tools;
And well remember, o'er that fence she looked,
And, while I paced along the foot-way path,
Called out, and sent a blessing after me,
With tender cheerfulness, and with a voice
That seemed the very sound of happy thoughts.

"I roved o'er many a hill and many a dale,
With my accustomed load; in heat and cold,
Through many a wood and many an open ground,
In sunshine and in shade, in wet and fair,
Drooping or blithe of heart, as might befall;
My best companions now the driving winds,
And now the 'trotting brooks' and whispering trees,
And now the music of my own sad steps,
With many a short-lived thought that passed between,
And disappeared.
           I journeyed back this way,
When, in the warmth of midsummer, the wheat
Was yellow; and the soft and bladed grass,
Springing afresh, had o'er the hay-field spread
Its tender verdure. At the door arrived,
I found that she was absent. In the shade,
Where now we sit, I waited her return.
Her cottage, then a cheerful object, wore
Its customary look,—only, it seemed,
The honeysuckle, crowding round the porch,
Hung down in heavier tufts; and that bright weed,
The yellow stone-crop, suffered to take root
Along the window's edge, profusely grew
Blinding the lower panes. I turned aside,
And strolled into her garden. It appeared
To lag behind the season, and had lost
Its pride of neatness. Daisy-flowers and thrift
Had broken their trim border-lines, and straggled
O'er paths they used to deck: carnations, once
Prized for surpassing beauty, and no less
For the peculiar pains they had required,
Declined their languid heads, wanting support.
The cumbrous bind-weed, with its wreaths and bells,
Had twined about her two small rows of peas,

And dragged them to the earth.
                              Ere this an hour
Was wasted.—Back I turned my restless steps;
A stranger passed; and, guessing whom I sought,
He said that she was used to ramble far.—
The sun was sinking in the west; and now
I sate with sad impatience. From within
Her solitary infant cried aloud;
Then, like a blast that dies away self-stilled,
The voice was silent. From the bench I rose;
But neither could divert nor soothe my thoughts.
The spot, though fair, was very desolate—
The longer I remained, more desolate:
And, looking round me, now I first observed
The corner stones, on either side the porch,
With dull red stains discoloured, and stuck o'er
With tufts and hairs of wool, as if the sheep
That fed upon the Common, thither came
Familiarly, and found a couching-place
Even at her threshold. Deeper shadows fell
From these tall elms; the cottage-clock struck eight;—
I turned, and saw her distant a few steps.
Her face was pale and thin—her figure, too,
Was changed. As she unlocked the door, she said,
'It grieves me you have waited here so long,
But, in good truth, I've wandered much of late;
And, sometimes—to my shame I speak—have need
Of my best prayers to bring me back again.'
While on the board she spread our evening meal,
She told me—interrupting not the work
Which gave employment to her listless hands—
That she had parted with her elder child;
To a kind master on a distant farm
Now happily apprenticed.—'I perceive
You look at me, and you have cause; to-day

I have been travelling far; and many days
About the fields I wander, knowing this
Only, that what I seek I cannot find;
And so I waste my time: for I am changed;
And to myself,' said she, 'have done much wrong
And to this helpless infant. I have slept
Weeping, and weeping have I waked; my tears
Have flowed as if my body were not such
As others are; and I could never die.
But I am now in mind and in my heart
More easy; and I hope,' said she, 'that God
Will give me patience to endure the things
Which I behold at home.'

                   It would have grieved
Your very soul to see her. Sir, I feel
The story linger in my heart; I fear
'Tis long and tedious; but my spirit clings
To that poor Woman:—so familiarly
Do I perceive her manner, and her look,
And presence; and so deeply do I feel
Her goodness, that, not seldom, in my walks
A momentary trance comes over me;
And to myself I seem to muse on One
By sorrow laid asleep; or borne away,
A human being destined to awake
To human life, or something very near
To human life, when he shall come again
For whom she suffered. Yes, it would have grieved
Your very soul to see her: evermore
Her eyelids drooped, her eyes downward were cast;
And, when she at her table gave me food,
She did not look at me. Her voice was low,
Her body was subdued. In every act
Pertaining to her house-affairs, appeared
The careless stillness of a thinking mind

Self-occupied; to which all outward things
Are like an idle matter. Still she sighed,
But yet no motion of the breast was seen,
No heaving of the heart. While by the fire
We sate together, sighs came on my ear,
I knew not how, and hardly whence they came.

    "Ere my departure, to her care I gave,
For her son's use, some tokens of regard,
Which with a look of welcome she received;
And I exhorted her to place her trust
In God's good love, and seek his help by prayer.
I took my staff, and, when I kissed her babe,
The tears stood in her eyes. I left her then
With the best hope and comfort I could give:
She thanked me for my wish;—but for my hope
It seemed she did not thank me.
                    I returned,
And took my rounds along this road again
When on its sunny bank the primrose flower
Peeped forth, to give an earnest of the Spring.
I found her sad and drooping: she had learned
No tidings of her husband; if he lived,
She knew not that he lived; if he were dead,
She knew not he was dead. She seemed the same
In person and appearance; but her house
Bespake a sleepy hand of negligence;
The floor was neither dry nor neat, the hearth
Was comfortless, and her small lot of books,
Which, in the cottage-window, heretofore
Had been piled up against the corner panes
In seemly order, now, with straggling leaves
Lay scattered here and there, open or shut,
As they had chanced to fall. Her infant Babe
Had from its mother caught the trick of grief,

And sighed among its playthings. I withdrew,
And once again entering the garden saw,
More plainly still, that poverty and grief
Were now come nearer to her: weeds defaced
The hardened soil, and knots of withered grass:
No ridges there appeared of clear black mould,
No winter greenness; of her herbs and flowers,
It seemed the better part were gnawed away
Or trampled into earth; a chain of straw,
Which had been twined about the slender stem
Of a young apple-tree, lay at its root;
The bark was nibbled round by truant sheep.
—Margaret stood near, her infant in her arms,
And, noting that my eye was on the tree,
She said, 'I fear it will be dead and gone
Ere Robert come again.' When to the House
We had returned together, she enquired
If I had any hope:—but for her babe
And for her little orphan boy, she said,
She had no wish to live, that she must die
Of sorrow. Yet I saw the idle loom
Still in its place; his Sunday garments hung
Upon the self-same nail; his very staff
Stood undisturbed behind the door.

                               And when,
In bleak December, I retraced this way,
She told me that her little babe was dead,
And she was left alone. She now, released
From her maternal cares, had taken up
The employment common through these wilds, and gained,
By spinning hemp, a pittance for herself;
And for this end had hired a neighbour's boy
To give her needful help. That very time
Most willingly she put her work aside,
And walked with me along the miry road,

Heedless how far; and, in such piteous sort
That any heart had ached to hear her, begged
That, wheresoe'er I went, I still would ask
For him whom she had lost. We parted then—
Our final parting; for from that time forth
Did many seasons pass ere I returned
Into this tract again.

                Nine tedious years;
From their first separation, nine long years,
She lingered in unquiet widowhood;
A Wife and Widow. Needs must it have been
A sore heart-wasting! I have heard, my Friend,
That in yon arbour oftentimes she sate
Alone, through half the vacant sabbath day;
And, if a dog passed by, she still would quit
The shade, and look abroad. On this old bench
For hours she sate; and evermore her eye
Was busy in the distance, shaping things
That made her heart beat quick. You see that path,
Now faint,—the grass has crept o'er its grey line;
There, to and fro, she paced through many a day
Of the warm summer, from a belt of hemp
That girt her waist, spinning the long-drawn thread
With backward steps. Yet ever as there passed
A man whose garment showed the soldier's red,
Or crippled mendicant in soldier's garb,
The little child who sate to turn the wheel
Ceased from his task; and she with faltering voice
Made many a fond enquiry; and when they,
Whose presence gave no comfort, were gone by,
Her heart was still more sad. And by yon gate,
That bars the traveller's road, she often stood,
And when a stranger horseman came, the latch
Would lift, and in his face look wistfully:
Most happy, if, from aught discovered there

Of tender feeling, she might dare repeat
The same sad question. Meanwhile her poor Hut
Sank to decay; for he was gone, whose hand,
At the first nipping of October frost,
Closed up each chink, and with fresh bands of straw
Chequered the green-grown thatch. And so she lived
Through the long winter, reckless and alone;
Until her house by frost, and thaw, and rain,
Was sapped; and while she slept, the nightly damps
Did chill her breast; and in the stormy day
Her tattered clothes were ruffled by the wind,
Even at the side of her own fire. Yet still
She loved this wretched spot, nor would for worlds
Have parted hence; and still that length of road,
And this rude bench, one torturing hope endeared,
Fast rooted at her heart: and here, my Friend,—
In sickness she remained; and here she died;
Last human tenant of these ruined walls!"

    The old Man ceased: he saw that I was moved;
From that low bench, rising instinctively
I turned aside in weakness, nor had power
To thank him for the tale which he had told.
I stood, and leaning o'er the garden wall
Reviewed that Woman's sufferings; and it seemed
To comfort me while with a brother's love
I blessed her in the impotence of grief.
Then towards the cottage I returned; and traced
Fondly, though with an interest more mild,
That secret spirit of humanity
Which 'mid the calm oblivious tendencies
Of nature, 'mid her plants, and weeds, and flowers,
And silent overgrowings, still survived.
The old Man, noting this, resumed, and said,
"My Friend! enough to sorrow you have given,

The purposes of wisdom ask no more:
Nor more would she have craved as due to One
Who, in her worst distress, had ofttimes felt
The unbounded might of prayer; and learned, with soul
Fixed on the Cross, that consolation springs,
From sources deeper far than deepest pain,
For the meek Sufferer. Why then should we read
The forms of things with an unworthy eye?
She sleeps in the calm earth, and peace is here.
I well remember that those very plumes,
Those weeds, and the high spear-grass on that wall,
By mist and silent rain-drops silvered o'er,
As once I passed, into my heart conveyed
So still an image of tranquillity,
So calm and still, and looked so beautiful
Amid the uneasy thoughts which filled my mind,
That what we feel of sorrow and despair
From ruin and from change, and all the grief
That passing shows of Being leave behind,
Appeared an idle dream, that could maintain,
Nowhere, dominion o'er the enlightened spirit
Whose meditative sympathies repose
Upon the breast of Faith. I turned away,
And walked along my road in happiness."

FRANK O'CONNOR

PEASANTS

WHEN MICHAEL John Cronin stole the funds of the Carricknabreena Hurling, Football and Temperance Association, commonly called the Club, everyone said: "Devil's cure to him!" "'Tis the price of him!" "Kind father for him!" "What did I tell you?" and the rest of the things people say when an acquaintance has got what is coming to him.

And not only Michael John but the whole Cronin family, seed, breed, and generation, came in for it; there wasn't one of them for twenty miles round or a hundred years back but his deeds and sayings were remembered and examined by the light of this fresh scandal. Michael John's father (the heavens be his bed!) was a drunkard who beat his wife, and his father before him a land-grabber. Then there was an uncle or grand-uncle who had been a policeman and taken a hand in the bloody work at Mitchelstown long ago, and an unmarried sister of the same whose good name it would by all accounts have needed a regiment of husbands to restore. It was a grand shaking-up the Cronins got altogether, and anyone who had a grudge in for them, even if it was no more than a thirty-third cousin, had rare sport, dropping a friendly word about it and saying how sorry he was for the poor mother till he had the blood lighting in the Cronin eyes.

There was only one thing for them to do with Michael John; that was to send him to America and let the thing blow over, and that, no doubt, is what they would have done but for a certain unpleasant and extraordinary incident.

Father Crowley, the parish priest, was chairman of the committee. He was a remarkable man, even in appearance; tall, powerfully built, but very stooped, with shrewd, loveless eyes that rarely softened to anyone except two or three old people. He was a strange man, well on in years, noted for his strong political views, which never happened to coincide with those of any party, and as obstinate as the devil himself. Now what should Father Crowley do but try to force the committee to prosecute Michael John?

The committee were all religious men who up to this had never as much as dared to question the judgments of a man of God: yes, faith, and if the priest had been a bully, which to give him his due he wasn't, he might have danced a jig on their backs and they wouldn't have complained. But a man has principles, and the like of this had never been heard of in the parish before. What? Put the police on a boy and he in trouble?

One by one the committee spoke up and said so. "But he did wrong," said Father Crowley, thumping the table. "He did wrong and he should be punished."

"Maybe so, father," said Con Norton, the vice-chairman, who acted as spokesman. "Maybe you're right, but you wouldn't say his poor mother should be punished too and she a widow-woman?"

"True for you!" chorused the others.

"Serve his mother right!" said the priest shortly. "There's none of you but knows better than I do the way that young man was brought up. He's a rogue and his mother is a fool. Why didn't she beat Christian principles into him when she had him on her knee?"

"That might be, too," Norton agreed mildly. "I wouldn't say but you're right, but is that any reason his Uncle Peter should be punished?"

"Or his Uncle Dan?" asked another.

"Or his Uncle James?" asked a third.

"Or his cousins, the Dwyers, that keep the little shop in Lissnacarriga, as decent a living family as there is in County Cork?" asked a fourth.

"No, father," said Norton, "the argument is against you."

"Is it indeed?" exclaimed the priest, growing cross. "Is it so? What the devil has it to do with his Uncle Dan or his Uncle James? What are ye talking about? What punishment is it to them, will ye tell me that? Ye'll be telling me next 'tis a punishment to me and I a child of Adam like himself."

"Wisha now, father," asked Norton incredulously, "do you mean 'tis no punishment to them having one of their own blood made a public show? Is it mad you think we are? Maybe 'tis a thing you'd like done to yourself?"

"There was none of my family ever a thief," replied Father Crowley shortly.

"Begor, we don't know whether there was or not," snapped a little man called Daly, a hot-tempered character from the hills.

"Easy, now! Easy, Phil!" said Norton warningly.

"What do you mean by that?" asked Father Crowley, rising and grabbing his hat and stick.

"What I mean," said Daly, blazing up, "is that I won't sit here and listen to insinuations about my native place from any foreigner. There are as many rogues and thieves and vagabonds and liars in Cullough as ever there were in Carricknabreena—ay, begod, and more, and bigger! That's what I mean."

"No, no, no, no," Norton said soothingly. "That's not what he means at all, father. We don't want any bad blood between Cullough and Carricknabreena. What he means is that the Crowleys may be a fine substantial family in their own country, but that's fifteen long miles away, and this isn't their country, and the Cronins are neighbors of ours since the dawn of history and time, and 'twould be a very queer thing if at this hour we handed one of them over to the police. . . . And now, listen to me, father," he went on, forgetting his role

323

of pacificator and hitting the table as hard as the rest, "if a cow of mine got sick in the morning, 'tisn't a Cremin or a Crowley I'd be asking for help, and damn the bit of use 'twould be to me if I did. And everyone knows I'm no enemy of the Church but a respectable farmer that pays his dues and goes to his duties regularly."

"True for you! True for you!" agreed the committee.

"I don't give a snap of my finger what you are," retorted the priest. "And now listen to me, Con Norton. I bear young Cronin no grudge, which is more than some of you can say, but I know my duty and I'll do it in spite of the lot of you."

He stood at the door and looked back. They were gazing blankly at one another, not knowing what to say to such an impossible man. He shook his fist at them.

"Ye all know me," he said. "Ye know that all my life I'm fighting the long-tailed families. Now, with the help of God, I'll shorten the tail of one of them."

Father Crowley's threat frightened them. They knew he was an obstinate man and had spent his time attacking what he called the "corruption" of councils and committees, which was all very well as long as it happened outside your own parish. They dared not oppose him openly because he knew too much about all of them and, in public at least, had a lacerating tongue. The solution they favored was a tactful one. They formed themselves into a Michael John Cronin Fund Committee and canvassed the parishioners for subscriptions to pay off what Michael John had stolen. Regretfully they decided that Father Crowley would hardly countenance a football match for the purpose.

Then with the defaulting treasurer, who wore a suitably contrite air, they marched up to the presbytery. Father Crowley was at his dinner but he told the housekeeper to show them in. He looked up in astonishment as his dining-room filled with the seven committeemen, pushing before them the cowed Michael John.

"Who the blazes are ye?" he asked, glaring at them over the lamp.

"We're the Club Committee, father," replied Norton.

"Oh, are ye?"

"And this is the treasurer—the ex-treasurer, I should say."

"I won't pretend I'm glad to see him," said Father Crowley grimly.

"He came to say he's sorry, father," went on Norton. "He is sorry, and that's as true as God, and I'll tell you no lie. . . ." Norton made two steps forward and in a dramatic silence laid a heap of notes and silver on the table.

"What's that?" asked Father Crowley.

"The money, father. 'Tis all paid back now and there's nothing more between us. Any little crossness there was, we'll say no more about it, in the name of God."

The priest looked at the money and then at Norton.

"Con," he said, "you'd better keep the soft word for the judge. Maybe he'll think more of it than I do."

"The judge, father?"

"Ay, Con, the judge."

There was a long silence. The committee stood with open mouths, unable to believe it.

"And is that what you're doing to us, father?" asked Norton in a trembling voice. "After all the years, and all we done for you, is it you're going to show us up before the whole country as a lot of robbers?"

"Ah, ye idiots, I'm not showing ye up."

"You are then, father, and you're showing up every man, woman, and child in the parish," said Norton. "And mark my words, 'twon't be forgotten for you."

The following Sunday Father Crowley spoke of the matter from the altar. He spoke for a full half hour without a trace of emotion on his grim old face, but his sermon was one long, venomous denunciation of the "long-tailed families" who, according to him, were the ruination of the country and made a mockery of truth, justice, and charity. He was, as his congregation agreed, a shockingly obstinate old man who never knew when he was in the wrong.

After Mass he was visited in his sacristy by the committee. He gave Norton a terrible look from under his shaggy eyebrows, which made that respectable farmer flinch.

"Father," Norton said appealingly, "we only want one word with you. One word and then we'll go. You're a hard character, and you said some bitter things to us this morning; things we never deserved from you. But we're quiet, peaceable poor men and we don't want to cross you."

Father Crowley made a sound like a snort.

"We came to make a bargain with you, father," said Norton, beginning to smile.

"A bargain?"

"We'll say no more about the whole business if you'll do one little thing—just one little thing—to oblige us."

"The bargain!" the priest said impatiently. "What's the bargain?"

"We'll leave the matter drop for good and all if you'll give the boy a character."

"Yes, father," cried the committee in chorus. "Give him a character! Give him a character!"

"Give him a what?" cried the priest.

"Give him a character, father, for the love of God," said Norton emotionally. "If you speak up for him, the judge will leave him off and there'll be no stain on the parish."

"Is it out of your minds you are, you halfwitted angashores?" asked Father Crowley, his face suffused with blood, his head trembling. "Here am I all these years preaching to ye about decency and justice and truth and ye no more understand me than that wall there. Is it the way ye want me to perjure myself? Is it the way ye want me to tell a damned lie with the name of Almighty God on my lips? Answer me, is it?"

"Ah, what perjure!" Norton replied wearily. "Sure, can't

you say a few words for the boy? No one is asking you to say much. What harm will it do you to tell the judge he's an honest, good-living, upright lad, and that he took the money without meaning any harm?"

"My God!" muttered the priest, running his hands distractedly through his gray hair. "There's no talking to ye, no talking to ye, ye lot of sheep."

When he was gone the committeemen turned and looked at one another in bewilderment.

"That man is a terrible trial," said one.

"He's a tyrant," said Daly vindictively.

"He is, indeed," sighed Norton, scratching his head. "But in God's holy name, boys, before we do anything, we'll give him one more chance."

That evening when he was at his tea the committeemen called again. This time they looked very spruce, businesslike, and independent. Father Crowley glared at them.

"Are ye back?" he asked bitterly. "I was thinking ye would be. I declare to my goodness, I'm sick of ye and yeer old committee."

"Oh, we're not the committee, father," said Norton stiffly.

"Ye're not?"

"We're not."

"All I can say is, ye look mighty like it. And, if I'm not being impertinent, who the deuce are ye?"

"We're a deputation, father."

"Oh, a deputation! Fancy that, now. And a deputation from what?"

"A deputation from the parish, father. Now, maybe you'll listen to us."

"Oh, go on! I'm listening, I'm listening."

"Well, now, 'tis like this, father," said Norton, dropping his airs and graces and leaning against the table. "'Tis about that little business this morning. Now, father, maybe you don't understand us and we don't understand you. There's a lot of misunderstanding in the world today, father. But we're quiet simple poor men that want to do the best we can for everybody, and a few words or a few pounds wouldn't stand in our way. Now, do you follow me?"

"I declare," said Father Crowley, resting his elbows on the table, "I don't know whether I do or not."

"Well, 'tis like this, father. We don't want any blame on the parish or on the Cronins, and you're the one man that can save us. Now all we ask of you is to give the boy a character—"

"Yes, father," interrupted the chorus, "give him a character! Give him a character!"

"Give him a character, father, and you won't be troubled by him again. Don't say no to me now till you hear what I have to say. We won't ask you to go next, nigh or near the court. You have pen and ink beside you and one couple of lines is all you need write. When 'tis over you can hand Michael John his ticket to America and tell him not to show his face in Carricknabreena again. There's the price of his ticket, father," he added, clapping a bundle of notes on the table. "The Cronins themselves made it up, and we have his mother's word and his own word that he'll clear out the minute 'tis all over."

"He can go to pot!" retorted the priest. "What is it to me where he goes?"

"Now, father, can't you be patient?" Norton asked reproachfully. "Can't you let me finish what I'm saying? We know 'tis no advantage to you, and that's the very thing we came to talk about. Now, supposing—just supposing for the sake of argument—that you do what we say, there's a few of us here, and between us, we'd raise whatever little contribution to the parish fund you'd think would be reasonable to cover the expense and trouble to yourself. Now do you follow me?"

"Con Norton," said Father Crowley, rising and holding the edge of the table, "I follow you. This morning it was perjury, and now 'tis bribery, and the Lord knows what 'twill be next. I see I've been wasting my breath.... And I see too," he added savagely, leaning across the table towards them, "a pedigree bull would be more use to ye than a priest."

"What do you mean by that, father?" asked Norton in a low voice.

"What I say."

"And that's a saying that will be remembered for you the longest day you live," hissed Norton, leaning towards him till they were glaring at one another over the table.

"A bull," gasped Father Crowley. "Not a priest."

" 'Twill be remembered."

"Will it? Then remember this too. I'm an old man now. I'm forty years a priest, and I'm not a priest for the money or power or glory of it, like others I know. I gave the best that was in me—maybe 'twasn't much but 'twas more than many a better man would give, and at the end of my days ..." lowering his voice to a whisper he searched them with his terrible eyes, "... at the end of my days, if I did a wrong thing, or a bad thing, or an unjust thing, there isn't man or woman in this parish that would brave me to my face and call me a villain. And isn't that a poor story for an old man that tried to be a good priest?" His voice changed again and he raised his head defiantly. "Now get out before I kick you out!"

And true to his word and character not one word did he say in Michael John's favor the day of the trial, no more than if he was a black. Three months Michael John got and by all accounts he got off light.

He was a changed man when he came out of jail, downcast and dark in himself. Everyone was sorry for him, and people who had never spoken to him before spoke to him then. To all of them he said modestly: "I'm very grateful to you, friend, for overlooking my misfortune." As he wouldn't go to America, the committee made another whip-round and between what they had collected before and what the Cronins had made up to send him to America, he found himself with enough to open a small shop. Then he got a job in the County Council, and an agency for some shipping company, till at last he was able to buy a public-house.

As for Father Crowley, till he was shifted twelve months later, he never did a day's good in the parish. The dues went down and the presents went down, and people with money to spend on Masses took it fifty miles away sooner than leave it to him. They said it broke his heart.

He has left unpleasant memories behind him. Only for him, people say, Michael John would be in America now. Only for him he would never have married a girl with money, or had it to lend to poor people in the hard times, or ever sucked the blood of Christians. For, as an old man said to me of him: "A robber he is and was, and a grabber like his grandfather before him, and an enemy of the people like his uncle, the policeman; and though some say he'll dip his hand where he dipped it before, for myself I have no hope unless the mercy of God would send us another Moses or Brian Boru to cast him down and hammer him in the dust."

ISAK DINESEN

SORROW-ACRE

THE LOW, undulating Danish landscape was silent and serene, mysteriously wide-awake, in the hour before sunrise. There was not a cloud in the pale sky, not a shadow along the dim, pearly fields, hills and woods. The mist was lifting from the valleys and hollows, the air was cool, the grass and the foliage dripping wet with morning-dew. Unwatched by the eyes of man, and undisturbed by his activity, the country breathed a timeless life, to which language was inadequate.

All the same, a human race had lived on this land for a thousand years, had been formed by its soil and weather, and had marked it with its thoughts, so that now no one could tell where the existence of the one ceased and the other began. The thin gray line of a road, winding across the plain and up and down hills, was the fixed materialization of human longing, and of the human notion that it is better to be in one place than another.

A child of the country would read this open landscape like a book. The irregular mosaic of meadows and cornlands was a picture, in timid green and yellow, of the people's struggle for its daily bread; the centuries had taught it to plough and sow in this way. On a distant hill the immovable wings of a windmill, in a small blue cross against the sky, delineated a later stage in the career of bread. The blurred outline of thatched roofs—a low, brown growth of the earth—where the huts of the village thronged together, told the history, from his cradle to his grave of the peasant, the creature nearest to the soil and dependent on it, prospering in a fertile year and dying in years of drought and pests.

A little higher up, with the faint horizontal line of the white cemetery-wall round it, and the vertical contour of tall poplars by its side, the red-tiled church bore witness, as far as the eye reached, that this was a Christian country. The child of the land knew it as a strange house, inhabited only for a few hours every seventh day, but with a strong, clear voice in it to give out the joys and sorrows of the land: a plain, square embodiment of the nation's trust in the justice and mercy of heaven. But where, amongst cupular woods and groves, the lordly, pyramidal silhouette of the cut lime avenues rose in the air, there a big country house lay.

The child of the land would read much within these elegant, geometrical ciphers on the hazy blue. They spoke of power, the lime trees paraded round a stronghold. Up here was decided the destiny of the surrounding land and of the men and beasts upon it, and the peasant lifted his eyes to the green pyramids with awe. They spoke of dignity, decorum and taste. Danish soil grew no finer flower than the mansion to which the long avenue led. In its lofty rooms life and death bore themselves with stately grace. The country house did not gaze upward, like the church, nor down to the ground like the huts; it had a wider earthly horizon than they, and was related to much noble architecture all over Europe. Foreign artisans had been called in to panel and stucco it, and its own inhabitants traveled and brought back ideas, fashions and things of beauty. Paintings, tapestries, silver and glass from distant countries had been made to feel at home here, and now formed part of Danish country life.

The big house stood as firmly rooted in the soil of Denmark as the peasants' huts, and was as faithfully allied to her four winds and her changing seasons, to her animal life, trees and flowers. Only its interests lay in a higher plane. Within the domain of the lime trees it was no longer cows, goats and pigs on which the minds and the talk ran, but horses and dogs. The wild fauna, the game of the land, that the peasant shook his fist at, when he saw it on his young green rye or in his ripening wheat field, to the residents of the country houses were the main pursuit and the joy of existence.

The writing in the sky solemnly proclaimed continuance, a worldly immortality. The great country houses had held their ground through many generations. The families who lived in them revered the past as they honored themselves, for the history of Denmark was their own history.

A Rosenkrantz had sat at Rosenholm, a Juel at Hverringe, a Skeel at Gammel-Estrup as long as people remembered. They had seen kings and schools of style succeed one another and, proudly and humbly, had made over their personal existence to that of their land, so that amongst their equals and with the peasants they passed by its name: Rosenholm, Hverringe, Gammel-Estrup. To the King and the country, to his family and to the individual lord of the manor himself it was a matter of minor consequence which particular Rosenkrantz, Juel or Skeel, out of a long row of fathers and sons, at the moment in his person incarnated the fields and woods, the peasants, cattle and game of the estate. Many duties rested on the shoulders of the big landowners—towards God in heaven, towards the King, his neighbor and himself—and they were all harmoniously consolidated into the idea of his duties towards his land. Highest amongst these ranked his obligation to uphold the sacred continuance, and to produce a new Rosenkrantz, Juel or Skeel for the service of Rosenholm, Hverringe and Gammel-Estrup.

Female grace was prized in the manors. Together with good hunting and fine wine it was the flower and emblem of the higher existence led there, and in many ways the families prided themselves more on their daughters than on their sons.

The ladies who promenaded in the lime avenues, or drove

through them in heavy coaches with four horses, carried the future of the name in their laps and were, like dignified and debonair caryatides, holding up the houses. They were themselves conscious of their value, kept up their price, and moved in a sphere of pretty worship and self-worship. They might even be thought to add to it, on their own, a graceful, arch, paradoxical haughtiness. For how free were they, how powerful! Their lords might rule the country, and allow themselves many liberties, but when it came to that supreme matter of legitimacy which was the vital principle of their world, the center of gravity lay with them.

The lime trees were in bloom. But in the early morning only a faint fragrance drifted through the garden, an airy message, an aromatic echo of the dreams during the short summer night.

In a long avenue that led from the house all the way to the end of the garden, where, from a small white pavilion in the classic style, there was a great view over the fields, a young man walked. He was plainly dressed in brown, with pretty linen and lace, bareheaded, with his hair tied by a ribbon. He was dark, a strong and sturdy figure with fine eyes and hands; he limped a little on one leg.

The big house at the top of the avenue, the garden and the fields had been his childhood's paradise. But he had traveled and lived out of Denmark, in Rome and Paris, and he was at present appointed to the Danish Legation to the Court of King George, the brother of the late, unfortunate young Danish Queen. He had not seen his ancestral home for nine years. It made him laugh to find, now, everything so much smaller than he remembered it, and at the same time he was strangely moved by meeting it again. Dead people came towards him and smiled at him; a small boy in a ruff ran past him with his hoop and kite, in passing gave him a clear glance and laughingly asked: "Do you mean to tell me that you are I?" He tried to catch him in the flight, and to answer him: "Yes, I assure you that I am you," but the light figure did not wait for a reply.

The young man, whose name was Adam, stood in a particular relation to the house and the land. For six months he had been heir to all; nominally he was so even at this moment. It was this circumstance which had brought him from England, and on which his mind was dwelling, as he walked along slowly.

The old lord up at the manor, his father's brother, had had much misfortune in his domestic life. His wife had died young, and two of his children in infancy. The one son then left to him, his cousin's playmate, was a sickly and morose boy. For ten years the father traveled with him from one watering place to another, in Germany and Italy, hardly ever in other company than that of his silent, dying child, sheltering the faint flame of life with both hands, until such time as it could be passed over to a new bearer of the name. At the same time another misfortune had struck him: he fell into disfavor at Court, where till now he had held a fine position. He was about to rehabilitate his family's prestige through the marriage which he had arranged for his son, when before it could take place the bridegroom died, not yet twenty years old.

Adam learned of his cousin's death, and his own changed fortune, in England, through his ambitious and triumphant mother. He sat with her letter in his hand and did not know what to think about it.

If this, he reflected, had happened to him while he was still a boy, in Denmark, it would have meant all the world to him. It would be so now with his friends and schoolfellows, if they were in his place, and they would, at this moment, be congratulating or envying him. But he was neither covetous nor vain by nature; he had faith in his own talents and had been content to know that his success in life depended on his personal ability. His slight infirmity had always set him a little apart from other boys; it had, perhaps, given him a keener sensibility of many things in life, and he did not, now, deem it quite right that the head of the family should limp on one leg. He did not even see his prospects in the same light as his people at home. In England he had met with greater wealth and magnificence than they dreamed of; he had been in love with, and made happy by, an English lady of such rank and fortune that to her, he felt, the finest estate of Denmark would look but like a child's toy farm.

And in England, too, he had come in touch with the great new ideas of the age: of nature, of the right and freedom of man, of justice and beauty. The universe, through them, had become infinitely wider to him; he wanted to find out still more about it and was planning to travel to America, to the new world. For a moment he felt trapped and imprisoned, as if the dead people of his name, from the family vault at home, were stretching out their parched arms for him.

But at the same time he began to dream at night of the old house and garden. He had walked in these avenues in dream, and had smelled the scent of the flowering limes. When at Ranelagh an old gypsy woman looked at his hand and told him that a son of his was to sit in the seat of his fathers, he felt a sudden, deep satisfaction, queer in a young man who till now had never given his sons a thought.

Then, six months later, his mother again wrote to tell him that his uncle had himself married the girl intended for his dead son. The head of the family was still in his best age, not over sixty, and although Adam remembered him as a small, slight man, he was a vigorous person; it was likely that his young wife would bear him sons.

Adam's mother in her disappointment lay the blame on him. If he had returned to Denmark, she told him, his uncle might have come to look upon him as a son, and would not have married; nay, he might have handed the bride over to him. Adam knew better. The family estate, differing from the neighboring properties, had gone down from father to son ever since a man of their name first sat there. The tradition of direct succession was the pride of the clan and a sacred dogma to his uncle; he would surely call for a son of his own flesh and bone.

But at the news the young man was seized by a strange, deep, aching remorse towards his old home in Denmark. It was as if he had been making light of a friendly and generous gesture, and disloyal to someone unfailingly loyal to him. It would be but just, he thought, if from now the place should disown and forget him. Nostalgia, which before he had never known, caught hold of him; for the first time he walked in the streets and parks of London as a stranger.

He wrote to his uncle and asked if he might come and stay with him, begged leave from the Legation and took ship for Denmark. He had come to the house to make his peace with it; he had slept little in the night, and was up so early and walking in the garden, to explain himself, and to be forgiven.

While he walked, the still garden slowly took up its day's work. A big snail, of the kind that his grandfather had brought back from France, and which he remembered eating in the house as a child, was already, with dignity, dragging a silver train down the avenue. The birds began to sing; in an old tree under which he stopped a number of them were worrying an owl; the rule of the night was over.

He stood at the end of the avenue and saw the sky lightening. An ecstatic clarity filled the world; in half an hour the sun would rise. A rye field here ran along the garden; two roe-deer were moving in it and looked roseate in the dawn. He gazed out over the fields, where as a small boy he had ridden his pony, and towards the wood where he had killed his first stag. He remembered the old servants who had taught him; some of them were now in their graves.

The ties which bound him to this place, he reflected, were of a mystic nature. He might never again come back to it, and it would make no difference. As long as a man of his own blood and name should sit in the house, hunt in the fields and be obeyed by the people in the huts, wherever he traveled on earth, in England or amongst the red Indians of America, he himself would still be safe, would still have a home, and would carry weight in the world.

His eyes rested on the church. In old days, before the time of Martin Luther, younger sons of great families, he knew, had entered the Church of Rome, and had given up individual wealth and happiness to serve the greater ideals. They, too, had bestowed honor upon their homes and were remembered in its registers. In the solitude of the morning half in jest he let his mind run as it listed; it seemed to him that he might speak to the land as to a person, as to the mother of his race. "Is it only my body that you want," he asked her, "while you reject my imagination, energy and emotions? If the world might be brought to acknowledge that the virtue of our name does not belong to the past only, will it give you no satisfaction?" The landscape was so still that he could not tell whether it answered him yes or no.

After a while he walked on, and came to the new French rose garden laid out for the young mistress of the house. In England he had acquired a freer taste in gardening, and he wondered if he could liberate these blushing captives, and make them thrive outside their cut hedges. Perhaps, he meditated, the elegantly conventional garden would be a floral portrait of his young aunt from Court, whom he had not yet seen.

As once more he came to the pavilion at the end of the avenue his eyes were caught by a bouquet of delicate colors which could not possibly belong to the Danish summer morning. It was in fact his uncle himself, powdered and silk-stockinged, but still in a brocade dressing-gown, and obviously sunk in deep thought. "And what business, or what meditations," Adam asked himself, "drags a connoisseur of the beautiful, but three months married to a wife of seventeen, from his bed into his garden before sunrise?" He walked up to the small, slim, straight figure.

His uncle on his side showed no surprise at seeing him, but then he rarely seemed surprised at anything. He greeted him, with a compliment on his matutinality, as kindly as he had done on his arrival last evening. After a moment he looked to the sky, and solemnly proclaimed: "It will be a hot day." Adam, as a child, had often been impressed by the grand, ceremonial manner in which the old lord would state the common happenings of existence; it looked as if nothing had changed here, but all was what it used to be.

The uncle offered the nephew a pinch of snuff. "No, thank you, Uncle," said Adam, "it would ruin my nose to the scent of your garden, which is as fresh as the Garden of Eden, newly created." "From every tree of which," said his uncle, smiling, "thou, my Adam, mayest freely eat." They slowly walked up the avenue together.

The hidden sun was now already gilding the top of the tallest trees. Adam talked of the beauties of nature, and of the greatness of Nordic scenery, less marked by the hand of man than that of Italy. His uncle took the praise of the landscape as a personal compliment, and congratulated him because he had not, in likeness to many young travelers in foreign countries, learned to despise his native land. No, said Adam, he had lately in England longed for the fields and woods of his Danish home. And he had there become acquainted with a new piece of Danish poetry which had enchanted him more than any English or French work. He named the author, Johannes Ewald, and quoted a few of the mighty, turbulent verses.

"And I have wondered, while I read," he went on after a pause, still moved by the lines he himself had declaimed, "that we have not till now understood how much our Nordic mythology in moral greatness surpasses that of Greece and

Rome. If it had not been for the physical beauty of the ancient gods, which has come down to us in marble, no modern mind could hold them worthy of worship. They were mean, capricious and treacherous. The gods of our Danish forefathers are as much more divine than they as the Druid is nobler than the Augur. For the fair gods of Asgaard did possess the sublime human virtues; they were righteous, trustworthy, benevolent and even, within a barbaric age, chivalrous." His uncle here for the first time appeared to take any real interest in the conversation. He stopped, his majestic nose a little in the air. "Ah, it was easier to them," he said.

"What do you mean, Uncle?" Adam asked. "It was a great deal easier," said his uncle, "to the northern gods than to those of Greece to be, as you will have it, righteous and benevolent. To my mind it even reveals a weakness in the souls of our ancient Danes that they should consent to adore such divinities." "My dear uncle," said Adam, smiling, "I have always felt that you would be familiar with the modes of Olympus. Now please let me share your insight, and tell me why virtue should come easier to our Danish gods than to those of milder climates." "They were not as powerful," said his uncle.

"And does power," Adam again asked, "stand in the way of virtue?" "Nay," said his uncle gravely. "Nay, power is in itself the supreme virtue. But the gods of which you speak were never all-powerful. They had, at all times, by their side those darker powers which they named the Jotuns, and who worked the suffering, the disasters, the ruin of our world. They might safely give themselves up to temperance and kindness. The omnipotent gods," he went on, "have no such facilitation. With their omnipotence they take over the woe of the universe."

They had walked up the avenue till they were in view of the house. The old lord stopped and ran his eyes over it. The stately building was the same as ever; behind the two tall front windows, Adam knew, was now his young aunt's room. His uncle turned and walked back.

"Chivalry," he said, "chivalry, of which you were speaking, is not a virtue of the omnipotent. It must needs imply mighty rival powers for the knight to defy. With a dragon inferior to him in strength, what figure will St. George cut? The knight who finds no superior forces ready to hand must invent them, and combat windmills; his knighthood itself stipulates dangers, vileness, darkness on all sides of him. Nay, believe me, my nephew, in spite of his moral worth, your chivalrous Odin of Asgaard as a Regent must take rank below that of Jove who avowed his sovereignty, and accepted the world which he ruled. But you are young," he added, "and the experience of the aged to you will sound pedantic."

He stood immovable for a moment and then with deep gravity proclaimed: "The sun is up."

The sun did indeed rise above the horizon. The wide landscape was suddenly animated by its splendor, and the dewy grass shone in a thousand gleams.

"I have listened to you, Uncle," said Adam, "with great interest. But while we have talked you yourself have seemed to me preoccupied; your eyes have rested on the field outside the garden, as if something of great moment, a matter of life and death, was going on there. Now that the sun is up, I see the mowers in the rye and hear them whetting their sickles. It is, I remember you telling me, the first day of the harvest. That is a great day to a landowner and enough to take his mind away from the gods. It is very fine weather, and I wish you a full barn."

The elder man stood still, his hands on his walking-stick. "There is indeed," he said at last, "something going on in that field, a matter of life and death. Come, let us sit down here, and I will tell you the whole story." They sat down on the seat that ran all along the pavilion, and while he spoke the old lord of the land did not take his eyes off the rye field.

"A week ago, on Thursday night," he said, "someone set fire to my barn at Rødmosegaard—you know the place, close to the moor—and burned it all down. For two or three days we could not lay hands on the offender. Then on Monday morning the keeper at Rødmose, with the wheelwright over there, came up to the house; they dragged with them a boy, Goske Piil, a widow's son, and they made their Bible oath that he had done it; they had themselves seen him sneaking round the barn by nightfall on Thursday. Goske had no good name on the farm; the keeper bore him a grudge upon an old matter of poaching, and the wheelwright did not like him either, for he did, I believe, suspect him with his young wife. The boy, when I talked to him, swore to his innocence, but he could not hold his own against the two old men. So I had him locked up, and meant to send him in to our judge of the district, with a letter.

"The judge is a fool, and would naturally do nothing but what he thought I wished him to do. He might have the boy sent to the convict prison for arson, or put amongst the soldiers as a bad character and a poacher. Or again, if he thought that that was what I wanted, he could let him off.

"I was out riding in the fields, looking at the corn that was soon ripe to be mowed, when a woman, the widow, Goske's mother, was brought up before me, and begged to speak to me. Anne-Marie is her name. You will remember her; she lives in the small house east of the village. She has not got a good name in the place either. They tell as a girl she had a child and did away with it.

"From five days' weeping her voice was so cracked that it was difficult for me to understand what she said. Her son, she told me at last, had indeed been over at Rødmose on Thursday, but for no ill purpose; he had gone to see someone. He was her only son, she called the Lord God to witness on his innocence, and she wrung her hands to me that I should save the boy for her.

"We were in the rye field that you and I are looking at now. That gave me an idea. I said to the widow: 'If in one day, between sunrise and sunset, with your own hands you can mow this field, and it be well done, I will let the case drop and you shall keep your son. But if you cannot do it, he must go, and it is not likely that you will then ever see him again.'

"She stood up then and gazed over the field. She kissed my riding boot in gratitude for the favor shown to her."

The old lord here made a pause, and Adam said: "Her son meant much to her?" "He is her only child," said his uncle. "He means to her her daily bread and support in old age. It may be said that she holds him as dear as her own life. As," he added, "within a higher order of life, a son to his father means the name and the race, and he holds him as dear as life everlasting. Yes, her son means much to her. For the mowing of that field is a day's work to three men, or three days' work to one man. Today, as the sun rose, she set to her task. And down there, by the end of the field, you will see her now, in a blue head-cloth, with the man I have set to follow her and to ascertain that she does the work unassisted, and with two or three friends by her, who are comforting her."

Adam looked down, and did indeed see a woman in a blue head-cloth, and a few other figures in the corn.

They sat for a while in silence. "Do you yourself," Adam then said, "believe the boy to be innocent?" "I cannot tell," said his uncle. "There is no proof. The word of the keeper and the wheelwright stand against the boy's word. If indeed I did believe the one thing or the other, it would be merely a matter of chance, or maybe of sympathy. The boy," he said after a moment, "was my son's playmate, the only other child that I ever knew him to like or to get on with." "Do you," Adam again asked, "hold it possible to her to fulfill your condition?" "Nay, I cannot tell," said the old lord. "To an ordinary person it would not be possible. No ordinary person would ever have taken it on at all. I chose it so. We are not quibbling with the law, Anne-Marie and I."

Adam for a few minutes followed the movement of the small group in the rye. "Will you walk back?" he asked. "No," said his uncle, "I think that I shall stay here till I have seen the end of the thing." "Until sunset?" Adam asked with surprise. "Yes," said the old lord. Adam said: "It will be a long day." "Yes," said his uncle, "a long day. But," he added, as Adam rose to walk away, "if, as you said, you have got that tragedy of which you spoke in your pocket, be as kind as to leave it here, to keep me company." Adam handed him the book.

In the avenue he met two footmen who carried the old lord's morning chocolate down to the pavilion on large silver trays.

As now the sun rose in the sky, and the day grew hot, the lime trees gave forth their exuberance of scent, and the garden was filled with unsurpassed, unbelievable sweetness. Toward the still hour of midday the long avenue reverberated like a soundboard with a low, incessant murmur: the humming of a million bees that clung to the pendulous, thronging clusters of blossoms and were drunk with bliss.

In all the short lifetime of Danish summer there is no richer or more luscious moment than that week wherein the lime trees flower. The heavenly scent goes to the head and to the heart; it seems to unite the fields of Denmark with those of Elysium; it contains both hay, honey and holy incense, and is half fairy-land and half apothecary's locker. The avenue was changed into a mystic edifice, a dryad's cathedral, outward from summit to base lavishly adorned, set with multitudinous ornaments, and golden in the sun. But behind the walls the vaults were benignly cool and somber, like ambrosial sanctuaries in a dazzling and burning world, and in here the ground was still moist.

Up in the house, behind the silk curtains of the two front

windows, the young mistress of the estate from the wide bed stuck her feet into two little high-heeled slippers. Her lace-trimmed nightgown had slid up above her knee and down from the shoulder; her hair, done up in curling-pins for the night, was still frosty with the powder of yesterday, her round face flushed with sleep. She stepped out to the middle of the floor and stood there, looking extremely grave and thoughtful, yet she did not think at all. But through her head a long procession of pictures marched, and she was unconsciously endeavoring to put them in order, as the pictures of her existence had used to be.

She had grown up at Court; it was her world, and there was probably not in the whole country a small creature more exquisitely and innocently drilled to the stately measure of a palace. By favor of the old Dowager Queen she bore her name and that of the King's sister, the Queen of Sweden: Sophie Magdalena. It was with a view to these things that her husband, when he wished to restore his status in high places, had chosen her as a bride, first for his son and then for himself. But her own father, who held an office in the Royal Household and belonged to the new Court aristocracy, in his day had done the same thing the other way round, and had married a country lady, to get a foothold within the old nobility of Denmark. The little girl had her mother's blood in her veins. The country to her had been an immense surprise and delight.

To get into her castle-court she must drive through the farm yard, through the heavy stone gateway in the barn itself, wherein the rolling of her coach for a few seconds re-echoed like thunder. She must drive past the stables and the timber-mare, from which sometimes a miscreant would follow her with sad eyes, and might here startle a long string of squalling geese, or pass the heavy, scowling bull, led on by a ring in his nose and kneading the earth in dumb fury. At first this had been to her, every time, a slight shock and a jest. But after a while all these creatures and things, which belonged to her, seemed to become part of herself. Her mothers, the old Danish country ladies, were robust persons, undismayed by any kind of weather; now she herself had walked in the rain and had laughed and glowed in it like a green tree.

She had taken her great new home in possession at a time when all the world was unfolding, mating and propagating. Flowers, which she had known only in bouquets and festoons, sprung from the earth round her; birds sang in all the trees. The new-born lambs seemed to her daintier than her dolls had been. From her husband's Hanoverian stud, foals were brought to her to give names; she stood and watched as they poked their soft noses into their mothers' bellies to drink. Of this strange process she had till now only vaguely heard. She had happened to witness, from a path in the park, the rearing and screeching stallion on the mare. All this luxuriance, lust and fecundity was displayed before her eyes, as for her pleasure.

And for her own part, in the midst of it, she was given an old husband who treated her with punctilious respect because she was to bear him a son. Such was the compact; she had known of it from the beginning. Her husband, she found, was doing his best to fulfill his part of it, and she herself was loyal by nature and strictly brought up. She would not shirk her obligation. Only she was vaguely aware of a discord or an incompatibility within her majestic existence, which prevented her from being as happy as she had expected to be.

After a time her chagrin took a strange form: as the consciousness of an absence. Someone ought to have been with her who was not. She had no experience in analyzing her feelings; there had not been time for that at Court. Now, as she was more often left to herself, she vaguely probed her own mind. She tried to set her father in that void place, her sisters, her music master, an Italian singer whom she had admired; but none of them would fill it for her. At times she felt lighter at heart, and believed the misfortune to have left her. And then again it would happen, if she were alone, or in her husband's company, and even within his embrace, that everything round her would cry out: Where? Where? so that she let her wild eyes run about the room in search for the being who should have been there, and who had not come.

When, six months ago, she was informed that her first young bridegroom had died and that she was to marry his father in his place, she had not been sorry. Her youthful suitor, the one time she had seen him, had appeared to her infantile and insipid; the father would make a statelier consort. Now she had sometimes thought of the dead boy, and wondered whether with him life would have been more joyful. But she soon again dismissed the picture, and that was the sad youth's last recall to the stage of this world.

Upon one wall of her room there hung a long mirror. As she gazed into it new images came along. The day before, driving with her husband, she had seen, at a distance, a party of village girls bathe in the river, and the sun shining on them. All her life she had moved amongst naked marble deities, but it had till now never occurred to her that the people she knew should themselves be naked under their bodices and trains, waistcoats and satin breeches, that indeed she herself felt naked within her clothes. Now, in front of the looking-glass, she tardily untied the ribbons of her nightgown, and let it drop to the floor.

The room was dim behind the drawn curtains. In the mirror her body was silvery like a white rose; only her cheeks and mouth, and the tips of her fingers and breasts had a faint carmine. Her slender torso was formed by the whalebones that had clasped it tightly from her childhood; above the slim, dimpled knee a gentle narrowness marked the place of the garter. Her limbs were rounded as if, at whatever place they might be cut through with a sharp knife, a perfectly circular transverse incision would be obtained. The side and belly were so smooth that her own gaze slipped and glided, and grasped for a hold. She was not altogether like a statue, she found, and lifted her arms above her head. She turned to get a view of her back, the curves below the waistline were still blushing from the pressure of the bed. She called to mind a few tales about nymphs and goddesses, but they all seemed a long way off, so her mind returned to the peasant girls in the river. They were, for a few minutes, idealized into play-mates, or sisters even, since they belonged to her as did the meadow and the blue river itself. And within the next moment the sense of forlornness once more came upon her, a *horror vaccui* like a physical pain. Surely, surely someone should have been with her now, her other self, like the image in the glass, but nearer, stronger, alive. There was no one, the universe was empty round her.

A sudden, keen itching under her knee took her out of her reveries, and awoke in her the hunting instincts of her breed. She wetted a finger on her tongue, slowly brought it down and quickly slapped it to the spot. She felt the diminutive, sharp body of the insect against the silky skin, pressed the thumb to it, and triumphantly lifted up the small prisoner between her fingertips. She stood quite still, as if meditating upon the fact that a flea was the only creature risking its life for her smoothness and sweet blood.

Her maid opened the door and came in, loaded with the attire of the day—shift, stays, hoop and petticoats. She remembered that she had a guest in the house, the new nephew arrived from England. Her husband had instructed her to be kind to their young kinsman, disinherited, so to say, by her presence in the house. They would ride out on the land together.

In the afternoon the sky was no longer blue as in the morning. Large clouds slowly towered up on it, and the great vault itself was colorless, as if diffused into vapors round the white-hot sun in zenith. A low thunder ran along the western

horizon; once or twice the dust of the roads rose in tall spi-
rals. But the fields, the hills and the woods were as still as a
painted landscape.

Adam walked down the avenue to the pavilion, and found
his uncle there, fully dressed, his hands upon his walking-
stick and his eyes on the rye field. The book that Adam had
given him lay by his side. The field now seemed alive with
people. Small groups stood here and there in it, and a long
row of men and women were slowly advancing towards the
garden in the line of the swath.

The old lord nodded to his nephew, but did not speak or
change his position. Adam stood by him as still as himself.

The day to him had been strangely disquieting. At the
meeting again with old places the sweet melodies of the past
had filled his senses and his mind, and had mingled with
new, bewitching tunes of the present. He was back in Denmark, no longer a child but a youth, with a keener sense of
the beautiful, with tales of other countries to tell, and still a
true son of his own land and enchanted by its loveliness as he
had never been before.

But through all these harmonies the tragic and cruel tale
which the old lord had told him in the morning, and the sad
contest which he knew to be going on so near by, in the corn
field, had re-echoed, like the recurrent, hollow throbbing of a
muffled drum, a redoubtable sound. It came back time after
time, so that he had felt himself to change color and to answer absently. It brought with it a deeper sense of pity with
all that lived than he had ever known. When he had been riding with his young aunt, and their road ran along the scene of
the drama, he had taken care to ride between her and the
field, so that she should not see what was going on there, or
question him about it. He had chosen the way home through
the deep, green wood for the same reason.

More dominantly even than the figure of the woman struggling with her sickle for her son's life, the old man's figure, as

he had seen it at sunrise, kept him company through the day. He came to ponder on the part which that lonely, determinate form had played in his own life. From the time when his father died, it had impersonated to the boy law and order, wisdom of life and kind guardianship. What was he to do, he thought, if after eighteen years these filial feelings must change, and his second father's figure take on to him a horrible aspect, as a symbol of the tyranny and oppression of the world? What was he to do if ever the two should come to stand in opposition to each other as adversaries?

At the same time an unaccountable, a sinister alarm and dread on behalf of the old man himself took hold of him. For surely here the Goddess Nemesis could not be far away. This man had ruled the world round him for a longer period than Adam's own lifetime and had never been gainsaid by anyone. During the years when he had wandered through Europe with a sick boy of his own blood as his sole companion he had learned to set himself apart from his surroundings, and to close himself up to all outer life, and he had become insusceptible to the ideas and feelings of other human beings. Strange fancies might there have run in his mind, so that in the end he had seen himself as the only person really existing, and the world as a poor and vain shadow-play, which had no substance to it.

Now, in senile willfulness, he would take in his hand the life of those simpler and weaker than himself, of a woman, using it to his own ends, and he feared of no retributive justice. Did he not know, the young man thought, that there were powers in the world, different from and more formidable than the short-lived might of a despot?

With the sultry heat of the day this foreboding of impending disaster grew upon him, until he felt ruin threatening not the old lord only, but the house, the name and himself with him. It seemed to him that he must cry out a warning to the man he had loved, before it was too late.

But as now he was once more in his uncle's company, the green calm of the garden was so deep that he did not find his voice to cry out. Instead a little French air which his aunt had sung to him up in the house kept running in his mind. —"*C'est un trop doux effort...*" He had good knowledge of music; he had heard the air before, in Paris, but not so sweetly sung.

After a time he asked: "Will the woman fulfill her bargain?" His uncle unfolded his hands. "It is an extraordinary thing," he said animatedly, "that it looks as if she might fulfill it. If you count the hours from sunrise till now, and from now till sunset, you will find the time left her to be half of that already gone. And see! She has now mowed two-thirds of the field. But then we will naturally have to reckon with her strength declining as she works on. All in all, it is an idle pursuit in you or me to bet on the issue of the matter; we must wait and see. Sit down, and keep me company in my watch." In two minds Adam sat down.

"And here," said his uncle, and took up the book from the seat, "is your book, which has passed the time finely. It is great poetry, ambrosia to the ear and the heart. And it has, with our discourse on divinity this morning, given me stuff for thought. I have been reflecting upon the law of retributive justice." He took a pinch of snuff, and went on. "A new age," he said, "has made to itself a god in its own image, an emotional god. And now you are already writing a tragedy on your god."

Adam had no wish to begin a debate on poetry with his uncle, but he also somehow dreaded a silence, and said: "It may be, then, that we hold tragedy to be, in the scheme of life, a noble, a divine phenomenon."

"Aye," said his uncle solemnly, "a noble phenomenon, the noblest on earth. But of the earth only, and never divine. Tragedy is the privilege of man, his highest privilege. The God of the Christian Church Himself, when He wished to experience tragedy, had to assume human form. And even at that," he added thoughtfully, "the tragedy was not wholly valid, as it would have become had the hero of it been, in very truth, a man. The divinity of Christ conveyed to it a divine note, the moment of comedy. The real tragic part, by the nature of things, fell to the executors, not to the victim. Nay, my nephew, we should not adulterate the pure elements of the cosmos. Tragedy should remain the right of human beings, subject, in their conditions or in their own nature, to the dire law of necessity. To them it is salvation and beatification. But the gods, whom we must believe to be unacquainted with and incomprehensive of necessity, can have no knowledge of the tragic. When they are brought face to face with it they will, according to my experience, have the good taste and decorum to keep still, and not interfere.

"No," he said after a pause, "the true art of the gods is the comic. The comic is a condescension of the divine to the world of man; it is the sublime vision, which cannot be studied, but must ever be celestially granted. In the comic the gods see their own being reflected as in a mirror, and while the tragic poet is bound by strict laws, they will allow the comic artist a freedom as unlimited as their own. They do not even withhold their own existence from his sports. Jove may favor Lucianos of Samosata. As long as your mockery is in true godly taste you may mock at the gods and still remain a sound devotee. But in pitying, or condoling with your god, you deny and annihilate him, and such is the most horrible of atheisms.

"And here on earth, too," he went on, "we, who stand in lieu of the gods and have emancipated ourselves from the tyranny of necessity, should leave to our vassals their monopoly of tragedy, and for ourselves accept the comic with grace. Only a boorish and cruel master—a parvenu, in fact—will make a jest of his servants' necessity, or force the comic upon them. Only a timid and pedantic ruler, a *petit-maître*, will fear the ludicrous on his own behalf. Indeed," he finished his long speech, "the very same fatality, which, in striking the burgher or peasant, will become tragedy, with the aristocrat is exalted to the comic. By the grace and wit of our acceptance hereof our aristocracy is known."

Adam could not help smiling a little as he heard the apotheosis of the comic on the lips of the erect, ceremonious prophet. In this ironic smile he was, for the first time, estranging himself from the head of his house.

A shadow fell across the landscape. A cloud had crept over the sun; the country changed color beneath it, faded and bleached, and even all sounds for a minute seemed to die out of it.

"Ah, now," said the old lord, "if it is going to rain, and the rye gets wet, Anne-Marie will not be able to finish in time. And who comes there?" he added, and turned his head a little.

Preceded by a lackey a man in riding boots and a striped waistcoat with silver buttons, and with his hat in his hand, came down the avenue. He bowed deeply, first to the old lord and then to Adam.

"My bailiff," said the old lord. "Good afternoon, Bailiff. What news have you to bring?" The bailiff made a sad gesture. "Poor news only, my lord," he said. "And how poor news?" asked his master. "There is," said the bailiff with weight, "not a soul at work on the land, and not a sickle going except that of Anne-Marie in this rye field. The mowing has stopped; they are all at her heels. It is a poor day for a first day of the harvest." "Yes, I see," said the old lord. The bailiff went on. "I have spoken kindly to them," he said, "and I have sworn at them; it is all one. They might as well all be deaf."

"Good Bailiff," said the old lord, "leave them in peace; let them do as they like. This day may, all the same, do them more good than many others. Where is Goske, the boy, Anne-Marie's son?" "We have set him in the small room by the

barn," said the bailiff. "Nay, let him be brought down," said
the old lord; "let him see his mother at work. But what
do you say—will she get the field mowed in time?" "If you
ask me, my lord," said the bailiff, "I believe that she will.
Who would have thought so? She is only a small woman. It is
as hot a day today as, well, as I do ever remember. I myself,
you yourself, my lord, could not have done what Anne-Marie
has done today." "Nay, nay, we could not, Bailiff," said the
old lord.

The bailiff pulled out a red handkerchief and wiped his
brow, somewhat calmed by venting his wrath. "If," he remarked with bitterness, "they would all work as the widow
works now, we would make a profit on the land." "Yes," said
the old lord, and fell into thought, as if calculating the profit it
might make. "Still," he said, "as to the question of profit and
loss, that is more intricate than it looks. I will tell you something that you may not know: The most famous tissue ever
woven was raveled out again every night. But come," he
added, "she is close by now. We will go and have a look at her
work ourselves." With these words he rose and set his hat on.

The cloud had drawn away again; the rays of the sun once
more burned the wide landscape, and as the small party walked
out from under the shade of the trees the dead-still heat was
heavy as lead; the sweat sprang out on their faces and their
eyelids smarted. On the narrow path they had to go one by
one, the old lord stepping along first, all black, and the footman, in his bright livery, bringing up the rear.

The field was indeed filled with people like a marketplace;
there were probably a hundred or more men and women in it.
To Adam the scene recalled pictures from his Bible: the meeting between Esau and Jacob in Edom, or Boaz's reapers in his
barley field near Bethlehem. Some were standing by the side
of the field, others pressed in small groups close to the mowing woman, and a few followed in her wake, binding up
sheaves where she had cut the corn, as if thereby they thought

to help her, or as if by all means they meant to have part in her work. A younger woman with a pail on her head kept close to her side, and with her a number of half-grown children. One of these first caught sight of the lord of the estate and his suite, and pointed to him. The binders let their sheaves drop, and as the old man stood still many of the onlookers drew close round him.

The woman on whom till now the eyes of the whole field had rested—a small figure on the large stage—was advancing slowly and unevenly, bent double as if she were walking on her knees, and stumbling as she walked. Her blue head-cloth had slipped back from her head; the gray hair was plastered to the skull with sweat, dusty and stuck with straw. She was obviously totally unaware of the multitude round her; neither did she now once turn her head or her gaze towards the new arrivals.

Absorbed in her work she again and again stretched out her left hand to grasp a handful of corn, and her right hand with the sickle in it to cut it off close to the soil, in wavering, groping pulls, like a tired swimmer's strokes. Her course took her so close to the feet of the old lord that his shadow fell on her. Just then she staggered and swayed sideways, and the woman who followed her lifted the pail from her head and held it to her lips. Anne-Marie drank without leaving her hold on her sickle, and the water ran from the corners of her mouth. A boy, close to her, quickly bent one knee, seized her hands in his own and, steadying and guiding them, cut off a gripe of rye. "No, no," said the old lord, "you must not do that, boy. Leave Anne-Marie in peace to her work." At the sound of his voice the woman, falteringly, lifted her face in his direction.

The bony and tanned face was streaked with sweat and dust; the eyes were dimmed. But there was not in its expression the slightest trace of fear or pain. Indeed amongst all the grave and concerned faces of the field hers was the only one perfectly calm, peaceful and mild. The mouth was drawn together in a thin line, a prim, keen, patient little smile, such as will be seen in the face of an old woman at her spinning-wheel or her knitting, eager on her work, and happy in it. And as the younger woman lifted back the pail, she immediately again fell to her mowing, with an ardent, tender craving, like that of a mother who lays a baby to the nipple. Like an insect that bustles along in high grass, or like a small vessel in a heavy sea, she butted her way on, her quiet face once more bent upon her task.

The whole throng of onlookers, and with them the small group from the pavilion, advanced as she advanced, slowly and as if drawn by a string. The bailiff, who felt the intense silence of the field heavy on him, said to the old lord: "The rye will yield better this year than last," and got no reply. He repeated his remark to Adam, and at last to the footman, who felt himself above a discussion on agriculture, and only cleared his throat in answer. In a while the bailiff again broke the silence. "There is the boy," he said and pointed with his thumb. "They have brought him down." At that moment the woman fell forward on her face and was lifted up by those nearest to her.

Adam suddenly stopped on the path, and covered his eyes with his hand. The old lord without turning asked him if he felt incommoded by the heat. "No," said Adam, "but stay. Let me speak to you." His uncle stopped, with his hand on the stick and looking ahead, as if regretful of being held back.

"In the name of God," cried the young man in French, "force not this woman to continue." There was a short pause. "But I force her not, my friend," said his uncle in the same language. "She is free to finish at any moment." "At the cost of her child only," again cried Adam. "Do you not see that she is dying? You know not what you are doing, or what it may bring upon you."

The old lord, perplexed by this unexpected animadversion, after a second turned all round, and his pale, clear eyes sought his nephew's face with stately surprise. His long, waxen face, with two symmetrical curls at the sides, had something of the mien of an idealized and ennobled old sheep or ram. He made sign to the bailiff to go on. The footman also withdrew a little, and the uncle and nephew were, so to say, alone on the path. For a minute neither of them spoke.

"In this very place where we now stand," said the old lord, then, with hauteur, "I gave Anne-Marie my word."

"My uncle!" said Adam. "A life is a greater thing even than a word. Recall that word, I beseech you, which was given in caprice, as a whim. I am praying you more for your sake than for my own, yet I shall be grateful to you all my life if you will grant me my prayer."

"You will have learned in school," said his uncle, "that in the beginning was the word. It may have been pronounced in caprice, as a whim, the Scripture tells us nothing about it. It is still the principle of our world, its law of gravitation. My own humble word has been the principle of the land on which we stand, for an age of man. My father's word was the same, before my day."

"You are mistaken," cried Adam. "The word is creative— it is imagination, daring and passion. By it the world was made. How much greater are these powers which bring into being than any restricting or controlling law! You wish the land on which we look to produce and propagate; you should not banish from it the forces which cause, and which keep up life, nor turn it into a desert by dominance of law. And when you look at the people, simpler than we and nearer to the heart of nature, who do not analyze their feelings, whose life is one with the life of the earth, do they not inspire in you tenderness, respect, reverence even? This woman is ready to die for her son; will it even happen to you or me that a woman willingly gives up her life for us? And if it did indeed

357

come to pass, should we make so light of it as not to give up a dogma in return?"

"You are young," said the old lord. "A new age will undoubtedly applaud you. I am old-fashioned, I have been quoting to you texts a thousand years old. We do not, perhaps, quite understand one another. But with my own people I am, I believe, in good understanding. Anne-Marie might well feel that I am making light of her exploit, if now, at the eleventh hour, I did nullify it by a second word. I myself should feel so in her place. Yes, my nephew, it is possible, did I grant you your prayer and pronounce such an amnesty, that I should find it void against her faithfulness, and that we would still see her at her work, unable to give it up, as a shuttle in the rye field, until she had it all mowed. But she would then be a shocking, a horrible sight, a figure of unseemly fun, like a small planet running wild in the sky, when the law of gravitation had been done away with."

"And if she dies at her task," Adam exclaimed, "her death, and its consequences will come upon your head."

The old lord took off his hat and gently ran his hand over his powdered head. "Upon my head?" he said. "I have kept up my head in many weathers. Even," he added proudly, "against the cold wind from high places. In what shape will it come upon my head, my nephew?" "I cannot tell," cried Adam in despair. "I have spoken to warn you. God only knows." "Amen," said the old lord with a little delicate smile. "Come, we will walk on." Adam drew in his breath deeply.

"No," he said in Danish. "I cannot come with you. This field is yours; things will happen here as you decide. But I myself must go away. I beg you to let me have, this evening, a coach as far as town. For I could not sleep another night under your roof, which I have honored beyond any on earth." So many conflicting feelings at his own speech thronged in his breast that it would have been impossible for him to give them words.

The old lord, who had already begun to walk on, stood still, and with him the lackey. He did not speak for a minute, as if to give Adam time to collect his mind. But the young man's mind was in uproar and would not be collected.

"Must we," the old man asked, in Danish, "take leave here, in the rye field? I have held you dear, next to my own son. I have followed your career in life from year to year, and have been proud of you. I was happy when you wrote to say that you were coming back. If now you will go away, I wish you well." He shifted his walking-stick from the right hand to the left and gravely looked his nephew in the face.

Adam did not meet his eyes. He was gazing out over the landscape. In the late mellow afternoon it was resuming its colors, like a painting brought into proper light; in the meadows the little black stacks of peat stood gravely distinct upon the green sward. On this same morning he had greeted it all, like a child running laughingly to its mother's bosom; now already he must tear himself from it, in discordance, and forever. And at the moment of parting it seemed infinitely dearer than any time before, so much beautified and solemnized by the coming separation that it looked like the place in a dream, a landscape out of paradise, and he wondered if it was really the same. But, yes—there before him was, once more, the hunting-ground of long ago. And there was the road on which he had ridden today.

"But tell me where you mean to go from here," said the old lord slowly. "I myself have traveled a good deal in my days. I know the word of leaving, the wish to go away. But I have learned by experience that, in reality, the word has a meaning only to the place and the people which one leaves. When you have left my house—although it will see you go with sadness—as far as it is concerned the matter is finished and done with. But to the person who goes away it is a different thing, and not so simple. At the moment that he leaves one place he will be already, by the laws of life, on his way to another, upon this earth. Let me know, then, for the sake of our old acquaintance, to which place you are going when you leave here. To England?"

"No," said Adam. He felt in his heart that he could never again go back to England or to his easy and carefree life there. It was not far enough away; deeper waters than the North Sea must now be laid between him and Denmark. "No, not to England," he said. "I shall go to America, to the new world." For a moment he shut his eyes, trying to form to himself a picture of existence in America, with the gray Atlantic Ocean between him and these fields and woods.

"To America?" said his uncle and drew up his eyebrows. "Yes, I have heard of America. They have got freedom there, a big waterfall, savage red men. They shoot turkeys, I have read, as we shoot partridges. Well, if it be your wish, go to America, Adam, and be happy in the new world."

He stood for some time, sunk in thought, as if he had already sent off the young man to America, and had done with him. When at last he spoke, his words had the character of a monologue, enunciated by the person who watches things come and go, and himself stays on.

"Take service, there," he said, "with the power which will give you an easier bargain than this: That with your own life you may buy the life of your son."

Adam had not listened to his uncle's remarks about America, but the conclusive, solemn words caught his ear. He looked up. As if for the first time in his life, he saw the old man's figure as a whole, and conceived how small it was, so much smaller than himself, pale, a thin black anchorite upon his own land. A thought ran through his head: "How terrible to be old!" The abhorrence of the tyrant, and the sinister dread on his behalf, which had followed him all day, seemed to die out of him, and his pity with all creation to extend even to the somber form before him.

His whole being had cried out for harmony. Now, with the

possibility of forgiving, of a reconciliation, a sense of relief went through him; confusedly he bethought himself of Anne-Marie drinking the water held to her lips. He took off his hat, as his uncle had done a moment ago, so that to a beholder at a distance it would seem that the two dark-clad gentlemen on the path were repeatedly and respectfully saluting one another, and brushed the hair from his forehead. Once more the tune of the garden-room rang in his mind:

> *Mourir pour ce qu'on aime*
> *C'est un trop doux effort...*

He stood for a long time immobile and dumb. He broke off a few ears of rye, kept them in his hand and looked at them.

He saw the ways of life, he thought, as a twined and tangled design, complicated and mazy; it was not given him or any mortal to command or control it. Life and death, happiness and woe, the past and the present, were interlaced within the pattern. Yet to the initiated it might be read as easily as our ciphers—which to the savage must seem confused and incomprehensible—will be read by the schoolboy. And out of the contrasting elements concord rose. All that lived must suffer; the old man, whom he had judged hardly, had suffered, as he had watched his son die, and had dreaded the obliteration of his being. He himself would come to know ache, tears and remorse, and, even through these, the fullness of life. So might now, to the woman in the rye field, her ordeal be a triumphant procession. For to die for the one you loved was an effort too sweet for words.

As now he thought of it, he knew that all his life he had sought the unity of things, the secret which connects the phenomena of existence. It was this strife, this dim presage, which had sometimes made him stand still and inert in the midst of the games of his playfellows, or which had, at other moments—on moonlight nights, or in his little boat on the sea—lifted the boy to ecstatic happiness. Where other young people, in their pleasures or their amours, had searched for contrast and variety, he himself had yearned only to comprehend in full the oneness of the world. If things had come differently to him, if his young cousin had not died, and the events that followed his death had not brought him to Denmark, his search for understanding and harmony might have taken him to America, and he might have found them there, in the virgin forests of a new world. Now they have been disclosed to him today, in the place where he had played as a child. As the song is one with the voice that sings it, as the road is one with the goal, as lovers are made one in their embrace, so is man one with his destiny, and he shall love it as himself.

He looked up again, towards the horizon. If he wished to, he felt, he might find out what it was that had brought to him, here, the sudden conception of the unity of the universe. When this same morning he had philosophized, lightly and for his own sake, on his feeling of belonging to this land and soil, it had been the beginning of it. But since then it had grown; it had become a mightier thing, a revelation to his soul. Some time he would look into it, for the law of cause and effect was a wonderful and fascinating study. But not now. This hour was consecrated to greater emotions, to a surrender to fate and to the will of life.

"No," he said at last. "If you wish it I shall not go. I shall stay here."

At that moment a long, loud roll of thunder broke the stillness of the afternoon. It re-echoed for a while amongst the low hills, and it reverberated within the young man's breast as powerfully as if he had been seized and shaken by hands. The landscape had spoken. He remembered that twelve hours ago he had put a question to it, half in jest, and not knowing what he did. Here it gave him its answer.

What it contained he did not know; neither did he inquire.

In his promise to his uncle he had given himself over to the mightier powers of the world. Now what must come must come.

"I thank you," said the old lord, and made a little stiff gesture with his hand. "I am happy to hear you say so. We should not let the difference in our ages, or of our views, separate us. In our family we have been wont to keep peace and faith with one another. You have made my heart lighter."

Something within his uncle's speech faintly recalled to Adam the misgivings of the afternoon. He rejected them; he would not let them trouble the new, sweet felicity which his resolution to stay had brought him.

"I shall go on now," said the old lord. "But there is no need for you to follow me. I will tell you tomorrow how the matter has ended." "No," said Adam, "I shall come back by sunset, to see the end of it myself."

All the same he did not come back. He kept the hour in his mind, and all through the evening the consciousness of the drama, and the profound concern and compassion with which, in his thoughts, he followed it, gave to his speech, glance and movements a grave and pathetic substance. But he felt that he was, in the rooms of the manor, and even by the harpsichord on which he accompanied his aunt to her air from *Alceste*, as much in the center of things as if he had stood in the rye field itself, and as near to those human beings whose fate was now decided there. Anne-Marie and he were both in the hands of destiny, and destiny would, by different ways, bring each to the designated end.

Later on he remembered what he had thought that evening.

But the old lord stayed on. Late in the afternoon he even had an idea; he called down his valet to the pavilion and made him shift his clothes on him and dress him up in a brocaded suit that he had worn at Court. He let a lace-trimmed shirt be drawn over his head and stuck out his slim legs to have them put into thin silk stockings and buckled shoes. In this majestic attire he dined alone, of a frugal meal, but took a bottle of Rhenish wine with it, to keep up his strength. He sat on for a while, a little sunk in his seat; then, as the sun neared the earth, he straightened himself, and took the way down to the field.

The shadows were now lengthening, azure blue along all the eastern slopes. The lonely trees in the corn marked their site by narrow blue pools running out from their feet, and as the old man walked a thin, immensely elongated reflection stirred behind him on the path. Once he stood still; he thought he heard a lark singing over his head, a spring-like sound; his tired head held no clear perception of the season; he seemed to be walking, and standing, in a kind of eternity.

The people in the field were no longer silent, as they had been in the afternoon. Many of them talked loudly among themselves, and a little farther away a woman was weeping.

When the bailiff saw his master, he came up to him. He told him, in great agitation, that the widow would, in all likelihood, finish the mowing of the field within a quarter of an hour.

"Are the keeper and the wheelwright here?" the old lord asked him. "They have been here," said the bailiff, "and have gone away, five times. Each time they have said that they would not come back. But they have come back again, all the same, and they are here now." "And where is the boy?" the old lord asked again. "He is with her," said the bailiff. "I have given him leave to follow her. He has walked close to his mother all the afternoon, and you will see him now by her side, down there."

Anne-Marie was now working her way up towards them more evenly than before, but with extreme slowness, as if at any moment she might come to a standstill. This excessive tardiness, the old lord reflected, if it had been purposely performed, would have been an inimitable, dignified exhibition of skilled art; one might fancy the Emperor of China advancing in like manner on a divine procession or rite. He shaded his eyes with his hand, for the sun was now just beyond the horizon, and its last rays made light, wild, many-colored specks dance before his sight. With such splendor did the sunset emblazon the earth and the air that the landscape was turned into a melting-pot of glorious metals. The meadows and the grasslands became pure gold; the barley field near by, with its long ears, was a live lake of shining silver.

There was only a small patch of straw standing in the rye field, when the woman, alarmed by the change in the light, turned her head a little to get a look at the sun. The while she did not stop her work, but grasped one handful of corn and cut it off, then another, and another. A great stir, and a sound like a manifold, deep sigh, ran through the crowd. The field was now mowed from one end to the other. Only the mower herself did not realize the fact; she stretched out her hand anew, and when she found nothing in it, she seemed puzzled or disappointed. Then she let her arms drop, and slowly sank to her knees.

Many of the women burst out weeping, and the swarm drew close round her, leaving only a small open space at the side where the old lord stood. Their sudden nearness frightened Anne-Marie; she made a slight, uneasy movement, as if terrified that they should put their hands on her.

The boy, who had kept by her all day, now fell on his knees beside her. Even he dared not touch her, but held one arm low behind her back and the other before her, level with her collar-bone, to catch hold of her if she should fall, and all the time he cried aloud. At that moment the sun went down.

The old lord stepped forward and solemnly took off his hat. The crowd became silent, waiting for him to speak. But for a minute or two he said nothing. Then he addressed her, very slowly.

"Your son is free, Anne-Marie," he said. He again waited a

little, and added: "You have done a good day's work, which will long be remembered."

Anne-Marie raised her gaze only as high as his knees, and he understood that she had not heard what he said. He turned to the boy. "You tell your mother, Goske," he said, gently, "what I have told her."

The boy had been sobbing wildly, in raucous, broken moans. It took him some time to collect and control himself. But when at last he spoke, straight into his mother's face, his voice was low, a little impatient, as if he were conveying an everyday message to her. "I am free, Mother," he said. "You have done a good day's work that will long be remembered."

At the sound of his voice she lifted her face to him. A faint, bland shadow of surprise ran over it, but still she gave no sign of having heard what he said, so that the people round them began to wonder if the exhaustion had turned her deaf. But after a moment she slowly and waveringly raised her hand, fumbling in the air as she aimed at his face, and with her fingers touched his cheek. The cheek was wet with tears, so that at the contact her fingertips lightly stuck to it, and she seemed unable to overcome the infinitely slight resistance, or withdraw her hand. For a minute the two looked each other in the face. Then, softly and lingeringly, like a sheaf of corn that falls to the ground, she sank forward onto the boy's shoulder, and he closed his arms round her.

He held her thus, pressed against him, his own face buried in her hair and head-cloth, for such a long time that those nearest to them, frightened because her body looked so small in his embrace, drew closer, bent down and loosened his grip. The boy let them do so without a word or a movement. But the woman who held Anne-Marie, in her arms to lift her up, turned her face to the old lord. "She is dead," she said.

The people who had followed Anne-Marie all through the day kept standing and stirring in the field for many hours, as long as the evening light lasted, and longer. Long after some of them had made a stretcher from branches of the trees and had carried away the dead woman, others wandered on, up and down the stubble, imitating and measuring her course from one end of the rye field to the other, and binding up the last sheaves, where she had finished her mowing.

The old lord stayed with them for a long time, stepping along a little, and again standing still.

In the place where the woman had died the old lord later on had a stone set up, with a sickle engraved in it. The peasants on the land then named the rye field "Sorrow-Acre." By this name it was known a long time after the story of the woman and her son had itself been forgotten.

ACKNOWLEDGMENTS

Grateful acknowledgment is made for permission to reprint copyrighted material as follows:

"A Country Doctor" and "The Bucket-Rider" by Franz Kafka from *The Metamorphosis, The Penal Colony, and Other Stories*, translated by Willa and Edwin Muir. Copyright © 1948 by Schocken Books and renewed © 1975 by Schocken Books. Reprinted by permission of Schocken Books, a division of Random House, Inc.

"The Wrecked Houses; The Big Thing" (Randall Jarrell's title) by Rainer Maria Rilke, from *The Notebooks of Malte Laurids Brigge*, translated by M. D. Herter Norton. Copyright © 1949 by W. W. Norton & Company, Inc. and renewed © 1977 by M. D. Herter Norton Crena de Iongh. Used by permission of W. W. Norton & Company, Inc.

"The Witch of Coös" from *The Poetry of Robert Frost*, edited by Edward Connery Latham. Copyright © 1923, 1969 by Henry Holt and Company, copyright © 1951 by Robert Frost. Reprinted by permission of Henry Holt and Company, LLC.

"The Nose" from *Tales of Good and Evil* by Nikolai Gogol, translated by David Magarshack. Copyright © 1957. Reprinted by permission of Doubleday, a division of Random House, Inc.

"Her Table Spread" by Elizabeth Bowen from *Collected Stories*. Copyright © 1981 by Curtis Brown Ltd, Literary Executor of the Estate of Elizabeth Bowen. Reprinted by permission of Alfred A. Knopf, a division of Random House, Inc.

OTHER NEW YORK REVIEW CLASSICS

For a complete list of titles, visit www.nyrb.com or write to:
Catalog Requests, NYRB, 435 Hudson Street, New York, NY 10014

* *Also available as an electronic book.*